THE STEPS

Considerations, Parables and Entertainments

by

Anthony Benn

First Edition

October, 2021

For Janet

For everything, even the rainbows on the ceiling

An Epitaph To Love

Is to give more than to receive
To know and to understand
It is to eat of the Grape
    to drink of the Wine
It is never to complain
It is always to trust
It is to be for now - yet
    It is to know the end
It is to be greater than me
    greater than you
It is to be that which is better;
You and me
    Entangled
The patience of intimacy
    The impatience of passion
It is private and it is free
It is not to be bought or sold
It is to share with those we love
And those we know
    For our happiness enriches

St Ignatius *Semper Virens*

The Steps

Contents

1

Introduction

What I do is me; for that I came.

G. M.Hopkins

Our World - and all life on it - is entering into a dark period. This is our own making.

*

A few years ago, I was in Kenya, the land of my birth, an event now long ago when the country was part of the British Empire. I was the eldest child of a 'settler farmer'.

After I had retired, I revisited the country and I was staying in an hotel on the shore of Lake Naivasha, near where we had lived. Coming back into my rondavel, I noticed that there was a bird flying around, trying to find its way out. I quickly opened all the windows and the door. When I had done so, I saw that the bird had settled on the lampshade hanging from the ceiling. Gently, ever so gently, I put my hand over its back from the rear, hoping to put it outside. Just as I was about to take hold, it darted away to its freedom. It left behind though, in my hand, its long, orange tail.

The bird was a Paradise Flycatcher. It is on the cover of this book, feeding its chick.

It must surely be one of the most beautiful birds.

This bird tells much about what I have tried to write about herein. In the first place, it is obviously so very beautiful, with its bright colouring, its blue head, white body and long, long tail.

It is about, too, generation, here in the form of mother and off-spring. It is also, about Evolution, for why did it leave its tail behind? Its speed of escape at first startled me, and then intrigued me. Its speed – as that of all the predated – was sufficient to escape the predator, in this case me. I was left holding the feathers, as any other predator night have done. A not very nourishing capture.

Furthermore, it said something about life in general, about survival and its purpose: to pass on genes to the next generation. And in order that one little creature might survive, another must die. It thus asked questions about the nature of life itself. The bird had found its freedom, at least from me; it was, if momentarily, free to be itself. And in that there was great relief.

These 'Considerations, Parables and Entertainments' are offered as reflections and experiences over many years, about freedom and joy, and about their opposite, the darkness in the human heart. They are not without such but they *are* written in hope, at least that they might communicate something and, indeed, entertain.

The former, the essays or 'Considerations', deal with Atheism, Evolution or at least its most renowned exponent, they deal with Jane Austen and the beginnings of modern society and the corporate world we live in today; they deal with our colonial past, a past that must be understood, however much we prefer to look away and idealise that past. And they deal with humanity's endless search for identity, exemplified in Literature and film.

The Parables, as I conceived them, are meant to depict, in simple yet direct terms, the nature of authoritarianism or totalitarianism and life for individuals suppressed in such a regime. These regimes are today sprouting up all over the world, as governments undermine the nature of democracy, even whilst they are praising it (and themselves). This is happening as much in *this* country as anywhere else.

And as for the entertaining pieces – well, I leave these for the reader's own judgement.

And as for the author of these pieces? I am now well into retirement and leading a contented life. I write as an ordinary man, not one with any especial experience of life. So, embodied here are thoughts and ideas that have lingered and festered in my mind for perhaps many years. And, as those of my generation live out the remainder of our days, one must be very concerned about the directions that our life – that is, the life of this planet we call Earth – is taking.

But let me also be clear – I am white, middle-aged, middlebrow and distinctly male. These pieces are written by one as such. And I must be frank, I am irremediably Woke. All creative work of any sort, entertaining or not, *must* challenge the status quo, the Establishment and, especially, the Government. *Telegraph* columnists and others such have created and declared war on anything they consider Woke. Well, I am very awake (or so I like to think).

I think that we are entering a dark and dangerous period – threats to democracy, pandemics, climate change, over-population *and* control through the Internet seem to mount by the day – a period that will last much, much longer than I have left to live. So, in a way, this book is for Millennials: it is very possible that this century will see the end of Humanity's evolutionary story.

It is our choice. It seems that our Evolution or our History (one and the same thing) has lead us to the potential for universal annihilation. This is to be of no concern to anyone, but us. Does it matter?

I have not touched on Climate Change in these pieces. I merely accept that the Science is correct, that it is urgent that all nations take immediate and far-reaching steps to counter this threat. Otherwise, for our children and grandchildren, life will be very, very far from how we have come to expect it.

Nor have I dealt with the other big issue of our time, the Pandemic. This one will pass in time – but the real fear is that more dangerous viruses will emerge in the years to come. Again, we must change something very radical here: to recognise that we are part of Nature and NOT apart from it.

I did not start to write these pieces with the intention that they demonstrate. There is much darkness that has emerged in their creation. I am particularly concerned, I must repeat, with the progress being made by autocratic governments, however much they might claim to be democratic, to undermine Democracy, through subverting the powers of the judiciary, to censoring the media, through diminishing powers of protest and debate and to actively denying the vote to certain sections of the electorate – 'voter suppression' as Republicans in the States call it.

In particular, I am most concerned about the use of the Internet. I take my cue here from Yuval Noah Harari's *Homo Deus*. In this now very widely read and most important work, he details how the Internet is being used to manipulate our everyday thinking, our very natures, to suit the aims of all dictators from time immemorial: to control peoples' thoughts. He is not the only one to write about this. So have such as Jeanette Winterson and Niall Ferguson. This is a very real danger, one mounting all the time. We need to become more and more aware of this.

The 'Dark Net' is not something hidden 'out there'. It is very much with us, every time we log on.

I write, too, about Religion and Evolution. The essay 'On Atheism' needs no explanation here, except to say that it cannot and should not be the wish of anyone to see Religion abolished. On the contrary, when Religion is, like Christianity, the religion of self-denial, of restraint and of care, one can only praise it. Or when like Hinduism, it is so vital, wonderfully colourful and possessed of multiple deities, little and large. Or, as Buddhism, it recognises the essential nature of being, that of suffering and the ways out of it. All religions have their wonders, their inspiration and their beliefs – the architecture and poetry of Islam, too. All religions, also, are based in the need to be grateful for nature's provisions and for uniting people.

But too often, religion, throughout history, has been the source of violence and of war, of the underpinning of nationalist arrogance, of imperialism and of class-structures. Indeed, if 'the survival of the fittest' is at the heart of Evolution, then Evolution and History are indeed synonymous.

So, philosophically speaking, if I am anything, I am an Existentialist, in so far as I accept that life has no intrinsic meaning, that we all live 'here and now' and only so, even if we reach back into the past for our direction and into the future with our hopes and fears, and that anything takes its meaning, including every word I have written, from its context and only so. However, neither the past nor the future exist. It is striking that both Existentialists and the Nazis seized upon Darwin's Evolutionary Theory. The former – correctly – recognised the principle characteristics of Evolution: that all biological life is a matter of chance, as the Anthropic Principle demonstrates, that there is no intrinsic meaning to life nor any purpose to it, but to survive in order to pass on genetic material. The Nazis, and other Fascists, seized upon the concept of 'the survival of the fittest' and used this to justify their evil philosophies, of racial and nationalistic superiority: 'Might is Right'. The consequences are only too well known. Have we forgotten the lessons?

Darwin offered, implicitly if not explicitly, Humanity a choice: to act responsibly or to act destructively. This choice, it seems to me, is at the heart of all that is written in these pages.

And, as I write this, I recall Borges' words – the title to a short, very short story about Shakespeare: 'Everything and Nothing'. Life, Borges suggests, is everything – and it is nothing. This we must recognise as the ultimate truth: that there is no intrinsic meaning to life, except as how it is lived.

Nevertheless, we have to also recall Descartes' famous dictum, 'I think, therefore I am.' Darwin's Evolutionary Theory stresses that we are as much part of Nature as the smallest microbe or the largest elephant. We are *not* apart from it. Except in so far as we think, that is reflect, understand and attempt to change our behaviour, we do not differ from the rest of Nature. This is our freedom and our responsibility.

And yet we have to be aware of and to confront the paradoxes of our existence – that Life is full of meaning, but only as we live it, for there is nothing beyond life; that we can love and we can hate, that the promises of the Divine have lead us into endless war, that seeking perfection too often leads to imperfection. Such, over the centuries, have been and still are the staples of thought and of our lives. We confront complexity all the time, though many retreat into simplicity, especially that offered by authoritarians of one sort or another.

In short, this work suggests that there need be only one commandment: 'Do no harm'. Of course, this is so very easy to say but infinitely more difficult to obey. In both our personal lives and in our relation to the wider political, religious or ideological world in which we live, we have been for centuries only too willing to do just the opposite. Despite the presence of religions throughout history, suffering has been at the heart of all existence, even though moral imperatives have been at the core of religion. Perhaps this is what T.S. Eliot was referring to by 'something infinitely gentle, infinitely suffering.'

All thought has its limitations; all writers will know that whatever they have written is incomplete. And however much a writer struggles for the truth, surely all writers recall the words of Carl Jung, 'Nothing is absolutely true, not even that.'

The beauty of the little Paradise Flycatcher surely denies that?

2

The Greatest Story Ever Told

The Steps and the Keys

It is with some trepidation that someone with my beliefs or absence of belief about God comes to preach in a chapel, even though I am grateful for the opportunity.

However, this is not going to be a sermon as such; I leave that for those who know better how to do it. Instead, this is going to be a story, the greatest story ever told. It tells of endeavour, experience rich in joy and deep in tragedy, of everything and of nothing. And, as ever in the story of humanity, there is practically no time to tell it in. It is called 'The Steps and the Keys.'

There are, in an arid and lonely valley somewhere in Tanzania, footprints, human footprints. Footprints, of course, cover the world in one form or another. But these footprints, embedded as they are in ancient rock, go back a million, two million years. There are two pairs of these footprints. They are of different sizes and they are obviously those of an adult and a child. There is only a step or two of each, they then disappear. No one knows anything more about these footprints, and the steps they were making. They come – and they disappear. And they are amongst the most poignant evidence of the ancient history of Humanity.

In fact, the only aspect of these footprints and the steps that were making them, so many aeons ago, were human at all is that those walkers were walking upright, that is they had evolved by their time from earlier creatures into hominids – not homo sapiens – of one type or another. If we were to meet them today, we would only just recognise them by this as being part of the same family as us. They would have had little or no language, their heads flatter, for no frontal lobes had yet developed, their jaws would have thrust much further forward that ours. And they would have been much hairier.

However, they had probably developed a capacity for memory, enabling instinct to be controlled by reason: 'I am hungry (and hunger would have been an intense and daily experience for such as these),' the older might have said to the younger. 'Let's go to where we last left or found some berries.'

And so they would have done, or clubbed to death a young deer. And then in the evening, the two proto-humans would have eaten their food; hunger would have been assuaged. The sky that night would have been filled with a million, million stars; a moon might have shone, and this daily ritual would have gone on for periods of time which we can only think of with awe, so long are they. A brilliant morning sun would have woken them, and they and their kin would have moved on a little further in the endless quest for food.

Then one day the elder of the two would have sat down. He would have released the hand of his child and without a glance he or she would have walked on. Sitting on the dry earth, he perhaps would call back, as the child walked to the crest of the hill. He saw his child silhouetted against the harsh midday sun; he knew, instinctively, that he had given up the keys to survival as best he could. He waved a feeble wave, but received no response. He closed his eyes; his jaw fell to his chest as he collapsed, his body rolled over. Above, a circling predator waited for death, descended, and began to tear the flesh from the bones, before putrefaction. Other predators followed, including worms and microbes, until all that was left were scattered and broken bones, which in turn sank into the soil, perhaps to be preserved for ever in rock, and to be dug up an eternity later by a descendant who rejoiced in the recovery of the bones of the most ancient of his ancestors.

Such is all human life: procreation, protection of one's own, the endless movement in the search for food and sustenance, the fear of hunger, the passing on of the keys to rooms we know we can never enter, and death.

But before this story is continued, it is necessary to go back, back to the beginning. Our ancient ancestors had not been the first on earth, they were no Adam or Eve in a Garden of Eden. Instead, they had evolved from earlier forms, which in turn had evolved from even earlier ones. At a time some 450 million years ago – and can you, reader, conceive of a time span such as this, can you imagine a million years, a hundred thousand years and of all the life that would have been lived in all that time? It is very, very hard, isn't it? – came something called the Cambrian Explosion. During this period, and it is a very, very long period, life as we recognise it today first appeared in ponds and puddles. Protoplasmic cells discovered movement, minute creatures squirmed in the sludge, moved, bumped into one another, fed, multiplied. Soon, and by soon I do not mean the next day or even the next year, these primeval creatures could move out of the water, develop legs, walk and hunt and live and die in all the multiplicity that life on this planet could sustain, be they microbes or dinosaurs. Billions of species came; they thrived – and died out or evolved into other creatures better suited to changing environments, thus passing on the genetic keys that were fit enough to survive. And bear in mind that 99.5 percent of all species that ever came into being and survived have, in time, perished.

And before this great explosion of life that produced you and me? Bear this in mind, too: we can only listen to the almost eternal silence, and wonder in awe. You cannot imagine half a billion years. Can you imagine a billion, four billion? For that is when the earth was formed, particles of rock agglomerating around a minor star in our galaxy, eventually, for so the laws of physics dictate, a round planet emerged, a violent, lifeless, storm ridden place. For billions of years. Perhaps a passing comet or asteroid, crashing onto the earth's surface, brought with it microbes or water. Perhaps lightning strikes it and the whole magnificent process, 'the greatest show on earth', began. And so our couple found life, and death.

But the boy or the girl who disappeared over the hill was not alone. The people to whom he or she belonged multiplied and spread. They had come down out of the trees, learnt to walk on two feet, thus making defence easier; and they had developed memory, thereby enabling reason and intellect. By five hundred or two hundred thousand years before our written history begins, society had evolved and developed, but forever driven by the elemental drives of life: to feed, to procreate, to survive in order so to do. At about this time, religion, too, might have begun. Indeed, today it is possible to see evidence of this. If you travel to Namibia in Southern Africa, and you go out amongst the hunter-gatherer people called the Khoi or the Khoi San, you will see this. An animal is hunted for the tribe, hunger as ever driving; it is killed. The clan or family are fed and for a few days, stomachs are full. The event is celebrated. A fire is lit for cooking, then, once the meal is eaten, it is stoked up, followed by dancing and singing. Above, the millions and millions of stars silently, minutely rotate, the flames and glowing embers somehow linking the infinitesimally small with mysterious and glorious majesty of the cosmos (not that the ancients yet had words such as these). Humans thus were first filled with intimations of the divine. Indeed, it is very possible that we are genetically wired to the experience of awe, because awe is linked to the place in which we first found food and shelter. Furthermore, today under the borders of Switzerland and France, a vast machine is working in a magnificent experiment to peer into the deepest substance of those very stars which filled ancient man with his first sense of awe.

But I digress. It is time to give our ancients names; after all, they are of the same flesh and blood as ourselves. Let is call them Sam and Daisy, his daughter. There were many such, as their people multiplied. And their names varied, of course. But there was also something else, something that this story is all about: the endless steps that humans have taken. Movement and migration, as well as their opposite, settlement, have always been the staple of our existence on this planet. About a hundred and fifty thousand years or a hundred thousand years ago, Sam and Daisy, now recognisably human, had spread through much of Africa, and they made then their most daring and greatest journey; it is a journey not yet ended. They left Africa. At a point where the Red Sea was then much narrower than it is now, perhaps in what is now called Eritrea, they managed to get to the other side, to what is now The Yemen. And from here, throughout the millennia that followed, they spread inexorably along the shores of Arabia eastwards and northwards, too. To what was to become Mesopotamia, to India, Central Asia and to China. They went to the north into our own continent of Europe. They crossed the Baring Straights into Alaska, spreading down to fill the Americas to Tierra del Fuego, the Land of Fires. Half a world away across the Pacific Ocean, the Far East and Australasia were also reached. Such were the endless, endless migrations of our race.

And as much as they travelled, they settled, as if contentment and impatience have forever been at the heart of the human psyche. The settled in valleys and on the sea shore, they settled by rivers and on plateaus – wherever food was easily attained, and above all, water found. Areas to us now deserts were to our ancestors lush, green and productive. When settled, and no longer nomadic (and there are still nomadic people in our own time), the ancients began to build. They built 'society'. In journeying across the face of the globe during the thousands and thousands of years, we changed. Some remained dark skinned; others' skin became pale. Facial features varied, as did size and shape and bone structure – all the result of adaptations to the environments in which mankind found itself. Some dwelt in mountains, some on great plains; some adapted to living in arid, desert areas, and some, like the English, in lush lands where nature was forever generous.

Cultures grew up, flourished, magnified themselves into empires, became corrupt and weakened; and were destroyed, sinking back into the sands from which they had grown. Even today, we can find evidence – shards of pottery, libraries half buried in the Nubian Desert, evidence of long-lost life and vitality. All this was, though, not millions of years ago, not even tens of thousands of years ago, but all in the last seven or eight thousand years.

But these cultures, kingdoms and empires needed one element, above all, to succeed. Think of the Pharaohs of Egypt, the Incas of Peru or even the France of Louis XIV. Think of the Pyramids, of Atahualpa, the Sun King of the Incas, of the great cathedrals and the wonderful litanies of religious music: a god was always needed to underpin, to explain and to justify existence. Conscious beings cry out for a god, for that crying out is a recognition that as well as awe-inspiring the Sun, the stars and the Moon might be, they are also force us to recognise the loneliness, the silence and the inexplicability of existence. Great empires grew up with great religions.

And as empires offer civilisation, they are also destructive in all that they do: they bring war and conquest with them, suppression and brutality. For such is human nature. I know: I was a child of empire.

Sam and Daisy instinctively love one another. This great story is summed up as follows. There is, in the Japanese Alps, a primate species known as Japanese Macaques. Some of you have seen these. This primate (we, too, are primates, remember) has adapted to the severe cold of the Japanese winter – and no primate, other than us, is capable of living at such an altitude – by developing a very thick fur and by taking to the water. Thermal pools, kept at a steady 41 degrees Centigrade act as a 'thermal spar'. In the pool, the infant macaques play; others groom themselves, as primates all over the world do, for thereby endures the sense of kinship essential for survival. Here a mother suckles her infant, an expression of blissful relaxation and maternal love on her face.

But turn your head: another little macaque is trying to get into the water – he is brutally repelled, first by other little ones, then by the alpha male who dominates the clan. The weaker monkeys sit on the water's edge, shivering in whatever shelter they can find. The difference between inside the hot spring and outside is 60 degrees – quite literally, the difference between life and death.

This is heart-rendingly cruel – who cannot be moved by the distinction. But it also entirely necessary. The environment these monkeys live in is harsh in the extreme. The monkeys expelled are expelled because they are weaker, and the genes of the weaker must not be passed on to the next generation, to ensure the survival of the clan and its gene pool. Without this, there would be no Japanese Macaques.

Does this not, also, stand as a symbol of all society? History is littered with the corpses of dominant males – and occasionally females. Sun Kings, Pharaohs, Monarchs, tyrants – a Stalin or a Hitler – and elected presidents, like in America? They arise out of their own families, clans and tribes (that is, gene pools) to offer order, control and even sense to their members, giving themselves divine status and characteristics? Is not the thermal pool of these Macaques just another Versailles, another Kremlin or White House?

And what of another question: what if all these gods of all the religions that have flourished and grown, deflated and died in the course of history, do they themselves not die? Very late in our journey from that lonely valley in Africa, a French writer and mischievous atheist asked this question (and he asked it in a time of religious certitude); "If God did not exist, then would we not have had to invent him?"

Or is there just one God, who has appeared in a multiplicity of guises throughout history and in every culture? One Absolute Being, divine in nature and the fount of all existence? Or is this God just the product of the need to fill the yawning gap between our genetic imperatives – even our altruistic ones – and our consciousness?

If the answer is yes, as I believe it to be, then what does this mean?

It means that, with the ancients, when we look up at the stars, when we take the steps of our lives, and when we ask such a question, we do so out of our own nobility, much of which is characterised by curiosity. It means that we can know everything, including the idea that when everything is known, there will be nothing left to know. As the playwright put it, "When we have found all the mysteries and lost all the meaning, we will be alone, on an empty shore." Human nobility means facing up to that, and facing up to the one other ineluctable truth, the one that is common to us as it is to all creatures that have and have had life: that it ends.

It means that we have the responsibility of choice, and of understanding. Of choice: to choose our attitude and outlook and behaviour. Of understanding: to know, as the poet and artist, William Blake, put it: "Life is made for joy and woe./When this ye rightly know, through the world ye safely go."

It means there is nothing beyond life; but it does mean that there is life, in all its wonder and tragedy. In my life, I have tried to pass on the keys to those who have come after me. I cannot go with them. You will pass them onto your children, in one way or another, and every step will be an ending and a beginning.

And our story might end in your lives, or in your children's lives or their children's, when the Ice-cap melts, and methane will fill the world. Maybe the human story will last another six billion years, when our Sun, running out of hydrogen and time will expand and inflate itself like a greedy emperor, gobbling up the planets nearest it, including ours. It will then collapse in upon itself, finally to extinguish itself, leaving not a rack behind, but a darkness and eternal silence in our little, unimportant corner of the universe, that will last for all eternity.

3

Walking in the Hills (1)

The past is another country.

L.P.Hartley

One morning, Joe was up early. As usual, it was a cloudless, if somewhat chill, start to the day and now in bright sunlight from the East, all was clear with everything in sharp detail. He took himself to where he and his friends had been digging some ditches, working out what need to be done that morning. He looked up, seeing the hospital, on top of the hillside which was, falling at first gently then more steeply, to a valley way below and out of sight. He knew where it went – down a steep incline, down to a stream, a stream that could not be seen from above. He walked some yards and seated himself. What he could see, to his young eyes, was breath-taking.

The hill rose on the far side of the valley, gently, roundly. In the distance, the slopes became ever higher and ever rockier. Some way up, perhaps a mile away, on the far hill, sat some huts, a half dozen, perhaps. Here people spent their lives, he thought. He could make out some patches of cultivated ground. There was not a breath of wind. All was wonderful in this bright yellow morning light.

He could see, too, a couple of men working the soil. They were some distance from each other.

And they were talking. Joe could hear them, loud and clear, the sound echoing across the valley. He sat, transfixed.

At that moment, he felt a movement beside him. Jane had come out to join him.

She stood for a minute or two. 'Lovely,' she muttered and walked back.

*

Mantsonyane.

How does one recall events of more than 50 years ago with accuracy and honesty, at least to oneself? Perhaps one doesn't, but Joe was to remember in some detail, or in his imagination, those few weeks spent in this place high in the mountains of Lesotho. Today it is still a country of no significance to the rest of the World. Beautiful, wild and natural it was then, though today, Westerners, seeking these qualities, are making the place one to escape to.

Joe had been there in his student days, to a 'work camp' organised by his university in Cape Town. It was in the summer vacation, the hottest time of the year, though high in the Lesotho mountains, it would be cooler. Joe pieced his memories together – how many were there? 6, 8? He does not recall. Who? One friend, Rina. The organiser, Mike, and the others. Dan. And Jane.

And, as he now recalls – and as he had recalled many times over the decades since – it was the heyday of Apartheid. Oh, he had done his bit, the occasional demo or sit-in. But that was just 'repressive tolerance', the State, The National Party allowing a bit of steam to be let off, to show its 'tolerance'. But white, middleclass students – what did they really know about the suffering of the system, of the pain and degradation? Study sufficiently, have fun – 'the future will be your oyster!'

A train from the Cape to Bloemfontein, change there, then onto Maseru, the capital, lying to the north west of the country, just on the border with South Africa. It is one of only three landlocked countries in the World completely surrounded by one other. So Joe had been reading. It had been a British colony until just a three years before his visit there.

Maseru – they passed through. A few modern buildings surrounded, as so often in Africa, by shanty towns, even back in 1969. And the countryside around? The city stands in a shallow bowl, with beyond open grasslands and rocky, irregular hills, for here begin the mountains of Lesotho.

He recalled that they had found a lorry which would take them to Mantsonyane and the hospital, where they were to help with manual labour for the next fortnight or so. Joe closed his eyes as he remembers the journey. One or two sat in the cab next to the driver, the rest, like him, found perches amongst the sacks and bags and equipment being taken into the depths of the country. Joe was settled, as they left the town, being driven on into the wide-open spaces. Few trees dotted the countryside, and occasional settlements – round huts of varying states of repair, all with straw rooves and most with the distinctive decoration on the top, like a sports cup. But for the sound of the vehicle, all was peaceful as it slowly climbed, on and upwards.

After a couple of hours, it stopped. Joe recalls the moment in much detail, or believed he did. There were a few trees – Blue Gums? – a stream and a young lad, the shepherd of a small herd of goats. With the engine cut, all was silent except that Joe heard only one sound, beautifully filling the air all around. It was the gentle tinkling of bells, held in the hands of a young boy. No wind, no other sound, just the wonderful clarity of the little bells, used, he learnt, to keep the tiny herd together and within range.

Soon they were off again. One or two had changed seats. Joe saw one of the girls settle herself down at the back of the lorry. Of course, they had talked occasionally on the journey up.

*

It was, as Joe said to himself, late afternoon that he and his friends arrived. Mantsonyane: a village of nothing more than a few huts, and a little way beyond, the hospital, St James's Mission Hospital. High in the Maluti Mountains on a tree-less ridge, it had originated in the early '50s. As they descended from the truck, Joe saw that there were some local people, wrapped in their characteristic, colourful blankets, gathering around – to help, to watch? – and then out, as it were, of the skies a man on a little horse, a local Lesotho pony adept at clambering over rocky hillsides, galloped up. Dressed in doctor's coat, a bearded young man jumped down from the saddle and started shaking hands. 'Welcome. Welcome! I'm Nick Cohen. And you're Mike. . . you're. . . ?

‘Yes, I’m Mike. We’ve been in touch. From Capetown Uni.’

‘Of course. Welcome!’

Mike made the introductions.

‘Dan, Jane, Joe, Rina,’ and the others.

‘Oh, yes. Welcome! Welcome1 I’m Nick, do just call me Nick. I’m in charge here. Well sort of.’

And so Nick, getting to know each of them, showed the group the hospital, shaking hands, small talk, big talk about the hospital and what was to happen. And led them to where they were to eat, sleep, put their things – in a small barn with a corrugated tin roof and earthen floor, set apart from the main building. This was long and single-storied, but for a central part which rose up one floor.

That evening, over a meal of mealies and a few vegetables, their stay in the hospital had begun. Joe thought with so much pleasure of that time, that time of youth, so long ago.

The hospital served many people in the surrounding district, though few were able to get to the doctor, hence his pony. In the morning, with breakfast being soon after dawn, there were ditches to be dug, walls to be whitewashed and various other jobs that Nick, the doctor, would in time make clear.

And then, as the students were settling down after their long day, they began to chat and to get to know one another. Was it then that Joe had chatted to the girl on the truck, he wondered? She was one who was happy to talk to anyone.

And Joe, searching the internet many years, many decades later, discovered who this young Doctor was. Perhaps he was one of Life’s natural saints. Though, Joe learnt, Nick had been born in Cape Town, he been brought up in London, the son of a doctor. But so much of his working life was to be spent amongst the poor and destitute, in Ethiopia, fighting smallpox, and in Bangladesh. But he had started just a year before, eschewing the opportunities that London might have offered, in Mantsonyane.

There was something dynamic about him, Joe had always thought, riding about on his pony, bearded and with a Lesotho blanket flowing behind, a young man only 31 years old. In an obituary in *The Lancet* – Nick died in 2010 of Parkinson’s, able to cure many but not himself - Joe read that Nick had learned in Mantsonyane, ‘what it means to live on a meal of maize flour a day, what it feels like to go barefoot, clothed only in a blanket in the freezing winter days, and how many children die of diseases that elsewhere are entirely preventable.’

*

Early next morning, the work began, as it would each day – then a break or two, lunch, then ending at about 5.00 pm. Joe’s first task was to dig a ditch from a spot where others, with some young local men, were removing large amounts of earth from a round area, marked out for a water-tank. Wheelbarrows of soil, turf piled high, muddied hands and clothes. Backbreaking, even for those as young as they were, using unfamiliar muscles – Joe knew the feeling only too well these days. But he knew that it was all in a good cause. Nowadays, most muscle were unused. Joe paused for some time.

In the evenings, after a shower, there was a meal, usually of maize in one form or another, and local meats. Afterwards, they gathered in their barn, chatted, told stories, played on musical instruments, singing 'We Shall Overcome!' and other songs that have come down through the decades as hymns of that happy Hippy time.

And now. . ?

Joe coughed. 'Bridge over Troubled Water'. Who was it by? Singing it, even in faraway Lesotho.

And they had talked politics. This was the heyday, if that is the right word, of a political system that at the time Joe knew little of. Of course, he had done the standard student things like a sit-in and protests down the centre of the city. But Nelson Mandela, now in the early years hacking rock in the stifling heat of the quarry on Robben Island? Never mentioned. Apartheid. Separateness. Joe remembered his journalist friend of a year or so later, a so-called 'coloured', excoriating people like him, just English 'liberals' leading a comfortable life, buying into a system that provided for them, especially as they might have moved to South Africa from newly liberated colonies to the north.

And it was Jane who lead conversations about this. It appeared that she and her family had had close contacts with black people, of whatever race. In time, they were forced to flee the country.

'How good it is,' he recalled her saying, 'to come to a country where all are equal. I love it!' She spoke passionately. 'Where there is no imprisonment or house arrest, no Robben Island. We should be treating each other, politically, socially, *naturally*, for God's sake, as equals. We all live on the same planet and we all have just one life.'

With such words, she held attention. Of course, others had their say, whilst Joe listened, watching her ever more closely.

Joe had had a photo of Jane, taken walking along a beach near Cape Town soon after their return. She always looked beautiful, not in a film star way, but in her own self, confident in herself, with her thick brown hair flowing behind. 'Film star? Joe thought. 'Yes, Katherine Hepburn?' Joe had loved the comparison. When had he made it?

*

One evening, after work, some of the team were invited by their newly made Lesotho friends to visit their home a rondavel, as it would be called in South Africa, but here a small round hut. Mud walled, it had a round, sloping roof, with the distinctive decoration on the top, a decoration that was on their hats: something like a sporting cup.

Outside were two ponies. As Joe and others, Jane included, entered, it was nearly all darkness, but for a couple of little windows. Seated around were other members of the family.

Moeketsi, who had invited them, made the introductions. 'Relebohile, my Mother. Father.' Something like that, though the last name had been forgotten.

The young white students from Cape Town smiled, shook hands and tried to remember.

'Lineo and Thabiso. My boy and my girl.' Moeketsi looked proud. 'Please. Please be seated.'

And so the meeting began. Joe recalled how colourful were the clothes being worn, but wondered how they all slept, ate, lived in so cramped a place. He had had no idea that life could be like this.

Soon, a drink was being passed around. 'Chwala,' Joe thought. The local beer. But Nick had told them not to drink this, because it might have had anti-freeze in it. He could not refuse, though. Joe sighed at the memory.

'What does it feel like,' Joe's attention was drawn to the conversation, 'to have your independence? No longer being a colony, no longer subject to another country?' Jane was the speaker. Joe had found himself coming to admire her passion.

'Well,' Moeketsi replied, 'we're free of Britain, but not free of South Africa! OK, we don't have Apartheid, no one goes to prison for their beliefs, but we are dependent for much from over the border.' Joe did not think his English was this good, but he recalled accurately enough what had been said.

And so they talked and chatted, though it was not the women who spoke. They remained silent and, it seemed, respectful. Jane listened and spoke so naturally with them, whilst Joe could only reflect on the vast differences between his life and the life he had just seen. He wondered if, after all these decades, things had really changed.

*

And so the days passed. A good day's work was done. Enjoyable evenings followed by well-earned sleep. And something happened. He could now recall only too well what it was, but when? Why? One moment they were al relaxing, chatting when Joe felt himself being overwhelmed. He was watching, listening. And Jane was not far from him. He chuckled to himself afterwards, but it was not just love or desire, for he knew nothing of these things yet.

And then it hit him. He did not will it, but he welcomed it, confused though he was.

It was, he would recognise later in life, both but not just these together, but an exalted feeling, of rightness, of goodness, inspired by the girl sitting nearby. It was as if Mantsonyane and her and this beautiful country were one. He knew now and he knew he would know for evermore, that he was in love, that *this* was love.

Joe sat as if facing something divine, high in the mountains of a lovely country.

He knew – or felt he knew, or hoped – that something was returned. A couple of days before the end of their stay, an idea had struck. Was it to him or to her it had come? It was that instead of returning to Maseru and to The Cape with the others, they would walk to South Africa, going in the opposite direction. Through the mountains. Of course, the idea was treated with some disdain and mockery. But this is what Jane and Joe were going to do. She seemed only too willing. The idea left him feeling nothing but happiness.

Of course, it was crazy. No maps, little money or food, no idea of distance or direction. But what did they care? They were young.

That last evening, the locals had provided a pig as a thank you, a pig to be roasted on a spit. Joe and Mike and the others gathered the wood together – an actual spit had been provided and the carcass had been prepared.

But as they were doing this, the clouds had gathered, building up high into the sky, their first rain in Mantsonyane. It became ever darker, though the fire had been lit and was gathering strength. For all those years since, this, of all the images of that time, had remained most powerfully in his memory. As the rain poured down and lightening flashed and thunderous claps shook the buildings and all around, immediately – did one even strike the spit? – the pig roasted. Pouring rain, rolling thunder and a roasting pig. A good meal was had, though.

*

Next day, they were off. There was not much comment from their friends, but Nick did say he was, well, sceptical. Did Jane and Joe really know what they were doing? 'Walking back to South Africa'! From the middle of a country a little bigger than Wales. Maps, food, money. Maps, again. It was always odd but happy, too, Joe had thought as the years passed, that neither of them allowed any doubt to enter.

Joe chuckled to himself, as he had done many times at the thought. What were he and Jane up to? In Wales, at least there were roads, towns and villages, pubs and youth hostels, and people who spoke the same language. Joe did not really recall these points being made, but it was fine, sunny morning and not too hot, when Nick offered to drive them some of the distance to the nearest town, Thaba-Tseka, some thirty miles away. Soon, their rucksacks and they were in the back of the pick-up.

What was on their minds? The two did not really know each other and Joe has always wondered why Jane had entrusted herself to his company. But luck would be with them.

They were young, after all. It's what you do – perhaps this was their thought, however unstated. In the years that have passed, Joe would sometimes liken stepping out that morning, that February morning, high up in the mountains of an unknown country, with a girl he felt he was in love with, as the beginning of his life. It was as if the barn doors had been flung wide open as they strode out into the bright, optimistic early morning sunlight and that life, adult life, with all its hopes and fears, with all that it silently entailed, welcomed them and drew them on. And now, decades on, Joe knew that the doors were now closing in on him.

What were those lines that Joe remembered from T.S. Eliot: 'At the end of all our journeying, we will end up where we started from and know the place for the first time.' And did he?

So, after a while, the pickup stopped, Nick got out and, helping them off, said, 'I have to go up this track here. Thaba-Tseka is just a few miles on, shouldn't take you long. Good luck!'

And so it was, after many thank-yous. The car drove up the rocky pathway towards some distant rondavels. Soon all was silence, open spaces and silence. A dusty road lay ahead of them. Joe and Jane were alone on it.

'Here we go, then,' Joe smiled. 'On with the backpacks!'

*

Thaba-Tseka then was a very small town, despite being a provincial capital. Joe recalled arriving there some hours later. But it was busy with its people, in their blankets and hats, their unhurried steps and hardly any vehicles. Joe suggested they buy some food at some stalls on the roadside. Just a few Loti. Dusty bags of mealies, some fruit, nuts, too. Enough to be going on with.

'Hey,' said Jane, 'there are some horses.'

So, after they had discovered that two or three of these were going to the Orange River – a possibility that had been mentioned before, they found that their bags were to be put on one of the ponies, and they set off again, this time led by another on a fine brown mare, not one of the normal ponies.

They had not as yet walked very far, though later Joe would reckon that, if they had made it, they might well have walked 100 miles. At one point, he took her hand. Jane let go, not long after.

Soon Jane and then Joe took of their shoes as the road, now nothing more than a track was smooth and sandy.

'Bugger!' Joe spat a little later on – a thorn had pricked his toe. Soon, the thorns multiplied.

'You'd better put your shoes on now!' It was the rider of the mare. Joe saw her face only once, at that moment and he had always remembered her voice, its best Oxford English. And that was all he ever knew of her.

Slowly the road wound its way down a long, sloping hill to the valley at the bottom. The Orange River. On the far side, rocky and steep, was a cliff some hundreds of feet high. 'You go that way,' said the woman,' I go to the right. You'll find someone who can help you cross the river.' And that was that.

*

Half a mile or so on, with evening settling in, they came to a small hut. Tied by it on the bank was a small rowing-boat. A solitary man sat nearby.

'Hi,' Joe called. 'Can you take us across the river, please? We need to go to the other side.'

The man turned slowly, smiled and got up. He shook hands. 'In the morning,' he replied. 'Tonight, you can stay here.' Joe recalled his broken English.

The man pointed to a hut. It was just a few yards from the water's edge, just big enough for the two of them.

'Where will you sleep, then?' Jane asked.

Joe and Jane looked at each other as the man pointed to a rough-looking bed – he would sleep under the stars. That, it was clear, was his custom.

They moved to the hut and made themselves at home, more or less. There were two low bunks on the earthen floor. After resting for a while, talking about how the day had gone and how well, they ate some of their food.

Outside the sun had long since settled. Instead, the Moon had risen, its silver light coming from upstream. Joe and Jane sat next to each other at the river's bank. The only sound was that of the water flowing almost silently past them, unstopping almost, it seemed to Joe, timelessly. The moonlight fell on it, glinting off the ripples, catching, too, the steep bank on the far side.

And with the river gliding silently, slowly by just feet away and with the stars, myriads of them in the black, black sky but soon to fall beneath the mountains, shining brightly, Joe hoped that this would be his chance. And how many times had he looked back to this moment?

And they sat there for a while. It was too beautiful and he longed to put his arm around Jane. Soon, though, she got up and went back to the hut. Joe remained for a while longer. The memory, though, lasted very much longer.

And Jane started to itch through the night.

*

The ferryman – Charon, as Jane called him, when, in fact he was just the opposite - had taken them to the other side. The great river behind them, they were faced with the cliff-face. 100 feet above, 200 feet? Some climb, as the day was warming up. Short, scrubby bushes, some with thorns, loose stones, rocks at the end of strata sticking out. Not quite vertical, though. No option, only one way. Bags on their backs.

In the end, Joe recalled, it was not too difficult, clambering up. 40 minutes or so, if hot and dusty. And there, as their boatman had told them, was a track. 'Go to the right. You will find some church people not far away.'

They stopped from time to time, drinking the fresh river water, but with the itches on Jane getting worse, she had to pause and scratch. Joe was feeling some itches, too.

The ever-warming sun seemed to illuminate the surrounding hills and the valley below in a glowing red. The straps began to irritate, now.

After a while, a corner was turned and there in the distance the sun shone off some corrugated roofs. Perhaps the man had been right.

A couple of hour's trudging, and they were there. To be met by a young missionary in his cassock. On seeing the young couple, he pulled pistol out from underneath, pointing it at them.

'No, no!' Joe exclaimed. 'We're not here to harm you. We need to rest. Jane's covered in itches.'

At that, the young priest apologised, explaining that there had been a *coup d'etat* in Maseru and that they might have had something to do with it – the British coming back to take over again, perhaps.

'We're on our way to South Africa. . . .'

'Hm. You have at least a hundred miles to go! High mountains, deep valleys, many rivers, few people. I hope you have fun! But,' he continued, 'you can stay here. In three days a plane will come and take you to Durban, if you want. Come, I'll show you a room where you can stay.'

And so it was. Joe and Jane were well looked after by this kindly man, whilst they did their best to get the better of their bites. Jane's were by far the worse. And so they agreed to take the plane, when it came.

The time passed quickly, but what was clear became obvious. 'That pony,' Jane exclaimed, 'that pony from Thaba-Tseka to the river, it must have been infested with fleas. Then our rucksacks and my sleeping-bag!'

Joe agreed. 'And mine!'

'But,' she went on, 'you know what?'

'No. What?'

'Those fleas might well have saved our lives.'

'Why? How do you mean?'

'Well, we can't go on can we? I've been thinking. . . .'

'And if the fleas hadn't been there, we might have gone on?'

'And on, and on, till we had to stop. In the middle of nowhere, in a valley, on a mountainside. . . .'

And so it was that three days after arriving, Joe and Jane waited outside. It was not apparent how or where the little plane would land, as the ground sloped steeply down on one side and up on the other. There was, though, a little field with one or two scraggy trees on either side.

And there was the light aircraft, circling in to land. Up the hill. Safely landed, it turned, its provisions unloaded and one or two passengers. They were invited to get in, saying their goodbyes and thank yous, and after strapping themselves in. the plane took off. Down the hill.

Soon, they were in Durban and making their way back to The Fairest Cape.

*

It was not long after their return that Jane made it clear to Joe that she was not interested in a relationship. Joe and she really did not see eye to eye politically speaking and so he had reluctantly to accept this and he hoped they would remain friends. She had been so angry with him, for his ignorance of Apartheid, of the Pass Laws of Robben Island, of 'miscegenation' and all the other horrors of the system design to protect racial purity and superiority. The mountains had not worked their magic and it was time to move on.

In a year or two, both had left South Africa, never to meet again, though over the decades on very rare occasions, Joe did hear of her. And for him, there was his Sarah – now no more – and the two boys, and the grandchildren – Mark and his girl, Alice. Where were they now, for they seemed to have vanished?

And anyway, Jane turned the other way.

4

The Torturer - *A Parable*

I am moved by fancies that are curled
Around these images, and cling:
The notion of some infinitely gentle
Infinitely suffering thing.

T.S. Eliot

1. Allegro: *Why is it that one human is so willing to inflict pain on another?*

The Colonel struck the top of the bar with his whip. The crack, the whiplash, caught the others by surprise. Silence from the thirty or so colleagues in the room.

They knew better than to continue talking. "Whiskey!"

Silently, the man behind the bar, poured – he knew the right brand.

The Colonel turned and faced the room. His uniform, black leather, was immaculate. His eyes, sharp and black. He was not used to being defied; he certainly wouldn't be now.

The room, with its original 18th Century furniture and artworks belonging to the ancient family who had owned the place before, waited, silent. Through the French windows, a cold evening was settling in. The men - all men - are drinking, some out of priceless 19th Century glasses, carelessly taken.

The Colonel was hitting his leather boots repeatedly. In every other way he stood quite still.

"Four!"

Usually at this time the Colonel and others would either be drinking convivially here or be back at home, in apartments created in the Castle.

"Four," the Colonel repeated. Though it was uttered more quietly than before the tone was sharp, even venomous. "Attacked and shot. Out of the blue."

Nobody moved. Nobody dared.

"Williams, Hartley, N'Guma and Ahmed. In cold blood! COLD BLOOD!"

One straightened himself up, attentive, but jogging the table on which was a vase of fresh, pale pink roses. The vase wobbled. One of the officers hurled his glass at the wall.

"We are supposed to know everything about every citizen. Aren't we, Esterhouse? Isn't that why we have the Internet of Everything, which you are supposed to run here?"

Esterhouse was just a few feet away. He could not move, even bat his eyelids. He knew what failure meant. The twist of the knife. The electric chair.

"Where they go, who they see, what they are thinking – we've got it all worked out, haven't we?" Aggression was barely concealed. *Someone* would take the blame. "What went wrong? What!?"

Silence. Esterhouse felt everything draining away, a river suddenly in drought, a mind suddenly emptied, a life going.

"I'll tell what went wrong. These four brave colleagues were sitting in a bar. What were they doing, sitting in a bar? Drinking!" He paused. "Wasting time!" He looked around the room. "And who was supposed to be in charge of them? Eh, Mr Donnelly?"

"I had given them. . . ."

The faces on the walls had more life than the faces in the room.

"You 'had given them. . .' their death sentences! Not so?"

The crack of the whip again, echoing the sarcasm. The door opened and two armed guards entered. The Colonel nodded slightly. There was nothing more to be said. Esterhouse and Donnelly stood. None looked at them; they looked at no one, but walked to the door. The guards closed it behind them.

There was a pause as the footsteps faded away.

"So. I will tell you. It was simple. A car pulls up, a window is wound down, a gun points out. It is fired. Death for the four is instantaneous. It drives off."

He turns to a remote control, switches the screen on.

"Look. You can see. Everything is filmed, noted, recorded. Everything!"

His listeners face the screen. The relevant footage soon comes up. The event is replayed. They all watch. Otherwise the Colonel would notice weakness.

"Their bodies have been brought here, to the Castle."

The Castle. Dark rooms, narrow corridors, battlements and castellations. Slits for widows, through which arrows would once have been fired. And dungeons. Darkness, a monument to the darkness in the human heart. No pleasure dome this.

"These killers are mad! We have been able to build a safe and happy society under our wise guidance from above. Why should anyone want to damage, even destroy it, unless they are mad!" One or two murmurs follow these words. "There is work, home, food, pleasure for all! People have been let down; people will pay!"

Someone coughed.

"Now look! Look!" A new image appears on the screen. On the steps of the old cathedral, now used for discos and political rallies and sex parties, state sponsored, a crowd has been gathered, men, women, children. They are huddling together. And not because it is cold. A drone is flying overhead. It has various cameras.

One shows the crowd; another shows lines of armoured police, all in black helmets, bullet-proof vests, with truncheons, lasers, handcuffs and other means of quelling 'the people' – as seen in images from around the world. And another camera picks out a machine-gun at one corner of the square, with another at the opposite. These are unmanned.

They do not need to be manned. Where just now the screen was split into three, now it is one again. The Colonel presses a button. The sound tells what is happening.

The guns are firing. Bodies fall, and screams can be heard. Blood and pain. Arms, torsos flail bend, twist, fall amidst terror and panic.

And then silence.

No one in the room moves.

When it is over – and this is after some time – the Colonel emits a low whistle.

He feels a twitch in his cheek. This he has recently noticed.

"It is done," he declares. "The bodies will remain there as a warning. It is on national television. In the National interest."

He drinks his whiskey down in one. He goes out.

Before going home, he reports to his superior – who knows not to cross him. Instead he commends the Colonel on his decisive actions.

He goes down, down into the heart of the Castle, of the darkness. It is so familiar to him. Those in the dungeon await him.

*

Home is a house outside the castle, but within walking distance. Still, Colonel Westerbrook must take a protected vehicle when he later goes home.

Light and airy, the house is clean and spotless. He would not have it otherwise. He has two sons – any sign of them enjoying themselves, having fun, has been removed before his return. What few books there are, are arranged neatly, in size order. Fresh air blows through the windows. Light and airy: after the castle, who would want anything else?

A vase of roses, pink and yellow, sits on the table by his chair. His slippers are in place as he enters. Mary, his wife, is careful not to let the smells of cooking leave the kitchen. The boys are upstairs waiting for him to come and say good night.

"Hello, my dear," says Mary as he enters. She kisses him on the cheek; he does not respond. She has seen the television news. It is good to feel safe, but she has never asked why she needs to feel this.

Taking off his coat, he asks not about her and her day. Instead, it is, "Is supper ready? As I asked?"

"Yes, of course, dear. Your favourite fish pie. And there has been a fresh bottle of white in the fridge waiting for you. Have you had a good day?"

"You have seen the television?"

She nods. “Of course. They got what they deserved. The boys saw it, too.”

“Good.”

“Peter bit Tom this afternoon.”

“Do you know why?”

She shrugs.

He leaves her, going up stairs. Tom and Peter, each in his own bed, are eight and ten. Their hairs are brushed, their pyjamas done up to the top. They look pleased to see their father; at least, that is what they are expected to show, though they can’t know why. Their room is neat and tidy; they are not allowed teddy bears.

“Hello, boys,” their father says. “Has it been a good day for the Westerbrooks?” Does he feel a little aggressive as he utters this?

“I got a star in Geography today,” says Tom. “I know where Peru is!”

Smiling, their father, the Colonel, ruffles his younger son’s hair. “Well done.” He turns to his elder.

“And you, young man? What have you achieved today? Anything?” Peter knows this tone only too well, now.

“Yes, Dad.” He is too old now for ‘Daddy’, he has been told. “I have learnt the sayings of the Leaders.”

“That is very good.” But the boy’s hair is not ruffled. “And anything else.”

“We played Rugby.”

“And did your team win?”

“No. but it was close.”

“And have you been good to Tom? Have you helped him at school?”

“Yes.” This is uttered with uncertainty in his voice.

“Then why did you bite Tom?”

Silence is Peter’s only reply. He knows what is to come.

“Was it out of spite? Did he take something of yours? Did he bite you?”

Peter knows that denial is fruitless, for Tom will be the only one to be believed.

“Get out of bed!”

The Colonel has brought his whip with him.

Peter slowly does as he is told. He is wearing only his pyjamas.

“Lower your trousers!” Peter does so. “Bend over your bed.” The order is snapped.

He does so. He knows Tom is watching.

Six. Oh, he can count, only the counting helps make it bearable. One, two. Pause. Three. He senses his father turn for a moment to ensure that the younger boy is watching. Three. Four, Five, then the last. The hardest.

The Colonel is pleased. He smiles. This happened to him as a boy. It made him tough. Tom is tough but he fears that Peter will grow up weak. He doesn't know how many beatings it will take.

He kisses Tom goodnight, as Peter gets back into bed, covering his face and turning to the wall. Peter knows he dare not cry.

Momentarily, Westerbrook recalls punching a peer at school. 10 years old; he got away with it.

He hears Tom snigger as their father turns out the light.

"Is everything all right?" Mary asks.

"I hope so. Can you bring me my whiskey?"

He sits himself down in his chair. A few moments later, his whiskey is beside him.

Mary knows only too well what she will do next. Is it a sigh? A moment during which her husband's eyes are shut? He doesn't have to ask.

It has often been like this. After the time with his superior, he had been down to the dungeon. The two young people were there, bound to chairs. Whatever else, he could see her beauty.

Mary kneels before him; at first her hands are on his knees. It is not to pray. She doesn't have to ask. She undoes his belt, lowers his zip.

And when it is over, something in her wants her to cry. But she can't. She is too empty.

The roses, fresh and beautiful, offer no comfort to her.

*

2. Andante: *con amore*

As was usual in those day, there was no one at the lake, just them, Mark and Alice. The water was ruffled by a gentle breeze, its gusts disturbing the leaves as if they were laughing with the couple, enjoying the summer afternoon, enjoying the sunlight as it appeared, occasionally masked by alto cirrus clouds. The breaking of the little waves on the shoreline, the sound of skylarks high above only emphasised the silence. There is a little jetty, placed there long ago by – who knows? It is a new world now. No one will come there now, for such individual pleasures are to be denied.

But Mark and Alice are there. At the time, when the authorities were otherwise engaged, they were able to make their way to the lake, for once unobserved. They have an old car, but its false number plates will not fool anyone. They have sat by the water's edge on a low, moss-covered rock. They have been here before. Alice has her knees brought up to her chest, Mark leans back. Both breathe in the air, the sound as it were in praise to the very being of the place. They are so used to doing everything as one. Delight fills their eyes, their nostrils and spreads through their bodies, as music, great music, too, fills their bodies as they listen to it with ears and muscles, bones and organs. As they silently watch – for there is no need of words between them – the sunlight on the water, the ripples of the wavelets and the splash of an occasional duck as it lands on the surface, they know that, for now, loves fills everything. She takes his hand ; he brings her towards him. There is no space between them. No more words.

For now.

Soon, Alice looks up at him. "Let's," she says. She turns to him and undoes his top button. She has no need to look him in the eye; she knows he watches even the lightest movement of her fingers, her hands, her head. All he adores. She knows, she feels, she loves.

He stands. She stands. He undoes her blouse. Her trust is absolute, for this he has done many times. Soon, his shirt is off, lying close by on the ground; so is hers. She turns away, so that he can undo the hooks at the back. Her breasts are free – free! He holds them, she turns and they kiss as they have kissed so many times. They remove their lower clothes, each dealing with the other's. Suddenly, she is gone, running the few yards to the end of the jetty.

When they came to this lake not many months ago, for the first time, they did not know if they could swim in it, if it was safe and healthy. But they had taken the plunge. The waters are clear and small fish can be seen, and each time they have come here, it is as if it is for the first time. She stands at the end, her back to Mark, her body silhouetted against the low hills on the far side, sunlight touching her shoulders, her head, her hair. Then she turns to look to him, to reassure herself that he is still there. Of, course he is, lighting up, in her eyes, this lovely place. Suddenly she dives backwards into the water. It is only a foot or so below, but deep enough to offer no risk. The splashing water reaches high above her, as Tom can see, it washes over her, as if swallowing her up, as if to wash her, to cleanse her and to free her to joy all the more.

Mark runs to the end, dives in, head first. It was at first a little chill, but it is fresh and, too, cleansing. When he comes up, he sees Alice standing there, just next to him, her hair wet and in streaks. He washes the water from her eyes. And as he has seen her so often before, he feels that all he wants to do is to hold her.

But at once she says, "Race you, race you to that point just over there and back again!" And she is off. She knows she is a stronger swimmer than him. He is not far behind. But he comforts himself with the thought that he has let her win.

She laughs; he is near crying with delight. With the water high to their midriffs, they hold each other without any movement.

After a time, during which they have swum and circled and splashed and laughed, they leave the water, hauling themselves onto the jetty. There, they stand and observe one another in all their nakedness. He takes her hands, they stand touching each other; then, they are in each other's arms.

Later, they rise, dress and walk hand in hand to the car. Every flower, every leaf is alive with and in them.

*

Back in their flat, they have seen the television. It is not possible to turn it off or the sound down when there is 'official' news. They hold each other tight, their eyes shut, but their ears only too aware. Though this kind of news is not new to them, each time the fear and the horror forces them ever more firmly into each other's arms.

The silent question: how is it that a human can experience such joy and beauty, both in nature and in another, and at the same time be witness to such horror? They know no answer, except to be as one together.

In time, they go to bed.

And at 5.00 in the morning, before it begins to get light, before even the earliest bird sings, their front door is brutally knocked in.

Ten men – armed with guns and batons, tasers and handcuffs, helmeted and wholly impersonal, as seen all over the world – seize them, ripping them from their bed, ripping them apart. Hurling clothes at them, they are ordered to dress. "Quickly!" one screams, watching Alice trying to understand. He slaps her. Mark reacts; another shoves him fiercely against the side of the door.

Within minutes, they are in the black van, huddled, terrified. Blindfolded.

They do not, cannot notice the drone overhead.

*

3. Allegro *con brutalità*

It is some hours later. Mark and Alice lie crumpled on the floor of a cell. They cannot tell where they are nor what time it is. Alice whispers.

"I love you." So faintly; Mark moves to her. They cannot see each other, nor touch, they are bound in. . . .

They know, of course, of the Castle. And, like all such, it is a monument to the darkness in the human heart.

"Alice. Alice." She can now feel his body against hers. Little though it is, it offers comfort. "Think of yesterday, of our time together by the lake."

She presses against him. "But why are we here like this?"

"You will soon find out!" Harsh words accompany the opening of the cell door. "Pick them up," commands Westerbrook. "Take them to the chamber." He rips off the blindfolds.

Though bruised, tired and shocked, Mark and Alice try to walk as normal, but it is hard. After a few short minutes, a few short steps, they are roughly led into a room, darkened around the edges, but with bright lights on two chairs in the middle. All in the room is painted white, even the floor.

The guards, with expressionless faces, undo the bindings and roughly remove their clothing. Forcing Mark and Alice onto the chairs they bind their feet to the legs of the chairs, then their arms are roughly bent back, tied tightly. They are quite naked. Westerbrook watches, waits, as do a couple of assistants.

On a table are implements, bottles, wires and his whip. Torture is cheap and simple.

There is a long silence. Alice looks – as best she can – at where she is, at whom she sees. She looks at Mark. Her look tells him, "Don't do anything to protect me!"

Nothing has begun. Yet.

Westerbrook notices one of the guards moving his hand at the sight of the naked woman. But he, the Colonel, will deny himself such pleasure. For now.

He cracks the whip across Mark's face. "You will tell us. Now!"

Mark, agonised, looks blankly at his opponent.

"Do you think we don't know what you were doing yesterday? Do you think we didn't follow your car, even with its false number plates? Oh, and we watched with pleasure as you two 'had it off' by the lake!"

"But. . . ."

"But what?" whispered the Colonel. "There can be no 'buts'."

Mark looked at Alice. She moved her eyes from side to side. "Give the bastard nothing!" Mark reads in them.

"Love! I scorn the word, the idea. Don't you know, don't you realise that we humans are all, each one of us, just cogs in a machine, just electronic information buried deep in a mountainside. Even me. But *we* are in charge, you mere fodder. So, before we have finished here, you will tell us who killed our four men. Won't you? And that will be all. After all, why did you choose to go to the lake, just think we would be otherwise occupied??"

"We know nothing. . .!"

Westerbrook nods. An assistant clips two leads onto Mark' genitals, two onto his feet, the wires going back to their source. His scream fills the room, rebounding of the white walls, the white floor. It floods into the corridor outside, so that others can hear. And it goes on till Mark faints. Alice has kept her eyes tight shut.

And so it begins. The wires, tweezers pulling out fingernails, water splashed again and again over his face. Mark faints, is revived, faints again, is whipped. In the end, a pipe is thrust into his mouth. A liquid runs through it – for some minutes. It is enough.

But, ultimately, there is no point to the torture, for nothing can be revealed. For one reason or another.

And then it is Alice. She is the real victim, perhaps because they see that she is stronger than him. It is when Westerbrook plunges a truncheon into her, deep into her, that he comes into his own. But still, he learns nothing, for they had nothing to do with the assassinations.

But after that he is bored. He instructs the guards to finish the session. "Then put their bodies with the others on the Cathedral steps."

Before that, the guard stands close in front of Alice, between her knees, his trousers down.

*

When Westerbrook gets home later, his need bursts forth. "Mary, come upstairs at once." His two sons are now downstairs eating tea. They hear footsteps above, a door slamming. Not long after, they hear music. Though they do not know it, it is the slow movement of Mahler's 5th Symphony. That stops abruptly; it is followed by the last, intense and aggressive last movement.

Tom has a slight smile, a smirk, on his face. Peter feels only an incoherent sadness.

*

Mark and Alice have been dumped on the steps, as ordered.

There is little left of them. Darkness has fallen. Other bodies provide cushions, bloodied.

After a while, Alice is able to move her hand. It is all she can do.

She finds and holds Mark's.

And she will remember, for all the years and the decades that will follow, only one thing. In time, she is able to put the torture, its brutality and its pain, behind her, more or less. But she will never, never be able to forget this.

Mark's hand is cold.

*

Postscript.

No apology is made for the Orwellian association. The lovemaking here may, or may not be, a 'political act'.

The massacre on the steps derives from Patrick Lee Fermor: in World War 2, whilst with the resistance in Crete, he captured a German general. The Germans massacred 100 Cretans in retaliation. A memorial to them stands on top of a cliff on the south side of the island.

The Internet of Everything: Yuval Noah Harari, *Homo Deus*.

Decades ago, knowing nothing and just out of University, in Capetown, I found myself a job as a teacher in a school for 'coloured' children, as they were then termed. It was during that year that I learnt the harsh and cruel realities of Apartheid. Ahmed Osman, older than me by as much as 30 years, took me under his wing, helped and befriended me – I became almost a member of his family. He taught me about Mozart and he read me his poetry, and about imprisonment, torture, solitary confinement and dehumanisation in the name of a perverted ideal. He had experienced all.

Ahmed Osman. R.I.P.

5

Darwin's Journey

We stopped looking for monsters under our bed when we realized that they were inside us.

Charles Darwin

It is surely the case, that amongst numerous others who have created the world that we live in, Charles Darwin must be the greatest of Victorians.

Darwin's life took him from happy but simplistic, youthful religiosity to a fundamental disbelief. Of course, in his Autobiography, edited and perhaps corrected by his widow and son, Frank, he declared himself to be a 'Theist'. This goes much against the simple understanding that his Theory of Evolution asserts: that there is no God. This was not just a reaction to the tragic death of his beloved daughter, Annie, at the age of 10 (and of two other of his children); rather, this was the inevitable consequence of having to recognise that the truth of Evolution denied everything that had been taught him – and Christian society at large – about religion and God. Furthermore, he recognised that all life – biological life – is a matter of chance survival and that there is no destination for life, no New Jerusalem, no theistic communist state, to be achieved. We know that 99.5% of all species that have existed, have perished, one way or another.

This is what beckons for Homo Sapiens, too.

He realised, too, that humanity – in general and individually – has only one choice: to pursue this inevitability or to do the opposite, that is to be responsible for our survival, even if this might still lead to the only conclusion for our species.

However, if there is to be found a void at the meaning of existence, other than 'the survival of the fittest' (*not* his words, but Herbert Spencer's), there is only one option for human happiness: to be responsible. 'To do no harm'.

For the young man who, on his famous journey on *The Beagle*, took great pleasure in shooting animals, what does this mean later in his life?

Socrates' dictum that 'the unexamined life is not worth living for a human being' is, to my mind, as well exemplified in the life that Charles Darwin led as it is in anyone's. Socrates emphasised above all else that reason must be applied to all that a human must do, to come to terms with and understand life as it is. Reason, with its accompanying characteristics of observation, examination and judgement, is the only tool that we have for this purpose, and it is this that establishes the higher faculties that distinguish humans. Reason, we are led to believe, has no place in the animal kingdom. For Darwin, as much as for Socrates, reason is the only religion.

When Charles Darwin was born in 1809, over-lapping with Jane Austen by eight years, the culture of the European world, at least, was undergoing fundamental changes, brought on by the Enlightenment. Darwin was perhaps to prove himself the greatest inheritor of these changes during the course of his life time. When he died, in 1882, his world, and the place of man in it, had changed completely. And it is possible that he made the single greatest contribution to that change. Indeed of all the most powerful ideas that have changed our understanding of life, Darwin's idea of 'Natural Selection', Copernicus' realisation that the solar system was heliocentric and Einstein's Theory of Relativity and Heisenberg's Quantum Theory, it has been claimed that the first was the most significant, for it directly and most immediately impinges upon our actions and our self-awareness, in relation to the world around us. Great ideas force us to see ourselves as we are, and not as we would imagine ourselves to be.

This paper is about Charles Darwin, not about Evolution as such. I will have to refer to it, in the hope that I have some grasp of the principles that Darwin set out in *On The Origin of the Species* and in his extensive other writings. I am sure I will be picked up on any failings in this respect. Rather, I want to try to capture something of the nature of the man himself, using principally his own words, but also words of his contemporaries, friends and family, together with reference to modern commentators. I want to consider to a degree the development of his thought in the context of his life and times, with reference to *The Origin*, to his 'Autobiography', journals, letters and such like. Darwin examined life as fully and extensively as anyone could. As far as I can tell, no one had a bad word to say against him, but what sort of man was Darwin? What was his cast of mind and what, by the end of his life, did he know? What lay between the small boy in the portrait, presenting a pot of flowers to his younger sister, and the old man, photographed by his son, Leonard, of whom the young Henry James said, "Darwin is the sweetest, simplest, gentlest old Englishman you ever saw. . . . He said nothing wonderful and was wonderful in no way but in not being so."[1] This last sentence needs bearing carefully in mind.

The Charles Darwin I have come to understand is a man of great complexity. The easy-going, energetic young man who boarded *The Beagle* in October, 1831 returned in 1836 if not troubled, then certainly perplexed by his travels. His loathing of the sea ensured he would never leave England again. By 1842, when settled in Kent at Down House, the man who had explored the World and was to give the most coherent explanation of life to date, retreated into fatherhood, the life of a small country squire and of gentlemanly scientific pursuits. His illnesses started from this time, restricting greatly his social life – and gregarious and warm in company he appears to have been, yet he was often teased for his hypochondria. He was a workaholic, a man of precise routines, a loving, liberal father and husband, and yet a precise, objective recorder of his children's growth and behaviour. This man who was to reshape our view of the world spent much of his time peering through his microscope.

He and Emma read widely in the classics and they would read the plays of Shakespeare as family evening entertainment. He was a prolific, and very good, writer himself – not just *The Origin* and the three books that accompany it, but also of four huge volumes about barnacles, numerous papers published in a wide range of journals and magazines, other books including one on worms published in the year before his death, together with an estimated 15,000 letters. He hated cruelty of any kind, though as a young man he was an avid shooter. He was, one can see from numerous portraits, such as those by George Richmond of Darwin and his young wife, Emma, a man of poise and self-possession, and he was possessed of an unforced and invariable charm that endeared him to all. On the other hand, he had a horror of causing offence, whilst being most rigorous and determined in his intellectual causes. If he was a man

---

[1] Keynes, R: 'Creation', p.254.

of paradox, then he lived with perhaps the most compelling paradox of all: that, whilst life is remorselessly and purposelessly cruel, it also possessed its wonders, that whilst he came to see that *all* life had no ultimate meaning, he lived his own as fully as can be expected of anyone.

In many ways, he was very privileged, both in terms of the intellectual milieu into which he was born as well as financially – he learnt as a teenager that he was never going to have to work for his living. It is worth recounting his background. He was the fifth of the six children of Robert Darwin, a doctor practising in Shrewsbury. He was also the grandson of Erasmus Darwin, himself a doctor, if unwillingly so, but far better known for his works, *The Botanic Garden* and *Zoonomia.* He, Erasmus, was very much a *bon viveur*, a philandering libertine (he appears to have run at least two families), and perhaps most famously, as a member of the Lunar Society, a group of like-minded intellectuals who would meet in Birmingham once a month at the time of the Full Moon, in order to get home when it was light enough to avoid highwaymen. This Society, I am told, has been revived, but in the latter part of the 18th Century, it was a focal point for Enlightenment ideas, liberal political thought and non-conformist religious understanding. It counted amongst its members not only Darwin, but also Benjamin Franklin and Joseph Wright of Derby, the artist. Erasmus Darwin, in his day was regarded as the 'most famous man in England'. His name was put forward for Poet Laureate – the works above are in verse – and it is his influence and Enlightenment thinking that permeated through his son to his grandson. In particular, *Zoonomia* forcefully advanced the idea of evolution.

But I am not just name-dropping. By the end of the 18th century, it is quite astonishing the range of connections within the intellectual life of the nation that Erasmus' generation had, and subsequent generations also had and maintained, not just as contacts, but also as friends and family. In the first place and perhaps most profoundly significant, was Erasmus' friendship with Josiah Wedgwood I, the founder of the Wedgwood pottery empire. The latter was born in 1733 in to a family of small potters; he started with nothing, and ended up by selling dinner services to Catherine the Great. He died enormously wealthy. Erasmus and Josiah I had much in common: temperamentally dynamic and creative, they shared the intellectual predispositions of the day, and were united in the Unitarian faith, which gave birth in turn to liberal Whig political ideals, including a hatred of slavery in all its forms. In particular, because of their anti-slavery attitudes, the Wedgwoods became friends and supporters of William Wilberforce and of the remarkable Thomas Clarkson, whose life was given to the Abolitionist cause, and was funded by Wedgwood, and whom Jane Austen 'loved'. All this would tell upon Charles Darwin's life and achievement. Bear in mind, one of the remarkable things about these two families is that, if I can put it like this, they came out of the soil of England. The Wedgwoods were almost literally of the earth, being potters for generations; the Darwins, initially from Nottingham, were small landowners.

However, it was the marriage between Robert Darwin and Josiah Wedgwood's daughter, Susannah, an occasion which was both inevitable and bound the families together. This marriage ended in tragedy, when Susannah died aged 54 in 1817, when Charles Darwin was just 8 years old. Robert is said never to have got over her death, and there is some discussion as to the degree to which his son was affected by it, as there is over the extent to which his theory of Evolution was a rebellion against his overbearing father, which is not a view I take, though the death of his mother appears to have been one of the two or three most important events in his life. I will refer to this later.

Charles Darwin's intellectual heritage is as rich as that by which he was surrounded. There is not the space to go into them all, except to say that anyone worth knowing came into his purview, and even friendship. His brother, Erasmus, trained as doctor but never practised; instead he led a life of ease in London, never married and remained Charles' closest friend. His connections were widespread, and include a very close (but platonic) relationship with that blue-stocking of all blue-stockings, Harriet Martineau and with the reprehensible Thomas Carlyle. George Eliot was part of the circle – she and Darwin and his wife later in life attended a séance together. Among Darwin's closest friends were Joseph Hooker, son of the Founder of the Botanical Gardens at Kew and later director of it himself, T.E. Huxley ("Darwin's Bulldog") and Charles Lyell, the father of Geology.

Finally, it is worth mentioning Darwin's descendants. Seven of his ten children survived into adulthood; three of his sons received knighthoods (Darwin himself was shamefully ignored in his life time). A grandson worked with Rutherford and Bohr on the atom in Manchester and became Master of Christ College, Cambridge, Darwin's own college. His granddaughter married Sir Geoffrey Keynes, brother of Maynard, whilst Ralph Vaughan Williams' grandmother was Darwin's elder sister, Caroline. Poets, writers, artists, musicians and academics abound in the family tree. Charles Darwin was the most remarkable of men, but just one member of a remarkable family tree.

I mention this, because Darwin worried greatly that he and Emma would do irreparable harm to their off-spring, in so far as they were first cousins. In the very Jane Austenish world into which Darwin was born, marriage between cousins was far from rare – one moved about in relatively confined social and familial circles. He feared that his sickness, whatever it was, was being passed down to his children. The death of his beloved daughter, Annie, at the age of ten in 1851 devastated him and Emma, and was all the more likely to confirm him in his fears. I will deal with this below. His children suffered frequent illnesses. His third child died in infancy, whilst their last son died from scarlet fever at the age of two in 1858. (This boy, also called Charles, appears to have suffered from Down's Syndrome, a likelihood, as I understand, of a very late pregnancy, his mother being 48 at the time of the birth. How ironic that he should have lived and died at Down House.)

By the turn of the 19th Century, both the Darwins and the Wedgwoods had moved inexorably, but only by their own gifts and efforts, into the burgeoning, newly-affluent middle class. They lived in large houses, were well-connected and educated. They had extensive libraries and read widely, in arts, Sciences and literature. Emma Darwin herself was, by all accounts and outstanding musician – she reportedly had lessons from none other than Frederic Chopin, and to have read *Paradise Lost* at the age of five. They supported causes, not only against slavery, but across a wide front, including the revolutionaries in France. They were anti-clerical and generous with their money (and good with it – Robert Darwin, whose appetite for life must have been enormous, made a great deal by investments and speculation; when he died at the age of 82, he weighed 24 stone. He left his son £40,000.) These families were what we might call aspirational; they certainly achieved.

Nevertheless, illness and death, in their cruel evolutionary way, stalked Victorian life. It is perhaps hard for us to understand how much this was the case, as we too are the inheritors of the Enlightenment and all the wonderful advances in medicine since Darwin's time. I hope that I have said enough about the background to his life; it is to what I consider the most famous episode of Darwin's life that I must turn, the voyage of 'The Beagle' and *The Origin of Species* notwithstanding. The Darwins, and Wedgwoods, had a tendency to great longevity, but they, as with so many, had their fair share of family tragedies. We are perhaps inclined to think of mortality in previous centuries as being regarded with a degree of fatalism, as being inevitable. However, the death of any child in any era must be the most terrible experience for parents, who will react in their own particular ways.

Annie Darwin died at noon on the Wednesday 23rd April, just after Easter in 1851. She had been ill for some months before (it is thought now with Tuberculosis, and not an inherited ailment). She died not at home, but in Malvern, whence her father had taken her in a last-ditch attempt to see if the very fashionable Dr Gully, whose water treatment had been some help to Darwin, could do something for his daughter. It was to no avail. Emma, though, had to stay at Down, which is just outside Bromley in Kent. She was pregnant with her ninth child, due at any time and could not travel. It is hard to imagine a more traumatic circumstance.

As Annie lay dying, Charles and Emma kept up a daily, even hourly, correspondence. He charted Annie's progress in every detail. "I am assured that Annie is several degrees better. . . . She looks very ill: her face lighted up & she certainly knew me. . . . My own dearest support yourself – on no account for the sake of our other children; I implore you, do not think of coming here." (17th April). Then a long letter on 20th April: "It is a relief to me to tell you: for whilst writing to you I can cry, tranquilly. . . . All night she has slept tranquilly. . . She, however, has taken less gruel this night and is fearfully prostrated. . . . Yet when Brodie (the family's nursemaid) sponged her, she asked to have her hands washed and thanked Brodie. . . ," the latter "put her arms around her neck, my poor child and kissed her. . . . 8 o'clock a.m. Dr Gully says *positively* no symptom is worse. . . . 10 o'clock. I grieve to say she has vomited rather much again. . . . Mr Coates (an assistant) seemed astonished at her 'fearful illness' & he made me very low; so this morning I asked nothing & then he felt her pulse of his own accord & at once said, 'I declare I almost think she will recover.' Oh my dear was this not joyous to hear. . . . But I must not hope too much. – The alterations of no hope & hope sicken one's soul: I cannot help getting so sanguine every now & then to be disappointed. . . . 12 o'clock. . . . 2 o'clock. . . . 3 o'clock. . . . 4.30. The chilliness has pretty well gone off & no more sickness, refreshing sleep."

And then on 23rd April:

> "My dear dearest Emma
>
> I pray God Fanny's note may have prepared you. She went to her final sleep most tranquilly, most sweetly at 12 o'clock today. Our poor dear child has had a very short life but I trust happy, & God knows what miseries might have been in store for her. She expired without a sigh. How desolate it makes one think of her frank cordial manners. I am so thankful for the daguerreotype. I cannot remember ever seeing the dear child naughty. God bless her. We must be more and more to each other my dear wife – Do what you can to bear up & think how invariably kind and tender you have been to her. – I am in bed not very well with my stomach. When I shall return I cannot say. My own poor dear, dear wife. C. Darwin."

Darwin did not stay for the funeral, but hurried back to be with his wife and family. He was heartbroken, as this letter, in its very brevity and disjointedness, bears strong witness to. It is not known when Emma heard first of her daughter's death, but its opening sentiments, about "her final sleep" being "tranquilly, most sweetly" reached is deeply poignant – and there is certainly no cause to sneer at the Victorian idiom. Then the short sentences, being somewhat random, suggest Darwin doing his best to control his feelings, including the worry that he might not have been a good enough parent, though he stresses that Emma was. A year or two before, the family had visited a society photographer in London, hence the daguerreotype: remembrance aided by modern technology. And then, "We must be more and more to each other my dear wife." Is there a sense of guilt here, in that he had prevented Emma from being at her daughter's bedside: she might not have been able to travel, but should Darwin have taken his daughter away from home in the first place? "My own poor dear, dear wife."

Darwin would never return to Malvern, for the associations it would bring; Annie's grave lies just outside the main door to the church, carefully maintained. Three weeks later, Emma gave birth to Horace and Darwin buried himself in his barnacles. They did not appear again till the summer of that year when they visited the Great Exhibition. And when some years later, family members tried to find Annie's grave, at first it could not be located. Weeds had grown all over it; today, it is easily seen.

Perhaps Annie's death brought home to Darwin most powerfully one of the central concepts in Evolution, namely, the utter wastefulness of life.

There were many consequences. Annie, by all accounts appears to have been an exceptional little girl (rather putting her younger sister, Etty, in the shade). The Darwins, according to the biography written by his great-great grandson, Randal Keynes[2], followed the advice given by Rousseau in his novel *Emile*, and of other writers regarding the upbringing of children. Above all, children should not be cast into chains the moment they are born. Freedom of expression, movement and of play and the imagination must be theirs of right. So the Darwins left their children to play and to roam as they would, through the house, the gardens and the woods beyond Down House. Discipline was never enforced, but learnt through the experience of learning to respect others. All grew up to be very successful adults. Except Annie, who would follow her father around the Sandwalk, skipping and laughing and observing, as children of that age do. Above all, she was as interested in everything as he was. He wrote, as apparently was the custom at the time, a memorial to his daughter. Written only ten days after their loss, it is remarkable in two ways: it reveals the passionate love he had for his daughter. It is also the writing of a scientist, with its careful, detailed observations in almost every line[3].

Not only did this sad event turn Darwin against religion – he never went to church again - it also informed, even confirmed, much of his thinking about natural selection. But before considering Darwin as a scientist, it is appropriate at this point to consider the question of Darwin and religion, and before doing this, a glance at his childhood is necessary.

Darwin's account of his earliest memories is given in an autobiographical work which was published after his death, originally intended only for his family to read. His youthful

---

[2] 'Annie's Box', later filmed as 'Creation', with Paul Bettany and Jennifer Connelly.

[3] He had kept a record of his children since the birth of his first son, William. They were as much his subjects as were barnacles, pigeons and finches.

memories have an almost Joycean quality to them, of wonder even: "I have an obscure picture of the house before my eyes, & of a neighbouring small shop, where the owner gave me one fig, but which to my great joy turned out to be two: - this fig was given me that this man might kiss the maidservant. . . ." There was "a walk to a kind of well, on the road to which was a cottage shaded with damascene trees, inhabited by an old man called a hermit, with white hair, (who) used to give us damascenes." However, even at this early age, young Charles demonstrated a love of collecting and organising. As mentioned previously, however, this childhood idyll was destroyed prematurely by the death of Darwin's mother.

This occurred when he was eight years old. The psychologist John Bowlby has written a most interesting biography of Darwin[4]. He considers this to have been a most crucial experience for the young boy. From his account, it would appear that the Darwin family reacted to their terrible loss in what would appear to us to have been an entirely negative way. So devastated, Bowlby argues, was Robert Darwin that his two elder daughters, who took over the running of the household, refused any mourning or reference to their lost parent. This repression took a serious toll upon young Charles, and, as Bowlby's theory goes, was the cause of his illnesses, for throughout his working life till his late years, he was chronically and, at times, debilitatingly ill for weeks, and even months, on end. Nausea, dizziness, rashes, eczema, the products of hyperventilation – all kept him bed-ridden so much that by his own reckoning he had lost "several years". A further symptom, according to Bowlby, was the little boy's tendency to take himself off for long walks and, upon his return, not know where he had been.

There is plenty of argument as to the causes and nature of his illness, but if Darwin did nothing else in his life, it was walk. As a boy, he walked and explored his home and its locality, collecting and organising insects all the time. He would take himself off fishing. At school he walked, at university in Edinburgh, instead of studying to be a doctor, he walked along the shore looking for specimens as instructed by his then mentor, Robert Grant. He walked in the Lake District, and after Cambridge, walked with another one of his early teachers, Adam Sedgwick, on a geological expedition in North Wales. He walked looking for beetles with John Stephens Henslowe, his university lecturer, through the Cambridge countryside – it was this latter who was to recommend Darwin to Captain Fitzroy of 'The Beagle'.

Darwin spent weeks, months even, walking and riding in the countries he visited on his famous journey – of the four years and ten months he was away, he is reckoned to have spent only 553 days on board ship. And once he had settled at Downe in Kent, he would walk every day, when he wasn't too ill, along the Sandwalk, a pathway through the woods adjoining the garden. Here he would do his thinking. He appears to have boundless energy and drive, was a workaholic as we would call it, and he possessed a quite remarkable capacity for observation, recognition and remembering what he had seen on his travels. 'He had an almost superhuman ability to see things other people did not notice. . . (and) not only the thing itself, but its significance."[5] This is a hallmark of all his work. His passion for all things natural started when very young – he recalls collecting stones and pebbles as a very little boy. He was forever looking and noticing. He read widely, too, one of his earliest influences being Gilbert White's *Selborne*, and a work called *The Wonders of the World*. Strangely, however, he took

---

[4] Charles Darwin – A New Life.

[5] Aydon, p.286.

up angling as a boy, and this developed into a passion for shooting, one might say an addiction. This he refers to in his autobiography with a real degree of embarrassment – Darwin hated cruelty of any kind and by the time of his move in 1842 to Down House had quite given it up. But what of religion and of God?

As a boy and young man, Darwin had taken on easily the religion of his forebears. His degree was in Theology, but had he become a village priest, one imagines he would have found plenty to distract him from his duties. In his youth, his religious attitudes were as received and little thought about. I feel that, though his faith waned and died in his maturity, for various reasons he does not seem to spend too much time thinking about theological issues. His ideas about evolution and about life in general simply precluded any faith – one of the reasons for his long procrastination over the publishing of his great work.

For example, on 13th December 1866[6], Darwin received a letter from one Mary Boole, some seven years after the publication of *The Origin*. She was an ordinary member of the public who had become somewhat disconcerted about the implications for religion in the idea of Evolution and Natural Selection. She asked him three rather direct questions: Did he consider that "knowledge is given to man by the direct Inspiration of the Spirit of God? That God is a personal and Infinitely good Being? And that each individual man has, within certain limits, a power of choice as to how far he will yield to his hereditary animal impulses, and how far he will rather follow the guidance of the Spirit Who is educating him into a power of resisting those impulses in obedience to moral motives." Mary Boole does not in her letter challenge Darwin's theory, since in it she saw a link – "not to say *the* missing link" – between Science and religion. However, as the debate had raged, her worries had grown that she might have been mistaken.

It seems to me that Mrs Boole had got to the core of the problem that many of her time faced; indeed, Darwin faced it all his life. However, in his response to her is very typical. He begins in a characteristically self-deprecatory way: "It would have gratified me if I could have sent satisfactory answers to your questions, or indeed answers of any kind." Then he goes straight to one of the great issues concerning evolution as a whole: the issue of whether "all organic beings including man have been genetically[7] derived from some simple being, instead of having been separately created [8], bears on your difficulties." In other words, Darwin does not know the answer, or as he further implies, is unwilling to give it, in order not to cause his correspondent distress. He asks her to consider that the amount of suffering in the world has natural causes, and is not caused by God. He can go no further than this rather equivocal answer, partly because he was fearful of causing offense, partly because he seems to shy away from all theological discourse.

Ten years later, in his 'Autobiography', he included a section dealing with religion. It is not long, but is very revealing. Bear in mind that this was not written for publication, but for his wife and family only. Nevertheless, the text was edited and perhaps censored by Emma, and their son Frank. Also, it should be born in mind that she and her husband, however entirely well-suited they might have otherwise been, differed absolutely in their respective attitudes to religion. She, when young, had developed a deep commitment to her faith in God, in

---

[6] In 'Evolution- Selected Letters of Charles Darwin, 1860-1870, p.155.

[7] The use of this word is curious. I don't recall it occurring in *The Origin* at all. William Bateson is said to have coined it in the 1890s, after CD's death.

[8] i.e. evolution against creationism.

salvation and in the after-life. Darwin, as he made clear form the days of his courtship, that he had no such faith. This was always a great source of tension, but I can find no evidence that either mocked or ridiculed the other's attitude.

Half way through the section on 'Religious Belief', Darwin writes these damning words: 'And this is a damnable doctrine.' For emphasis, these six words stand alone on their own paragraph. What had brought them on?

In the preceding paragraph, Darwin accounts for his initial loss of faith. Apparently, whilst on 'The Beagle', the sailors teased him for his simplistic religious beliefs. But after his return, in October 1836, his faith began, slowly, to disappear. "Thus disbelief crept over me at a very slow rate." By the end, he felt "no distress" at this loss. The lack of evidence for the existence of God, the incomprehensibility of the Old Testament, the improbability of the miracles ("the more we know of the fixed laws of nature the more incredible do miracles become"), the unlikelihood of the Gospels being written at the same time, with all the inaccuracies and contradictory narratives that these reveal – all these contributed to his growing disbelief. Then he writes this:

> I can indeed hardly see how anyone ought to wish Christianity to be true; for if so the plain language of the text seems to show that men who do not believe, and this would include my Father, Brother and all my best friends, will be eternally punished.
>
> And this is a damnable doctrine."

Darwin here is not damning Christianity as a whole, merely this particular aspect of its teaching. Well, not entirely, since, as we have seen, Annie's death had removed any vestigial faith. Had he been writing a hundred years earlier, he might well have had to consider his own safety. His loss of faith began in his late twenties, long before his daughter's death, when he was putting together his understanding of evolution; by 1838-9, this he had done. And he was fully aware of its implications.

Mrs Boole's three questions seem, as I said, to have gone to the heart of the issue. In the first place, is the question of knowledge. It is plain, from everything that he wrote, that knowledge – that is, recognition, understanding, insight – depends entirely on the logical connections that only observation – noticing, experimenting – can allow for. Darwin is, above all, a scientist. There is no divine gift in this. Secondly, Mrs Boole refers to God as being "a personal and Infinitely good Being." The simple response to this, as it has always been, is to ask why, if God is such, does he allow so much suffering. Darwin had recognised the overwhelming prevalence of suffering in the world and in nature. In one letter, he asks angrily why God should have designed an insect which works its way into the belly of a caterpillar, where it feeds on the organs of that caterpillar, thus destroying it. This is indeed a very perverse God.

However, Darwin – from an evolutionary point of view – considered that in his judgement, "happiness decidedly prevails."[9] Thus, "if the truth of this conclusion be true, it harmonises well with the effects which we might expect from natural selection." He then goes on to advance a reading of the idea of natural selection, based upon the pleasure principle. However, and this is essential, "pain or suffering of any kind, if long continued, causes

---

[9] Autobiographies, p.51.

depression and lessens the power of action; yet is well adapted to make a creature guard itself against any great or sudden evil -" in other words, adapt.

How paradoxical that in all the profusion of suffering in the natural world, of destruction and extinction, that "happiness" should serve its purpose in the propagation of species! "There may be," he goes on, "an excess of happiness over misery." However, "such suffering is also quite compatible with the belief in Natural Selection" which "tends to render each species as successful as possible in the battle for life with other species." So, "pleasurable sensations . . . may long be continued without any depressing effect; on the contrary they stimulate the whole system to increased action." These pleasurable sensations serve as "habitual guides", in other words are themselves both the driver *and* the product of evolutionary processes.

The third question, as to the relationship between morality and "hereditary animal impulses", Darwin argues as follows. The standard view of suffering and punishment is that this "serves for moral improvement. . . . Whilst suffering and pain might be good for humans, there is any amount of such in the animal kingdom, with no visible moral benefit. . . . A being so powerful and so full of knowledge as a God who could create the universe, is to our finite minds omnipotent and omniscient, and it revolts our understanding to suppose that his benevolence is not unbounded, for what advantage can there be in the suffering of millions of the lower animals throughout almost endless time."[10]

There are two points here: the first is that Darwin *deliberately* equates man and animal as being part of the whole scheme of things. There is *no* special place for humanity. Secondly, he counters the argument that suffering is predicated upon the existence of God by predicating its existence instead on Natural Selection: "the presence of much suffering agrees well with the view that all organic beings have been developed through variation and Natural Selection." He had carried this stark distinction with him since the early days of the formulation of his theory. Thus Darwin deals with the question of good and evil in the natural world.

Though Darwin admits "that the religious sentiment was never strongly developed in me", it must surely be that he sees, or at least hints at, an evolutionary *purpose* to deep religious feelings[11].

Nevertheless, he then goes on to declare himself to be a theist, for it is quite possible to argue the "extreme difficulty or rather impossibility of conceiving this immense and wonderful universe. . .as the result of blind chance or necessity. When thus reflecting I feel compelled to look to a First Cause having an intelligent mind in some degree analogous to that of man."

Perhaps, though, he added this to placate his wife and family?

However, no sooner has he said this, than doubt rises in his mind. Religious feeling "probably depends upon inherited experience." Is religion not just the inculcation of a belief in God in the minds of young children just part of this process? But, as so often in personal responses,

---

[10] Ibid, p.52.

[11] Modern genetic research indicates as much. See 'Time Magazine', November 29th, 2004: 'Is God in our Genes?' This offers a most interesting and, to me, quite plausible explanation for the origin of religious feelings such as awe, wonder, reverence etc.

he self-deprecatingly sits on the fence: "I cannot pretend to throw the least light on such abstruse problems."

Instead he ends the passage most curiously, with a delightful anecdote about his atheist father. An old lady, suspecting unorthodoxy in Robert Darwin declared to him, hopefully, 'Doctor, I know that sugar is sweet in my mouth, and I know that my redeemer liveth.' One wonders to what extent the workers on sugar plantations would have recognised this; and Darwin himself, so fiercely against slavery?

Darwin, throughout his adult life, was ever keen to avoid giving offence. In the first instance, he was well aware of what pain his absence of religious belief gave to Emma throughout their marriage. Our view of the 19th Century is perhaps a false one; it was, indeed, a century of great changes and developments as the effects of the Enlightenment got under way. Every aspect of the Darwins' life and work was part and parcel of this. Darwin resisted publication of his work on evolution for twenty years, precisely because he did not want to create difficulties. But by the 1860s, secularism had taken hold and attitudes were changing fast.

However, religion was not giving up without a fight and neither were many rebarbative ideas, especially those regarding race and class. Darwin has been considered a radical scientifically, a liberal politically and a conservative socially. The first two points are clear and I don't wholly agree with the third. Nevertheless, Darwin lived very much as the country squire, a benevolent one maybe, and he was wealthy beyond the dreams of the vast majority. Politics never engaged him and whilst he beavered away in privilege, revolutionary movements swirled around him. And as part of that rural establishment, Emma Darwin and her family regularly attended the local Anglican church though, after Annie's death, without their paterfamilias.

To whom else might he have given offence? Before answering this, perhaps one should try to give some sense of the religion lived by the average person in Victorian England. This is not the place for theological exegesis. However, it is hard nowadays to get the whole picture of what Darwin felt he was up against. Non-conformism – the strand of the Christian religion that both the Darwins and the Wedgwoods came from - notwithstanding, society was overwhelmingly Protestant; Catholics were not emancipated in any way till the late 1820s. Church going was more or less compulsory, at least once a week. The parish priest, often a younger son or relative of the local squire, in whose gift the 'living' was until relatively very recently held, exerted enormous sway. The rectory, after the manor house, was often much the largest building in the village. The 39 Articles and the teaching of the Bible in all its aspects were, well, gospel. The divine was ever-present, in the form of Bible stories and teachings, miracles and the immanent. The original sinfulness of man was the first lesson to be learnt, punishment of the eternal kind an ever-present threat and redemption and salvation an ever-present promise in the life hereafter. For the religiously minded, like Emma Darwin, this underpinned everyday experience of life. Its living intensity we should not forget.

Nor should we forget that, for Darwin, mankind had no special place in creation; this was only too evident from his evolutionary theory. For those who had read *Paradise Lost*, as the Darwins had, would have known only too readily the task that faced men and women as a result of the Fall. Nevertheless, humans were, traditionally, the 'Special Creation', by virtue of being sentient beings, to be regarded as having a particular relationship to God. Charles Darwin was always very clearly aware of this. He would also have been aware that white, indeed European races were especially favoured. And, indeed, were white, European males. Darwin risked not only offending his beloved wife, but the entire establishment of church and state. He was also, incidentally, very wary of losing his reputation as a scientist.

Darwin's life work as a scientist can be said to have centred on the notion that all organic life had one common source which produced the 'Tree of Life'. In a world which would seem to us to be hideously and ruthlessly racist, Darwin did not, of course, stand alone. Nevertheless, as Adrian Desmond & James Moore make resoundingly clear[12], *The Origin of Species* became in time one of the central planks in the fight against discrimination. I have mentioned above the connections between the Wedgwoods and William Wilberforce. Darwin inherited a loathing of slavery. His *Beagle* journals make this abundantly clear. However, slavery took much of its justification from the notion of the 'Special Creation'. Thus, in taking on religion, Darwin was also taking on slavery, and vice versa. He loathed cruelty of any kind, whether it be towards other humans or to animals. He took particular offence at those such as the 'Shropshire squires' who sent seven-year-old children up their chimneys. However, whilst he let his writings do his work, others would engage the world beyond Downe.

But it was as a scientist that Darwin would have to prove himself. By the age of 30, he had achievement enough. The happy but somewhat directionless young man of 22 who had boarded 'The Beagle' in October 1831, was by the end of the decade a man of very considerable achievement. He had circumnavigated the world in what was to become one of the most famous journeys of all time. He had made a considerable name for himself through sending huge amounts of specimens and reports back to England; he was now secretary of the Geological Society on the basis of major contributions to geology, a study of coral reefs and evidence of the gradual uprising of mountain ranges in particular, a fellow of the Royal Society, married and very busy – though the illness that was to try him so sorely for so many years now began to strike him. He had published a best seller, known to us as *The Beagle Journals*[13]. This work, to my mind, establishes quite clearly that though he does not articulate his theory of the origin of species in it, is full of just those sorts of observations, details and reflections that form the substance of the theory. There are endless remarks about contrasts and differences throughout, with implied the question of why these differences exist never far from his mind. One might say that the obsession took root almost from the outset, even if it had not been there from his earliest days in Edinburgh.

Thus, by 1840, he had also formulated into a complete theory the idea that was to make him so famous, for it changed for ever the way in which we understood our place in the scheme of all things natural.

In the next few years, he had moved to Downe, started a family and had written a 242-page draft of his great work, with a much shorter abstract. He also wrote a letter to Emma, giving instructions to her to have published this work should he die – such was the state of his health at this point. Then he put it away, and was not to touch it again for another fifteen years. Then two things happened.

First, there appeared in 1844 an anonymous and very voluminous book called *Vestiges of the Natural History of Creation*[14]. Published anonymously, it created a storm. Darwin was

---

12 In 'Darwin's Sacred Cause – Race, Slavery and the Quest for Human Origins'.

13 1839

14 Written by a well-known publisher, the founder of the dictionary company, Robert Chambers

thought to have been the author. Like his grandfather's *Zoonomia*, Darwin found this book easy to dismiss even though it propounded the very theory he was working on. Its ideas were just that, having no scientific validity at all. Nevertheless, it showed that the idea of evolution was already in the public domain.

This, secondly, also forced Darwin to recognise that *he* would have had to have proved himself *as a scientist* and not just a speculative country squire with time on his hands and an on-going obsession. Indeed, a casual remark by Joseph Hooker in a letter to him ('I am not inclined to take much for granted from someone who . . . does not know what it is to be a specific naturalist'[15]) convinced Darwin that he had to demonstrate that he *was* a genuine scientist. It is said that if he had published nothing more than his four volumes on cirripedes, or barnacles, Darwin would still have been regarded as a scientist of very considerable standing.

Although he thought that his study of barnacles would take just a few months, in fact Darwin spent eight years at it, from 1846-54. There is only time to spend a few moments now on the subject. Barnacles are everywhere on the sea shore and on the bottoms of boats and ships; no one knew anything about them and their classification was totally incoherent. From what one can see, they are, in evolutionary terms, quite extraordinary. There tends not to be much humour in Darwin's most scientific writings; indeed, one needs a pretty sound training in biology to grasp anything of what he writes on the cirripedes. Nevertheless, this passage might give something of the flavour of his observations and understanding:

> . . . the probosciformed penis is wonderfully developed, so that in Cryptophialus, when fully extended, it must equal between eight and nine times the entire length of the animal! These males . . . consist of a mere bag, lined by a few muscles, enclosing an eye, and attached at the lower end by the pupal antennae, it has an orifice at its upper end, and within it lies coiled up, like a great worm, the probosciformed penis . . . there is no mouth, no stomach, no thorax, no abdomen, and no appendages or limbs of any kind. . . . I know of no other animal in the animal kingdom with such an amount of abortion.[16]

This creature, nicknamed Arthrobalanus, was the size if a pin-head. Darwin had found it, boring into a conch, on the shores of Chile some ten years previously, and had forgotten about it until he began his researches. Some such barnacles had *two* such penises. But what this study, of which this is only the smallest fragment, allowed Darwin to do was to show that there was an evolutionary process involved in the development of barnacles. This progress was from hermaphrodite to bisexual and thence to diverged sexes. However careful he had to be not to allow the theory to determine his interpretation of his observations, but to let the evidence speak for itself, Darwin was sufficiently confident that he was on to something after only two years that he could write to Hooker:

> I should never have made this (the separation of the barnacle sexes) out had not my species theory convinced me, that an hermaphrodite species must pass into a bisexual species by insensibly small stages, and here we have it, for the male organs in the hermaphrodite are beginning to fail, & independent males ready formed. But I can

---

[15] Aydon, p.170, et al.

[16] Quoted in 'Darwin and the Barnacle', p.220. Hooker was *not* referring to Darwin here, but to someone else.

> hardly explain what I mean, & you will perhaps wish my Species theory al Diablo together. But I don't care what you say, my species theory is all gospel.[17]

'All gospel!' In simple terms, if this process can be seen as being paradigmatic, Darwin could demonstrate, in physical terms through observation, that evolution *does* take place. He also observed that numerous varieties of barnacle could exist in close proximity to one another. This gave him the clue to the answer as to why there is such great and profligate abundance in nature. No wonder he sounds triumphant. By the end of the process six years later, however, he was thoroughly sick of the whole matter. It exhausted him, brought on frequent bouts of his illnesses – and he had to endure the death of Annie during it.

This very brief summary of Darwin's barnacle research gives an idea of its significance in various ways. Of course, he observed anything that came within his scope. Especially important, though, is another long study he made into pigeons. This gave him the basis for the argument that embodies *The Origin of Species*: that all organic life has a common source. He spent much time visiting and befriending pigeon-fanciers in London; he bred his own and researched them in his characteristically detailed way. What he was able to demonstrate was that *all pigeons*, pouters, tumblers or whatever, were derived from one species, the rock pigeon, or *Columba Livia.*

Thus barnacles gave him the status as a genuine scientist that he so needed in order to face up to the demands that his great project threw upon him; they also gave him the paradigm for the process of Evolution. Pigeons gave him the clue to the origin. He returned to his 1844 text and set about writing what he termed 'his big species book'. He was never to complete it.

But what, in the first place, motivated, what compelled Darwin to write this work, to struggle for all those years through doubt and endless, debilitating illness? How did he even manage it? Why did he not, like Gilbert White, settle down to life as a country parson, spending his spare time, which he might have had plenty of, just observing the wonders of nature around him?

I think it was St Augustine who said that the first condition of mind for anyone who wishes for understanding must be one of wonder. Wonder brings curiosity, and curiosity understanding. As a small boy Darwin started with pebbles, and then moved on to small animals, learning their names, trying to organise and to classify them. In school, he was bored silly by endless Latin and Greek and Maths (about which he later regretted); whenever he could he rushed home, or out into the fields. At Edinburgh, he was again bored silly by tedious lecturers, and could not take the suffering without anaesthetic of a small boy being operated on[18]. Robert Grant, one of the junior lecturers, who encouraged Darwin to help him collect crustacean and the sea-shore life from the nearby beaches, provided Darwin with his first disciplined lessons, though informal, in natural history; indeed, he annoyed Grant on occasion by making observations that he, Grant, had not made[19]. Although Darwin had taken his first steps, he was in Edinburgh to train as a doctor. This he gave up after two years.

---

[17] Darwin to Hooker, 10/5, 1848. Quoted in 'On Evolution'.

[18] Anaesthetics did not become available until the 1840s. Darwin, because of the late arrival of the doctor, administered chloroform himself to his wife when her last child was delivered. Queen Victoria also gave birth using chloroform.

[19] In 'Darwin and the Barnacle', p.37.

Thence at Cambridge, to study Theology with a view to taking orders and a life in the priesthood, Darwin had the same rooms in Christ College in which William Paley had once studied. Paley in the decades at the end of the 18th and beginning of the 19th centuries, was a very important figure. His *Principles of Moral and Political Philosophy* was the standard work for all who wished to study as Theology. Whilst powerfully against slavery, as against any form of cruelty, he nevertheless advocated a form of belief in which design had a central place: since the creator is divine, then all creation must be so too. Initially, Darwin "was entranced"[20] by Paley's Argument from Design for the proof of God's existence and he felt encouraged to go "bug-hunting" – he developed an obsession with beetles. He was taken up, though, by Adam Sedgwick and by John Stephens Henslowe. With the former, after he had finally taken his degree, Darwin went "geologising" in Wales; with the latter, he went for many walks in the Cambridgeshire countryside, observing all the time the works of nature around him.

In short, there was nothing to inhibit Darwin's natural sense of wonder. It must have been this, as well as his obvious high intelligence, which encouraged Henslowe to recommend him to Fitzroy. And there was wonder enough to be found during the famous voyage.

Thus, in a wonderful passage, he describes a trip into the Brazilians jungle on the 29th February, 1832:

> The day has passed delightfully: delight is however a weak term for such transports of pleasure: I have been wandering by myself in a Brazilian forest: amongst the multitude it is hard to say what set of objects is most striking: the general luxuriance of the vegetation bears the victory, the elegance of the grasses, the novelty of the parasitical plants, the beauty of the flowers. – the glossy green of the foliage, all end to this end. A most paradoxical mixture of sound and silence pervades the shady parts of the wood. – the noise from the insects is so loud that in the evening it can be heard even in a vessel anchored several hundred yards from the shore. – Yet within the recesses of the forest when in the midst of it a universal stillness appears to reign. – To a person fond of Natural history such a day as this brings with it pleasure more acute than he may ever again experience.[21]

And again, he recalls the following experience. 'The Beagle' was sailing from Rio Plata towards Port Desire at the very tip of South America.

> December 6th, 1833. Several times when the ship has been some miles off the mouth of the Plata, and at other times off the shores of Northern Patagonia, we have been surrounded by insects. One evening, when we were ten miles from the Bay of San Blas, vast numbers of butterflies, in bands of flocks or countless myriads, extended as far as the eye could range. Even by aid of a glass it was not possible to see a space free from butterflies. The seamen cried out 'it was snowing butterflies,' and such was in fact the appearance.

Darwin never forgets that he is a scientist, even on wondrous occasions. Observation, understanding, naming – even at intense moments, both the poetic and the objective go hand in hand.

---

[20] Charles Darwin His Life and Times', p.32.

[21] Beagle Diary 1831-1836, p.69

In passing, the following from his work on barnacles might entertain

> I will allude to the marvellous assemblage of beings seen by me within the sack of an *Ibla quadrivalvis* – namely an old and young male, both minute, worm-like, destitute of a capitulum, with a great mouth, and rudimentary thorax and limbs, attached to each other and to the hermaphrodite, which latter is utterly different in appearance and structure: secondly, the four or five, free, boat-shaped larvae, with their curious prehensile antennae, two great compound eyes, no mouth, and six natatory legs; and lastly several hundreds of the larvae in their first stages of development, with horn-shaped projections on their carapaces, minute single eyes, filiformed antennae, probosciformed-mouths, and only three pair of natatory legs; what diverse beings, with scarcely anything in common, yet all belonging to the same species![22]

As quite often, he employs an exclamation mark when he gets excited, even in the most scientific of passages. And all this was observed through his microscope. There are four volumes of such prose. He was surprised that the book did not sell!

Darwin's expression of wonder is no less the case on many occasions in *The Origin.*

Then, on the 18th June, 1858, Darwin wrote to his friend, Charles Lyell[23]: "He has today sent me the enclosed & asked me to forward it to you. It seems well worth reading. Your words have come true with a vengeance that I should be forestalled." On various occasions, Lyell and others had urged Darwin not to take so long to complete his work on the origins of species; he had taken twenty years so far. Their concern reflects not only their friend's seeming procrastination, but also the sense that the idea of evolution was very much in the air by the middle of the century, as we have seen with *Vestiges*. Darwin *had* dithered because of his fear of the offence his work would cause; it was also a major work, capable of taking up volumes. Darwin was also meticulous in all that he did.

"He" was Alfred Russel Wallace. Wallace had sent from what is now Indonesia to Darwin a 20-page manuscript outlining his own theory of evolution. "If," Darwin continues, "Wallace had my M.S. sketch written in 1842 he could not have made a better short extract! Even his terms now stand as heads of my Chapters."

This famous interjection into the course of Darwin's work by someone living far away caused him rather more disturbance than is revealed in the letter just quoted. Darwin was not ambitious for himself; he was for his work. Although Wallace had indeed arrived at a coherent explanation of Evolution *independently* of Darwin, it is right and proper to consider the latter the true originator of the theory. The two had corresponded in the previous three or four years; they were to do so hereafter, at least until Wallace abandoned evolution (and Science) for spiritualism. They got on very well[24]. Nevertheless, Darwin knew now that he had to produce something very rapidly or indeed someone, if not Wallace, would get there first. The result was *The Origin of Species or The Preservation of Favoured Races in the Struggle for Life*. This 'abstract' of his ideas in fact is 155,000 words long, and it has become one of the most famous books ever.

---

[22] From 'A Monograph of the Sub-Class Cirripedia' (1851). Quoted from 'On Evolution', p.126

[23] 'Origins – Selected Letters of Charles Darwin', 1822-1859, p.192

[24] David Attenborough attests eloquently to this in one of his 'Life Stories' broadcasts, BBC Radio 4, April 2011. This is available as a podcast.

The central theme is that all organic life has a common source, and that there is not only in a ruthless and never-ending conflict between organisms, but also, in the great profligation of life in the natural world, the central paradox brought on by the struggle for survival. It was a direct challenge to the idea that each individual creature had been placed on earth by a creator, and was thus a challenge to all established systems of religious belief, as it remains today. Both Darwin and Wallace had read – and seen vividly exemplified in both nature and in the behaviour of human beings – the works of Robert Malthus, with his stress on the endless and remorseless struggle for control of natural resources.

I am moderately capable of reading *The Origin* as a work of Literature. Darwin wanted to present a text that was accessible to the general reader, to the lay person. I see it in terms of the quality of its writing as the author expands on his 'argument', as he puts it, and on the sense of the nature of the individual behind the words. It is, in effect, a polemic, as much as a work of scientific enquiry. Once one has got used to the idiom, the terminology and the ways in which Darwin structures and organises his thoughts paragraph by paragraph, the quality of the prose becomes abundantly, even radiantly clear.

The work is in fourteen chapters; the whole seems to me to work as if it had a musical form to it, rather as if it were a suite in fourteen movements. Each chapter has its own theme, with variations including development, recapitulation, and points illustrated comprehensively and sources acknowledged. Darwin is well aware of opposing arguments, so the whole has the feel of a fugue, with point and counter-point effortlessly and lengthily being played out.

By the time of the formulation of his theory, Darwin had quite given up the Panglossian view of life so favoured by William Paley, as he had done of God. An example against the Argument from Design is in Darwin's account of the structure of the honeycomb, it being not an example of Design but rather a mechanism for ensuring survival of the bee (or rather of its genes). It is written with characteristic passion and insight:

> Numerous, successive, slight modifications . . . led the bees to sweep equal spheres at a given distance from each other in a double layer and to build up and excavate the wax along the planes of intersection. The bees, of course, are no more knowing that they swept their spheres at one particular distance from each other, than they know what are the several angles of the hexagonal prisms and of the rhombic plates. The motive power of natural selection having been economy of wax: that individual swarm which wasted least honey in the secretion of wax, having succeeded best, and having transmitted by inheritance its newly acquired economical instinct to new swarms, which in their turn will have had the best chance of succeeding in the struggle for existence.[25]

But there is of course the dark side. Thus he concludes the chapter on Instinct:

> Finally, it may not be a logical deduction, but to my imagination it is far more satisfactory to look at such instincts as the young cuckoo ejecting its foster-brothers, - ants making slaves, - the larvae of the ichneumonidae feeding within the live bodies of caterpillars, not as specially endowed or created instincts, but as small consequences of one general law, leading to the advancement of all organic beings, namely, multiply, vary, let the strongest live and the weakest die.[26]

---

[25] 'The Origin of Species', p. 256
[26] 'The Origin of Species', p. 263

And again, from, Chapter III, 'Struggle for Existence':

> Nothing is easier to admit in words the truth of the universal struggle for life, or more difficult – at least I have found it so – than constantly to bear this conclusion in mind.

Annie was never far from his mind, even years after her death:

> We behold the bright face of nature bright with gladness, we often see the superabundance of food; we do not see, or we forget, that the birds which are idly singing around us live mostly on insects or seeds, and are thus constantly destroying life; or we forget how largely these songsters, or their eggs, or their nestlings, are destroyed by birds and beasts of prey; we do not always bear in mind, that though food may now be superabundant, it is not so at all seasons of each recurring year.[27]

And what of God in all this? For Darwin, there is no place in the natural world for a creator.

> The fact, as we have seen, that all past and present organic beings constitute one grand natural system, with group subordinate to group, and with extinct groups often falling between recent groups, is intelligible on the theory of natural selection with its contingencies of extinction and divergence of character.

In other words,

> It must be admitted that these facts receive no explanation on the theory of Creation.[28]

Nevertheless, we can recall that in his *Autobiographies* Darwin wrote this:

> Another source of conviction in the existence of God, connected with the reason and not with feelings, impresses me as having much more weight. This follows from the extreme difficulty or rather impossibility of conceiving this immense universe, including man with his capacity for looking backwards and far into futurity, as the result of blind chance or necessity. When thus reflecting I feel compelled to look to a First Cause having an intelligent mind in some degree analogous to that of man; and I deserve to be called a Theist.[29]

He was, of course, writing before Einstein and Relativity, before Quantum Theory and before Heisenberg's Uncertainty Principle; and perhaps he was being kind to Emma, in resorting to the ontological argument, albeit with an anthropic twist.

But it is with Charles Darwin that I must end. He had seen how enormously cruel and wasteful life, and yet how superabundant it also is, through natural selection, variation and speciation. He had seen how multiplicity helped to ensure the survival of the fittest, and he had seen how little, or none, was the purpose of it all. And he would have seen this in his own life, and in the lives that he was progenitor of.

The last chapter of *The Origin* is in fact musically entitled 'Recapitulation and Conclusion'. In it Darwin does just this, advancing as it does to a wonderful vision of the future of human understanding; it includes the famous sentence, "Light will be thrown on the origin of man and his history." *The Origin* never deals with humanity at all, though any intelligent reader of

---

[27] 'The Origin of Species', p. 2115-6
[28] 'The Origin of Species', p. 450
[29] P.53

his day would have recognised that the work as a whole must include man, with its constant references to "child"," off-spring", "parents". It would not be until 1871 when Darwin published *The Descent of Man, and Selection by Relation to Sex* that he dealt with humanity.

The Origin ends in a stunning coda, in the last few paragraphs. Whilst this final chapter sums up the whole of the book, so in effect does the last paragraph. I quote it here:

> It is interesting to contemplate an entangled bank, clothed with many plants of many kinds, with birds singing on the bushes, with various insects flitting about, and with worms crawling through the damp earth, and to reflect that these elaborately constructed forms, so different form each other, and dependent on each other in so complex a manner, have all been produced by laws acting around us. These laws, taken in the largest sense, being Growth and Reproduction; Inheritance which is almost implied by reproduction; Variability from the indirect and direct action of the external conditions of life, and from use and disuse; a ratio of increase so high as to lead to a struggle for life, and as a consequence to Natural Selection entailing Divergence of Character and the Extinction of less-improved forms. Thus, from the war of nature, from famine and death, the most exalted object which we are most capable of conceiving, namely, the production of the higher animals, directly follows. There is grandeur in this view of life, with its several powers, having been breathed into a few forms or into one; and that, whilst this planet has gone on cycling according to the fixed laws of gravity, from so simple a beginning endless forms most beautiful and most wonderful have been, and are being, evolved.

The beauty, the musicality of this paragraph cannot go unnoticed, both for its content and its expression and structure. It begins with the mild, disarming "It is interesting" and proceeds through three sections. The first is almost a vision of the Garden of Eden. The 'entangled bank' is a bank near Down House, perhaps the one he built in the front to the building. It echoes Shakespeare's "I know a bank where the wild thyme grows. . . ." But here, too, is Darwin's garden, the fauna and flora of which he studied in minute detail for forty years – his last book, published in the year before his death, dealt with worms and their significance[30]. Insects innocently are "flitting about". But then, does a memory of his lost daughter flit across his mind, of her enthusiastically following him through the garden and along the Sandwalk? The section ends with reflection on the interconnectedness of all things living. And here lies the great paradox at the heart of Darwin's vision, profligate destruction and creation at one in nature.

Then he gives a final recapitulation of the "laws" or principles of evolution – Darwin's love of lists, both as rhetorical and poetic devices, is used to wonderful effect here, as in the penultimate sentence, where once again he reiterates the paradox.

At last, he comes to his final sentence, perhaps the greatest sentence ever written. The beautiful musicality of it cannot be missed: "There *is* grandeur . . .": the minute evolutionary process is set against the workings of the Cosmos, life against utter, beautiful impersonality. The pauses and the repetitions serve the final emphases in "have been, and are being, evolved."

---

[30] 'The Formation of Vegetable Mould, through the action of Worms, with Observations on their Habits'. 1881

This is indeed a vision.

*

And the tired and gentle old man, whom Henry James had met, died early in 1882. Against his wishes, his body is buried, at the instigation of Thomas Huxley, in Westminster Abbey, lying next to the tomb of Sir Isaac Newton.

6

Aquae Vitae

Nothing is softer or more flexible than water, yet nothing can resist it.

Lao Tzu

The Red Eyed Frog clings to a little branch, as green as the little creature is. The frog has survived because it is so small, it rarely grows to more than a centimetre – easily hidden. Round, staring red eyes, centred by black pupils, are watching, waiting.

Inches away, a rain drop plops onto a leaf that is as green as the frog.

A second drop passes the frog, just out of range. A third.

The frog's tongue – half its body-length - darts out. The drop is caught.

The frog drinks.

More rain drops fall, and ever more. Soon, the jungle is almost invisible from rain, so heavy is the fall. The frog's body is awash. This is normal: it washes and refreshes the tiny creature.

The rain saturates all as it falls. It falls and keeps falling. And refreshes, reawakens all that makes up the jungle.

Charles Darwin, in his journals of The Beagle voyage in the 1830s, recalls how, one day, the little survey boat stopped off the coast of Brazil. Darwin took a short walk into the jungle and stood amazed at what he saw. But he knew at once: the jungle was all of life, from the tallest trees, the canopy of which held most of the rain as it fell, to the smallest creatures: new-sprouting plants, insects and, though he did not yet know it, a multitude of life too small for him to see.

And yet all around was decay, death, destruction: fallen branches and trunks of once great trees; decaying leaf-mould, dead bodies. The cycle of life lay before him.

A while later, as The Beagle sailed away, the sound, the endless, humming, throbbing sound of the jungle followed the boat even a mile or more out to sea.

The little boat sailed on, moisture evaporating from the sea and forming clouds that daily grew heavier and darker. Until they deposit their waters on all below.

And sustain the frog in its life.

And hasten decay.

A million miles away, a million years apart, the ageing farmer sits on his veranda, his stoep. His pipe is worn and nowadays holds little tobacco. Inside, his wife is moving restlessly, and without rest. His children have left long ago.

It is four in the afternoon. As with every day, days which begin with bright sunshine and cloudless blue skies, by midday, the clouds are building up, growing and darkening. He sits there now, looking at them, looking at the land that is before him.

It is parched and more than parched. Grasses lie dried, deadened, desiccated. There are no flowers, some of his cattle, the remaining ones, thin and emaciated, are doing their best to find sustenance. There is little, so little. The farmer thinks that soon he will have to leave, leave the land inherited from his father and from his father beforehand. He will be as arid as the soil before him.

The clouds have banked up and all is ever darker. There is no wind. Stillness, darkness. As every afternoon, for months now. The weather forecast offers no hope, each morning. Lightning and thunder, yes.

He draws on his pipe. Little satisfaction. Drought kills, he knows that now.

Perhaps he drops off, a moment. He cannot spend all his time watching the clouds, waiting, hoping. He is tired. Tired of the battle.

He glances down to the earth before him. The earth, shrunken, dried out, has cracks, zig-zagging away from him. An occasional ant scurries somewhere. Across the way, a cow looks up, at him.

He dozes off.

A drop on the corrugated roof above him does not wake him.

Nor does a second or third.

A hand on his shoulder does wake him.

'Look!' she cries. 'It's rain!'

Rainwater *is* falling. Ever faster, ever heavier.

He jumps up.

Runs forward, into the now streaming water. As much as it comes down, it splashes off the hardened ground. He grabs his wife, dances, shouts spins around and around. Cheering, shouting. Laughing.

Refreshed, washed, cleansed.

And wherever there has been water, in ancient times, these places, springs, rivulets, lakes, have become places of pilgrimage. They become holy sites, temples and churches are built, civilisations are created.

And empires.

Water. Water is God. Creator - and Destroyer.

'The way is to the destructive element submit yourself, and with the exertions of your hands and feet in the water make the deep, deep sea keep you up.... In the destructive element immerse.'

So said the trader. But Jim had, in an act of cowardice, left the pilgrims on *The Patna*. But he will die, by his own hand, for moral weakness.

He could not hold himself up, by his own efforts.

But the man, chest deep in water, muddy water, holds a basket above his head. In it, a very small child. The great river, at once a great brown god and an agent of destruction, has, once again overflown. Flood waters lie for miles around. Homes, shops and houses, lost.

They will be rebuilt. For the next rainy season.

The man, after finding a dry spot, leaves the basket with one sitting there. He returns to the ruin that was his home. His wife is fearful, sitting still with other children. A scene, common from across the world

And yesterday evening, the sea glistened with the setting sun, warm with gentle waves breaking on the sandy shore.

And as they fled the hotel, a man and his wife found a tree to climb, for the water, up to their waists, was full of debris. Furniture, branches, clothing. . . . Just minutes ago, the tsunami had smashed against the shoreline, smashed and roared and flailed, breaking against all that was living and not living, against all that was normal. They stayed in the tree for several hours, appalled, the destruction becoming more and more apparent. Nothing of the resort was as it had been. Broken, destroyed. Bodies floating.

Saved by the concrete of the hotel, they will never forget the size, the noise, the force of the giant wave. Once home, they would freeze. Shock, delayed, took hold.

And it was recorded that there was a scuba diver beneath the wave. It affected him not.

Still, the brothers love to be at the water's edge. No great waves disturb this Scottish tarn. They throw a small branch into the water for their long-haired Labrador to fetch. In he goes, tail wagging, nose held up. Doggy paddle. He snatches at the twig as it drifts away, returns and drops his prize at the boys' feet. 'Again, please!' he seems to say. And again. Then, after one more time, he suddenly vigorously shakes himself, the water flying off him in a great corona. The boys leap back, laughing.

And, at the end of the day, she will sit there, all day, with such memories. Her boys. And her daughter. The waves lap against the shore, each time a little weaker, a little further out. And each time, the light is dimmer. There is now not much for her to look forward to, not much at all. For a while, she could chat and do jigsaws, read magazines. Slowly, inexorably, these are dropped by the wayside, like so many memories, like so many waves fading, weakening against the shore. Like her time at the end of the war as a Wren, driving sailors – ratings, admirals – from place to place. Her first love: a lieutenant, handsome in his uniform. Of Africa and her life there. And dogs - Poppy, Joey, Vicky, Jasper. Dog-training and croquet, mountain walks. Such and such like now drift through, like so many ancient lakes and rivers, seas and rainy seasons in years gone, long gone by. Slowly, day by day, the memories drift into dreams, the dreams into sleep and more sleep. Now she can no longer walk – nor do the daily things that have to be done. Cared for so well, she feels no discomfort nor pain. In this way, Life has treated her well, as now Death does. More sleep. Then the last sight. The last little wave. Her last breaths.

The waters of life are drained away and she no longer eats or drinks. Dry, still, darkening. Noiseless.

Her breath falters, stutters, weakens.

The river, once giant, pouring its waters into the sea, has retreated, back through towns and cities, back through cataracts and falls, through narrowing valleys and on high up into the hills, where it is but a small, trickling stream, a stream that narrows and becomes indistinguishable amongst ancient reeds and ferns, back into the darkness of the earth.

7

Address from the Leader of the Opposition

The native hue of resolution is sicklied o'er with the pale cast of thought.
Shakespeare

First, before I try to answer this, I must thank you, colleagues and friends, for electing me Leader of her Majesty's Opposition, of our great Labour Party, and for the distinct yet positive way in which you have done this. And what an opportunity! Let us grasp it, create it and enjoy it!!

But *first* I must ask, 'Whither Labour?'

Together we are, I hope to show, going make our mark in a way that is so very different from any of our predecessors as the Opposition Party. This is not the easiest of times. In many ways, conventional politics is now in abeyance, though we have been making pretty good mincemeat of our Prime Minister, who stumbles and lies makes U-turns every day, but we do not now have a lead in the polls, even a small one. In a sense, it should be easy: you have just had to sit back and allow the Government to create its own woes. But, we have to do more than this, *much* more.

But, as political commentators are now beginning to say, it is time for us to start laying out proposals for the sort of country Labour would like to realise and to hand on to our children and grandchildren.

Our first and perhaps greatest challenge is to affirm – loud and clear – our democratic principles. I consider myself a Social Democrat. I affirm this most definitely! Socialism, in its literal sense, means all taking part in the democratic process for the good of all. It can *never* be authoritarian in any sense. One person, one vote. Proportional Representation and democracy working from the ground up, from the parish and village hall to Westminster. Choice, information and argument are, I believe, essential as definitions of this sense of democracy. I will elaborate on this later.

So why am I saying this? Come with me, for what I say is me.

First, because the present Government, taking its hint from The Horror in America, is eating away at our democracy, day by day, by controlling elections in ways that suit it. And I believe – and hope – that our forthcoming Government will vigorously and determinedly be thoroughly reformist, recreating our national image and identity of ourselves, including a thorough redistribution of wealth. This *will* be done through the true democratic processes.

I will offer you a vision of the sort of country we would like to leave behind, once it is time to hand over to a younger generation. It will be far more sophisticated than the ideas that I have. Yet I feel strongly enough about them to want to express them. No, *declare* them. Again and again.

I remember well the catchphrase used by Labour at the time of the 1964 General Election: "Thirteen Years of Tory misrule." By the time of the next general Election it will be 14 more, unless the Government repeals the Five-Year Term Parliamentary Act. During this time, the Government will have been dealing with the current pandemic and Brexit, with changes to many aspects of life as we know it: shackling the BBC, weakening the Supreme Court, putting the Electoral Commission in the hands of ministers rather than maintaining its independence from Government, upturning planning laws, even, indeed, as we see daily, weakening the authority of Parliament itself and – more frighteningly – through control of the Internet. I fear, no, *I know* that our democracy is seriously under threat.

We need a new vision, a new idea of what this country *is* and what its future should be in the decades that follow, decades that are going to prove very difficult for our children and grandchildren. We need a vision, too, that provides for everyone, in terms of what a civilised society should offer now to enhance the lives of all and so that this can be handed on.

This vision must *not* be derived from the past. – the past is dead! Empire, the World Wars, Queen Victoria, Shakespeare and all the rest of 'history' as it has been taught for so long in school – a history that is wholly idealised and very far from the truth – so much government propaganda! Of course, these must not be forgotten, but these truths must be told: endless exploitation, imperialism, slavery and all its terrible brutality which we *must* acknowledge, colonialism (which is slavery with a few pennies thrown in), class conflict and the cruelties of industrialisation must never be forgotten – only recently, I was watching the actor, Jodie Whitaker, discover how her great-great-grandfather worked down a mine from the age of 8. *Millions* have died unnecessarily and cruelly for our national history and prosperity.

So what exactly do I hope for Labour? What exactly will make me believe in the future and in the society we could be developing and handing on? There is much that really appals me about the contemporary state of British politics. I do not advocate a bloody revolution, but one that does indeed change every way in which we as a nation regard ourselves and how we relate to the world at large.

First, **Social Democracy**. If I am to say I am a Social Democrat, what does this mean? The best answer to this that I can find is from a colleague of ours, Peter Hain:

> Democratic socialism should mean an active, democratically accountable state to underpin individual freedom and deliver the conditions for everyone to be empowered regardless of who they are or what their income is. It should be complemented by decentralisation and empowerment to achieve increased democracy and social justice. [...] *Today democratic socialism's task is to recover the high ground on democracy and freedom through maximum decentralisation of control, ownership and decision making.* For socialism can only be achieved if it springs from below by popular demand. The task of socialist government should be an *enabling* one, not an enforcing one. Its mission is to disperse rather than to concentrate power, with a pluralist notion of democracy at its heart. (My italics.)

Here are some key phrases: 'democratically accountable state', 'everyone to be empowered', 'socialist government should be an enabling one, not an enforcing one'. And 'a pluralist notion of democracy at its heart'.

And in this context, I will be proposing to you that the Leader of the Labour Party must put themself forward for re-election between each General Election. This should *not* be a job for life.

These are clear and perhaps, obvious to us. Yet we must be prepared to declare these ideas at every opportunity. We are not and *never* have been an autocratic party as the right wing press so enjoyed calling as at the last General Election. This was a perfidious lie. But what should we expect from The Telegraph, The Mail and other such right-wing owned media outlets?

But I must begin by asserting that our Party *must* be both democratic and representative of the people as a whole. Therefore, I will be insisting that at the next General Election, 50% of our candidates must be women. In today's world, I assume that this is so obvious that it is written on everyone's heart.

We must also, if we are to say anything to the people of this county, make sure that all our MPs in future must reflect the cultural and racial diversity that is today's nation. We can no longer linger in the past! This, too, will be enshrined in our selection procedures.

And I ask, why should the attitudes of those no longer with us determine our rules for today?

The most important implication of this for today is that a true and proper democracy must involve people in their everyday lives. Our democracy is seriously under threat, if it has not gone already, as I have described above. Thus in our manifesto for the next General Election, I hope that we will offer **Proportional Representation**, of one kind or another. The Labour Party has just celebrated its 120th anniversary. It has been in power for just 38 of those years, 13 of which were under 'New' Labour. Remember Peter Mandelson's assertion that he was perfectly happy for people to get 'filthy rich'? This is *not* a good record. Indeed, one wonders how much of a Labour Party New Labour turned out to be. I understand – *we* must understand - that Labour has stood firmly against PR for a long time. This *has* to change. And democracy must be allowed to operate at the most local of levels. If this means smaller government, a smaller state, as Tories like to have, then to the good. Tories, too, may want a smaller state, but ever more power in the hands of the few.

So, let me be absolutely clear: there is *no point* in Labour being the party of opposition. Nothing can be achieved thus. To share power, with the number of seats in Parliament reflecting accurately the number of votes cast, will *still* enable us to be creative and positive in bringing about a renewed and optimistic nation.

Of course, there are countries in which PR doesn't work. But there are many more where it has been so very successful – Germany, France, Spain and all practice PR in one way or another.

I do appreciate that the Liberal Democrats appear, for the time being at least, a spent force. I was very sorry that Layla Moran lost the election to be Leader, especially as she made it clear that she favoured PR. But only 57% of party members could be bothered to vote in the leadership election. Still, you may well need their support in the future. We will need to learn to work with other parties and not back away from PR in the hope of gaining sole power, something I fear will *never* happen. But, perhaps, never should.

And let me be clear, political idealism does not mean we can ever achieve the 'perfect state'. Just look at countries whose leaderships have proclaimed this. They are and have been tyrannies. Political progress is always incremental, bit by bit, government after government (though, of course, the Tories will always be stealing our policies, as soon as they appear popular). Hard work is all it takes.

First, we live in a multicultural and multi-racial society – not to say multi-party one, one whose people offer so much, but this variety cannot ever be given its true political voice under the current system which caters only for very broadly defined electoral categories. I quote again: 'The task of a socialist government should be an enabling one, not an enforcing one.' 'Enabling: giving all the right to determine the course and nature of their own lives, as individuals, as members of their community or of their work environments, in which each must have a share of ownership'. A government must surely reflect as many aspects as possible of our society in all their individuality.

A government that trusts the people is *never* an authoritarian one. 'All power corrupts. . . .' PR protects the people from this.

Furthermore, surely the case must be that the number of seats in the Commons *must* reflect the numbers of votes gained. This is, of course, the standard argument for PR. Given what I have said above, this seems all the more important. However, Labour *shamefully* has stuck with the Tories over the decades in rejecting this argument wanting, in effect, to impose policies that may or may not be fine, but nevertheless can *never* command a popular majority. Labour must be able to govern with such.

And you will also be aware that the Conservative Party nationally numbers about 170,000 members. Average age? 55. Predominantly male and with about 90% white membership. How many members of our party? About 500,000. Representative government, please!

And if PR had been in place long ago, Labour would have a far greater share of power than the mere 38 years it has had.

But, there is much more than just PR that I wish to propose to you. At the heart of our next government will be *a wholesale* reconstruction of our national Constitution. Well, a wholesale construction of a new one, as we don't have one already.

We do have, indeed, a body of law that guides and directs our governance, but this can be undermined easily – as the present government is doing. I think that you will all agree that parliamentary processes are antiquated in the extreme. I have published a document which I am sure all will have read. But let me repeat the main proposals. First, the abolition of The House of Lords as being fundamentally undemocratic. Instead we will have a Senate. Its constituencies will not be simply geographic, but elected to this new body will be representatives (*not* delegates) of interest groups, from the Sciences, from Business, from the Arts and from Agriculture and from Sports, as much as from politics. All these are just examples. The purpose and role of this new Senate will be to assess, examine and to question legislation before it goes to its final reading in the House of Commons, using the knowledge and expertise of its members. I also propose, as you will have read, that there will be no Three-Line Whip in this new Senate. All will be elected proportionately, as will the Commons. I have proposed, too, that a General Election will happen every three years. And here we take our example from America, with one third of all seats being subject to election by rotation, at each and every election, even the seats of cabinet ministers. The Prime

Minister will have no freedom to call an election when he – or she – wishes, as if this were a gift to the people.

There will be a Supreme Court, as at present, but candidates for it will be appointed by the legal profession and approved by the members of the Senate, to avoid political bias. We will also put in strict laws to empower local political organisations, down to the very lowest level. Corporate interests will no longer be able to circumvent local decisions by taking the relevant minister out to lunch. The power of The Lobby will be broken, too. Political influence should never be the property of the rich.

Talking of which, our new Government will do all in its power to eliminate **Sleaze**. For example, no MP will be allowed to have two jobs, for their whole commitment must be to their constituents. Again, the Lobby will be abolished. We have seen only too often that this is a means solely for enriching those already enriched. It also seriously undermines local democracy.

And finally, we need to decide if we need to be a **Monarchy**. I am a republican and the question of monarchy will be put to the people in a special referendum. Why, I will argue, should one family be born to immense wealth, power and significance without having earned a penny of it?! Is this why we should have Monarchy? Why should this Monarchy 'symbolise' our nation, why should it hold us 'all together'? Think about it. Our monarchs were imposed upon us centuries ago and they have presided over as much iniquity as anyone else. Let us bury this kind of history!

So you will ask, who will be head of state? I will answer, no one. Why do we need one? Or we might say, let's draw lots for it. Anyone, *anyone* could be selected in a lottery, for a period of a couple of years, his or her job being safeguarded and their expenses paid for. He or she will meet people at airports. No more 'royal consent'. How about that?

These are some of the principle measures that our new constitution will contain. As I have said, our country needs renewal. Now is the time to seize the opportunity. Do not let us fail again!

One other point: *all* school children should be taught, from a young age, the nature and practise of democracy so that it becomes part and parcel of their everyday lives. Religious Education need only be a choice. It will, though be taught alongside the teachings of the great Philosophers, those who asked, 'Who am I?' All education should begin with this question.

It seems very clear to all that Labour has a mountain to climb if it is to win power at the next General Election. If Labour wants to be a fair and genuinely popular government, then surely a proposal for PR *must* be in our next manifesto, as must the Nation's wholly new Constitution. The latter will be put before the country to vote on, once its details are made quite clear. The proposals for this new Constitution will be put to the people as soon as possible after we have come to power. This Referendum will need to be passed by a clear majority and will only be reversable by a similar majority after a specific time. And there will be in this Referendum on our new Constitution a provision that it, as a whole or in detail, can be changed only by a further Referendum.

Secondly, **Taxation**. If I am right in this, Labour has significantly failed – *drastically* so, in fact – to put into effect a real, substantial and meaningful redistribution of wealth, much though this has always been at the heart of its mission. The gap between the haves and the have nots grows wider all the time. I read just today that 1% of the people own 25% of the wealth of this country. And we are still suffering the effects of Austerity, with resources – financial as well as material – being steadily drained from the governance of this country. Ask any county councillor.

I understand that British tax laws run to some *17,000* pages. This is quite incredible, except when you realise that the vast majority of these pages represents, in effect, a fine lifestyle for tax lawyers. Whilst the great majority of us are happy with PAYE and NI payments, the rich can work the tax-deductible games and siphon off their millions to offshore accounts in the Bahamas or Singapore or elsewhere. I understand that some trillions of Pounds is hidden away thus. *Trillions*! This applies both to individuals and to multi-nationals: Volvo, I know, pays no Corporation Tax here. Why? Because it runs at a loss. How come? Its profits are sent through Luxembourg.

Let's be quite clear about this: a new Labour Government will make it illegal for British nationals to put their money on off-shore accounts, far from the reach of the taxman.

Here is a challenge: to sit down for an afternoon and write a completely new tax code in about 30 pages. In fact, it has often been suggested that *all* taxes should be abolished, except taxes on expenditure and purchases. How simple would that be? It would be a tax code that reflects a most important idea, at the heart of the nation we want to become: that, ultimately, if all is shared, if all is participatory, that is better for all. Having read *On The Origins of Species*, the maverick economist, Herbert Spencer coined the phrase 'the survival of the fittest'. He understood Victorian commerce better than anyone. But he was only partially right. Evolution teaches that the strong *do* survive. But it also teaches us that co-operation is essential for survival. Let us never forget this!

But to be most serious, a complete reconsideration of the very nature of tax would be part and parcel of the restructuring and redefining the nature of the British state: a tax system that was straightforward, transparent, progressive and supportive of all the activities of the state, without destroying entrepreneurial and creative drives. A tax system that would see the wealth of this country shared *much* more equitably.

Be not mistaken. I am not and our party cannot be anti-business whether in private ownership, whether multi-national or under government supervision. Business – provision and exchange - has been with us throughout history. It defines the relations between people in providing for their needs and desires. It is, let it be recalled, one way of defining creativity. Yet, and I cannot repeat this too often, business needs to be under democratic control. It must *never* be able to act and conduct itself as if beyond government control. In this regard, too, our future government will put in place very strict controls regarding party funding. We will begin all this by ensuring worker representation on boards and worker shareholding in their companies. I am sorry, tax lawyers. Your time is up!

Therefore, I look forward very much to our new Labour government, on day one after the next election, tearing up all those 17,000 pages, having developed for your next Manifesto a fair, concise and effective system of taxation.

Of course, taxation is closely tied in with the **Economy**. It is not for me at this point to go into details about this – our Shadow Chancellor will be doing this. However, I need to suggest one or two principles that will guide our government.

First, the economy *must* serve all the people, all of time. We will stand firmly against the Thatcherite idea that 'You can't buck the market', but we will not put in place a programme of renationalisation. Tony Blair was right to get rid of Clause Four. We will never be against free enterprise and wealth creation but your government will enact laws that will enable investment to be guided by the government. We will, in short, be working with the banks and pension funds, and with the Stock Market, to ensure that the wealth created in this country is *for* this country. There are trillions stuffed away in pension funds. We will find better ways of using this money, for education, for the elderly and the frail and for the NHS.

To that end, whilst we will not nationalise big business, we *will* nationalise all hire purchase agreements and processes. This should have been Labour's task in the great post-World War 2 government of Clement Attlee. A National Investment Bank will be set up for this purpose. This will, through time, create a vast fund to enable development throughout all regions of our nation. It will be *us*, not Mr Johnson, who will do the 'levelling up'! Not that he is going to do so, anyway.

We will never tax the poorer parts of society to make up for Government shortfalls. But at the heart of our economic policy – to repeat – will be what is good for everybody.

Next, I think that there are three institutions that lie very close to the hearts of the people of Britain. One is the **BBC**, another, **The National Health Service**. Both are, as they say, National Treasures, both are perhaps the greatest achievements of the post-War era. Both are now under threat from this Government. It must be remembered that the former belongs to the general public, through the License Fee. The BBC is often derided by both sides of politics for its 'bias'. Perhaps one can only say that it is therefore doing its job properly, to 'inform, educate and entertain': *The BBC belongs to the people.* Let no Tory ever tell otherwise. It is paid for by us through the License Fee. We will develop this by giving the License Fee payer the right to vote for the senior management of the BBC. Otherwise, please leave it alone!

And as far as other aspects of the media are concerned, we will make it illegal for anyone not British to own or part own a British media outlet. This is the case in America. It should be so here and that the same time, we will ensure complete editorial independence, regardless of the predilections of the owners. I remember the day when The Times was known as The 'Thunderer'. It is a pale shadow of its great past.

Present Tory philosophy respects nothing unless it is driven by market forces. 'You can't buck the market,' to repeat what Thatcher infamously said. One implication of this is that any state organisation is, by its own existence, a burden on the state and therefore should be privatised and be properly run by private companies – probably American ones and/or owned by Tory party donors. Such is the Conservative view. The implication of this is that everyone will be expected to take out private health insurance, at great profit to the insurers and great expense to ordinary citizens, like you and me.

But the move to privatisation has been going on for some time already, at least in minor aspects of its provision. For example de-waxing of ears, formerly free on the NHS has now been farmed out. A ten-minute cleansing of the ears can now cost £80 or more, so I discovered to my disgust. Physiotherapy is another such example.

This means that the basis of the NHS is being slowly undermined: treatment 'free at the point of delivery' is increasingly *not* the case.

On the other hand, financing the NHS is indeed increasingly expensive. Nevertheless, with a proper tax system in place and greater control of those companies that supply the Service, together with an examination of the extravagant consultants' and management's fees, these should, in time, make NHS provision financially entirely viable. The health of a nation is, literally, embodied in the health of its individual members.

Perhaps, too, we might consider ways of improving the national diet. But that's another matter.

Finally, recall what Tony Blair said when asked what his three main priorities were: 'Education, education, education.' Our next government will continue the process of making **Education** available to as many as possible and at as high a level as possible. To this end, we will copy the French example: the basics of politics and philosophy will be taught in all schools, as I have mentioned. We will, also, put in place radical procedures to reduce average class-sizes across the country. Finally, though we cannot and should not abolish them, a fair tax system will be imposed on private schools to circumvent their 'charitable' status.

Next, historically speaking, our armed forces have played a central role in our imperial power and for **Defence**. As mentioned above, armed interference (i.e. brutality) in other countries has been a dark secret of our history, as, indeed, has heroism in defence of liberty and justice been celebrated. A clear and unequivocal understanding of the former role is, I accept, essential. We must have the courage not to appeal to voters' patriotism. At its best, this is solely backward looking.

Of course, I rejoice when England (or Britain) wins a World Cup or a Briton wins a Nobel Prize. But what did Dr Johnson mean when he said, 'Patriotism is the last refuge of the scoundrel'? He meant that one who has run out of argument turns to this basic, atavistic impulse, one who considers thinking of the priority of 'the nation' over individual welfare and morality, one who has no other argument to fall back on, e.g. Edmund Burke. Patriotism is to be downplayed at all costs.

Of course we need a Defence Force. Defence is just that; we accept that there are great risks in this world of ours. but there is one aspect of defence which is, to put it mildly and literally, indefensible. This is our **Nuclear Deterrent**. This will be scrapped immediately on the first day of our premiership. 'Deterrent' it is not. It is just the opposite. Mr Johnson, though, is intent on *increasing* our nuclear weaponry. 'Global Britain'? What totally dangerous nonsense!

Our nation must stand for the morality that embodies peace, co-operation and shared responsibility for peace across the world. And if our foreign policy reflects the morality of the ways in which our nation is governed, then and only then will be able to suggest to the world that we might have something to offer.

The nation has four Trident submarines, each carrying eight missiles armed with forty nuclear warheads each, in turn, much more powerful than that which was used at Hiroshima. The submarines are built and owned by Britain, at great cost; the hardware – the weaponry – is built here in this country by companies 70% American owned. The cost of these is, again, vast. These all have to be serviced in American naval bases, again at great cost to Britain.

Furthermore, at the time of an international crisis, with nuclear exchanges imminent or perhaps even taking place, these weapons of mass destruction cannot be launched without America giving the appropriate permission and thereby the launch codes. This cannot be done within less than 24 hours, during which time an enemy, say Russia, will not wait to see what happens. They will simply launch pre-emptive strikes upon us.

Can one imagine a 50-megaton bomb falling, say, on Birmingham? I don't need to elaborate on the horror of this. Defenders will say but the Russians will not, cannot know where our Trident (or Dreadnought successor subs) are. Perhaps not, perhaps yes. It does not matter. They won't wait to have up to 90 nuclear bombs fall on their country.

Furthermore, America is supposed to come to our defence in such a situation. Will they? I doubt it, when they see such horror. It will not be welcome in their country.

In short, our nuclear defence is in fact nothing more or less that a forward offensive-defensive position for the American military.

Thus it *must* be cancelled *immediately* we take office.

And there is a further reason for its abolition. In doing so, Britain will be taking the lead in a more general process of nuclear disarmament *internationally*. At a time of growing international tension *as well* as being a matter of principle, a British government will be setting an important political *and* moral precedent.

This should be a simple, *instinctual* matter for a Labour government. And why? Labour has always believed in the only and proper role in Defence: just that, with the proviso that our forces should, in a limited way, help where difficulties elsewhere arise and under United Nations leadership.

And of the major policy issues, of paramount importance is **Brexit**. Let me put my cards on the table here. I am a committed European, voting to remain in the 2016 Referendum. I regard the creation of the European Union as *the* greatest geo-political achievement of mankind. Born out of the horrendous suffering of two World Wars which were brought upon the World largely by European imperialist struggles and after centuries of territorial, dynastic, religious and imperial fighting, European unity has brought peace and prosperity to this continent, with one or two relatively minor but unpleasant exceptions.

Our membership of the European Union, through its principles of the free movement of people, finance trade and services, has allowed ordinary people, you me and all Europeans the right to live and work throughout our continent. To mix and marry, to trade and create new businesses and new cultures and to live new lives free from nationalistic pride and fear. This has been one of *the* greatest geo-political achievements of mankind. The 20th Century was marked by horrendous wars. No more!

And all this has been *democratically* achieved. Between 1870 and 1940, Germany invaded France three times; in my life time, it has not done so once. And nor has any other nation done or intended similar. Leaving the EU has been and is *monumentally* pointless as we see and learn more and more as the weeks and months go by.

Peace and prosperity have been the major achievements of the Union. Of course, charges against it can be made, but no government is perfect (and that is why we have democracy). Of the four basic principles of the EU – the free movement of finance, services (up to £225 billion p.a.to the UK), trade and people – the latter is the most important, to repeat, for it allows ordinary people to live, work, create, intermarry, build businesses and create new cultures free of anxiety, fear and any sense of national superiority, difference yes, and I celebrate difference, but *not* superiority.

Those in favour of Brexit claim to be *re*claiming our sovereignty. It is no matter to them that the EU has embodied in it the sovereignty of its members nations. Each member state has the right of veto. However, what does this word 'sovereignty' mean? It means that there is a ruler over us – a ruler who has never been elected. It means, therefore, that people are *subjects* and not citizens. And the European project is considerably more democratic that our democracy.

Of course, we now know at this stage on what exact terms we relate to the EU since December 31st. Well, we don't really. The 'deal' was forced through Parliament just before Christmas last year, without proper scrutiny at all, all 1,200 pages of it! There are years of argument to follow. A 'no deal', destroying jobs in their thousands - tens, maybe hundreds of thousands - is becoming disastrous. And American economies of scale (and Chinese?) will make us all the poorer should we turn to the US in our need, deal or no deal. And the Americans seem, as I speak, not to be concerned at all to 'do a deal' with us.

Even as I speak, we are seeing the impact of leaving upon distribution of basics – food, gas, fuel – rapidly impinging on our everyday lives.

Thus, I hope to see in our next manifesto a commitment to the renegotiation of whatever has passed. At the very least must be a commitment to the free movement of people. Re-joining the EU: yes. But I suspect that this could only be done in stages – quick stages. Free trade would soon follow, though.

For centuries, the blights of nationalism, of patriotism and of 'exceptionalism' have led to untold suffering. If you wish, by the time of your retirement, to be able to look back on what you have achieved, surely a contribution to international peace and understanding must be high on your intentions.

You will want to govern for the people, for individual people to live productive and meaningful lives. All people. Wealth should never be the only mark of this, only the well-being of all. At the core of it all should be a commitment to 'the greatest happiness of the greatest number of people'. Free trade, and the free movement of people, allowing them to mix, marry, to live, be creative and to start and build business across Europe – Yes!

And then there is the greatest issue of our day: **Climate Change**. It is the greatest because it concerns the *whole* world as is independent of any one country. It is here, it's in the East, the West, the North and the South, as we see with the ice-caps melting more and more each summer. Its causes are multiple and it will be with us for as much of the future as far as we can see. So, if we are to bring into being a society in which our children and grandchildren are not just to prosper but also to survive, we *have* to act now and decisively.

To his credit, Johnson addressed the matter recently at the United Nations – and he was right to do so. But in his childish way, he told the world to 'grow up', and he quoted – indeed – Kermit The Frog's song, 'It's not easy being green'. Of course, Kermit was *not* referring to the environment!

I doubt very much that world leaders will take kindly to being told to 'grow up' (something that could easily be levelled at him), and I am not sure that Xi Ping of China will have much knowledge of Kermit or how he will take to being told to mature. But there you go.

But Kermit was right and Johnson very wrong, as he is about most things, in so far as he has *no* feasible policies in this area – as we have seen at his recent Party's conference, with him it is all bluster. So, he has declared very recently, all electricity will be green by 2035. He does not explain how his government will achieve this. Even as new nuclear power plants are being built at Hinckley and soon at Broadwell! And a new oil field of The Shetland Islands. Indeed, it *is* very difficult to know what to do, both nationally and internationally. But act we must. Now!

It will not be easy, it will take time, but we must be serious about this. My predecessor in this role once declared education to be his most important subject. Mine will be 'Renewables, Renewables, Renewables!'

Let's think about this. We will be happy to work with The Greens on this. But what will be our proposals? First, all new oil and gas drilling will be terminated. *All* new construction will have to be entirely ecologically sound, insulated as fully as possible. We will need to wean ourselves off the motor car, much as we love our cars. To that end, for example, we will give tax breaks to reflect the lower the distance from work and home, we will encourage the sale of bicycles, of small, minimum consumption vehicles, we will encourage supermarkets to stock produce form regional and local sources. If this mean not being able to buy prawns from Madagascar, so be it. And, of course, we will be using and developing, as a matter of urgency, renewable sources of energy. Every new house will have panels and small windmills. Wave technology will be essential part of the process. And we will give tax advantages to the oil and petrol companies which follow these demands to develop these new technologies.

These are just some of the ideas we will follow. It won't be easy. And sure, since the war, society has got ever richer. Our standard of living has, inexorably, improved unimaginatively during these decades. And we, as individuals, continuously ask for those standards to ever improve, especially as education has spread ever more widely through the nation.

But be absolutely sure that this *cannot* continue. If we are to avoid ecological catastrophe – and all the Science stresses that this is not just possible but inevitable, not just then, but *now* – we must act *now*.

And it will *not* be cheap. I cannot and will not hide this from you. Nor from our children – and their children.

So, on many fronts, to save our planet will not be easy. But we will have to do it together. Here and internationally.

I have, of course, not mentioned various vital areas of public policy, social services, education, devolution (yes!), the role and power of the corporations, racism - and so on. I merely assume these will be important priorities for you and for the next Labour Government. But there is one more I wish to touch upon.

I spoke about the state of our **Democracy** above. I believe it to be under serious threat. I have just finished reading this summer Richard Norton-Taylor's *The State of Secrecy* on the role that the Secret Services play in our society and democracy; it also deals with the ways in which successive governments have used these and the law to cover up ministerial incompetence, misdeeds and indeed corruption. Using the catchphrase 'a danger to national security', governments are able to hide behind a fog of vagueness, silence and the law. So much so, that the people themselves have become 'a danger to national security'. I mention, for example, the government's refusal to publish the review into Russian interference in last year's General Election. Even as I write the media is making it absolutely clear that The Conservative Party has been bought, through 'donations' by Russian oligarchs, Arab sheiks and other malignant and corrupt owners of vast wealth. It is becoming enormously difficult for the truths of all this to be revealed. The Investigatory Powers Act of 2016 which gives government extensive and detailed powers to follow all our movements, communications and relationships, is one such instrument. There are numerus other Acts – Theresa May's infamous Supervisory Powers Act of 2019 for example, which could be mentioned, not the least Blair's Freedom of Information Act which he, it appears, much regretted, as it left gaps through which truths, uncomfortable truths, could well come out.

Yuval Noah Harari has written most cogently about 'The Internet of Everything' in *Homo Deus*. This must be essential reading for us all in our great Party .

This is one aspect of my concern. Others include the independence of the BBC and Supreme Court, both of which are under threat from this government, as mentioned before. I discussed, above, my desire to see PR adopted by the Labour Party. With an 80-seat majority in parliament, Johnson and his gang are using this power in such a way as to reverse our Constitutional belief that all government is answerable to Parliament. Increasingly Parliament is answerable to those in No. 10, Downing Street, though this is not a new phenomenon. There is a whole range of devices that governments can use, for example statutory instruments and hidden clauses in Bills, to bypass Parliament.

On top of this is the fact that 70% of the media is owned and controlled by right-wing proprietors; the new Culture Secretary is very much part of this. This, too, will be a problem for you to deal with in our time. Labour lost a string of seats in the North in December 2019, the so-called Red Wall, seats that had *never* returned conservative members. Deeply shocking though this was, how did it come about? Thus, much of today's media output is, one way or another, mere propaganda.

As mentioned, we will limit the power of oligarchs and *any* political party to own and control the media. We will also make foreign ownership illegal. Furthermore, we will ban all shell companies and make it illegal for British citizens to stash their money in 'tax havens' overseas.

Whilst Norton-Taylor makes clear that such widespread powers leads not just to the abuse of power but also of almost universal inefficiency, including leaks, he also makes it clear that a root and branch reformation and redefinition of the roles and natures of the secret services is essential if our democracy is going to survive a time when more and more power is accrued by central government.

We will act upon this.

'All power corrupts; absolute power corrupts absolutely.' I am sure that you will remember this everyday whilst in office. In France, democracy works effectively right down to the level of the local commune; even America demonstrates a democracy that works, too, in a most local way. And if I were to come back to this country in 30 or 40 years after I have finally left it, what would I expect to find? What will this green and pleasant land be like?

I have deliberately kept away from mentioning the **Pandemic**, as there seem to be fewer and fewer answers to it. However, I feel I must say one thing. Governments of all sorts play much upon people's fears, fear of illness, yes, but also of immigrants, unemployment and even of change and so on. This current government is no exception, again and again playing to fear of Covid. Whilst there may be a degree of justification for this, this is not my point. How will a future Labour government do in this regard? How will it make optimism its main modus operandi?

A future Labour government will *recover the high ground on democracy and freedom through maximum decentralisation of control, ownership and decision making.* 'Maximum' is here the key word. The environment protected, a people happy, and a state that serves them and not itself? A democracy that doesn't work just at election time but at all times in in respect of all decision-making, at national as much as at local level and at work? A rich and prosperous one, but one that recognises limitations ? A nation respected and admired throughout the world, *not* for its history, but for its present contribution? And a nation that shares in life – trade, cultures, people – with its neighbours and with all nations?

And as I have stressed above, a nation which allows for *all* to live fulfilling, productive and contented lives.

'All political careers end in failure,' once declared Enoch Powell (yes, him: his did). Prove him wrong: be courageous without being flamboyant, determined without becoming autocratic and dedicated without being self-centred. All these, I hope, will have echoes in my heart, not the least for one whose first name is that of the founder of the Labour Party. Let us forget internal divisions, though debate amongst us – much mocked in the right-wing press – is essential, for what on earth is democracy without debate? What matters – and it matters enormously and it will be done with great difficulty – is that we *must* win the next General Election. That must be our resolution!

Otherwise, wither our Party?

8

Damn You, Johnson

A simple desultory philippic

Simon & Garfunkel

Damn you, Johnson.

No, I'm not going to call you by your familiar, with which you ingratiate yourself with the Great British Public, it and your scruffy hair. I would not allow you through my front door!

Mind you, the Great British Public is pretty gullible. As you know only too well. But hey, who cares? You're Prime Minister!!

Damn you, though, for the charlatan that you are. OK, your hero, Winston Churchill, once commented that talk to the ordinary man in the street about politics for five minutes, and you wonder why you bother. You've played on that for years.

Damn you for the lying philanderer that you are. Sacked from the New Statesman, sacked from The Spectator, your wrote illogical articles in The Telegraph (well, why wouldn't they employ you?) earning a quarter of a million a year. And still you pleaded poverty. Poor you.

Damn you for so obviously serving yourself. Oh, you can amuse, you can charm, you can be irreverent – people like this. But when you have no values hidden beneath this, what are you? What do you believe in? Sorry. Only in your own power and aggrandisement.

Oh, I know. When you were a young schoolboy, you declared that you were going to be 'King of the World'. Well, OK, you wouldn't be the first child to aspire to this. But when you were at Oxford, you still went around claiming this. 'King of the World'!

Damn any 'King of the World'. Do you not know what hubris is? Oh, you'll be brought down, sooner or later, even though you have beguiled this great people. Any 'King of the World' is going to be a tyrant.

Damn you, but you are already showing signs of this in your ill-gained role. You are – or you will be – feeling that you have rights over and above those which your fellow country people have. After all, you are better than us, aren't you?

Damn you for your personal life. How many marriages? How many children? How many mistresses? Damn you, Johnson – how many abortions and miscarriages with your various mistresses have you 'fathered'? Allegra, Petronella, Anna, Helen – and how many others?

All just 'an inverted pyramid of piffle.' So very just.

Damn you for your treatment of your three wives, especially the second, Marina Wheeler, she who threw you out and took you back again, on more than one occasion. Yet whilst your marriage to her was breaking up, she was diagnosed with cervical cancer and you were carrying on with Jennifer Arcuri when you were Mayor of London. And you were so poor that you could not afford £3.10 to buy your American lady a drink!

Of course, there have been philandering prime ministers before you – and will be after you. But none quite so amoral or opportunist politically as you.

So: Damn you as a politician.

Damn you for the opportunism that saw you write two articles, for and against leaving the European Union – only to choose the one that would serve your interests best. You cared not a jot for the greatest issue of our day.

Damn you, too, for taking the Nation down the Brexit road, a road that is monumentally pointless. 'Get Brexit Done!' won you the 2019 Election. But what on earth did you mean by this? I don't suppose you know, for one minute. And judging by your actions regarding the Northern Ireland Protocol, which you signed as an International Treaty and you now seem quite happy to ignore, you are the ultimate charlatan.

Of course, most of its developing damage is hidden by the endless confrontation with the pandemic

Damn you for wanting to increase the stockpile of the nation's nuclear weapons. Damn you for not knowing that Trident – and Dreadnought to follow – makes us just a forward/defensive positions for the US military. Our nuclear weaponry is meant to be 'independent' It is far from it. As you ought to know. Probably you don't.

Damn you for spending this money *and* for cutting the international aid.

- And damn you for these:

- Police, Crime, Sentencing and Courts bill, now going through the Lords. This is designed to be no doubt the first of moves to delegitimise debate and argument against our Government, sorry, your Government. It gives the police the power to determine that even one protester is causing too much noise!
- The Nationality and Borders bill, which will, I effect, send back victimised asylum seekers to the countries they came from, to other countries *en route*, e.g. France, regardless that this breaks international treaties and agreements that go back to the Geneva Convention 0f 1951. But as with the Northern Ireland Protocol, to hell with that treaties and international agreements. Even the one YOU signed.
- The requirement for voters to bring photo ID – passports - to polling booths on the specious claim that fraud is a systemic problem. Despite the fact that there is virtually no evidence of voter fraud in this country (despite what the notions of the former horror in The White House might have to say and will have encouraged you). But this will also deny the vote to many who don't have passports, most likely those not disposed to vote for you.
- For the repeal of the Five-Year Parliamentary Term Act. Flawed though this may be (it should have been three years), it nevertheless does what should have been in place decades, centuries ago: a General Election is NOT and should never be the gift of the sitting Prime Minister to the British people. Rather, an election belongs to the people, the electorate. It is for them to elect you in and to boot you out , not for *you* to select the most opportune moment.

- And now your plan to update The Official Secrets Act. 'No journalist will be stopped from doing his job properly,' you announce. You liar, you!

But this is not all: you wish to weaken the Electoral Commission's powers and role and you have every intention of reducing the powers of the Supreme Court in revenge for its perfectly proper finding your proroguing of Parliament in 2019 as unconstitutional. Furthermore, it hands conduct of elections, campaigning and financing of elections to ministers. So much for you and your dreadful Party's love of democracy. (And what else has the Republican Party in America prompted you to do to create 'voter suppression'?)

Each of these has been described as 'seismic constitutional changes' and 'the most brazen assault on democratic freedoms that our country has ever seen.'

But this is all grist to the mill to you and your ilk Don't you just love it? Damn you!

And when you are addressed and questioned about matters of policy or those concerning current events, you waffle and flounder and evade and revert to your schoolboy language. Here you are, before the House of Commons Liaison Committee on Wednesday, 7th July:

You were asked if you had sacked the then Health Secretary. This was your reply: "We read about the story concerning Mr Hancock and CCTV on the Friday and we had a new Health Secretary on the Saturday. That's all I have to say on the matter."

Again, you were asked about your Government's approach to China and its growing power, particular how you proposed to get the Chinese to abandon coal, when at the G7 he couldn't even persuade his six closest allies. Your response, "I don't want anti-China spirit to lead us to pitchfork away Chinese investment.' (Yet you send a vastly expensive carrier fleet to The South China Seas. Hah! Global, Imperial Britain!)

Just three examples of many before this Committee, representatives of the people of this country, of each party. You appeared bored, ignorant and supercilious.

And then there has been the big issue of the day: the pandemic. One cannot feel but compassion for any political leader who has had to take initiative and make rules and regulations to deal with this most threatening disease. How many of the 130,000 deaths in this country are a result of your dullard's approach in the early days? And of the result of your slowness to react?

And, as we approached the end of Lockdown on July 19th, your messages to the Public were confusing to say the least. What was or was not going to be enforced for the public good? Well, you didn't seem to know, did you? As ever, you floundered away.

You have been lucky (well, you have been all your life haven't you?) in that miraculously vaccines were developed in time to prevent the spread of the disease from being serious to absolutely disastrous. But how much money and profit have your friends and Tory party and donors made out of this? What happened to the 570 vaccines the Government appears to have purchased? Sold off to . . . ? Those PPE purchases. . . to chums down at the local pub?

And now, as your 'route map' reaches its final 'irreversible' conclusion, why are you acting so complacently when a further huge increase is threatened? Why did you not stop travel from India at the same time as you stopped travel from Bangladesh and Pakistan – oh, because you wanted to hob-nob with Mahendra Modi and do a deal with him – a trip you were forced to cancel?

And what a muddle our much-vaunted 'Freedom Day' has become. Look to yourself!

Damn you for all this!

And why are you where you are? Well, you're not 'King of the World', however much you might like to deceive yourself. Instead, you are, as someone has recently said, 'driven by no ethos nobler than the appetite for power without accountability.'

Nothing you do touches you; you are the judge of all things: Lord Geidt and your £845 rolls of wall paper, Jennifer Arcuri, your trip to Cayman islands - etc, etc and etc. This good Lord, quintessentially Establishment, a former Private Secretary to The Queen, found that there was nothing particularly wrong with your No 10 refurbishment. You were considered 'unwise' to accept your Mustique holiday last Christmas, then told everyone you had in fact paid for it – and, damn you – your own employee found that there was nothing 'improper', politically or financially, in your relationship with Ms Arcuri. Oh, really.

But then, you have declared that you will be the final judge of matters such as these.

And now, with COP26 upon us, you have taken up the cudgel, warning in darkest terms about its failure. Such cynicism! Only recently your Chancellor did little or *nothing* to reduce our carbon emissions. All it is to you is, if it does fail, then you will be able to blame all the other nations taking part – and if it succeeds, you will take all the credit. SUCH monstrous cynicism! What on earth have you and your government done to even begin reducing our carbon emissions?? Open up new oil-field off the Shetlands? Look to open a coal mine in Cumbria. Do you have ANY programme for the nation to follow??

None at all.

And today, you have legalised sleaze. But at least there have been 51 members of your Party who voted against this. Even so, yours is Government of All the Sleaze.

You claim to be – quite falsely – an expert on Shakespeare, as you claim also to be on Empire.

Well, damn you!

'Stand not upon the order of your going, but go at once.'

. . .and

Bless You, Sir Keir

Well, after the Batley & Spen result, you beamed away, happy and delighted after a victory of just 323 votes. Great, I was delighted by the result and by you so happy. Bless you!

But it has not always been thus. One can only admire you decency, intelligence and achievement in life. Up to now you have appeared uncertain, tentative, not knowing where to take The Labour Party, or how. But, bless you. Things may well now be different.

I long to see you on the steps of No 10! But you have a mountain to climb, a huge mountain.

Your Party – the largest political party in Europe, with 430,000 members – is riven between left wing idealists and Marxists on the one hand and pragmatic centre-left members on the other. Stamp your authority on them all! There is only one thing that matters: winning the next General Election (which may well be much sooner than you'd like). Bless you, if you do!

But the system is going ever more against you. See what I have said above to your dreadful opposite number – you will know what I mean.

But how on earth did Johnson and the Tories (whose lust for power purifies their every breath) win the last election with an 80-seat majority? Cambridge Analytica! Algorithms, micro-advertising. Play them at their own game, then. No other way to beat them.

Politics is a ruthless game, isn't it? As they say, you have to be in it to win it! Bless you.

Your Party, the founder of which after whom you are named, was launched on 27th February, 1900 – as this is written, 121 years and 8 months ago. Your party has been in power for under 38 of those years, not counting the War time coalition. Not really very good, eh?

I have been a supporter of your Party all my adult life, believing in justice and fairness for all, in The NHS ('free at the point of delivery'), in the separation of powers, in the eradication of poverty and the redistribution of wealth, the abolition of Britain's nuclear power and in, above all, democracy. (I also believe that no one should *want* to be Prime Minister. But there you go.)

All these are now under threat, serious threat. The very nature of democracy, following the example of Putin, Modi, Erdogan, Orban and others across the World, is being destroyed. Here and now. And in our country.

You are looking much more cheerful now, but you are a politician now. Get your Party in order, make yourself heard, not just in the left-wing press. Go for it!

If, on the next Election day, I see you at the door of No 10 – well, you will be blessed!

And what do you want? To lead? Or to be lead??

Are you still a lawyer – a fine and good one, no doubt – or are you a politician????

SPEAK UP!

9

A Party Political Manifesto

Government of the people, by the people, for the people, shall not perish from the earth
Lincoln

The following has been presented to the Central Committee for approval.

The State/The Party – Never forget that we are for you, with you. We are only your servants

We look after your health. We look after your education, your safety, your defence. We have been so successful – why would you want to change??

We have been with you, for you, for the last several years. Many years, in fact.

We know how you think, we know how you feel. We know your anxieties and your hopes and we know how to ease them and to help you fulfil them.

You are you. We are the Party. And the State.

But, of course, this is a democratic state. You can choose your government. This is your right. You must VOTE!

And what will you be voting for?

These are our priorities –

> First, your Health.
>
> We do not have enough hospitals nor staff to look after your needs. So, in the first year we will increase expenditure by 10%, by 20% in the second year until we will have doubled the cost of your most essential service.
>
> Second, your defence.
>
> As ever, the external threats to our safe and secure society. You know we have developed the World's most advanced and effective rocketry and drones. We will also increase our nuclear warhead numbers. 'Safety First!'
>
> Education remains a most important priority, especially in the skills needed to maintain our superiority, technical skills in all fields.
>
> Then, of course, is internal security. We will continue as we have done. Political protest is no longer necessary. It is a truth long since held that any objection to our way of life, now nearing its perfection, must indicate in any individual a disturbed state of mind. He or she will be most carefully looked after in our Mental Hospitals.
>
> Our sporting triumphs. . . . .

"Yes, yes, yes," muttered the Chairperson. "All very good. We all approve. Don't we? Much the same as ever. The algorithms will do it all for us. Anyway, we don't have an Opposition, do we?"

With that, the Committee dispersed, no one really in any position to disagree. They did not look each other in the eye.

10

On Atheism

If God did not exist, then would we not have had to invent him?
Voltaire

Introduction

Sorry, but there is no God.

Well, in fact there are very many gods, gods of the hearth, of the weather, of the seas, of the forge and of, well, you name it.

There are gods of polytheistic and monotheistic religions, gods that are gentle and offer hope and a place for love in our Life, there are gods who are vengeful, demanding and fantastic. There are gods who offer peace and gods who underpin wars and repression and cruelty. Gods who are severe and austere and gods who are colourful and spirited.

But a being 'greater than which nothing can be conceived'?

We'll see.

*

The purpose of this essay is an opportunity for discussion of a topic that is only too infrequently mentioned in our world today without some degree of opprobrium – all the more strangely so, since we live in a secular society: Atheism. To echo Oscar Wilde, it is the faith that dare not raise its name. In so doing, I want to consider the meaning of the word, give some account of its history, to consider its place in contemporary discourse, and to provide some perhaps rather fanciful considerations of my own.

In the first place, Atheism is not a faith at all, however much defenders of religion might like to suggest it is. It has no creeds, no priests and makes no demands on anyone to accept what it has to say, beyond the demands of the rational. Indeed, its very meaning is in antithesis to faith, in so far as faith is in reference to something beyond the rational. When seen in contrast to religious ideas, Atheism espouses no faith at all, though it is an attitude of mind, even a philosophy, allied as it is to Secularism, Rationalism and Humanism.

It has been the focus of considerable attention in recent years, with the publication of several notable books on the theme, in particular Richard Dawkins' *The God Delusion* and of Christopher Hitchens' *God Is Not Great*. These are, I would suggest, required reading for both believers and non-believers, for it is my opinion that the values and nature of Atheism, or of a world view that does not require a deity of one sort or another for its validation, is seriously under threat. One only has to think of militant Islam, the terrible tragedy of Palestine-Israel, and the fact that , apparently 50% of all Americans consider themselves of the 'religious right', to be only too aware that the achievements of the last several centuries are seriously under threat.

However, a full discussion of the issues in this broad context is not possible in just a brief paper, though I want them to be kept in the back ground. I have to make, to begin with, though, one or two points. I offer no apology to anyone who thinks that, in what follows, is meant as an insult to religion; it is certainly not meant as such. However, anyone who feels offended needs to consider carefully the strength of their own faith: a few ideas from one such as me are hardly going to be as Samson in the temple.

Again, for those who might like to think that, even on a subconscious level, I am trying to work myself around to some kind of acceptance of faith need be under no such delusion. Finally, you may fancy putting me on the rack and then hanging, drawing and quartering me; but before you do this, I will happily recant, in imitation of Galileo. As Camus put is so perspicaciously[1], he, Galileo, was not going to die for the ontological argument. The joke will be on the torturers.

I will, though, make one apology. My mind is not of an analytical cast; rather, I tend, lazily, to synthesise ideas. So, my technique here is more polemical and less rational than it ought to be. But it is only a mild apology. I must also warn that I will be treading in fields in which I have perhaps no right to trespass; I won't apologise for this, however. I will try, though, to put paid to the Ontological Argument. I will discuss Cosmology and The Anthropic Principle as they refer to this subject, followed by a look at stories and revelations. Finally, I will offer a brief discussion about Love.

What, then, is Atheism? There are numerous approaches to it. I have indicated above what it is not. My starting point is this: it is the denial of a set of beliefs I assume held by all those who profess a faith of one sort or another, however 'God' might be considered. It rejects belief in a bearded gentleman of infinite wisdom and goodness, the creator of this world and the Universe and all that is in it, or more seriously of a prime mover and the source of all that this universe contains. Thus it rejects the divinity both of such a creature and in anything that follows from it, especially the transcendental and metaphysical.

As an atheist, I do not believe in an after-life, in miracles, in salvation and redemption, resurrection or in any of the other innumerable other attitudes or beliefs, stories or myths that are held by religious people across the world, however enjoyable they might be and however much they give meaning to faith. Furthermore, I understand that my existence is a matter of chance – fortunate for me if not to anyone else - and that I am a mere fragment of a fragment too miniscule in cosmic terms to have any significance at all, except as human society determines it (and even then, very little indeed).

I do not believe that human consciousness is somehow divinely created or ordained, rather that it is a product of our material and physical being, this being evolutionarily determined. I understand, also, that when I die, then that is that and, for me, *when* I die has no meaning, since on death all meaning is eradicated. You may well say that my understanding is faulty. What follows, then, is an explanation of it.

I suppose that one reason for my disbelief is the fact that I do not *feel* any sense of the divine or of awe or any impetus to worship in me; I never have done so. This is not to say that I don't like sitting in an ancient church, feeling its silences, feeling the echoes of countless footsteps, of innumerable sermons and prayers and hymns that have been offered up there. Larkin's 'footfalls of snow' and light from stained glass windows are beautiful evocations of how the ages have given meaning to the experience of being alive in such a place. Nor does it mean that I don't acknowledge that religion has been a wonderful impetus to the creation of great works of art. Haydn's *Creation* is surely one of the highest examples of this: it can easily reduce me to tears. No less moving are the oratorios of Bach, the stained-glass windows in a great cathedral and the language of Eliot's *Four Quartets.* Other religions have their own wonders, too.

However, Haydn's work is energised entirely by a sense of the here and now, of the physical properties of being. Bach could write a cantata for coffee, amongst other things. Yet one has to remember that most religious art is religious because religious institutions were for so many artists throughout the centuries the only source of patronage and income. In the case of each of these, though, it is not the transcendental elements that engage, rather the means whereby they express a profound joyousness at being alive, or at the endless capacity that human life has for the tragic. Or, if you like, for Damnation and Salvation.

I acknowledge, too, the nature and worth of prayer, and its concomitant, confession. This is a common place of human experience, whether it takes place in a pew in a church, on the psychiatrist's couch, in the silence of one's sitting room, as one reflects on life, on one's weaknesses and failings and anxieties, or simply on the day that has passed. Self-criticism needs no further comment, vital as it is to our mental well-being.

Furthermore, I have some respect for the role of religion in the up-bringing of children, if only because I was educated in its shadow and because I still regard myself, culturally speaking, as a Christian having been brought up in a Christian society. I do not respect it when religion - and in some senses I am with Dawkins and others who assert that a religious education amounts to cruelty to children – is one-sided, repressive and limits awareness of other approaches to life, especially when it succumbs to religiosity. Furthermore, it may well be possible to say that childhood requires religion; it is, though, something which we have to grow out of. But one thing I won't do is worship.

To my way of thinking, worship can be a dangerous activity. In the first place, the human capacity for worship has only too easily been appropriated by tyrants and dictators (as have some of those things mentioned above) to exercise control over whole populations – I don't have to elaborate upon this. However, even as a boy, I found it difficult to worship. It wasn't just that prayers never seemed to get answered, for whatever I was praying for, but that there increasingly appeared something undignified in the activity. It was not just a matter of growing disbelief; rather that there was something humiliating in it, subjection and abnegation being two ideas that come immediately to mind. I learned early on about the dangers of worship. Worship is not the same as prayer.

I said rather mischievously above that I did not believe in a bearded man sitting in heaven ruling all life and existence. I am quite willing to accept that such naivety no longer is of any concern amongst theologians, even though a trawl through the God channels on Sky TV might well leave you with the impression that such a man – yes, man - has indeed not been pensioned off. However, there have been innumerable images of the deity from one century to the next, from one culture to the next and from one religion to the next. I am quite willing to accept that a divinity that offers meaning to our existence, that can be regarded as the creator of all things, and is a god of love in all its various forms and has the further characteristics of omniscience and being all powerful and divine, is probably sufficient definition to be going on with.

Christians, Jews and Moslems would probably accept this, though Hinduism, which is polytheistic, and Buddhism, which some do not really regard as a religion at all, would be outside this range of meaning. I hope, then, that for the purposes of this essay, this list of characteristics will suffice. I feel no need to add anything, except to say that the one requisite of all religions is that humans humble themselves before such a deity, or deities. However, in a sense, it is just the word 'meaning' that this essay is concerned with.

I should also add that I have no desire to see religion abolished as I do not regard my attitude as being political; also, it would be quite impossible to do so. In the first place, who am I to deny the right to those many people in many religions who find comfort, solace, peace and a sense of belonging in their faith, prayer and worship, in their participation in the community of faith, as I understand it to be? Furthermore if religion is to be seen as a source of moral teaching, then so be it. There are reasons for this approach. In the first place, democracy must be allowed its way. Then again, theistic belief seems to me to reflect the human condition; it is the purpose, I suppose, of this essay, however feebly, to try to offer some consideration of this condition.

What this paper is *not* about is agnosticism, that is the notion that one is in doubt about the existence or otherwise of God. A blanket denial of God's existence is, however, not satisfactory either: even Dawkins' position is not this one, if only because he is a scientist and, on the black swan principle, a scientist is motivated by scepticism and not absolutism. That Science has been so successful in the last four hundred years does not mean that it aspires to absolutism. But as Science has grown, both in its pure and applied forms, so religion has increasingly receded from any role in defining or describing the nature of existence. Of course, it is possible to be religious and a scientist. For such people, dogmatism is as much a foe as it is to someone like Dawkins.

One final point: Atheism is a philosophical position and is not political, though, of course, an atheist can be a politician or hold political views, though religion is easily made political: the 'Established Church'. Atheism can never demand that faith be abolished, impossible though that would be. The essence of human consciousness is its capacity for choice.

Thus I lay out my cards, in general and personal terms. The history and nature of Atheism must now be considered.

A Brief History of Atheism

In this brief outline, I want to suggest that, in the Western world at least, Atheism has been growing for at least four or five centuries, recognising that life might well be meaningless; on the other hand, whatever is said is based on the idea that what is said is meaningful. This paper rejects the view that Atheism is synonymous with Nihilism or its cousin, Anarchism. There is no essential disparity between Atheism and Rationalism, Humanism and Secularism, except in so far that each offers a different approach to understanding Life without the presence of an Almighty. How, then, has Atheism been regarded in the past and what has been its place in at least Western philosophy over the centuries? What follows is a resumé of some ideas about Atheism that have come down to us, though it may appear to be egg shell without any egg.

I suppose that the most crucial moment, at least for western thought, is the moment when Descartes famously declared, 'I think therefore I am.' Or maybe it was when Erasmus published 'In Praise of Folly', or when Shakespeare gave to Hamlet – well, any number of phrases that suggested, with Alexander Pope, that 'the proper study of man is man himself'. Maybe it was when Luther declared his doctrine of 'justification by faith alone'. What all these have in common, though, is that while of course each of these was in his own way a man of faith, (Pope especially being determined to keep Rationalism and Faith separate), a sense that the human was becoming the central source of understanding of what human existence was all about. In other words, during this period began that long process that led through the Reformation and the Age of Enlightenment, Romanticism, Marxism and Darwinism and made it clear that there is increasingly little relevance for the existence of God. Perhaps hand in hand with this come all the other Sciences as we know them today. How many of us are ungrateful for the development of anaesthetics?

However, there is plenty of evidence that there were atheistic thinkers going all the way back to the ancients. Earliest atheists include Epicurus, Democritus and Lucretius[1]. The former's materialism has its parallel in later centuries, nearer to our own time, his philosophy denying the influence of the gods in human affairs and his empiricism determining that all knowledge came only through the senses; it was not just a matter of eating and drinking and having a good time. And like Epicurus, Lucretius' words, 'Fear holds dominion over mortality only because, seeing in land and sky cause whereof no wise they know, men think divinities are working there. Meantime, when once we know from nothing still nothing can be created, we shall divine more clearly what we seek: those elements from which all things alone created are, and how accomplished by no tool of gods,' would seem to me to be a fitting epigram for the whole endeavour of modern thought. Perhaps it was the fear of nothing that forced early mankind, and mankind since, to impose meaning on experience.

Giordano Bruno, burnt at the stake in Rome in 1600 for heresy, had endeavoured to counter the religious beliefs of his day, his approach having been forged by his understanding of Lucretius.

310 A.D. saw the establishment of Christianity as the State religion in Rome, and there followed 1800 years of – well, it depends on one's point of view. Christianity came to dominate all European life, from the smallest of parishes to the vast expanse of empires. It determined how life was to be lived, it teachings providing a morality by which all could live and provided meaning for millions. But was this not built upon at least one lie? It is perhaps astounding that Latin was the *lingua franca* of Christianity, a device deliberately designed to confound ordinary people. 'Hoc est Corpus Christi.' To all and sundry, it was just hocus pocus.

In *Homo Deus* Yuval Noah Harari argues very cogently that the domination of Europe by Christianity came about because of 'The Donation of Constantine'. This Emperor had, in 310 A.D., turned his realm into a Christian one. And five years later, he divided his rule in two, giving to Christianity, in effect, the whole of Western Europe, whilst he kept control of the Eastern Empire, ruling from Constantinople.

Harari points out that in reality this 'Donation' did not take place at all. Scholars now accept that it was forged as late as the Eighth Century A.D.

So, what of it? Latin was the official language of the Church, even though vast numbers of its members spread throughout Europe and later throughout the World, could have no idea what was meant. Sexual repression, intolerance of difference or divergence, willingness to torture, to underpin corrupt and violent rulers and corrupt political systems – are these not also the inherited History of Christianity?

And the Body of Christ? How does a little Eucharistic biscuit or little bit of bread, whether actually or symbolically, represent this Body? And The Crucifixion, Christ's Resurrection and Ascent into Heaven? How real are these? And how do we know? The Gospels were written – it is not even clear by who – some 40 to 90 years after the supposed death of Christ.

How can anyone attribute factual accuracy to this and all the other myriad aspects of doctrine, teaching and faith?

Nevertheless, from the Fall of Rome through what we call the Dark Ages and beyond, Christianity grew, flourished and determined the lives of millions.

However, in Shakespeare's time, there was reference to The School of Atheism or The School of Night, about which there remains considerable speculation. It is thought that it was Sir Walter Raleigh who was at the heart of this secret group – it had to be secret because to have been an atheist was to have been a traitor and thus under threat of death. Christopher Marlowe, Thomas Harriot, George Chapman and others, might have belonged to this secret group. Whilst its existence remains a mystery, even though it is thought to be parodied in *Love's Labours Lost*, it does seem that wild and intellectually adventurous men, contemporary with Shakespeare, at least flirted with disbelief. Marlowe's *Tamburlaine*, it seems to me could be read as paean to Atheism. And we don't really know what religious faith Shakespeare held.

In the Enlightenment, Voltaire might or might not have been an atheist; others might well have been, too, but the case of d'Holbach is interesting. Paul-Henri Thiry, Baron d'Holbach (1723 –1789) was a rich Franco-German aristocrat whose salon, in the years leading up to the French Revolution, became, in effect, the seedbed of modern Atheism. He collaborated greatly with Diderot, contributing to his famous Dictionary; amongst others who attended the *salon* were Condillac, Condorcet, D'Alembert and Helvetius, and from Britain Adam Smith, David Hume and John Wilkes amongst others. This was largely a secret gathering as there were penalties in place against Atheism at the time.

Whilst Voltaire railed against d'Holbach, for he found d'Holbach's materialism too extreme, the latter made himself famous through various works, the most significant of which was *The System of Nature*. In this he found "no necessity to have recourse to supernatural powers to account for the formation of things." He fiercely denied that human nature and being have any Divine origin; rather, following contemporary Rationalism, and at the heart of which was enlightened self-interest: "let a man always recollect, that his solid happiness should rest its foundations upon its own esteem, upon the advantages he procures for others; above all, never let him for a moment forget, that of all the objects to which his ambition may point, the most impracticable for a being who lives in society, is that of attempting to render himself exclusively happy." Indeed, d'Holbach's philosophy might well be most attractive to anyone of entrepreneurial nature.

Perhaps he died fortuitously in January, 1789. Nevertheless, his works inspired many, even those such as Danton and Desmoulins, even though their followers were to try to establish their own religion.

If the French Revolution succeeded in overthrowing the old religion and establishing a new religion of Reason, it was only following the thinkers of the Enlightenment. In so far as the Revolution failed to do anything of the sort, The Age of Enlightenment's attack on religion is perhaps paradoxically a monument to the power of religion and superstition, embodying as it did that fear that Lucretius rejected in *On The Nature of Things:* "To avoid bodily pain, to have a mind free from anxiety and fear, and to enjoy the pleasures of the senses." In other words, his rejection of religion (including there being nothing to fear beyond death), was echoed by d'Holbach and his contemporaries so many centuries later, for personal and social well-being is *not* for them to be found through religion.

However that may be, it is surely important to take into consideration the progression of thought as the Enlightenment gave way to the Age of Romanticism, for just as the former stressed that nothing was inaccessible to thought, so the latter, amongst much else, taught that both individuals and society could change and be changed. Thus, it should be remembered that the young Marx saw himself as a Romantic; it was only after his confrontation with the realities of poverty, as he and Engels discovered in Manchester and other cities, that the radicalism of Marxism was developed as we have known it since the *Communist Manifesto* of 1848. The point is that Marxism and Romanticism together made people realise that societies were not to be forever fixed in hierarchical class structures, and that such structures were man-made and had no divine sanction. When Marx declared that 'religion was the opium of the people', what he meant was that people allowed themselves to be drugged into belief in another, better world, rather than being willing to take responsibility for their lives and throw off their shackles and their poverty through revolutionary action.

This message, of course, persisted long in to the 20th Century. Its teleology, its purpose and end-point, as distinct from the Christian one of attaining a New Jerusalem through salvation and redemption, saw the creation of what has been called a 'communist City of God' here on earth. The new Jerusalem was to be achieved not beyond this world but in it, in a global and classless society in which all would be free and equal. God would have nothing to do with it.

This will the touched on again later.

Marx also established that there was no such thing as the discrete individual mind. For him, mind did not precede society, but society preceded mind, the mind is a product of material conditions, of economic and political circumstances, and *not* a factor of the Divine. In this way, and to an extent, Marxism and Evolutionary Theory can be said to have a similarity of outlook.

Of course, not believing in God does not necessarily mean that one is a Marxist, though it seems that the tendency to be left wing is more likely to be discerned in those that are sceptical about the claims of religion. Although I am appreciative of the place of religion in the transformation of society – for example, William Wilberforce was a devout evangelical, and one might like to consider that his inheritance was far more to the good than that of Marx. Nevertheless, there have been plenty of other ideas which have, to my mind, forced a diminishing of the role of a creator in our understanding.

For example, Darwinism and Freudianism both replaced God, the former by demonstrating conclusively that there is nothing in our make-up that separates us from all living life other than genetic differences and that these have evolved over the millennia, the latter that Freud showed that god was a product of our subconscious, indeed *was* the subconscious. Other advances in, say, psychology, pharmacology and neuroscience have further displaced god, explaining such things as revelation in scientific terms.

One recalls that Darwin, through the early part of his life, practised an easy-going Protestantism; during the voyage of *The Beagle*. Nevertheless, by the time That he had returned, married and settled in Down House, his faith was greatly diminished, given what he had discovered in those early years of his life. Then, in April, 1851, his ten-year old daughter, Annie, died. He never entered a church again in his life (though he was buried in Westminster Abbey, next to Sir Isaac Newton).

His study of Evolution had taught him that it was only its blind forces had created organic life, that there was no purpose to it and thus no meaning. However, if there was no meaning, no teleology, what was there? He would not have agreed with Ivan Karamazov that 'everything is permitted', just that 'everything is possible'. The implication for Darwin was that if human life is to have any value, *responsibility* must be at the heart of it and this, of course, involves *choice*.

Choice and responsibility: these words must be added to 'Do no harm'.

And this is an interesting thought: on the biological level, all that we do or think or feel serves one purpose, that is to ensure the survival of that organism and the transmission of its genes to the next generation. And harm, almost universally has accompanied this. For centuries, power, money and place were at the behest of the Church, at the heart of which are, as we see later, religious experiences of one sort or another. Its over whelming power ensured that, to put it simply, the best genes would have been situated in those who held that power, that is genes that provided for those experiences. However, with the decline of religion from the Enlightenment onwards, with increased power and wealth to be found, say, in the new and rising middle classes, the genes that caused religious experience died away, in favour of those that favoured rationalism and practicality. The Industrial Revolution might well be termed The Genetic Revolution.

Nevertheless, Darwin died an exhausted man, 'Wonderful for not being wonderful at all,' as the young Henry James recalled him, in 1883. We still have to learn and understand this fundamental aspect of Evolution and of Atheism.

It can be of no surprise that Existentialism sees in Darwinian theory the basis for its own understanding of Life. We live in the here and now, language has no meaning except as is contingent and relative. Thus there is no meaning beyond what we experience now. Yet we do live, here and now. Perhaps Leonard Cohen's song, 'Closing Time', echoes this with its vitality, love of song and music, yet it is a song about death. This theme will be elaborated on later.

Nevertheless, the Ontological Argument needs now to be addressed, since it can be argued on various grounds that God has allowed humanity to develop Science. Since his main gift to us after life itself, as the religious – especially Luther - would have it is Reason, then it must follow that he gives us the freedom to use Reason to explore the nature of existence, however much that might mean eating of the forbidden fruit. Reason is also, one presumes just as Luther did, an aspect of Divinity itself (though one understands that Luther regretted this: Reason became for him 'The Devil's Handmaid'). Therefore God, it can be said, stands outside and yet participates in existence. This idea needs now to be considered.

The Ontological Argument

What is the nature of the Divine, of The Creator and of God? Ontological Argument tries to put some clarity on the matter. That is, if one is allowed to know.

The standard source for this is St Thomas Aquinas, though it derives from St Anselm of Canterbury in 1078. There are various ways in which it can be presented, but the usual one is: 'It is possible to conceive of a being than which nothing greater can be conceived.'[2] Aquinas put it thus: 'When we know the meaning of *whole* and *part* we instantly agree that any whole is greater than any one of its parts. Well then, as soon as we grasp the meaning of the term *God*, we are bound to see immediately that his existence is implied. For it signifies that than which nothing greater can be conceived.'

I can conceive of anything, of a divinely beautiful woman interested only in me, of a flamingo which has evolved to having only one leg, since it tends to stand on one leg only when feeding, or of an elephant driving a suitably adapted sports car. This is my choice. I can give names to these entities, even though I doubt very much that they exist. But can I also conceive of and give a name to an entity that is greater than anything else?

Normally, we are able to identify anything by contrasting it to that which it is not – simple linguistics. Since I can have no knowledge of anything except in so far that it can be conceived of or sensed, by which I mean through use of another being that I can contrast it to and make distinction, I can call that being 'God', or 'Yahweh,' or 'Allah'. Therefore God exists. ('Yahweh', of course, means in Hebrew, 'that which cannot be named'. Yet creating the word. . . .)

The argument is obviously nonsensical, demonstrating only a capacity for the use of language.

Nevertheless, Aquinas was a most serious man, who had a profound influence; I have no doubt he was a good man, too. But it is perhaps trite to say that he was a Dominican monk, that he lived in a time of universal belief in God, and that these conditions might have predisposed him to come to the conclusion that he did so believe. It is important, though, to consider his *Quinquae Via*, or *Five Ways* in which the existence of God can be proved. These are[3] outlined as follows.

One: that everything is in movement; there therefore has to be a prime mover, which itself is unmoving.

Two: the world is one of cause and effect. Going back through this chain of being, one comes eventually to the start of it, which itself is uncaused.

Three: we live in a world of 'contingent possibilities', that is, that whatever is might *not* be. There must therefore be a 'guarantee' of contingency: God.

Four: we can make comparisons; there therefore must be a 'standard' against which we make all comparisons. That is, the world is one of imperfection and has to be compared ('contrasted'?) with that which is perfect.

Five: the teleological argument, or argument from ends. All things that are deemed to exist, serve a purpose. Since there is implied a design to anything, there must be an ultimate designer, to life as a whole.

To modern minds, these arguments must sound simplistic at best, if not plain daft. Do they not all rest on the assumption, however unspoken, of God's existence? Each has circularity about it: everything moves, therefore there must be a prime mover. Possibly; even so, why should this prime mover be God, unless you want it to be him? They are, in short, all *a priori* arguments pretending to be *a posteriori,* that is, versions of the Ontological Argument. This is the same with the contemporary Creationist arguments for the existence of God: F.R.E.D.: First Cause, Revelation, Experience, Design. Sometimes, O is added, for Ontological.

There is a witty refutation of the Ontological Argument, quoted by Dawkins[4]. It goes like this: The creation of the world is the most marvellous achievement possible. The merit of this achievement is the product of (a) its intrinsic quality and (b) the ability of its creator. The greater the disability of the creator, the more impressive is the achievement. The most formidable handicap for a creator, the more impressive the achievement. The most formidable handicap would be non-existence.

Therefore, if we suppose that the universe is the product of an existent creator, we can conceive a greater being – namely one who created everything while *not* existing. An existing God would not therefore be a being greater than which a greater cannot be conceived because an even more formidable and incredible creator would be a God which did not exist. Ergo, God does not exist.

But let us try one or two other possible arguments against the Ontological Argument. One might go like this. Dawkins and others take the idea of God too literally. Often, for example, he asks, if God exists, how do we account for his existence. Or, what produced the first creator? Granted, we can arrive at some sort of idea of Big Bang, but this is not to say that this is God. It is just a Big Bang. However, if you ask me to conceive of a being greater than that which can be conceived, let me try. It is called 'nothing'. If I assume that the Ontological Argument is correct (for the purposes of this argument), one must surely be at liberty to assume that the world, the universe was created out of nothing, for at least so we are told in creation myths. (The Big Bang theory to some extent agrees with this argument). Therefore, 'nothing' must be at least as great as God; or, the since Ontological Argument will have it both ways, God is nothing.

Thus two arguments from the Ontological Argument lead to absurdity. How about a third? It is the argument from Linguistics, and links Aquinas' arguments from comparison and contingency. God is so supremely powerful that he can both exist and not exist, he can be both something and nothing. Monotheistic religions would define this as the absolutism of the deity, beyond and absorbing all duality. We can know no more about him, for want of a better term, than just this. But, if I am not prepared to allow God to be both nothing and something, absurd and reasonable, I have to declare my own understanding of at least one of Aquinas' Ways, the fourth one. I recap: 'we can make comparisons; there therefore must be a 'standard' against which we make all comparisons.' That is, the world is one of imperfection and has to be compared with that which is perfect.'

Ignoring the *a priori* conclusion to this argument, let me offer another interpretation of it. Let us assume that the opposite of absolutism, in the sense above, is relativism, in the sense that indeed everything is contingent. This is all the more so the case where language is concerned. I know a tree is a tree and not breeze block, not because they are there standing together for me to inspect, though this is part of it, but because words – sounds - have been ascribed to them according to their differences, such as they may be.

In the same way, you might say to me, look at the differences between a God-defined absolutism and relativism. One of those differences must be, since absolutism is what it is, that it must contain everything, indeed everything that is relative. On the contrary, I will say: this is only words. I see the world as being marked in all respects by difference established by comparison, therefore your absolutism is only relative to and as relative as my relativism.

And so the argument will go on, but the point will have been made. God exists, does not exist, is absurd and not absurd, is relative and absolute. Since reason, according to Christian belief, is what most separates us from the animals (and from those who do not share this belief, perhaps), and is God's most precious gift to us after life itself, it might be of help that a rational understanding of the Ontological Argument were available. I repeat that Luther called reason 'the Devil's harlot', but his cantankerousness is far less important than anything else he left us; might he, though, have argued that God is rational and irrational?

Cosmology

If there is nothing in the above argument for God's existence, what about the argument from cosmology? Can this provide us with any hope? When Camus said that Galileo, in recanting from the heliocentric view, was not prepared to suffer for the Ontological Argument, Camus was not, to my mind, being entirely mischievous, for Galileo, having been tried by the Inquisition in 1633, was forced to spend the last nine years of his life under house arrest. The story of the heliocentric solar system had been around for many centuries, before Copernicus had realised, somewhat to his horror, the falsity of the traditional understanding, only publishing his understanding in 1543 not long before his death.

However, the Church, for ever keen to prefer, even to the extent of vicious persecution, meaning and doctrine when it flies in the face of the truth, was not prepared to have its authority threatened twice, first by the Copernican revolution, and then by the Reformation, and perhaps by Erasmus as well. In fact, it was not until the late Pope, John-Paul II, shortly before the end of his reign, finally pardoned Galileo that at last the Roman Catholic Church recognised the truth of what everyone else had understood several centuries beforehand. It is possibly the case that mathematicians in ancient Alexandria prior to the Christian era are thought also to have predated Copernicus in their understanding, which was ruthlessly suppressed, as of course did the Orientals.

What, though, is the significance of Cosmology in this debate? There is something rather enchanting and beautiful in the idea of the universe being centred upon the earth, with mankind as its very special recipient of life. The Sun, the Moon and the stars orbit the earth (together with the angels and other celestial, intermediary beings), while the stars are the portals through which God's Divinity shines through. Whilst the planets moved around in an observable way, and since all movement must produce sound, in such a way as to create the beautiful music of the spheres, then there was a harmony to all existence. This, it was taught, is from the Divinity, in which mankind has been given its divinely ordained place. Whilst comets and other manifestations of celestial disturbances were bad omens, it is amazing how this nursery version of the cosmos persisted for as long as it did. Such is the power of theocracy.

It is interesting to think that the young John Milton, whilst travelling on the continent met Galileo, in the same house, strangely enough, in which Mary Shelley's *Frankenstein* was conceived almost exactly two hundred years later. Galileo is referred to in Book 1 of *Paradise Lost*. There is some difficulty in Milton's conception of the Universe: his fantasy is certainly not post-Copernican; nor is it entirely heliocentric. It is entirely his – and very beautiful. However man's place in it is special and reserved only for him (and her). It is:

> Far off the empyreal heaven, extended wide
> In circuit, undetermined square or round,
> With opal towers and battlements adorned
> Of living sapphire, once his native seat;
> And fast by hanging in a golden chain
> This pendent world, in bigness as a star
> Of smallest magnitude close by the moon.

This is Milton's heavenly vision of Earth from *Paradise Lost*. Yet, it is just here – and now - that Satan plans to attack God as a consequence of his expulsion from Heaven. Of course, Milton's Universe is very much his own creation; it is certainly not Galileo's, nor ours.

The modern view of the Universe that has emerged in the Twentieth Century out of contemporary cosmological thinking out of contemporary Astrophysics and Astronomy needs now to be addressed. I do not need to revisit the explanation of the universe as we have come to understand it since Edwin Hubble in the 1920s realised, through the use of red-shift analysis, that light must be travelling to his telescope from way beyond what we had long considered to be our own galaxy. Nowadays, it is accepted that the Milky Way is just one out of perhaps billions of galaxies, each containing in turn billions of stars of one sort or another. Furthermore, this universe of so many galaxies is possibly just one of an infinite number of universes, the so-called Multiverse.

If the Copernican revolution was so shocking and disturbing in his day and in the centuries that followed, what on earth does Hubble's revolution say to us and our view of our place in existence? What indeed does the work of Einstein and others? It should be remembered in passing that the latter was very definitely an atheist[6], even though he could not quite accept Quantum Theory, declaring that 'God does not play jokes'. Perhaps the existence of the

Multiverse is indeed an idea greater than which nothing can be conceived. At least we don't have an Inquisition to worry about.

I am not sure that people pay too much attention these days to cosmological questions, unless you are a fan of *Dr Who* or of Philip Pullman's *Dark Materials* trilogy (another Miltonic reference, by the way), or you take a special interest in branes, wormholes and in the myriad sub-atomic particles that seem to be around. However, just to be able to conceptualise for oneself String Theory, quasars, black holes, the Horse Nebula, let alone the very size and age of our Universe, is indeed to fill one with awe and wonder. I will come back to this aspect of religious feeling below. In the meantime, I wish to consider something called the Anthropic Principle, for it offers a contemporary, and indeed, very strange understanding of our place in the universe. And a very strange God indeed.

As I understand it, this works on various levels, each offering an explanation of our place in the Universe, at least as we know it, for what cosmology has ever accurately offered anything else? I attempt to outline three of these: the 'soft', 'hard' and 'participatory'. Dawkins deals with the first two; I refer to Heather Coupar for a consideration of the last, though even such as Bill Gates has talked about it. It is a concept that goes back to the 1960s.

The concept is useful to Dawkins, in so far as he sets it in contrast to any design theory one may offer, such as Milton's pendant globe or anything creationists might intelligently try to think of. At the risk of over-simplifying the matter, this notion of the Anthropic Principle, which Dawkins calls the 'planetary version', operates thus: given that there are at least a billion galaxies in our Universe, with a conservative billion planets similar to our one dotted around in these, it is not unreasonable to say that life, as we know it, might exist in one or more of them. After all, it does exist in one.

However, Dawkins argues that within a reasonable degree of probability, this has a billion to one chance of occurring – that is, an exceedingly small one. This still leaves, nevertheless, about a billion planets potentially capable of supporting life – and that is quite a large number of them. Furthermore, since we surely agree that we exist, then our particular planet, maybe alone in that billion, must be entirely suitable for the evolution of life as we understand it.

Now, this 'planetary' Anthropic Principle works in this way. It asks us to accept that life has taken place on this planet, and that there is a distinction between the origin of life, which is a matter of chance, and Evolution itself, which is determined by adaptive capabilities. The pre-existent causes of life are not biological, but chemical, in conjunction with electricity. Dawkins makes some fun of the idea of a bit of pre-biological soup being sprung into life by some divine fire. However, in *The Selfish Gene* he does indeed suggest that a puddle of this primordial soup might have been struck by lightning, thus starting off the whole thing - hardly divine fire, except to the primitive mind. Thus, as he puts it, the earth is in a 'Goldilocks zone' – neither too hot nor too cold for the whole process to have been initiated by chance and evolutionary development through natural selection to be possible.

The second version, the 'cosmological version', goes like this. Again, shortage of space and time forces simplification. Just as we live on a planet that is friendly to life, so therefore we live in a Universe that is similarly so. This is because those universal constants, which are understood to hold all the forces and energies in the appropriate balance for the advancement of life, happen to support life as we know it. Dawkins refers to six constants, given as numbers suggested by the Astronomer Royal, Martin Rees, and deals with one of them: "the magnitude of the so-called 'strong' force which binds the components of an atomic nucleus." In order for the atom to be split and other atoms to be made, this force has to be overcome. It seems that, in the hydrogen atom, this is measured at 0.007 – this measurement, the understanding goes, pertains to all chemistry as we know it, and thus for life to exist by allowing some hydrogen to persist. Dawkins continues: if this strong force were 0.006, then the universe would consist entirely of hydrogen, and if 0.008, all the hydrogen produced by the explosion of a supernova, such as occurred with the creation of the earth, would have all been used up in the creation of other, heavier elements and there would be no hydrogen. In either case, life as we know it would not have been possible.

We accept, at this point, the Science as here presented. However, Dawkins tackles various religious arguments for the idea that God is present or represented by such constants, mainly on the grounds that those theologically inclined do not seem to understand the ideas that they are propounding. Thus, God stands outside the universe, 'twiddling knobs' so that the constants are always correct. But, Dawkins asks, the universe as we know it is immensely complex and does this not this suggests a God even more complex, an improbable consideration? He also is not averse to the idea of the multiverse, for here indeed would be opportunities for those constants to be varied, but not in our universe. Finally, he addresses those who consider God to be 'simple', the ambiguity of which does not seem to strike those who use this argument.

These seem to me, however, to be a variant of the Ontological Argument since they depend upon cause and effect, and therefore of little interest, whatever their limited rationality.

Finally, there is the third or 'participatory' Anthropic Principle, solipsistic in its nature. Dawkins alludes to but does not deal with this. Simply put, it means that the Universe exists because 'I' exist. This does not mean, as will be shown, that 'I' have created the universe, or have any power over it. In a strange way, this would seem to put the human back in the centre of the Universe, but this is only so far as it has any reference at all to pre-Copernican belief. On the other hand, it implies a final demonstration that all our consciousness is indeed solipsistic in the extreme. It is an idea that derives from Quantum Theory.

That amorous German, Erwin Schrodinger, conceived it thus: given that at the sub-atomic level relationships do not have the same cause and effect relationship that they have above that level, their existence, or occasioning, is a matter of probability. He may or may not have had a cat; however, if, as he put it, his cat was placed in a box, there would be an equal probability of the cat being dead or alive when the box was opened. The reason for this is because either event is as likely as the other, his cat thus being a metaphor for events on the sub-atomic level. Therefore, the particles that make up 'me' are as likely to have made up any variations of 'me', in any condition and in any possible universe, alive or dead. As a consequence, the Universe is said to exist because 'I' exist.

Thus: because 'I' exist, the Universe exits; if 'I' do not exist, then nor does the Universe.

The same will apply to you. You, though on the evidence that life affords, would continue to exist after my death. If so, therefore you must live in a different Universe from me, or the theory is a false one.

However, it is to Quantum Theory that one must go, if only incoherently. It seems, to one who is not a scientist, to beg an all-important yet ancient question: who am I? Or, indeed, what am I?

Furthermore, whilst a pre-Copernican, earth-centred universe will have given assurance as to mankind's place in it all, his revelation of the helio-centric nature of it, began a process that sees mankind in an ever-diminishing place in the scheme of things. The challenge that this gave to the religious authorities was enormous: it is no wonder that Galileo was under house arrest for the last 9 years of his life.

Although the Newtonian understanding of the Universe might have offered an explicable interpretation of it all, this was swept aside by Einstein's Theory of Relativity. Although the latter was prepared to make jokes at the expense of his fellow scientists, he did not believe in God. In a universe in which all is relative, that is, can only been seen in terms of relation to something else there therefore can be nothing outside the universe as we see it. As with what follows, our place in the universe becomes increasingly a complete matter of chance and equally as insecure.

Quantum Theory was an idea that precedes Werner Heisenberg. It derives, indeed, from the earliest realisation, by James Clark Maxwell, of the atom. It was developed by Planck, de Broglie, Einstein himself and others. So, just has Darwin inherited the *idea* of Evolution, so Heisenberg inherited the notion of Quanta.

Carlo Rovelli, in his recent work, *Helgoland*, puts the story most poetically. The young German scientist, just 23 years old, has discovered the theory of Quanta and has taken himself off to the island of the title of this work. Here he isolates himself, until he has worked out what it is all about. Here and at this time his famous Uncertainty Principle unfolded. And he had found something disturbing indeed.

Whereas the work of Einstein and others had dealt with the very large, the cosmic, Heisenberg had been considering the very, very small, the sub-atomic. He discovered that what we call reality was not reality at all.

Delving as he did, as Rovelli puts it, Heisenberg realised that, at the very smallest levels, it is impossible to detect or determine any definitive idea of what we like to call reality. For example, a photon is both a particle and a wave. Again, an electron circulating around a nucleus, can disappear. And there is 'Strange Entanglement': 'entanglement is a physical phenomenon that occurs when a group of particles are generated, interact, or share spatial proximity in a way such that the quantum state of each particle of the group cannot be described independently of the state of the others, including when the particles are separated by a large distance.' (Wikipedia).

However, a problem appears with this: how to describe or characterise a particle. Again, one resorts to Wikipedia, as it introduces Heisenberg's famous Uncertainty Principle: 'Such variable pairs are known as complementary variables or canonically conjugate variables; and, depending on interpretation, the uncertainty principle limits to what extent such conjugate properties maintain their approximate meaning, as the mathematical framework of quantum physics does not support the notion of simultaneously well-defined conjugate properties expressed by a single value. The Uncertainty Principle implies that it is in general not possible to predict the value of a quantity with arbitrary certainty, even if all initial conditions are specified.'

Thus – and indeed, as Quantum Theory was developed in the 20th Century - it became increasingly clear that if it cannot be determined what the nature of the Universe is at the very smallest levels, then it must mean that, one the one hand, our existence is a matter of chance.

There are, though one or two consoling factors. First, that, random though the initiation of quanta seems to be, Quantum Theory and its derivatives, are highly predictable. For example, I am not going to wake up in the morning with a green nose or on Alpha Centuri. It thus allows us to remain securely in our day to day world. It also has provided us with enormous technical skills and advantages, the working of this laptop as I type being an obvious example of this. I come back to this later.

Paradox is essential in Quantum Theory. One may well recall the cat that Erwin Schrodinger declared would be dead and alive according to random sub-atomic activity. However this maybe regarded today – and Rovelli makes a complicated story about this poor cat – it highlights uncertainty.

Michael Frayn puts this very cogently in his play, *Copenhagen*, as being a consequence of Werner Heisenberg's Uncertainty Principle.

As a young man, Heisenberg had visited Nils Bohr, the great Danish physicist. They became friends and the young German became the latter's protégé; they were friends and colleagues. In the years to come they would work together with numerous others, to develop their famous theory.

Then, some twenty years later in 1941, Heisenberg visited the Danish physicist, Nils Bohr, in Copenhagen. In brief, he wants Bohr to sanction his, Heisenberg's, involvement in the development of a Nazi atomic weapon. Frayn uses the Uncertainty Principle as a metaphor for his, Heisenberg's, own moral failing in his involvement, at Hitler's behest, as Germany's leading physicist in the process, and vice versa.

Formerly Bohr's student, colleague and friend, he is now a member of an occupying force intent on discovering how to make an atomic weapon and in so doing, trying to subvert Bohr. In other words, Heisenberg's desire for *certainty*, in his adoption of a role in the Nazi state, flies in the face of his own discoveries about the *uncertainty* of the nature of the universe and of perception itself. He even goes so far as to remind Bohr of the Principle: the nucleus at the heart of the atom is surrounded by protons, on a scale of roughly 10,000 to one. If you try to measure the nature and the movement of this proton, there is considerable difficulty: it can't be seen and it is always moving. In order to see it, you have to introduce a third element, say a photon. In so doing you immediately change the nature of the proton, thus making any measurement of it impossible.

Of course, Bohr did not like to be used in this way at all. However, the point is clear: whilst the Participatory Principle does allow for objective existence outside our minds, the Uncertainty Principle allows for existence only by the same probabilities that occasioned 'my' mind.

And God would seem to be just another of those probabilities.

There are one or two rather interesting further ideas associated with this, that need mention. It seems clear to me that with death there comes no survival of the ego that is ‘I’. The probabilities that had produced me, had pertained to give me existence must now operate differently, otherwise ‘death’ would be meaningless, in the sense that I must live for ever, a palpable nonsense. Another consideration is this. If ‘I’ have consciousness and I am of the same stuff as the universe and, furthermore, that it exists because ‘I’ exist, then ‘I’ must be the same as the universe. Yet ‘I’ have consciousness, and ‘I’ am conscious of saying this. ‘I’ am, as it were, the universe aware of itself. Right?

This somewhat curious idea might disturb; I find it comforting to reflect on what Bohr declared to Heisenberg about Quantum Theory putting man back at the centre of the universe. At least I know where I belong, in a Universe so wondrous, though not necessarily benign, as to force us to ask nothing more of it. For beyond the Universe must indubitably be nothing. To me this seems as great a concept as any other that I can think of.

Thinking such as this cannot, therefore, produce a cosmology that can accommodate God. Thus, at the extreme ends of our understanding of the Universe – the very, very small and the very, very big – there is little scope for a principle, call it God or what you will – that orders or even created such a universe. So far, at least, no one has been able to find a theory that unifies an understanding of the sub-atomic with the cosmic. Stephen Hawkins said that to do so will be to come to know the mind of God. This is, at best, plainly rhetorical. Of course, if reason has its limitations, then we can take recourse into faith, if one wishes to.

So, if the Anthropic Principle works in all three of its versions, it offers us a very different cosmology in our own time from that of previous eras. Gone is the comfort that Copernicus tried to recover; gone is the Newtonian, mechanistic Universe that Einstein threw over; we are left with a relative, uncertain and solipsistic universe, the place of humanity in which is equally strange, even inconceivable.

And does the Anthropic Principle matter? Except as to offer some explanation of the possibility of life existing in this part of the Universe where it does, not a jot.

It is, therefore, very hard to accommodate a place for God in all this, especially if the Ontological Argument is false. None of the thinking behind all this makes any reference to God. Merely to respond with, ‘Well, it ought to have done,’ seems facile in the extreme.

However, all this may seem very abstract and perhaps even sterile, even though mankind has tried for millennia to put existence into a cosmology that provides meaning to that existence. Perhaps it is not surprising that few pay much attention to cosmology these days, outside rather highly selected and educated circles. And God has been slowly but firmly pushed further into the background for the last four or five centuries, as I indicated in my opening paragraphs.

To end this section, let me develop one or two thoughts, in recapitulation.

It is the case, I understand, that the relative size of the nucleus at the heart of the atom to a proton circulating about it can be compared to a football paced on the centre spot at Wembley Stadium with objects circulating around the walls of the stadium.

String Theory, as I can grasp it only very simply, suggests that the relative size would be to objects (super strings) circulating the football as far away as Jupiter. These kinds of dimensions are impossible to conceive and they will always remain theoretical. Nevertheless, they are extraordinary. And conceivable? Yes, indeed.

On the other hand, as one recalls from Hubble's discoveries and from on-going developments, the universe itself is conversely enormous. Before him, the stars were the glorious Divine shining through the covering of darkness. Recall, though, what Hubble discovered and all the discoveries thereafter: that the Earth – our home – is just one amongst perhaps billions in our Galaxy, The Milky Way, itself perhaps just one galaxy amongst billons of others. And then there is the Multiverse in which, apparently, exists an infinite number of variations of every arrangement of all the atoms that this planet is made up of. If so, is this not quite incredible? Or is it not, you might say, just what is meant by the Ontological Argument: than which nothing greater can be conceived? Well, it has been conceived.

If the universe exists because I exist, then, for the sake of argument, let us suppose that the Universe exists because God exists. There is no logical, empirical connection between the two statements, but having played with the former, let us play with the latter. A deist would claim the second statement as a matter of faith, if not fact, regardless of its *a priori* nature. How about the reverse: that God exists because the universe exists? Well, we have certainly created God. . . . But what about the fact that it is possible to say that the universe exists because God does not exist. Does the universe disappear?

Please don't tell me that God allows me to say this, even though you might like to remind me of Pascal's wager: there is a lot more to be gained in believing that God exists than if he did not. Just a choice but one that is forced upon us and to Pascal's 17th Century readers, this must have been at least challenging. I am not sure that I would waste my money.

Well, then you say, is not God the Universe, the Universe God? Do you not know what tautology is? I reply. It is 'the saying of the same thing twice over in different words,'

For example, in basic sentence structure of subject, verb and complement, when the latter repeats the former. Here you will be just replacing one word with another, with no illustration. Say, 'God is God' or 'The Universe is The Universe'. What do you mean?

Consider, furthermore, that whilst we are told that the Universe in 16.3 billion years old, a time period incomprehensible to normal human perception, it is continuing to expand. By expansion, one understands, is meant that the space between atoms and sub-atomic particles is expanding, even as this is being written, even inside my fingers. And what drives this endless expansion – and why? 'Well,' you say, 'God moves in mysterious ways.' It is speculated that this expansion will go on *ad infinitum*, leaving the Universe, in due course, in total darkness, because light will never be able to travel its expanse, even at 176,00 mile per second. How odd of God.

But then, surely, your God and our place in the Universe is no more odd than Milton's.

Now we know, of course, from Einstein's Theory of Relativity, that Time & Space are, well, relative to one another. If I travel in a train going at the speed of light leaving my beloved in the station platform, and I travel for what to her is 100 years, when I have returned she will have aged accordingly, though I will not have.

Of course, we live in time. We cannot do otherwise. But how do we perceive time on these scales? How do we perceive distances and number on these scales? Is there a God who can offer explanations?

Seems unlikely.

But let me end with another speculation.

Why the Universe should exist is thus of the profoundest importance – or perhaps none at all. The Anthropic Principles suggest that we exist at a precisely suitable place in the Solar System to allow for life. Or that we, in perceiving the Universe, might in fact be creating it. Or defining it.

Then: if the Universe exists because 'I' observe it, I must be observing 'I' observing it. What is either 'I'?

And, if I look at myself in the mirror, who – or what - is doing the looking?

It might be, though, that in time (oh, yes) we might be able to unify the beginning and end of time. For example, what if the enormously large is contained in the infinitely small, the infinitely brief with endless eternity? Yes, we live in History, but we also live in Space-Time. The former will always be our determinant, but could we live, too, with an awareness of the relative nature of our existence?

Nothing absolute in this, is there? How could there be?

Well, whilst understanding of how matter works at the sub-atomic level has provided us with so much that has enriched our lives, as mentioned above, it has also provided us with the means to destroy all life in its entirety on the planet. Between them, Russia and The USA have about 7,000 nuclear warheads.

On Stories, Experience and Revelation

But there are other reasons, I accept, for believing in and having experience of God: revelation and experience, feeling, hope and faith. These are the very stuff of religion. How much these have contributed to the conduct of human relations over the centuries? Before the Cartesian revolution, perhaps everything; since it, increasingly little – though, it must surely go without saying, that they have contributed much to the destruction of human relations. One only has to think how quickly Islam descended into violence and imperial conquest so soon after Mohammed's death; Christianity has done no less.

However, as Christopher Hitchens spent many angry pages detailing, much of these justifications for faith evolve into stories that are just that – stories. I do not feel his anger about religion, in so far as I have lived in a free and democratic country for most of my life, and I have been allowed to hold my opinions as I think fit. Nevertheless, stories are just that – stories, fictions.

They grow up around any great charismatic leader to create a sense of wonderment and of awe at the sense of what lies behind those fictions. Of Siddhartha Gautama, we are told, flowers sprouted in his earliest footsteps; there are innumerable Hindu Gods, each with his, her or its magical powers. Mohammed, an illiterate trader, was able to fly from Mecca to Jerusalem on his horse, leaving a hoof print on the wall of Al Aqsa Mosque. Christian stories are too numerous and well known to recall here. Narratives accumulate, reverse themselves, turn in and contradict themselves, and they are used to give meaning to our lives, to direct our morals and to lead us towards one New Jerusalem or another. But they remain fictions, just perhaps as our lives do.

However, the point is not to belittle the vast contribution to culture that religion has made. More important it is to offer an understanding, even a celebration of that culture. Nevertheless, it is my firm belief that human life has been, is and always will be determined by the contingent, the relative and the temporary and that there is no God to whom we can make recourse to in the search for Salvation, Redemption or even an understanding of the purposes of existence that derives from the Divine.

As far as we know, we are alone in the universe, and even if the there are others out there, they too are alone in a similarly existential way. Human existence, furthermore, has no meaning outside that existence; it is defined only by the ways in which we inhabit this planet, determined by whatever sub-atomic, atomic, chemical, molecular and cellular imperatives that blindly drive life. When we understand everything that there is left to understand, there will be only nothing left to understand about life.

‘What will we do,’ asks the 13-year-old Thomasina in Tom Stoppard’s’ *Arcadia*, ‘when we know everything? We’ll dance on the seashore.’

Indeed, I would advance another, perhaps even more disturbing idea: that there is, in fact, no such thing as ‘life’. At some point, as Fritjof Capra puts it, in the processes involved in the conception and development of the cells that make up the foetus something we call life appears. As Noah Yuval Harari puts it, we are nothing but molecules and electricity.

However potential it might be, something happens which will end up as Beethoven, Hitler or me, a flower or a tiger. But is there really any such distinction to be made between the animate and the inanimate, other than the differences in the make-up of the chemicals that distinguish them? The elements that make up the Periodic Table are those that make up both the animate and inanimate. They derive from one source: from the explosion of a super nova, or from the Big Bang itself. The energy that does distinguish them is just as much part of the stone as it is of the frog. ‘We are made of the same dust as the stars,’ as the astronomer, Carl Sagan, put it. Is this not a story wonderful enough?

And there is much to wonder at in life, as artists, musicians, sculptors, architects have amply demonstrated throughout the centuries and in all cultures to express awe, wonder and devotion, beauty and pleasure. Bearing in mind that too often these have been in the service of theocracy, since the Church had money, this does not belittle them at all. Culture, at its highest, is a monument to human creativity, as much in the arts as in the Sciences. Edwin Hubble was the first who realised that we lived in a galaxy; we know now that ours is just one amongst billions of galaxies. Photographs from the orbiting satellite named after him and launched more than thirty years ago, have greatly enhanced our understanding of and indeed awe at the nature and immensity of the universe.

How strange it is, too, that Haydn's *Creation* should give musical representation to at least an approximation of the Big Bang, composed as it was three hundred or so years before the concept came into usage. How remarkable that the music of Bach, the sculptures of Bernini, the Sistine Chapel's ceiling, all tell such human stories. Culture is an expression of the human condition. And do not these – and all the other myriad art forms - exist only because of the one thing that seems to distinguish humans from animals – a conscious ability to adapt our own DNA through learning, expression and being creative?

You may call this God-given if you will, and one can think of it as an aspect of the meaning of spirituality. Recent research has shown that we possess, at a certain point in our DNA, genes that preconditions humans to experience awe. This might have evolved as a survival mechanism to ensure our nomadic ancestors recognised and felt some degree of ownership of a place where water and food were abundant, thereby ensuring return to that place or possession of it. I consider it, however, nothing more than good luck. Thus it is, to me, what characterises human existence.

And about Love

But I hear you say, what about love? Isn't this the most important aspect of existence? Is not God, the God of love? Does not the very nature and existence of love in our everyday lives indicate that this is proof of God's existence? Did not God send down to Earth his only Son? And did we not learn the nature of love through that Son's Crucifixion?

Some obvious questions: how do we know Jesus was the 'only' son? Why 'son', too? And to quote Howard Jacobson, 'Messiah does not mean "Son of God". Nor did Jesus ever claim to be the Son of God. The idea would have been a nonsense to him. The long-awaited Messiah (the word simply means "anointed one") would prepare the way for God, not assume the title of a God.'[31]

And why should such a God have created a race so cruel and dangerous – just for the fun of it? Or, more sensibly, for what purpose do the Fall, Salvation and Damnation serve – except in a Manichean Universe where God has two faces. Only two? And what veracity can Biblical stories have when they were written years, even decades after the events they are supposed to commemorate?

But without it, is not life meaningless? As with other arguments for the proof, or at least here, of the nature of God, the response is similar: humans can and do love, because they are human (and I don't think that love is restricted to humans). And there is an evolutionary necessity for love.

I conclude with the following story because it tells of the destruction of love, of hope and of happiness in the name of 'the perfect state', of Man's inhumanity to Man and in this case, as in so many others, to Woman, as she is, of course, lumbered with the Curse of Eve. Set during Stalin's Terror of the 1930s, it exemplifies the nature of tyranny. It needs retelling now because we see around us in today's world the rise of dictators, petty or not so, of such

---

[31] Howard Jacobson, 'Behold the Jewish Jesus' in The Guardian of January 11th, 2009.

as Erdogan in Turkey, Duterte, as 'Uhuru' Kenyatta, as Orban and indeed as Johnson may well prove in our country – or Trump in America. And Yuval Noah Harari recalls an anecdote, in *Homo Deus*, about Frederick the Great of Prussia. 60,000 men, uniformed and armed to go forth and slaughter 150, 000 Poles or whoever, are lined up on parade before him and a few generals. 'Here we are,' said the great Monarch, 'unarmed and defenceless. Any one of these men could easily kill us here and now. And why doesn't one?'

Why is it that ordinary men – and some women – can be so easily persuaded to torture, kill, rape and destroy?

Sophocles' *Oedipus Rex*, perhaps the greatest political drama ever written, tells us of all human fallibility, either in our person or in our fates. Oedipus, its flawed eponymous hero has achieved fame and reverence because he has saved Thebes from the Sphinx, the cause of plague. Its greatness, as in all ancient Greek tragedy, lies in its message: The Chorus – the people – must be freed from devotion to the 'strong leader', the autocrat, the dictator. Strength and human contentment can only be found through the democratic process. But how much suffering is needed for this to be achieved?

The following story is taken from Orlando Figes' *The Whisperers* (2007). This very remarkable book, by the Professor of History at Birkbeck College, gives an account of the Great Terror in Stalin's Russia, from 1917-1953, the year of Stalin's death. Although there is a great amount on the history of the period, this work primarily and deliberately gives voice to all the millions who died and suffered in Russia during this period. It is based upon interviews and records, oral and written, opened to view since the fall of the Soviet Union and he had access to many archives. These have now been closed under Putin.

It is a long and very thorough work, recording as it does how the Revolution of 1917 devoured its own children, Stalin excluded. In so doing, it focuses on numerous individuals and families, some inter-connected. Figes was able to interview many of the remaining survivors, though they are now, of course, a generation quickly dying off. In my view, it is a very timely and moving work.

Before I tell it, I need again for a moment to be somewhat personal. I have led, as has everyone I imagine reading this, a life far removed from the suffering I am going to reflect upon. In contrast, the many years since I was born have been, for me, a blessed time. I have known tragedy, and I experienced, though by no means suffered from, the iniquities of Apartheid. However, I have been happy, healthy, sufficiently well born and educated to give me a life of considerable freedom, privilege and contentment. I have much to be thankful for, including the benefit I have gained from the goodness of those around me. If this is the working of Love, then I acknowledge it. I, for one, have never suffered from man's (yes, man's) infinite capacity for inhumanity.

And this Love – where is it to be found? In the ordinary, in the individual? Or in the dreams of the idealist?

This story tells of the fate of one Julia Piatnitskaia[5]. It is like that of so many, many others. Her husband, Osip, was arrested at 11.00 pm on 7th July, 1937. His arrest was expected. It occurred at the height of the Terror, during its most dreadful phase. He was a senior Bolshevik, a member of the old, pre-revolutionary underground, a 'professional-revolutionary', who was dedicated 'entirely to the party, and lived only for its interests,' as

Lenin's widow, Nadhezda Krupskaia, put it. After the revolution, he worked tirelessly for the establishment of the Soviet system, becoming the head of the Comintern, the Communist International. However, he fell foul of Stalin and his henchmen in the NKVD because he was an outspoken critic of the growing 'bourgeoisification' of the Party, of Stalin's growing rapprochement with Western powers in the face of the threat from Nazi Germany, and of Stalin's growing control over the Party and the State. Piatnitsky was thus seized; his life was destroyed, as was that of his family. He died soon after in the Gulag.

Julia was, as Figes recounts it, a spirited, beautiful and idealistic woman, some seventeen years younger than her husband. Of Polish origin, she ran away from home at 16, enrolled as a nurse in the Red Army after October 1917, and married a general, who subsequently died. She then worked as a spy for the Red Army during the Civil War after October 1917, in the headquarters of Admiral Kolchak, the leader of the Whites, making a quick escape to Moscow when her cover was blown. There she had a nervous breakdown, recovered, married Osip, and produced two sons with him.

The Piatnitskys were of the generation that grew into adulthood before or during the First World War; they were highly idealistic and dedicated – and paid the price for their idealism. Julia had a strong sense of justice rooted in her religious upbringing; she was also, 'adored by everyone,' being remembered many years later by a daughter of one of her husband's colleagues thus: 'We children were always calm in her presence. . . . We forgot our worries. . . . She was always full of life.'

After her husband's arrest, her life fell apart, as it would do for so many others who found themselves in similar circumstances, at that time. In due course, her sons were arrested, although they were still teenagers, 16 being the age of 'criminal' liability. However, they survived; Julia did not.

Julia, who at first found it impossible to believe that her husband had been an 'enemy of the people', and a fascist, capitalist spy, began to have doubts, such was the pressure of the times. She even believed that it was right that those with whom Osip was supposed to be involved, like Bukharin and Rykov and the supporters of Trotsky, should be shot. Gradually, her life became ever harder and more desperate. Figes quotes from her diary: "My life has become an endless downward spiral. I talk with myself, in a whisper, and feel complete despair." She records her despairing thoughts of her sons, locked away in prison. However, she increasingly blames her husband for what has happened to them all and comes to believe that he was indeed guilty: "Perhaps Piatnitsky really was bad, and we must all perish on his account," she wrote. Her younger son had been released and then rearrested; she herself was finally taken in on 27th October, 1938.

She was sent to work in a labour camp in the north, near Murmansk; sometime later she was denounced, and sent to the notorious Karaganda labour camp, in Kazakhstan. Figes records her fate thus: "Physically frail and mentally unbalanced, Julia was in no condition to withstand the hardships of camp life." Refusing the sexual advances of the camp commandant, she was punished by him, being forced "to work as a manual labourer on the construction of a dam. For sixteen hours every day she stood waist high in freezing water, digging earth. She became ill and died on an unrecorded date in the winter of 1940."

Many years later, in 1958, an old woman, a family acquaintance who had known Julia in the camp, told Igor the truth about his mother's death. Figes recounts it thus: 'No one wanted to tell Zina, the woman, when she went to look for her, where Julia was, but then someone pointed to a sheep pen on the steppe and said that she could be found there. Zina walked into the pen. Amongst the sheep, lying on the ground, was Julia. Zina told Igor: 'She was dying, her whole body was blown up with fever, she was burning hot and shaking.' Julia begged Zina, through her delirium and her swollen lips, to find her little boy, Igor, and to help him to survive. Soon a guard came to Zina, and roughly frog-marched her away, telling her to say nothing.

Thus Figes ends his chapter on 'The Great Fear': 'Julia died in the sheep-pen. She had been left there when she fell ill and no one was allowed to visit her. She was buried where she died.'

I do not recount this haunting and terrible story just because it is thus. Julia and her husband and family and all the twenty-five million who died in the Terror, as well as the twenty-five million who died in the war in Russia alone, do indeed need to be memorialised, as do the six million in The Holocaust, the 45 million who died at the hand of Mao Tse-Tung. And how many at the hands of Empire-building nations?

But, as the late Bernard Levin once put it, there must have been those who, in the darkness of the Holocaust, cried out, 'Where are you, God?', as might have done those who were herded into churches in Rwanda to be slaughtered or who came out of their cellars and ruined houses in Berlin in 1945 to greet their final nemesis at the hands of Russian soldiers, who raped and killed them, in revenge for the devastation wreaked upon them by Hitler's armies. Examples from the 20th Century and its terrible wars are too numerous for us to seek much comfort in the thought that some of us have had easy lives. It is a strange God indeed who makes us pay for such idealism, for being young. Or for being human.

In the great Greek tragedies, of which *Oedipus The King* is perhaps the greatest, the Chorus, that is ordinary people, suffers as it sees its saviour's flaws and weaknesses exposed. As their story progresses thorough its various stages, including 'anagnorisis' or 'recognition' that they are alone and no saviour can possibly save them from this, they experience 'catharsis' or 'cleansing': a ridding of themselves from dependence. Aristotle, in his *Poetics*, defines this as being, 'From too much love of living, from hope and fear set free'.

The answer to Levin's question is perhaps as brutal as the action of a concentration camp guard's: 'There is no God.' One doesn't have to indulge in Nietzschean rage, nor believe with Ivan Karamazov that 'Everything is permitted!' It means that, as Jimmy Porter puts it in *Look Back in Anger*, 'We are alone in the freezing forest with only our breath before us to follow.' It means that we have created God in our own image for far too long, that we need to accept the responsibility of being alone, for the planet, for our lives and for each other, and that rationality defines for us our limitations, just as death does life. It means that we can love, but that this love is contingent upon acts of will and of self-restraint, of empathy and being fully human.

Is Love Life? Like Schrodinger's cat, it probably is and it probably is not. Just like God, who is and is not, but who is, in Jorge Luis Borges' resonant phrase, 'everything and nothing'. And this means that Life is, happily or unhappily, only what we make of it.

And 'it leaves not a rack behind.'

And yet. And yet. . . .

Why is that, in evolutionary terms, *Homo Sapiens* has not speciated, that is into other species that cannot procreate with the original one? Why is that, when 99.5% of all species that have ever existed, our one is still very much with us? One can suppose that Humanity has always, through the development of suitably powerful weapons, been able to fend off predators. Survival of the fitter?

However, having argued against God, I now recognise a new one. This God is being created now, by us. It will know everything. And it will never go away.

Homo Deus is the title of the work (2015) in which Yuval Noah Harari develops and explores the idea that what he calls 'Big Data', or 'The Internet of Everything' is being rapidly developed. In short, through the uses of algorithms and micro-advertising, Big Data will, in time have assembled all information about humans – both individually and collectively – in such a way as to control, predict, modify and control not just our thoughts, desires, hopes and fears. It will make us buy, achieve, desire and vote for as it requires. To be human is, in a very crucial sense (amongst others) is to be able to choose. This will become a pretence.

This god will have no metaphysical or spiritual dimension or characteristics, universal though it will be. Harari's title derives from Hegel, who declared that 'God is Man'. The latter's idealism was turned upside down by Karl Marx, who declared that 'Man is God', as we have seen. Marx meant by this that through revolutionary processes and actions, humans could overturn the oppressive status quo under which the great majority lived to create a new and ever more perfect society. Both declarations were wrong, as the history of the 20th Century so abundantly shows.

Harari's title is ironic. He demonstrates most persuasively that humanity is in the process of depriving itself of its evolutionary superiority on this planet. He never suggests what humans will do, once the Big Data take-over is complete. Maybe, as is depicted in *The Matrix*, humans will be bred as sources of energy for The Matrix

Others, like Niall Fergusson in his latest work, *Doom*, and Jeanette Winterson, have also commented and warned us about this. It is happening now: the Chines are perfecting it and are selling programs to countries with authoritarian leaders that will enable them to control their people. One wonders how exactly the Conservatives won the 2019 election, after 10 disastrous years in government.

Dictators throughout History have wanted to control their subjects' thoughts. This ability is now becoming ever-more realisable. The One Party State is upon us. Permanently.

This potentiality will come to pass as Big Data persists and perfects itself, so becoming 'God'. Its powers will be rather more than that of the gods of old, for it cannot be challenged. It will be unseen, unrecognised, but ever present and eternal. No one will control it. It will control us and, suggests Harari, we will wither away.

Is it too late for humanity to recognise this and to choose or to deny it? What can be done about it?

Don't use the Internet.

Don’t use the Internet?

Easier said than done.

11

Heart of Darkness

Numberless are the world's wonders but none more wonderful than man

Sophocles

As she was being put into handcuffs by the police officer, other pedestrians thought, not unnaturally, that the young woman was being arrested. One does not interfere when something like this is happening.

How, after all, does one know what is really going to occur next?

The officer puts her in his car and though one does not know what her reactions are like at this particular moment, these must have rapidly become more and more terrified, for, it must be clear, she had done nothing wrong and she had therefore no idea of the reason for what had happened to her – just a young woman walking home through a park, one evening in Spring.

One can only imagine her anxiety and then growing terror. A terror that gripped as she was driven away from the city to the country. And in a wood, she was dragged out of the car, raped and then murdered. Her body was then burnt and her remains thrown into a lake.

This terrible story has been much in the media of late.

The perpetrator of this terrible crime has pleaded guilty and has been sent to prison for the rest of his life. Can one have any sympathy for his apparent courtroom contrition? Can anything expunge this? Is expiation possible, *any* expiation? The judge plainly thought not. No one could disagree with this.

It should go without saying that the victim's family are utterly devastated, for they have lost a loved one who can never return. It is one thing to lose a son or daughter in an accident, quite another in circumstances such as these. Her extended family and friends must share in this and will do all they can to support each other.

There is, though, the other family, the family of the murderer, in particular their two small children. His wife, too, must be shattered – there is no indication whatsoever of her having any knowledge of her husband's intentions, intentions they must have been since it seems to have been carefully planned, though the hire car he used could be traced back to him. And since he was a police officer, one would have thought that he would have been aware of this. Thank goodness for his oversight.

One hopes that these children, who will be identified at school and in their community, will have help and support. They will have to live for many years – decades, indeed - with the knowledge of what their father did. He has destroyed his family, too.

I am not concerned at this point with the nature of the correct punishment or retribution for such a crime. What drove this man to do it is the subject that needs to be considered and discussed most widely. I write this as a man.

I will say this: I suspect, I hope wrongly, that there are *very* few men who have not, at some point or another, in one way or another, misbehaved towards a woman, however mildly. I am not innocent, except to say, in some degree of mitigation, that when she has said, 'No, please don't!', I have stopped.

I suppose – and I have no doubt that this will apply to the vast majority of men – that a sense of shame or of morality (putting it as vaguely as this) has slipped in between my intention and the act and thus brought a halt to what I had intended to do.

'For most of us, even a flickering awareness of the consequences of our imagined aggression triggers negative feelings that prevent us from going through with a violent act.'[32]

As one gets older, one hopes that this sense becomes all the more imperative. But not always.

Perhaps I ought to add more about myself. I am now in late middle age, in a relationship which brings much happiness. Although well educated, I am no genius. My understanding is in the Arts, not Sciences and I can claim no special insight, therefore, into the pathologies of the psychopath.

But I cannot make this as an excuse for *not* trying to come to some understanding of this behaviour. I am a no murderer, but I am man.

In short, unlike the vast majority of men who will hold themselves back as asked, why did this man not do so? What drove him to the most awful of acts? He knew what he was going to do some weeks beforehand.

And can we learn anything from this? We observe the horror (from a distance, of course), we suffer for the victim in our imaginations. The perpetrator is sent down for life. We soon move on, forget – until the next young woman is similarly treated.

But learn we must. Is it any good to damn this man as an 'evil monster', like the Yorkshire Ripper, or like Dr Harold Shipman or Rose and Fred West? Brady and Hindley, and Dennis Nilson? None would ever want to identify with such as these, but they are – or were – human. My question is, do we 'demonise them' at some future cost?

It has been remarked that when a man sees a woman for the first time, he thinks whether he would like to go to bed with her; he then thinks of what chance he might have. Does this mean that there is an instinctual and primal aspect to the male psyche that is essentially sexual? And being so, empowering?

For Freud, it is the libido that is the powerful motive force. And for Adler, the desire to control, to exercise power.

---

[32] I am much indebted here for help from the following: *Dangerous Minds: A Forensic Psychiatrist's Quest to Understand Violence by Taj Nathan, published by John Murray. Extract from The Guardian.*

One knows only too well that the sexual drive, starting as it does early in puberty, might well go on till late in life. Social constraints attempt to regulate this. Indeed, Christianity and other religions have all developed dogmas and practices to regulate this drive, most repressing it, but some celebrating it. Isn't every Greek statue a monument to the beauty of the human body, both male and female? But then, ancient Greek culture was entirely male dominated.

But again, I ask, what drove this man to this dreadful act? I ask again, because I must and not the least because he had – appallingly, extraordinarily - spent some weeks prior to it planning it. Not once, not once does it appear to have come to him that he was being ridiculous, bad and about to do something wholly, utterly wrong.

Was it because of the police culture in which he worked?

We have heard, too, that, as a serving police officer, he had been very much part of a macho world that denigrated women, not the least those who were his colleagues. One wonders how much the forthcoming enquiry into this culture will reveal.

It appears that very many similar charges have now been made against policemen.

We have been told too that there are suggestions that had exposed himself in public. Why was he protected by those in authority over him?

A young man walks through a park one darkening evening; he sees a young woman. He imitates exposing himself, without actually doing so. On another occasion, he does so expose himself. He gets away with it. He feels, does he not, a freedom, a sexual freedom? A sense of entitlement?

He masturbates, but he also feels, if indistinctly, something else: that the female is something that is, in fact, untouchable by him, unavailable to him. He does not, cannot, articulate this. But this is the foundation that drives his urge. He objectifies the female. Is it an urge for revenge? Self-pity? Arrogance?

Pornography. The male gaze. The use of prostitutes, even the myth of 'conjugal rights' – all such are miles away from what he would really like, which is *not* loveless sex. But he has no means of understanding this, as he is free only to act upon his impulses.

And the Internet, where there is no control, no barriers, moral or otherwise to prevent abuse, for there is the infamous Telecommunications Act, passed by Congress in the 1990s, when Clinton was President. Deep in it is a clause that defines websites – Facebook, Instagram, Google and such – as 'platforms', not publishers. A publisher is responsible for libel, inaccuracies, abuse and so on. A platform is not. So these 'platforms' get away with it.

A headline in the The Times: 'They put their daughters to bed, then go online and send me rape threats.' A famous young actor recounts the abuse she receives. She continues: 'These are the sort of men that go out and rape and kill women, surely. . . . OK, you haven't physically done anything to someone, which is why it's not taken as seriously, but it is as serious, because it could lead on to that," she said. "If you're threatening to rape me online, then you're having rape thoughts. So you want to rape a woman. Whether you act on it or not, you're having thoughts about raping a woman. So you need help, or you need to be in prison."

And here the word ‘psychopath’ comes to mind, for its suggestion of a disconnect between instinctual and moral feelings. What is the meaning of this?

Here, Wikipedia is perhaps helpful. It offers, inter alia, the following:

‘Low fear including stress-tolerance, toleration of unfamiliarity and danger, and high self-confidence and social assertiveness. Poor impulse control including problems with planning and foresight, lacking affect and urge control, demand for immediate gratification, and poor behavioural restraints.’

And: ‘Lacking empathy and close attachments with others, disdain of close attachments, use of cruelty to gain empowerment, exploitative tendencies, defiance of authority, and destructive excitement seeking.’

This murderer – I almost wrote ‘our’ – displayed some, if not all ,of these characteristics – he certainly seemed capable of planning. I read that he could also be depressive.

‘Women are to be had, to be played with, to be subject.’ To male desire, as he believed it.

Was this a start for this offender, for any sexual offender?

And he was a married man. Was this not enough?

No. The drive, the male libido, was too strong for him, in his arrogance.

He shamed his colleagues – or they are to be shamed with him, for their culture.

He destroyed a life. He destroyed a family. He destroyed his own family. And himself.

He thought that he had freedom.

12

Frankenstein's Heirs

For me as a human being, Nagarjuna teaches the serenity, the lightness and the shining beauty of the world: we are nothing but images of our images. Reality, including ourselves, is nothing but a thin and fragile veil, beyond which. . . there is nothing.

C.Rovelli, referencing Nagarjuna

What follows is, in its way, a history of mankind, not from the usual perspectives of dynasties and empires, wars and battles, of philosophical trends and fads or of religions, but of humanity's search for identity. It will also be a consideration of love and how it can be felt, achieved and, above all, needed.

And, perhaps, about its failure.

From Pygmalion to Frankenstein, from Prometheus to Utz – and many more left out – this essay will consider conflict, war and suffering even as love is sought for. This piece will end with an examination of some Science fiction films, with the creatures, monsters and heroes in each, especially with the figure of Ripley. It will contend that *all* these creatures are in fact, emanations of the potential of anything that is human, its heroes, saints and monsters, be they 'human' or 'machines'.

But what is this identity? What is love?

Plainly, no discussion of this subject can avoid reference to the Christian 'God of Love' and to Jesus Christ. Atheism is considered at some length elsewhere in this book. I merely ask this: if Jesus came to earth to save us all – from ourselves? did he do a good job? I leave the question unanswered at this point.

This paper has been stimulated by the idea that, so I like to think, human beings are most fully human only when being creative, not just with pianos and paintbrushes but with any activity that is new and capable of being developed. However platitudinous this might seem, it does not seem to be an entirely unambiguous idea. Whilst creativity provides meaning for us, it can also do something else: those meanings can, in certain circumstances, prove extremely dangerous, impelling one to be – paradoxically – destructive: Nazism was, after all new. It is possibly also the case that all creativity involves artificiality, thereby only compounding the problems of the nature of the word 'meaning'. Furthermore, there has always been, at least since the 16th Century, the distinction between artistic and scientific knowledge, activity and creation, though this distinction is often blurred. This paper explores, through reference to various different media, these ideas, hence its title, 'Frankenstein's Heirs'.

It considers how Victor Frankenstein tasted of the fruit of the Tree of Knowledge, just as Rabbi Loew did before him, and Adam before that. I will discuss how Prometheus, too, in a slightly different way, gave mankind the sense, not only of how to feed, look after and be creative, but also into the nature of the Divine; Utz, Caliban & Professor Higgins will be part of the story, as will Neo and Ripley and the Terminators,. All suffered terribly as a consequence of their actions, of their desire and their ambition. Perhaps in our own time we, too, have trod where we might not have done, as some of the films I am going to discuss suggest. In my title for this essay, 'Frankenstein's Heirs', I deliberately leave ambiguous to whom I am actually referring, for I want to bear in mind both the creator and the monster that is created.

However, all 'history' starts with myth, myths of origin, of creation and of a creator being, all of which give meaning and purpose. These myths abound around the world. My account of history, my privileged account, is not chronological, but thematic.

In Prague

The story goes back sometime before – and after – the first publication of Mary Shelley's masterpiece. I first came across the Golem in the late Bruce Chatwin's last and, I think, finest novel, *Utz*. The Golem 'was an artificial man . . . a mechanical man . . . a prototype of the robot', as Chatwin's fictional narrator puts it[1]. In brief, this is how Chatwin expands on this idea: the word 'golem' comes from the Hebrew and means 'unformed' or 'uncreated'. A righteous man could, in ancient Jewish belief, create the World by repeating, in a prescribed order, the letters of the secret name of God. In this way, we are told, Adam himself had originally been a golem, the size and shape of the World, till Yahweh reduced him to human scale, and 'breathed into his mouth the power of speech'[2].

Thus it was that the celebrated Rabbi Loew created his golem, for he wanted a servant. At first, this golem was obedient and diligent till one Sabbath, when the Rabbi omitted to let it sleep for the day of rest (as all creatures must do). The golem went 'berserk'; 'he pulled down houses, threw rocks, threatened people and tore up trees by the roots.' The Rabbi was forced to destroy his creation, by removing its 'shem', its power source[3]. This destructiveness is, of course, later much displayed by Frankenstein.

The lesson to be learned from this was that 'the golem-maker had acquired arcane secrets: yet in doing so had transgressed Holy Law. A man-made figure was a blasphemy. A golem, by its presence alone, issued a warning against idolatry – and actively beseeched its own destruction.'[4] We will find this blasphemy – of man playing at being God - over and over again in what follows, for a golem can be seen as a paradigm of human creativity, in particular in the sense man imagines he can act and be as God. In this way, Loew's story foretells that of Victor Frankenstein's.

An author, too, plays God, any author. *Utz* – the novel – is steeped in Central European history and experience. Utz – the eponymous hero – is a victim, first of the Second World War and second of Communism. Both denied him his inheritance as a minor aristocrat, and his lands. In response, he retreats into a world of make-believe, at the core of which is his vast collection of porcelain – mainly of Meissen and Dresden pieces, collected from childhood and throughout a lifetime spent avoiding the horrors of the real world around him. Utz, we are told, is a nondescript man, short, moustachioed and unprepossessing, yet obsessed with his porcelain. And as Chatwin makes clear Utz's collection has for an almost alchemical power for him, what he terms – and recognises as such -'porcelain sickness', or 'the Porzellankrankheit'[5] that had affected other collectors in the past. Chatwin gives the reader wonderful descriptions of the pieces in Utz's collection[6]; as Utz shows it to Chatwin's narrator, it seems as if Utz is breathing life itself into the models and figurines, with a joy that is, if not quite idolatrous, both innocent and complicit, for his motive is derived from the fact that he inhabits what is to him a sterile and very material world. Thus, paradoxically, Utz gives himself divine characteristics.

The novel is replete with ideas of breathing life into objects and ideas. Just as Rabbi Loew breathed life into his golem, so Utz does into his; so, too, does the absurd regime in which he lives: Communism's 'new man', released from the shackles of the repressive class system, strides forward, strong-jawed and vigorous into the bright new, post-revolutionary future – the subject of so many Soviet social-realist paintings. It is to be found in the many sexual conquests that Utz makes, and in the ever-faithful wife, Marta, that Utz had taken – but never publicly acknowledged as such - in 1952. And of course, Utz, in both meanings of the word, is a work of fiction just as much as any of the others mentioned above. It is possible, too, that in a parallel way, we are the golems of one another, even that we make golems out of ourselves. Just as Utz made meaning out of the insensate material of earth, so do we, out of the previously unformed nature of self-hood as we embark upon relationship, as much as when that relationship is within as without. And if this is the case, what, to Utz, *is* love?

And before moving on, it is worth mentioning that Chatwin goes out of his way to give the reader the meaning of the word 'utz': ' "drunk", "dimwit", "card-sharp", "dealer in dud horses",' or ' " any old Tom, Dick or Harry".'[7] In other words, he is both a nobody, and yet Everyman, for do we not all act to create ourselves - and in ways that may well be equally fictional? Perhaps the crowning of Utz's life lies in the triumph of his self-creation. Chatwin's narrator, who may or may not be Chatwin, is admiring Utz' huge collection of porcelain figures, among which are those representing characters from *Commedia del Arte*. Finally, he comes to the last:

> And Harlequin. . . . *The* Harlequin. . . the arch-improviser, the zany, the trickster, master of the volte-face . . . would forever strut in his variegated plumage, grin through his orange mask, tiptoe into bedroom, sell nappies from the children of the Grand Eunuch, dance in the teeth of catastrophe. . . Mr Chameleon himself.
>
> And I realised, as Utz pivoted the figure in the candlelight, that I had misjudged him: that he, too, was dancing; that for him, this world of little figures was the real world. And that, compared to them, the Gestapo, the Secret police and other hooligans were creatures of tinsel. And the events of this sombre century – the bombardments, blitzkriegs, putsches, purges – were, so far as he was concerned, so many "noises off".[8]

Here I end, for now, Chatwin's story, for Utz embodies much of what I will be saying, but note for now that Chatwin does not leave us with anything as final as this. It suffices at the start to identify various elements in this brief outline. There is first of all, the desire to create life, to assume the role of God in so doing; this is closely associated with the idea of inspiration, especially as it is exercised 'breathing life' upon matter. There is the idea of guilt and retribution: the golem, acting freely, acts dangerously, to others as much as to his maker, who at least is shamed. Violence is going, too, to be an important part of my theme, as will vengeance; so will their opposites – justice and peace. Embodied, too, in this, is technology – after all, what does the Rabbi require a golem for, but to be a domestic help; modern technology has given us all the help we need around the house. But behind technology lies Science, that is, that which tells us how the universe works and on what principles. Furthermore, as I will hope to show, in contrast to this is the idea of artistic creation, of appearance and reality, and indeed, perhaps, all creativity. And fundamentally, the purpose of this essay is to explore the tense dichotomy between metonymy and metaphor, between reference in terms of attributes and cause and effect on the one hand, and the associative and imaginative nature of language on the other, both being facets of the mind. Metonymy is the language of Science and logic, metaphor that of imagination and religion. Of course the distinction is not quite as neat as this.

And, with the development of the Internet, I will suggest that this dichotomy is to become wholly irrelevant.

Awareness

However, I had been conscious of the idea of man taking the powers of creation for himself for some time before I had read Chatwin. The most immediate example of this that comes to mind is Shaw's play, *Pygmalion*, which was later made in to the film, *My Fair Lady*. Professor Higgins, a phonetician, takes on the challenge of turning the pretty young Cockney flower-seller, Eliza Doolittle, into a 'lady'. He succeeds triumphantly after Eliza, now dolled up to perfection and uttering her syllables as if she had been born to them, triumphs at a society ball. This process of making the raw material of Eliza, just as the Rabbi had made the golem out of soil, is analogous to Eve having been made out the substance of Adam, who himself had been made out of the primeval mud. However, just as the golem takes revenge upon his maker, so does Eliza on hers. On return from the ball, she cannot understand Higgins' indifference to her – he'd won his bet, he'd educated her, he'd made something out of her; now all he wants is a little bit of attention, with no credit going to her. Not surprisingly, she is furious, hurt and upset. Her temper astonishes Higgins – 'Why can't a woman be more like a man?' he bewails. But more damage has been done, for Higgins has in fact fallen in love with his creation. Her turning him over for the safe Freddy Eynsford-Hill, is not just for love, but an act of revenge.

Around this delightful story, of course, Shaw spins social satire, the English class system being his foremost target, as is the nature of patriarchy. But Shakespeare also uses this idea: Caliban, the unformed 'monster' of the island on which Prospero and his daughter have been abandoned, is 'educated' by the former, who had 'breathed into his mouth the power of speech': 'You taught me language and my profit on it / Is I know how to curse.'[9] Though he, Caliban, is given some of the loveliest language of the play, he remains a perpetual threat both to Prospero and to the integrity of Miranda: 'This thing of darkness, I acknowledge mine.' Again, although there are multiple themes in this play – the nature of colonialism, of rule and authority, of revenge and retribution, of love and desire, and of artistic creation - it is the significance and nature of Caliban that is relevant in this context. As the oppressed – and uneducated - colonial subject, he must act as Prospero's servant, hewer of wood and carrier of water, his values and nature debased through alcohol and the deliberate destruction of pre-colonial society. The syndrome is a commonplace of colonialism, as I well remember from my African days.

The idea of the golem was also explored in Shakespeare's time by his younger contemporary, John Marston, whose earliest extant poem, *The Metamorphosis of Pygmalion's Image*, of 1598, deals with just this subject. Shaw took the title of his play, as did Marston, from the ancient Greek legend, *Pygmalion and Galatea*. Pygmalion, although a worshipper of Aphrodite, Goddess of Love, at the same time 'saw so much to blame in the sex that he came at last to abhor women'. Nevertheless, being so desperate to find love, he created a beautiful young woman out of a branch of wood. This he did and presented the image to Aphrodite at the forthcoming festival. The goddess breathed life into the figure, and as this event took place on Cyprus – or Paphos, the 'Island of Love' – the birthplace of Aphrodite. There are no recorded damaging consequences arising from this arrangement.[10]

However, it is historically much before any of these that I need to go; my account must start with *Prometheus Bound*. Prometheus, whose name means 'wise before his time' or 'forethought'[11], is the subject of one of the seven extant plays by Aeschylus, and of one that no longer exists except in a small fragment, *Prometheus Unbound*. He steals fire from the Gods, he rebels against them and gives fire to humanity. For his pains, he is chained by Violence and Strength to a rock; there he will languish for eternity, for Zeus is an unforgiving god. Furthermore, Prometheus has the art of prophecy; he foretells to the timorous Chorus the downfall of Zeus. Hearing this, the god increases the punishment: each night, Prometheus will be buried in the rocks of the mountain on which he is chained, to be raised again in the morning for an eagle, 'the dark-winged hound of Zeus', to tear at his liver. This will last for thirteen generations.

To what does all this amount? It is indeed an intense and vivid account, even lurid. First of all, Prometheus seems to me to be central to our understanding of human consciousness, of what this is, and of what it consists. Philip Vellacott, in his Penguin translation of the play, suggests that it reflects 'the transition from the primitive to the civilised world, from the life of nomadic tribes and village settlements to that of walled cities and states.' Prometheus was 'he Who hunted out the source of fire, and stole it. . . . And fire has proved for men a teacher in every art.'[12] Prometheus becomes, then, a stage in humanity's *evolutionary* development.

What did this allow? He 'gave them mind and reason.' Where before the life of humanity was 'confused and purposeless', he taught it carpentry, the nature of the seasons, how to write and to count, to farm by yoking 'beasts'; he taught medicine, 'various modes of prophecy' and how to interpret signs. In short, he taught the basis of everything that we consider to be the elements of civilised society, rational, purposeful and ordered.

Nevertheless, it seems to me that he taught something else. The years approximately from 500 B.C. to 1 A.D. have been referred to as 'The Anvil Years'. It was during this period that the modern mind was developing, in the West with Greek Philosophy, in the East, for example, with Confucian Thought, and the rise of the great religions. This is typified by the change from hunter-gatherer to settled, village and town-based communities.

The so-called Socratic Maxim, 'Know Thyself', is the term that sums up this development. The conception of Prometheus also taught awareness, or self-awareness, that sense of being aware and knowing that we are aware. Indeed, Prometheus is the very model of this himself. He knows what he has done: 'Do you think I quake and cower before these upstart gods?' he demands of Hermes, Zeus' messenger. He has chosen to act as he has done, for the good of humanity. In his mythological conception, he is half god, half human. Just as with Adam and the golem, he is made of the soil of the Earth. Earth (or Themis) was his mother, to the ancient Greeks the source of wisdom and understanding. Again, like Milton's Satan, he rebels with pride and, perhaps, because of pride. The Chorus warns him, 'A wise man will speak humbly, and fear Nemesis,' to which Prometheus scornfully replies, 'Always fawn upon the powerful hand! For great Zeus I care less than nothing.' Prometheus has acted impetuously, for Zeus was intent on getting rid of mankind, replacing the race with a perfect being. Of course, Zeus was never going to do anything of the sort, for he never existed, except in the minds of Ancient Greeks.

Perhaps, therefore, what Prometheus fictively represents in his rebellion is not one rebelling against a god or creator of the universe, but against the *absence* of such a god. In other words, if the abandonment of meaning through recognising the absence of God is in fact the only meaning humanity can grasp, then humanity is truly left up to its own devices, as humanity senses this truth. In this context, it might seem that the only appropriate word that we can use to describe the experience of this fearful awareness is that of 'trembling', to borrow Kierkegaard's famous response to his realisation of God.

So it is possible to see Prometheus as Aeschylus' golem: he is fashioned out of the soil, he transgresses against what might be termed Olympian Holy Law, and he is disruptive and dangerous. It can also be said that the whole course of Greek drama charts the course from a god-centred universe to a man-centred one with democracy and human choice at its core. Aeschylus' play and Sophocles' *Oedipus Rex* are perhaps the two most important plays in this process. In each, the Chorus, the fearful and limited representatives of the people, have to make a choice. How do they respond? Here, by accepting Prometheus and his challenge, rather than the old ways, the old inevitabilities, the old determination. The people of Thebes, in Sophocles' play, have to accept that their dependence on the heroic leadership of the flawed Oedipus, who, however unwittingly, has married his mother, is immature. They must stand on their own feet, they must be aware, however great the terror of so doing might be. This is not an attitude that a Zeus, a tyrant or any one with anti-democratic instincts might like. No wonder that they might tremble, that the birth pangs of democracy and the overthrow of autocracy or tyranny can be so painful.

Thus, in being Aeschylus' golem, what more can be said about Prometheus? In the first place, I would like for a moment to consider the connection between *Prometheus Bound* and Milton's *Paradise Lost.* Both are engaged with stories involving the very earliest human experience, at least recorded or conscious. Both are myths; both tell of rebellion against an overwhelming deity and both attempt, in differing ways, of that deity's plans for mankind. Aeschylus, as Vellacott puts it, wanted to tell of 'the ways of God to man': man should learn wisdom, and this wisdom is to be learnt through the inexorable condition of life: that of suffering [13].

Milton alternatively, saw his great epic of humanity's existence in terms of his desire to 'justify the ways of God to man'. In committing the 'necessary sin', after their temptation by Satan, Adam and Eve eat of the fruit of the Tree of Knowledge. This is not quite the knowledge that Prometheus has given to humanity, that of reason and its application, but knowledge of awareness – awareness of, in the first place their nakedness, symbolic of their innocence, but knowledge of their awareness. And on eating the Forbidden Fruit, in the instant they are expelled from the Garden of Eden. Their existence is to be marked with suffering and toil, to be redeemed only by Christ's incarnation, crucifixion and resurrection.

Only in falling for Satan's ploy, in other words and paradoxically, can humanity be finally redeemed, and Satan overcome. Satan's confidence is not perhaps of the same nature as Prometheus'; nevertheless, it seems remarkable that through the agency of both Satan and Prometheus, as they both rebel against the higher deities, God and Zeus, humanity comes into the potential fullness of its own being. This being is embodied in the freedom to choose, aware and yet capable of being both comic and tragic. Or even absurd.

There is, perhaps, a further interpretation available to us. It might have been noticed that if Prometheus and Adam are golems in the senses that we have been using the term, then they have one conspicuous difference from Utz's: they do not rebel against humanity, in ways that Rabbi Loew's did, or indeed as Eliza did against *her* creator. Could it be, then, that it is not so much they who are the golems, but their respective creators, Zeus and God, for certainly they are vengeful when their Law has been transgressed? For if we know that Zeus did not exist, and if we accept the parallel, if not identical roles of Prometheus and Adam, then we might assume that God also does not exist. It is in this vein, atheist and humanistic, that this paper is written in.

The rest of it is concerned with exploring aspects of this condition, tragic, comic or absurd as it may be. It is a journey both outwards and inwards.

The Great Experiment

'Frankenstein' is perhaps the most famous golem of them all. I use speech marks here, since in popular culture the name of the creature has taken on the name of its creator. There is perhaps good reason for this: one who creates such a monster must be pretty monstrous himself. However, Victor Frankenstein, the eponymous hero of Mary Shelley's 1818 novel, is far too human for this confusion. The way in which this story came about is worth bearing in mind.

Mary Shelley was travelling in the Summer of 1816 with her husband, the poet Percy Bysshe Shelley and her step-sister, whom the latter was enjoying as well. They arrived at a small house on the shores of Lake Geneva. Next door, in the Villa Diodati (a house in which, strangely, it appears that John Milton had stayed nearly two centuries before, when meeting Galileo), Lord Byron and had taken up residence, a refugee from England, like the Shelleys. Mary was at this time in her nineteenth year. One wet evening, Byron suggested a challenge: each was to tell a ghost story, in order to entertain one another. All that has come down to us are fragments of stories by Byron, by his doctor, John Polidori, and Mary Shelley's masterpiece. At first, somewhat in awe of the company she was keeping, she found it very difficult to come up with anything. However, one evening Polidori and Shelley were talking about 'the nature and principle of life', 'the mysterious powers animating life'[14]. There is, of course, much more to the inspiration and conception of this tale than is revealed in this, but suffice it for the moment to quote Mary Shelley in her own introduction to the 1831 edition of her novel. That night, she could not sleep, for 'My imagination, unbidden, possessed and guided me. . . . I saw. . . the pale student of unhallowed arts kneeling beside the thing he had put together. I saw the hideous phantom of a man stretched out, and then, on the working of some powerful machine, show signs of life, and stir with uneasy, half-vital motion. Frightful it must be; for supremely frightful would be the effect of any human endeavour to mock the stupendous mechanism of the creator of the world. His success would terrify the artist; he would rush away from his odious handywork, horror-stricken.'[15]

Her account of this powerful epiphany continues somewhat longer, but the essence of it is here. And so she began her telling her tale to her friends, with Victor Frankenstein's words that open Chapter 5: 'It was on a dreary night of November that I beheld the accomplishment of my toils. . . .'

I wonder how well known her story is. 'Very, very!' is surely the answer. Through numerous films, including a rather flawed attempt by Kenneth Branagh, and many plays, the first of which was produced almost as soon as the book was originally published, and even through the appropriation of the term 'Frankenstein' or 'Frankensteinian', it has entered the modern consciousness, as a warning of the of horror and terror, of a particular kind, of Science run riot and destructive of all that it is meant to serve. This is, though, a most limited and limiting representation.

Christopher Frayling, in an illuminating BBC documentary[16], points out that the progression of these representations of the story (the first stage version of which was made as early as 1825, the first film in 1905) reduce it more and more to the conflict between the monster and his creator – and there have been many different representations of the monster, including as a robot. However, there are many discourses and themes that animate this story; its very creation at the time it appeared being of the highest significance. Furthermore, the characterisation of both the main protagonists, gives each a genuine intelligence and sensitivity, without which the story would be much diminished.

Shelley makes it clear that her hero (or anti-hero), Victor (*sic*) Frankenstein, who becomes a young student at Ingolstadt University, is caught between the ancient philosophies and disciplines of ancient magicians and alchemists, like Paracelsus, Albertus Magnus and others, and the modern 'natural philosophers' – or 'scientists', as we call them today, a term that came into current use only in the 1830s. He is torn, as it were, between metaphorical, the imaginary and the fantastical on the one hand, and objective, metonymic and rational understanding of the world on the other, though he doesn't know it. He comes under the influence of a Professor Waldmann. Young Frankenstein is a man of high ideals, a powerful sense of enquiry and a deep desire to put his studies to good use for humanity. However, he is passionate and highly energetic. Perhaps these are all the ingredients that go to make monomania. What, though, does he do, and what are the consequences?

He creates his monster (this time out of base materials and electrical stimulus, and not earth or wood), and thereafter, the two are bound inextricably in a narrative that leads to the death of Frankenstein. (Some think that it leads to the death of his monster, too. But I doubt this.) Immediately on completion of his task, Frankenstein is horrified: the creature (who remains, significantly, unnamed), is hideous and huge, being, we are told over eight feet tall. It escapes from the laboratory, to its creator's relief, and Frankenstein feels that his life can recover a degree of normality: during this period he has ignored his family and friends, his appearance and his health.

However, the creature has gone to hide in the woods and mountains. There he comes across a tumbled down farmhouse, in which a family is living. During a long digression which the creature in due course tells his creator, he tells of how he hid in a hovel next to the house, became fascinated by this family, which is called de Lacey, whose story is of no concern here, except to say that they are good, impoverished French people, who have escaped injustice. From them, the Monster learns speech, reading (in particular *Paradise Lost*), the civilised arts and so on. Shelley makes it quite clear that he has in him human qualities of the highest sort; in her introduction she tells how he looks at his sleeping creator with 'speculative eyes'. In return for their unknowing succour of him, the creature provides wood and food.

However, in a crucial passage, this idyll comes to a sudden and dramatic end. The creature decides that he must make himself known to the family, 'my heart yearned to be known and loved by these amiable creatures; to see their sweet looks directed towards me with affection was the utmost limit of my ambition'[17]. He takes his chance when the younger ones are out to present himself to the father, who is blind. The old man shows him warmth and appreciation, for he cannot see what exactly is before him. The son returns and is horrified at what he sees and, in a rage, he beats the creature out of the house. Thus a moment of great tenderness between two disadvantaged ones ends in violence, and expulsion.

And from that moment on he, 'declared ever-lasting war against the species, and, more than all, against him who had formed me, and sent me forth into this unsupportable misery.'[18] For all that the Monster had wanted was to love and to be loved.

In consequence, the creature kills Frankenstein's little brother, William, implicating a girl who had been a part of the family, Justine Moritz, in the boy's death. Justine is subsequently charged, tried, found guilty and executed. He also kills Frankenstein's friend, Henri Clerval (Horatio to Victor's Hamlet) – all of whom are emblematic of love of one kind or another; and, after he has induced Frankenstein to meet him at Le Mer de Glace, near Chamonix (a place visited by Mary and Percy in 1816), he persuades him, Victor, to make him a female 'companion', promising to leave Europe for good and to live in some isolated part of the world. Victor initially agrees, though after deliberation, breaks his promise, fearing that the creature will people the world with his off-spring (as Caliban threatens, with Miranda). The creature understands this, and further threatens Victor: '*I will be with you on your wedding-night.*' In other words, if the creature is to be denied his own partner, then Victor will not have his. However, Victor does marry Elizabeth Lavenza, his long-suffering childhood sweetheart, who is indeed killed on her wedding-night bed: 'She was there, lifeless and inanimate, thrown across her bed, her head hanging down, and her pale and distorted figure half covered by her hair.'[19]

This terrible event – made all the more so by the sweetness and goodness of Elizabeth's character – leads to only one conclusion: just as the creature has sought his own revenge, so now must its creator have his revenge. The latter part of the story continues the dance of death in ever an increasing sense of desperation, loneliness and horror. Eventually, they are hunting each other in the Arctic wastes, where Victor Frankenstein finally dies, leaving his creature to vanish into the nothingness, though not, I stress, to die, even though many a version has them dying together, Branagh's on a funeral pyre in the ice flow.

Before going any further, it is necessary to comment briefly on narrative techniques employed by Shelley, for she, too, seems caught on the problem of the nature of language. Structurally, the story is in the epistolary form, that is, in the form of letters – a form common to the period; even Jane Austen used it. It begins with the letters of one Robert Walton writing from Russia to his sister back in England. He is planning a journey of exploration into ‘the icy climes’ of the far north. Shelley is not more specific than this. He sets off, and in his fourth letter, he recounts how first of all he saw in the distance the figure of the creature; soon after, Victor appears, exhausted to the point of death. However this does not prevent him from recounting the whole of his tale to Walton. This is the content of this fourth letter. At this point, guilt-ridden (for it is his creature who has killed those he loved most), Frankenstein dies. The story is then concluded by Walton recounting how he then found the creature in the room in which Victor had died; the monster has taken one last look at his creator, and disappears into the icy wastes through the cabin’s window.

The purpose of this epistolary device is quite complex. First it is to frame the principle narrative. Since Frankenstein dies at the end of his story, he cannot be alive to tell it. Thus, this allows for the first-person narrative of the tale, thereby bringing it paradoxically all the closer to the reader’s attention, and all the more powerfully so, given its principle themes.

Second, the device allows for the setting of the tone of the story. Walton is as lonely and as obsessive as Victor. Furthermore, his narrative is set in the Arctic. The symbolism is clear. Journeys of travel and exploration had become very familiar in European consciousness for more than two hundred years. This journey, echoing as it does that of the search for a northwest passage, offers no return in commercial terms, but only fame for Walton. Thus for Frankenstein. What setting could be more suitable for the idea of a lost and loveless humanity, whose only idea of how to fill this void is through ‘fame’, or should one say ‘celebrity’?

Furthermore, it is used – albeit unconsciously - to exploit the tension between metonymy and metaphor, between the literal and logical on the one hand and the metaphorical or imaginary on the other. The facts, as Shelley gives Walton to expand on, are clear; within them, the imaginative powerfully finds its place, but it is a place that cannot be sustained for long, hence the enduring power of the story. It bursts out of it in almost terrifying excess. For example, everyone knows of Frankenstein, but not of Walton. It is one reason why the Monster must not be allowed to die at the end.

And Mary Shelley’s own position must be considered, too. Loneliness and death were very much part of her life. Her mother, Mary Wollstonecraft, the author of *A Vindication of the Rights of Woman* (1792), died giving birth to her in 1797. She was brought up by her then notoriously radical father, William Godwin, who, it appears, was able to give her plenty of intellectual stimulation but little emotional warmth, and by his second wife, also called, confusingly, Mary, who completely lacked the intelligence and sensitivity needed for one like the future author of *Frankenstein*. The step-mother was the ‘bane’ of Mary’s life. [20] Mary was exceptionally gifted, she grew up in a brilliant household, and by the age of 16 was prodigiously well read. It is perhaps not surprising, given all this, that at this time she fell in love and eloped with Percy Bysshe Shelley. This central relationship of her life, however powerful and passionate, was to have almost nothing but tragic consequence: Shelley was already married at the time, and his first wife, Harriet, soon after committed suicide, an eventuality that must have acted powerfully upon the young Mary – guilt is a principle theme in her novel. Three of Mary’s four children by Shelley died at birth or infancy, and within eight years of the conception and telling of her story, all the men present in the Villa Diodati to hear Mary’s tale, were dead, Polidori, Byron in Greece, and Shelley himself in a boating accident in the Adriatic. Mortality was, of course, much more familiar to those of earlier centuries than it is to us, but Mary had her fair share of sorrow. It is not surprising, then, that

Frankenstein seems so death obsessed, and why metaphor appears to triumph, for with it come hope and love but they cannot, in the end.

That said, Shelley brought much more to her novel, as we cannot escape its literary and philosophical context. Maurice Hindle, in his excellent Introduction to the Penguin edition, explores both the personal and the intellectual and philosophical backgrounds to the novel. There is not space to go into it all here, except to mention some: the influence of her father, the presence of people in the household or at the family's printing and publishing house such as Thomas Paine and even William Blake. Of great significance, too, was the figure of Humphrey Davy, who powerfully influenced people of the time not only with his discoveries, but also with his belief that Science – the metonymic - , as opposed to alchemy and magic, could do untold good for humanity. But above all – at least as far as the story goes – was Giuseppe Galvani, who first demonstrated the effects of electricity upon matter.

Hindle also accounts for the influence of writers such as Cervantes, Coleridge and Locke, whose conception of the soul as a *tabula rasa* provides Shelley with the idea that not just the body, but the mind could be created by human effort – an idea she deliberately undermines in her novel. But above all, there was *Paradise Lost*, which appears to have been required reading in the Godwin household, together with *Paradise Regained.*

I have indicated above the connections between Prometheus and Adam. It is of great significance that the full title of Shelley's novel is: *Frankenstein, or the Modern Prometheus*. Mary lived in a time of great change, excitement and challenge. For the radical left, it must have felt as if the New Jerusalem was imminent. The Ancien Regime in France had been overthrown, and the British State sensed itself under real threat; the old ways could be challenged and overthrown, injustice replaced with justice, and Science would offer a panacea for all ills. Shelley (though she might have not known her own mind at 18, as Muriel Spark suggests[21]) is sceptical, perhaps for the reasons I have pointed out above.

If Victor Frankenstein is to be seen as a new Prometheus, his destiny is certainly tragic, as is his literary ancestor's. As Prometheus, Victor is transfixed, not to say transfigured by the ideas of Professor Waldmann: '. . . soon my mind was filled with one thought, one conception, one purpose. So much had been done, exclaimed the soul of Frankenstein, - far more, far more will I achieve; treading in the steps already marked, I will pioneer a new way, explore unknown powers, and unfold to the world the deepest mysteries of creation.'[22] Thereafter, his tale is one of unending suffering.

At a revealing moment in his narrative, Frankenstein says that he had 'a fervent longing to penetrate the secrets of nature'. His hubris had taken him too far: 'I had gazed upon the fortifications and impediments that seemed to keep human beings from entering the citadel of nature, and rashly and ignorantly I had repined.'[23] It is striking here that it is Nature that is referred to; God seems absent from any thinking that Frankenstein at this period is engaged in, and it is also striking how this highly poeticised language is used at just this crucial point (we will meet it again in a different context). Frankenstein imagines metonymy and metaphor working hand in hand; but for him, they do not and cannot.

Being tempted, Adam /Prometheus/Frankenstein falls. However, Shelley herself, of course, is not unaware of the spiritual dimension of her story, and there are, before I conclude this section on *Frankenstein*, three further points that need to be considered.

In the first place, her story is replete with references or allusions to Divine Grace. These are to be found in the beautiful descriptions of the mountains and lakes of Switzerland; they are to be found in the human relationships that exist within the family of Frankenstein, the love and tenderness that is shared, the self-sacrifice of Elizabeth Lavenza, the innocence of children and in the devoted friendship of Henri Clerval for Victor Frankenstein; it is to be found in the dignity and suffering of the de Lacey family. Above all it is to be found in the nature of the monster himself, who, as has been suggested above, has embodied in him all that is fine, intelligent and sensitive.

Until love is denied him. I cannot help feeling that the creature might make a fascinating study of the malcontent, the sociopath who has no moral instincts. He represents two sides of human nature, an almost psychotic humanity that can on the one hand sense what it is to be divine, and knows only too well what it is to be evil, on the other. We will meet this idea later on in a very different context.

Furthermore, he came out of the being of a very young woman. Hindle points out that Frankenstein can be identified with Percy Bysshe Shelley – a passionate believer in mankind's capacity for redemption, and of his own capacity to bring this about. Shelley himself, it appears,[24] had experimented in the manner of Galvani whilst at Oxford; he had also written his own *Prometheus* and *Prometheus Unbound*. Anyone reading *Ode to the West Wind* must understand what passions Mary must have felt excited in her - and what guilt must Mary have felt in her relationship with him. In a recent article[25], furthermore, it has been suggested that even as early in their marriage, when in Switzerland, Percy Shelley was conducting an affair with Claire Clairmont, Mary's pushy step-sister. She was with them when the couple fled England to escape the scandal of their marriage, with them at La Mer de Glace. Claire and her mother, according to Hindle[26] were highly opportunistic social climbers. One can only speculate on the rivalry between the two young women; perhaps something of it is reflected in the Monster's desire for a mate, on the promise that he would go with her to live in some isolated part of the World.

Finally, of course, it is a staple of modern consciousness that *Frankenstein* is warning about the dangers of Science, of the dangers of presuming to tread on the secrets of the processes of life, on Holy Law. This is a theme that I will myself fearfully touch upon below. Suffice it to say here that Galvani's discovery of the properties of electricity had, well, an electrifying effect. Not only did he demonstrate on frogs, but his son experimented with the corpses of recently executed prisoners, to much the same effect. It is not surprising that many of those of Mary Shelley's generation might have thought that they had the keys to Utopia in their hands. Such was her golem. The effects of electricity I now want to explore, by looking at representations of the golem in modern cinema.

Towards a View of Paris

The common theme that links the films I am going to discuss is that of the fear of Science, of Science being irresponsible, of taking over, in some subtle if not mysterious, but no less overwhelmingly powerful ways, our lives, of Science giving much, but demanding a price we are not really sure of, nor sure we want to pay anyway. This is, of course, to speak metaphorically, personifying Science as having a mind of its own; it doesn't, but we can feel this none the less. I am sticking only to films, since they are a principle medium of popular culture, and anyway, I am not a reader of Science Fiction. There have, of course, been very many films concerning this theme – I apologise for any that I have not and should have considered, but the ones I have chosen are all powerful in their different ways, and provide enough thereby to illustrate what I am trying to say. I am not offering any critical understanding of these films, merely a look at the treatment of the theme, and its related ideas and characterisations.

This is not, for one moment, to deny the manifold benefits that Science has brought to us. These do not need to be elaborated on. However, in evolutionary terms, we now have two nations on this planet with sufficient armaments to destroy not only each other, but all life on the planet. Wars throughout the centuries have been determined by whichever side was the 'fitter', in one form of power or another. When two sides are more or less equal in strength, whether they are Zulu impis or Russia and the USA, there is stalemate or, at best, shadow-play.

It may well be the case, as Harari suggests, that humanity has learnt to control its violent instincts, but I doubt it. He may well be right, though, to warn us of the development of war in another area: cyberspace. What follows is an examination of this theme as it is represented in film.

I mentioned above that the first cinematic representation of the Frankenstein story was apparently made in 1905 – within ten years, that is, of the Lumiere brothers frightening their Parisian audience with the sight of a train seemingly rushing at them out of a screen. Strangely enough, Charles Dickens wrote a short story, called *The Signalman* (1866), which gives voice to a visceral fear of Science as represented by the new-fangled railways, following as it does the Clayton Tunnel train crash of 1861, in which 23 died and over 170 were injured. And by the end of the First World War, enough evidence had been shown to suggest that the widespread deployment of technology, Science's younger brother, was a Moloch in the process of being born. On the other hand, those like the Futurists saw scientific progress as inevitably leading to the liberation of mankind.

Just this kind of ambiguity lies at the heart of the first film I wish to consider, Fritz Lang's 1926 *Metropolis*. This is perhaps not just a great silent movie and the first of the truly great 20th Century films. Developed in the form of a parable, it is an intensely political film, with society rigidly stratified into the workers who provide an existence of luxury and indulgence and privilege for the ruling class. Here, the city of the film's title is a multi-layered organism, with passageways and aerial roadways – a vision of life separated entirely from nature, with towering buildings dwarfing all humanity. It is ruled over by one Joh Fredersen, whose workers trudge duly to their toil everyday with their heads down in serried ranks of beaten and cowed humanity. They are fodder for the great figure of Moloch. This is the central image of the early part of the film, of defeated humanity walking into its great, steaming maws.

However, Frederson's son, Freder, falls in love with a lovely young teacher called Maria; in doing so, he undermines all the inhumanity of his father's regime. Frederson commissions Rotwang, an inventor, to reproduce a likeness of Maria, who has been stirring up the workers towards rebellion, in order that the new Maria should confuse the workers. Rotwang has in fact already been building an android, called Hel (not so far from HAL); he now sees his chance to gain revenge on Joh Fredersen, who had bettered him in love in the past.

There is not space enough here to go any further into the story; it is complicated and at the same time graphic, using many new techniques in producing the images that we see. Nevertheless, this rather somewhat curious imitation of the Frankenstein motif is interesting for a number of reasons. In the first place, the two Marias, both played with astonishing verve by an 18-year-old actress, Brigitte Helm(1906-1996), show two distinctive aspects of femininity, the one gentle, tender and loving, the other, the android, violent and deranged. Though put to use in the service of what we might nowadays call the military-industrial complex, it is the latter image that persists. I will be considering the relation between gender and Science below.

A second reason why this film is significant is because of its Orwellian vision. I don't know if Orwell had seen this film prior to writing *1984*, but there are obvious parallels. The dystopic vision presented by both works is a vision that will be repeated in later films. We have an all-powerful ruling element, and a subject or underground residue (for want of a better word), acting in various degrees of rebellion. Where they differ is that the film ends on an optimistic, though very trite note: "The mediator between brain and hands must be the heart,", whilst *1984* concludes with Smith and Julia destroyed, and we are left with an image of the boot coming endlessly down upon the human face. In some ways Ridley Scott's *Blade Runner* explores exactly this theme.

Finally, Henry Ford once famously declared that 'History is Bunk!' Subjecting his workers to a vigorous and exhausting time and motion regime to produce his cars, they became as if taken directly from *Metropolis*.

We do indeed live in the here and now, but each one of us must know, needs to know how we came to be where we are. (Nowadays, it seems, robots do much of the work to produce cars.)

These dystopias are, indeed, godless. Despite the intervention of the director of the film, there can be no appeal to entities over and beyond the respective narratives. Both *1984* and *Metropolis* present visions of an isolated and lonely humanity. Orwell, Lang and Chatwin are worlds apart from one another; but whilst the latter's *Utz* and its eponymous hero are guided by the spirit of play, the former two most certainly are not. Perhaps, though, each of these narratives, in its extreme nature, is looking for a way to rediscover the grace that Victor Frankenstein so recklessly destroyed. To what extent, however, can we look at these films with one eye on some kind of Holy Law being hubristically taken by Mankind for itself?

To discuss the three *Terminator* films in this context might seem risible. Nevertheless, they and the sequence of *Alien* films, as well as the three *Matrix* films, seem to take as their starting points just that dystopia brought about by Science unrestrained and controlled by a ruthless political elite. It is as if Mary Shelley's monster, having left Victor Frankenstein to die in the Arctic, has roamed the world in the intervening centuries, leaving nothing hut destruction and endless human suffering. If, in other words, her reading of *Paradise Lost* had left Shelley with a profound sense of anxiety, for if those electrical impulses with which Galvani appeared to stimulate life promised to reveal and to give to man the secrets of life, so we too must view the monster's freedom and survival with equal concern. This is not to deny the value of scientific progress; we can be grateful for anaesthetics, but it does not take much perception to grasp its dangers, especially in the year of the 76th anniversary of Hiroshima and Nagasaki.

The *Terminator* films, the first two directed by James 'I'm King of the World' Cameron[27], the third by Jonathon Mostow, have six 'Terminators', good and bad. Here, Victor Frankenstein's creatures have been designed and programmed to, well, terminate; they have neither conscience nor vulnerability, thus following their 19th Century antecedent. Arnold Schwarzenegger plays three of the Terminators, a 'bad' one in the first episode, and 'good' ones in the two others.

These films take as their starting point the idea that human society has put itself on the verge of destruction through scientific processes that have run riot and overwhelmed their creators. The first images are of war and destruction on a massive scale: tanks crush beneath their tracks human skulls by the hundreds, as a war between the machines and humanity is raging in violent progress.

In *The Matrix* films, though these end optimistically, if not without ambiguity, the 'real' world of ordinary human life is pitted against a 'virtual' world of highly sophisticated computer programs; however, the sequence of four *Alien* films (there is a fifth, *Alien versus Predator*, which is not worth mentioning in this context) ends despairingly: the final image is of Ripley and Call (a clone and an android respectively) sitting on a hill above a destroyed city, apparently Paris. Call, (Winona Ryder) asks Ripley, "Where shall we go now?", to which Ripley replies, "I don't know. I am a stranger here, too." A devastating nuclear war, in which three billion people die, is the ending of *Terminator 3*.

These are indeed very different dystopias. Violence – together with a highly critical attitude towards American gun culture – is at the heart of each. As the Terminator explains, "It's in your nature to destroy yourselves." Again, in another recent film, the genial *I, Robot*, the robots (however paradoxically) take over and attempt to destroy humanity because humanity is inclined to destroy itself anyway. To wipe out all humans to prevent themselves from wiping themselves out might be an ingenious idea, but, of course, the programs that created these robots were in the first place created by humans. At the heart of the *Terminator* story is a program called Skynet. It becomes "self-aware" in *Terminator 3*, and sets about acting as a massive virus in the defence systems of the American military, thus initiating a cataclysmic war.

The virtual world of *The Matrix* is highly self-aware; indeed, it has no doubt about the 'reality' of its existence. It is represented by Agent Smith (so chillingly played by the Australian actor, Hugo Weaving); Smith, like all other entities in the virtual world of the Matrix, is a construct, an amalgam of programs that give immense power, even to the point of being self-replicating – and of challenging, Satan-like, the authority of the Source, or the Creator. As Morpheus explains to Neo, the hero of the story, "The Matrix is everywhere. It is all around us. It is the world that has been pulled over your eyes to blind you to the truth." In his discovery of the Matrix, indeed of himself, Neo (in the 'real' world, a computer programmer called Mr Anderson) learns some horrifying truths. In undergoing an *Alice in Wonderland* journey of discovery, in entering the world of the Matrix, he is told that his self-hood is only a construct: "It exists only as a neural inter-active simulation." Furthermore, when humanity gave birth to a virtual world, "We marvelled at our brilliance", in spawning a race of machines.

Yuval Harari, I expect, must have watched and learnt from these films. 'Big Data', the 'Internet of Everything', is, indeed, The Matrix.

These machines are driven by electricity (and its off-spring, electronics); this electricity is generated by human beings. In short, the machines 'farm' humans in endless fields, no longer born but grown and used. Thus the original order of things has been reversed: where before, humans created the machines, now machines manufacture humans. There is a horrifying image of this that recurs on occasion during the films.

But what is The Matrix? "It is a computer-generated dream world" created to keep humans under control. And, "As long as the Matrix exists, the human race will never be free." Rabbi Loew's Golem has come a long way.

The situation is not quite the same in *Alien* and its successor films. There are, to be sure, robots or androids in these films – Ash (Ian Holm) in the first, the kindly and gentle Bishop in the second, and third films, and Call in the fourth. Bishop is in fact the doppelganger of his creator (note the essential vanity of those wishing to be cloned); the 'real' Bishop is an executive of United Military Systems, that is, the military-industrial corporation that has been behind all the attempts to get the alien back to earth to put it into service for 'defence' purposes. Ash senses that Ripley might have other ideas (if you watch him carefully from the start, there are distinctive signals of his intentions right from the memorable moment when Kane, played by John Hurt, 'gives birth' to an infant alien at the start of the epic). Ash attacks Ripley, who is saved by other crew members. Ash is then destroyed. Bishop – the human – tries, in the climactic scene of *Alien 3*, to deceive Ripley into returning to Earth so that she can have the alien gestating inside her removed. She believes, rightly, that he wants it for his evil intentions and that, if he gets it to Earth, it will destroy all life on it. Call, on the other hand, is an android who has rebelled against the system, a 'good' android, about whom Ripley has her suspicions before the truth is out: "You are too humane to be human," she tells her.

In the *Alien* films, then, it is not the androids themselves that are Frankensteinian monsters (though they may serve such purposes), but two other elements. The first is the 'zenomorphs' that people these films, and are the principle source of the terror. They are not, of course created in the same way that other monsters have been created; instead, they come out of the imagination of the original authors of these texts, and they find their place in the atavistic responses of the audience: the golem is inside us all, as it is inside Ripley. The second is the Corporation itself. Just as Cyberdyne Corporation in *Terminator* produces Skynet, which must be destroyed before it can wipe out humanity, is itself the principle golem of these films, so UMS (the initials are so close to *USA*), is bent on the blind destruction of mankind, as well as of itself, by gaining possession of the zenomorph. These are the Frankenstein monsters of these films, and perhaps of our day, too.

Now, the concept of colonial exploration and exploitation is, of course, a common one in Western Culture, if not in other cultures. Indeed the vast space ship in the first *Alien* film is called 'Nostromo', reminding us of Joseph Conrad and perhaps his greatest novel, in which the main theme is the greed and corruption of colonial exploitation. The sequence of *Alien* films uses this idea, transposing the territory to be explored into outer space. Here it is easy for the directors to exploit our fear of the unknown. This magnificent 'quadrilogy' of films vary in quality – the second, directed by James Cameron, being by far the worst. It involves the vastness of space, which is dark, threatening and lonely, like Shelley's icy north but unlike the cosmos in Stanley Kubrick's wonderful *2001: A Space Odyssey*.

Such films involve shock, human tenderness and extreme violence; they involve, also, a real sense of the question, "What am I doing here?" a question once asked by Bruce Chatwin and by so many throughout history. 'Space' can thereby be seen as metaphor for existence, the huge spaceships that traverse it as one for the trajectory of human life, individual or collective; the whole, by accumulation, can be seen as a metaphor for human consciousness; indeed, 'Nostromo' translates from Italian as 'our man'. They provide, on the one hand, a powerful evocation of a universe absent of love, decency and order, a melancholy sense of humanity's isolation, and on the other they reach out to some sense of hope, of redemption. However, just as Richard Hakluyt and others terrified and fascinated their Jacobean readers with tales and visions of monstrous creatures , just as Shelley did, so do Ridley Scott and the other directors, with their Terminators, computers and aliens to modern film-goers.

In essence, the alien, or zenomorph, born as it is out of a human, incubated in the chest, having been laid there by the 'facehugger', is a mirror image of us. Just as Frankenstein's monster has legs and arms and breathes and eats, moves with great rapidity and inspires great fear, so does this creature. Just as the former acts utterly without moral compunction, as do the 'bad' Terminators, so does this alien. Destruction is its mode of existence. And just, strangely, as Frankenstein's off-spring cries out for love, so in the end does this alien. Though *Alien 3* sees the end of Ripley and her incubus, *Alien Resurrection* has her and her foetus brought to life again. This, in fact, is made to work to very poignant effect; but by the end of it all, in order to destroy the alien, Ripley has to come to love it – it is her child. This, despite the violence of the creature, its hideous ugliness and despite what one might call its ontological horror – that is, Kierkegaard's 'trembling', not in the presence of God, but of the void.

It is worthwhile to give a description of the alien, or zenomorph, as it is referred to. Though the product of a short story by an American writer called Dan O'Bannon, its visual representation was first conceived of by a tortured Hungarian artist called H.R.Giler. When Ridley Scott first met him, he was offered some opium. Scott turned this down, but asked why Giler was taking it. "To keep the monsters from my mind," was his reply[28]. As well he might have wanted to.

There are numerous images of the alien in the documentaries that accompany my set of the films. Initially, in Giler's first drawings, it had a skeletal figure, metallic, rubbery and shiny in texture, with a huge head, a head, incidentally, that was distinctly and deliberately phallic in its suggestiveness. It has a tail, part fish, part crocodile. The whole is like a prehistoric creature, and it moves, when we see it so doing, like a cat. Its face is, I suppose, its most memorable feature. We see the head first – it is only in *Alien 3* that we get a glimpse of the whole creature. It first appears, as mentioned, out of the chest of Kane, one of the crew of the 'Nostromo'. This neonate pierces through the skin with its skull. It is bloody and slimy, and, again, with obvious phallic suggestion. It snarls, bears its teeth and scampers away. It is its teeth we see from time to time thereafter. It has grown very quickly and now haunts the spaceship. The adult's teeth are metallic, numerous, deadly sharp and slimy; and out of its mouth, instead of a tongue comes a miniature version of the main head and face, snarling and bearing its own teeth.

In later films, we see further births - Ripley has hers removed by what we might refer to as a Caesarean section. And we see the whole for the first time in *Alien 3*, though, of course, its presence is felt, or at best seen only partially, or implied where the body parts of someone who has been attacked and killed are left lying or dangling. Finally, it is not without intelligence, though that intelligence is, of course, totally lacking in moral content. Adolph Eichmann?

The horror and the excitement – we like to be made to feel frightened when, having suspended our disbelief, we can relax in the fastness of the cinema – are, of course, part and parcel of the genre of these films. *The Matrix* is, indeed, conceived of as a comic strip film. However, it is my contention that, as they act upon the minds of an audience, and being powerful elements in modern consciousness, they have serious elements. I am, after all, talking about Frankenstein's heirs. I have indicated above that in these films humanity is, in one way or another, debased, corrupted, abused, threatened and challenged. Do these films offer any redemption from an existence that is lonely, hellish and full of despair?

At the end of *The Matrix Revolutions,* after a cataclysmic battle in which swarms of sentinels have attacked and are about to destroy Sion, the vast underground city that rebellious humanity has developed to escape the Matrix, Neo (Mr Anderson) finds his final destiny. There is much made of the nature of choice and identity, of fate and of the pointlessness of human existence. In *Terminator 2: Judgement Day*, there is an expression that becomes almost a mantra of hope: "The future is not set. There is no future but what we make for ourselves." Again, there is much mumbo-jumbo in *The Matrix*. However, Neo is constantly being asked to make choices; when he confronts the Architect (the prime mover of the Matrix, the 'Big Brother' of these films), he is warned of the illusory and futile nature of choice. And at the end of these films, after Neo has returned from the Source (and after he has lost his Ariadne, Trinity), he confronts Smith in a magnificently staged finale. This fight Neo loses, when Smith after a tumultuous duel thrusts his fist into him and 'converts' him into a Smith, just one more of the multitude that now exists. But before this happens, however, Smith delivers, in words of coruscating mockery, the following speech to the prone Neo who is lying at his feet in muddy water. It is worth quoting in full:

> Why, Mr Anderson? Why? Why? Why do you do it? Why get up? Why keep fighting? Do you believe you're fighting for something, for more than your survival? Can you tell me what it is? Do you ever know? Is it freedom or truth, or perhaps peace? Could it be for love?
>
> Delusions, Mr Anderson, vagaries of perception, temporary constructs of a feeble human intellect trying desperately to justify an existence that is without any meaning or purpose – and all of them as artificial as the Matrix itself, although only a human mind could invent something as insipid as love. You must be able to see it, Mr Anderson. Why, Mr Anderson, why? Why do you persist?

To which, Neo replies, "Because I choose to." And is this not the essential, natural characteristic of humanity?

They fight some more. However, the choice is a futile gesture and defeat is inevitable for Neo; the machine wins as described above. However, in sacrificing himself, in imitation of Christ, and in response to the bargain made previously with the Source, Neo saves humanity. The Source attacks and destroys the Smiths, and the sentinels meekly disappear from Sion, which is now saved. Perhaps, though, we are meant to regard this with irony.

There are two other moments when similar sacrifices are made, both at climactic moments. The first is in *Terminator 2*, when the good Terminator, having destroyed his opponent TX by forcing him into a cauldron of molten metal, follows him. This is because the chip that controls him is lodged in his brain; he voluntarily destroys himself, or rather has John Connor (the boy he has been sent to protect), lower him into the cauldron, because he has not been programmed to self-destruct. This is meant to ensure that the future that has been set, which includes the forth-coming nuclear war, will not come to pass. It does, of course, because there must be a *Terminator 3*, subtitled *The Rise of the Machines*.

Ripley's death, at the end of *Aliens 3* is strangely similar. In many ways, this episode, directed by David Fincher, is the best of these films. Set on an isolated planet used as a prison, there is a real sense of melancholy about this film, a sense of humanity lost, terrified and on the edge of extinction. The prisoners and Ripley are abandoned without arms to fight against the zenomorph. The cold, the bleak, and the lonely: all are powerfully present. This group of violent convicts is ruled over by their warder, played with reptilian nastiness by that estimable actor, the late Brian Glover. Nothing must disturb their world; they practise a form of apocalyptic, fundamentalist Christianity.

At the start of the film, the craft, in which Ripley has been floating about the universe for numerous years, falls to their planet. During this time, she has been impregnated by a 'facehugger'. This she discovers during the nightmare of their attack by a second zenomorph, which has gestated in the belly of a bullock, or in a dog in one version. After a rather confusing final episode, in which the alien is destroyed after being trapped in cauldron of molten lead, comes the final climax of the story. Rescuers have at last arrived, with express orders to take Ripley back to earth so that her alien can be used by UMS. As recounted above, Ripley rejects this. Rather than be rescued, she falls into the lead, her arms outspread as if in crucifixion. Thus is humanity saved, as the evil in her dies with her.

This brings me naturally to endings, though not quite to the final one. I must make a digression into the treatment of gender in the films under discussion. At the end of the first *Alien* film, Ripley, the last survivor of the 'Nostromo' has, she thinks, escaped the zenomorph, which she imagines has been left to die on the spaceship when it blows up after her escape in a smaller module. However, the alien has hidden itself in the module, only to reveal itself on the destruction of the mother ship. Ripley at this time has undressed to her underwear prior to putting herself into hyper-sleep for the return journey. There are other incidents when Ripley is nearly naked – well, Sigourney Weaver is a strikingly beautiful woman – but here the sexual vulnerability of the feminine is clear. She hides in a closet, and as she puts on a space-suit, the camera observes this from a complicitly low angle. She opens the hatch in which the alien is hidden, it thereby being sucked in to the vastness of space. Only then can she relax.

The symbolism is obvious: the male, as represented by the alien (I have previously drawn attention to the phallic design of the head), is expelled, leaving the female at peace, accompanied only by the ship's cat, which Ripley had earlier rescued. The tender, the caring, the feminine survives; the violent male is destroyed. Is this, thereby, an instance when metonymy is sacrificed to the metaphorical, of male Science outwitted by female sexuality, and thus a reversal of the case with Shelley and her monster?

At this point, indeed, it is worth returning to *Frankenstein*. Shelley, again with preternatural understanding, gives us a clear insight into the relationship between scientist and nature. As Hindle points out, in the revealing passage in Chapter 2 referred to above, she details Victor Frankenstein's thoughts as he approaches the self-imposed task (my italics). He had long been 'imbued with a fervent longing to *penetrate* the secrets of nature'. The (natural) philosophers of old 'had partially unveiled the face of nature but *her* immortal lineaments were still a wonder and a mystery', but Frankenstein had '*gazed upon* the fortifications and impediments' that kept man outside the '*citadel of nature*'. Now, the new scientists had '*penetrated* deeper', and he was to enter 'with the greatest diligence into the search for the philosopher's stone or the elixir of life'. This anticipation is expressed in terms of clear pubescent excitement: he, Victor, was 'mingling, like an unadept, a thousand contradictory theories'. . . 'floundering desperately'. . . only 'guided by an ardent imagination and childish reasoning'[29]. The language and imagery here need no explanation, but I wonder what Mary Shelley would have made of Ripley's story and destiny.

The final image of the four *Alien* films is of two women, Ripley and Call sitting on a hill looking over the destroyed Paris – a city destroyed by male Science and corporate greed. Throughout the films, this has been a major theme, embodied first by the egregious and charming but fundamentally deranged J. Carter Buck, the UMS executive who is prepared to betray the trust the Ripley holds for him in the name of his greater god; there is Dr Wren, who, in the fourth film, is decidedly evil in his service of UMS. The male gender is, therefore, throughout these films if not wholly, then largely to be distrusted. Indeed they make it clear that it is male control of the processes – financial, political and scientific - which leads to the eventual destruction of life on earth, which I take to be the significance of this final image. What sense are we to make of all this, as Ripley and Call ponder their next moves on how to escape the military which will soon come searching for them?

This sense of the masculinity of Science is echoed in *Terminator 2* This is a passably good film, in so far as the characterisation is not totally dependent upon plot; Linda Hamilton does a pretty convincing job as Sarah Connor, the mother of John Connor, the boy – the Christ-figure who must be saved if the world is not to succumb to nuclear devastation. In order that it is not, then Dyson (interestingly), the inventor of Skynet, together with Cyberdyne Technology, must be themselves destroyed before the damage can be done. She attacks the home of the inventor, wounds him but does not kill him. At one point, she loses her temper with him: "Fucking men like you, built the hydrogen bomb. . . . You don't know what it's really like to create something, to create a life, feel it growing inside you. All you know how to create is death and destruction." This sense of the antagonism on this level between the genders has been undermined, however, by the way in which Sarah Connor is de-feminised in order to prepare for her vengeful attack – arming herself with an array of weaponry, dressing in battle fatigues, for example. Cameron cannot get away from testosterone-fuelled dynamics nor, of course, from shoddy dialogue.

And indeed, all these films in one way or another adhere to the staples of Hollywood blockbusters: fight sequences in *The Matrix* films that go on far too long, as with car chases, powerful guns and other weapons which have an obvious sexual connotation when deployed. Even Trinity, as she plummets to her death in the second *Matrix* film, shoots off her guns between her legs, even though she otherwise signifies much else that is feminine, though not necessarily submissive. She is characterised with strength, intelligence and fortitude, and, though she does die for Neo, I don't think this diminishes her.

There are other women: the T101, the female terminator in the third of these films is female only in appearance. Then there is the Oracle in *The Matrix*, the stereotypical wise old woman, and Lambert in the first *Alien* film. She is more tearful and fearful, in contrast to Ripley's aloof self-control.

And it is to Ripley that I must return, for there are few other female roles of any significance in the *Alien* films, a fact striking enough in itself. It appears that it was Alan J. Ladd Jnr, then head of 20th Century Fox, who were putting up the money for these films, who first suggested that Ripley should be a woman. It seems to me to have been an intuition of almost genius, for the films make sense only in this way: on the moral, scientific and psychological levels. To be fair, there are occasions when Ripley is, as one might say, 'masculinised', for example, when she has her hair cut off in the third film, ostensibly to remove any nits, or when she is carrying fire-arms around. Nevertheless, it is as a woman that she is characterised from start to end, and as a woman that she survives.

There are innumerable examples of this. Ridley Scott knew immediately, it appears, that Sigourney Weaver was to be Ripley: tall and with clear, strong features (these not too dissimilar from Jane Fonda's), she had had considerable acting experience on Broadway before she came to audition for her first film role. Stage, or screen presence, self-control balanced by a strong sense of humour, together with a clearly strong intuitive and caring side to her nature: all these seem to have been brought to the role. Ripley's saving of the ship's cat, her patience whilst all around her lose their cool, her tender understanding of the lost girl, Newt, in the second film and her determination not to believe in her own death but to try to rescue her despite the obvious dangers, and perhaps her final self-sacrifice at the end of *Aliens 3*, as described above are all obvious example of what I mean.

However, I have suggested above that it is as a mother that her role is most significant. In between films two and three, she is impregnated. Though she is very good at dealing with the testosterone-fuelled men or the devious company executives that surround her, and although she does have one sexual relationship, with the lonely but decent Dr Clements in *Aliens 3*, it is in her understanding of what she is bearing that is really significant. This is her golem, her Frankensteinian monster.

Some explanation is needed. After her death, she is 'rebuilt' from genetic material found on her ship; rebuilt with her, or in her, is the foetal alien, which is then extracted from her. However, this cloned Ripley is not the same as the original, which in terms of characterisation and the credibility of the fourth film is a masterstroke. Physically, she is altered, as she can feel no pain and her blood is highly acidic. But mentally, her feelings have been destroyed, and she seems to be, to some degree, obsessed with death. How does the story chart her recovery from this *anomie*? This descent had been, of course, brought about by men. It is they who cloned her - though there is a female scientist involved, she is hard to distinguish from her male colleagues, yet she immediately breaks down and panics when the zenomorphs break loose. They have cloned Ripley because of the incubus. However, at the start of the film, a small private spaceship, with a cargo of captured spacemen and scientists from another vehicle arrive at 'S.S.Auriga', to sell their captive cargo. These poor creatures are needed because the alien has to incubate in a human or other animal body. Thus, the link between the human and the alien is repeated once again.

Once the aliens have broken loose, and the ship abandoned by its regular crew, Ripley joins with the pirates in order to make their own escape. There are two very striking and powerful incidents during this episode. The first is perhaps the most horrifying.

Whilst they are walking towards their craft, Ripley stops and enters a laboratory. Here she finds numerous cloned versions of herself, all dead, but for one of them, and stored in formaldehyde. These terrible images of distorted, ugly and failed human life are perhaps some of the most shocking things in all these films. Their inhuman shapes and expressions are those of pain, horror, madness and despair; these are golems of true horror. The one who is still alive – a hideous, distorted figure lying on a bed, begs Ripley to kill her. In doing so, Ripley paradoxically acts, though with great pain and anger, compassionately, thus waking up, or beginning to wake up, characteristics of the original Ripley. She also destroys the poor captured souls, whom she finds in cocoons incubating their aliens. In other words, in the face of Science gone mad, she rediscovers, it is suggested, her humanity, an humanity which is essentially feminine.

Secondly, as they are running to reach the escape craft before the 'S.S.Auriga' crashes into the Earth (in order that the aliens might be destroyed), Ripley and her off-spring have one more meeting. The zenomorph that she has given birth to has grown into a queen, and is now giving birth herself, though she has mutated. No longer must the off-spring be gestated in human bodies, as she has now a womb, a genetic mutation derived from Ripley. Thus there is a further identification between monster and human. Though the new zenomorph immediately destroys its mother, it offers to Ripley (effectively her grandmother) tenderness and love. This is repeated a scene or two later, when this monster has found its way onto the escape craft. Ripley has to show it great affection; only then can she be free of it. Only now can she kill it. This she does by splashing a porthole with her acidic blood so that the external vacuum pulls the alien into outer space, an idea, I presume, that is taken from one of the Bond stories, when at its climax, 007 shoots a hole through an aircraft window, thus having Odd Job sucked out the plane.

However, Ripley is not Bond, however much we might have been shaken or stirred by her Herculean endeavours. The point is, it seems to me, is that Ripley has learned the wisdom of Prospero, whose recognition at the end of *The Tempest* that Caliban, "This thing of darkness, I acknowledge mine"[30], can be seen, in the terms of one discourse as confirming the slave-master relationship, but in another the connection between the rational and conscious mind and the irrational or subconscious. Perhaps, too, in a feminised language, metaphor and metonymy can at last approximate to one another.

Perhaps this is what is meant when we refer to coming to terms with our dark side. Thus, though Frankenstein's monster never found the love that he deserved, and destroyed his maker and all those he loved and Utz was lucky, to the extent that he deceived himself even to death, Ripley found a conditional deliverance, in that pride of conquest has to give way to tenderness and perhaps to regret. But Professor Higgins, well, he just had to do without.

Finally, it is necessary to add a few considerations about, Stanley Kubrick's *2001: A Space Odyssey*, which is perhaps one of the most significant if not the greatest films ever made. Fundamentally, it tells of Humanity's evolutionary history. At the end of the opening sequence, set in some distant prehistory, an ape-like creature, not yet a hominid nor even Homo Sapiens, discovers something absolutely vital: a weapon. He is using a bone to kill n animal he has predated. Suddenly the bone spins off into the air. And in one of the most remarkable pieces of photomontage ever, it is transformed into a spinning space ship, circling far above the Earth. The film then goes on to tell this story.

If all that the above has done is to reflect upon the greatest story ever told, this film surely tells it. There is not time or space here to go into the film in any detail; nevertheless, the symbolism of the golem is of very great importance in an understanding of it. At one moment during the very famous sequence of space travel in the fourth part of the film, a stewardess bends down to collect a pen that is floating in the weightlessness of space, and hands it to its owner. In some ways, this essay has been to outline a history of humanity's need for and use of tools; the pen is one, the computer is another perhaps ultimate tool. HAL (or *H*euristically programmed *Al*gorithmic computer - if these italics are displaced by one letter they give IBM) runs all the systems on the spaceship *Discovery* which is taking five astronauts to Jupiter to see if they can find out about the curious monolith, the meaning of which is the central idea of the film. However, just as implements and weapons, tools and technology have served mankind since the dawn of history (which Kubrick relates in the early part of the film), now HAL dominates these spacemen, in so far as there is nothing or little for the astronauts (who are all men) to do, when they are not hibernating. Everything is managed for them, everything is predetermined and foreseen.

Bearing in mind the suggestion above that these spaceships might represent human awareness of and experience in a lonely universe, it is as if the rather bleak determinism in the earlier films discussed is present here too in all its glory: HAL, it seems to me, is a metaphor, a paradigm for a kind of scientific determinism, controlling all human life. And when the astronauts plot to turn off HAL, in order to break free from him, because he appears to be getting things wrong, he attempts to kill them. He succeeds in killing four of them, with the same lack of emotion that we saw with both the Terminators and with Frankenstein's monster. He kills them because he has been programmed to ensure above all the safety of the mission, and he has not been programmed to accept his own demise. He acts with all the logic of the gas-chamber operator. However, as he fades away when Bowman closes down all his higher-order systems, he regresses to childhood. For the one thing that he cannot do is criticise and reprogram himself.

Now, HAL's death is highly significant, in that his death implies irrevocably the death of Bowman, who is Everyman, for in freeing himself from that which has controlled him, Bowman is free, paradoxically, for one further purpose only, to meet his destiny, a destiny that may or may not be tragic.

This seems to follow, if I may be allowed to stray a little, the conventional tragic course that Aristotle first outlined in *The Poetics*: mankind's tragic flaw is his hubris, to be found in his evolutionary trajectory from ape-man to astronaut, at each stage delving deeper into the secrets and processes of life. It is a journey he has taken, a *peripeteia* which is the whole of history. If this is the case, however, it is a history, Kubrick seems to be suggesting, in which imagination and courage, two fundamental human characteristics, again and again recur.

When the surviving astronaut, Bowman, turns off HAL's higher functions, he is acting in just this way, but knowing that the outcome can only lead to his death. This is his – and thereby, our - recognition, or *anagnorisis*, that comes before the tragic ending. Does Kubrick offer, though, a conditional *catharsis*, to be found in the figure of the Star Child[31]?

Is this film a tragedy? The film was made in 1968, just a year before the first manned Moon landings, at a time when we were all wildly excited about the great adventure that mankind seemingly was about to embark on. It was also made at the time of the Cold War (to which there are plenty of allusions), and of the Hippy revolution with its obsession with hallucinogenic drugs and 'Peace, man!'. The final sequence takes its cue from the 'trip' that such drugs induce. It is violently vivid, explosive and strange, but the key to this 'ultimate trip' is the sequence where Bowman, now facing his final journey, arrives at a large house, one that is at once destination, home, deathbed and womb. Here he will go through a rapid progress from young man to old age and to death; out of the shaft of his dead body, at the prompting of the monolith on its fourth appearance, comes the foetal image of new life, new birth – a foetal human, evolutionarily metamorphosed into the Star Child.

In the film, the giant figure looks down on a glowing Earth; Arthur C. Clarke's novel ends thus:

> There before him, a glittering toy no Star-Child could resist, floated the planet Earth with all its peoples.
>
> He had returned in time. Down there on that clouded globe, the alarms would be flashing across the radar screens, the great tracking telescopes would be searching the skies – and history as men knew it would be drawing to a close.
>
> A thousand miles below, he became aware that a slumbering cargo of death had awoken, and was stirring sluggishly into orbit. The feeble energies it contained were no possible menace to him; but he preferred a cleaner sky. He put forth his will, and the circling megatons flowered in a silent detonation that brought a brief, false dawn to half the sleeping globe.
>
> Then he waited, marshalling his thoughts and brooding over his still untested powers. For though he was master of the world, he was not quite sure what to do next.
>
> But he would think of something[32].

Kubrick wanted to tell the history of all humanity in this film. It is both bleak and optimistic, bleak in that, despite the wonderful use of the music of Strauss and Ligeti, and the beauty of the universe, it is silence that is so often the prevailing impression we have; indeed there are only about 40 minutes of stark dialogue in the film. Kubrick seems to be asking, what will we know when we know everything, when there will be nothing left to know. Kubrick, in telling of 'this strange eventful history'[33], means us to understand that mankind has reached its evolutionary peak, and that decline and extinction are now to follow, as Clarke's image of Armageddon suggests. On the other hand, the extraordinary images of re-birth and of human creativity, provides us with the final message. In this context, too, it is worth reminding ourselves that Prometheus acted precipitously: legend has it that Zeus was anyway going to do away with humanity, and start again from the drawing board, to create a perfect race.

And yet, Kubrick's final image of his film is as stark as Clarke's, for what does he make the Star Child see? Nuclear explosions taking place across the world below him.

However, to my mind, the overall effect is perhaps weakened, and the tragic dimension diminished, by one, central element: the monolith itself. And yet, its very vagueness suggests the indeterminacy of Evolution, for it appears at crucial moments in the evolutionary history told in the film. Appearing as it does at four crucial moments, affects human behaviour and development, for example giving to the ape-man the idea of the possibility of using a bone as a weapon. Though one may take it that this is an appeal to God, as Adam and Eve might have done as they left their Garden, an act which Prometheus might have scorned, it seems to me that this monolith is nothing more than a *deus ex machina*, a mere device that allows Kubrick to avoid resolving the issue of whether mankind's progress is indeed tragic (as the cathartic image at the end suggests) or plain absurd, that is, meaningless. 'He would think of something.' He probably won't.

Paradise Regained?

So, we might like to remember Blake's saying,

> 'Man was made for Joy and Woe;
> And when this we rightly know
> Thro' the World we safely go.[34]

It seems to me that despite the wonders and fascination that Science produces (in particular anaesthetics), I wonder if there are any lessons that can be drawn from what has gone above. Ripley and Call will wander an Earth ravaged by destruction and on which they are strangers. The Matrix may have been destroyed, but its Architect ('I'm not human, remember'), still walks the planet, whilst Frankenstein's monster, well, who knows where he is? And the Terminator was not able to prevent nuclear war. In the 76th anniversary of the end of the Second World War, perhaps some of the following considerations might be of interest.

I was brought up in the era of the cold war. Rudyard Kipling's words

> Oh, East is East, and West is West, and never the twain shall meet,
> Till Earth and Sky stand presently at God's great Judgment Seat[35]

reminded us that a knowledge of particle physics might have placed mankind in just that position. What did J. Robert Oppenheimer, the 'father' of the atom bomb, say after Hiroshima? 'I am become Death, the Destroyer of Worlds.'[35] Though we are ever more dependent on nuclear power for the conduct of our daily lives as we have become used to it, we are terrified that such power and resource should fall into the wrong hands (let alone being utterly confounded as to what to do with thousands of tons of nuclear waste). A leading Pakistani physicist, now recently dead has, it appears, happily sold nuclear secrets to all the most undesirable types of people.

Again, we are now in possession of all the secrets of Biology, or we will be soon. The genome has confirmed 'triumphantly' Darwinianism, despite what those who favour 'intelligent design' (the smart term for 'creationism') might have to say about it. Cloning can ensure that one's genes in their entirety are passed on to another generation, whilst stem cell research promises what in effect might be eternal life, since diseased parts of the body could simply be regrown. And nanotechnology promises similar wonders: 'faster computers; cell-specific drugs; powerful new chemical catalysts (used in the processing of petroleum); sensors monitoring everything from crops to crooks to customers; stronger, lighter, smarter, more durable materials, etc. Nanoscale technologies are poised to become the strategic platform for global control of manufacturing, food, agriculture and health in the immediate years ahead.'[36]

'Oh, Death,' we might cry, 'where is thy sting?'

Prometheus gave us fire, and Faraday electricity. Today, its binary scion enables us to communicate, calculate and create with power inconceivable a hundred years ago. Yet this power seems to be giving to those that rule us or determine our lives the liberty to restrict our freedoms. Our shopping habits are monitored, our conversations noted and recorded, and, even, if you open GoogleEarth.com, I can be traced, or will be able to be traced, anywhere in the world. 'Quis custodiet custodiens' is as relevant today as it was in the past. The organs of the state become ever more repressive, paradoxically in the name of freedom. The rules of the game have been changed, and our rulers are taking full opportunity of it.

In *The Matrix* films, Agent Smith and his cohorts are able to replicate and mutate at will. A recent newspaper article announced the arrival of a robot that can, indeed reproduce itself: 'In the long term, the scientists envisage a day when armies of self-replicating robots will be able to mend themselves when broken, expand their populations, explore space and even establish self-sustaining colonies on other planets' through the use of what are termed 'molecubes'. These 'demonstrate that mechanical self-reproduction is not unique to biology.'[37] Whilst it might be better to send such robots to Mars or elsewhere than humans, since the latter face almost certain death in such environments, despite the hopes of the vain-glorious man formerly in the White House, one might ask how they are to be controlled.

In these films, too, we have come across divided societies. In *The Matrix*, in *Blade Runner*, in the *Terminator* films and especially in *Metropolis* (to which all these later films are explicitly or implicitly indebted), there are active subterranean societies working to one degree or another to rebel against the power of technology that rules or threatens them. Many of the advances mentioned above in biology and genetic engineering will favour the rich and privileged societies of the developed World, since their use will be enormously expensive, or by dynamic countries like China, which is rapidly producing a class system as rigid as any. Even as I write, there is, one reads, a growing 'underclass' in Chinese cities, living in cellars, sewage systems, and so on literally underground. And someone, in some particle accelerator, might well, one day soon, fire the nucleus of an atom of gold in some carbon, and suddenly turn us all and everything in to anti-matter.

Finally, what about human self-hood and identity? The discrete, self-determining individual, the individual of free choice, handed down to us over the centuries, the Socratically 'the self-aware', may well be becoming something of a museum piece. Let us imagine a few decades hence, when there is every likelihood that androids or robots will have been created that look and behave exactly like humans. Then we might find the ultimate, perfect sexual partner; but what will this say about the nature of human relations?

Never mind, you might say, but please bear in mind what Ripley saw when she walked into that laboratory, and knew that a lost paradise will remain for ever lost.

And A Conclusion?

But I offer two different conclusions to this essay. Take them as you will.

For each, I return to Utz. In a mad world, he lived in his imagination, breathing life into his porcelain. He believed to the end that this was where reality lay for him (well, there and in his sexual conquests, but what was the difference?). Chatwin kills him off, the author playing a joke on the reader, for he has Utz's collection disappear. It cannot be found anywhere. Thus we have a double death, of the collection and of its owner. Was the collection real? Was Utz? What is the meaning of 'real' when asked about a work of fiction?

Chatwin's novel seems to suggest that what is real is what we make of ourselves. As we go through life, we constantly create and recreate ourselves, trying to know ourselves. Perhaps in this sense we are our own golems, perhaps even our own Frankensteinian monsters. Chatwin's most significant literary and philosophic antecedent was the great Argentinean writer and fabulist, Jorge Luis Borges, whose grandmother was in fact from Derby. This mixture of the poetic and the prosaic would have amused him, since appearance and reality was Borges' playground, as it was for *his* antecedent, William Shakespeare. Borges wrote the following short, very short story. It is called *Everything and Nothing*, and this is how it ends. All his life, Shakespeare, as Borges has it, has been pretending to be everyone and everything in order to try to hide an overwhelming sense of inner emptiness that has possessed him since boyhood.

> For twenty years he persisted in that controlled hallucination, but one morning he was suddenly gripped by the tedium and the terror of being so many kings who die by the sword and so many suffering lovers who converge, diverge and melodiously expire. That very day he arranged to sell his theatre. Within a week he had returned to his native village, where he recovered the trees and rivers of his childhood. . . . His friends from London would visit his retreat and for them he would take up again his role as poet.
>
> History adds that before or after dying he found himself in the presence of God and told Him: 'I who have been so many men in vain want to be one and myself.' The voice of the Lord answered from a whirlwind: 'Neither am I anyone; I have dreamt the world as you dreamt your work, my Shakespeare, and among the forms in my dream are you, who like myself are many and no one.'[38]

On the other hand, Utz was survived by his ever-faithful wife, Marta, the peasant girl whom he had saved from the village youths, who were mocking her for her friendship with a swan. Chatwin's fictional narrator, who may or may not be Chatwin, finds her living in the village of her childhood. When she opens the door, and the narrator has introduced himself and told why he has come, she says, with her face 'lit up with an astounded smile', and her eyes lifted to 'a rainbow', 'Ya! Ich bin die Baronin von Utz.'[39]

In other words, we may take it, perhaps with Ripley or with Victor Frankenstein's betrothed Elizabeth Lavenza, that all this proves, in Larkin's words, 'Our almost-instinct almost true: / What will survive of us is love.'[40]

Doesn't it?

I end by recalling the Japanese film of 1954, *Gojira*, directed by Ishiro Honda. Much that has been discussed above has apocalyptic undertones. This film tells the story of the destruction of humanity by a giant gorilla (in the trashy Hollywood version, *Godzilla*, the ape is seen atop of the Empire State building). In this film, the gorilla represents that destruction that befell Hiroshima and Nagasaki in 1945.

13

Nocturnal upon St Lucy's Day – A Parable

Do I dare disturb the Universe?
T.S. Eliot

Monday, 21st December: *'Tis the year's midnight, and it is the day's.*

Mark was still alive, wasn't he?

He had been taken from the Cathedral's steps, just alive. Alice had been left there. After some months, Westerbrook had had him released. Just like that. Bedraggled and hungry, Mark was lead out to the street. He had to make his own way home. It was the shortest day of the year.

How long had he been in the dark of the cell? He knew that it had been summer when he and Alice had been seized, tortured, separated. He remembered the bodies on the Cathedral steps, Alice taking his hand and being roughly separated from her.

Six months. A small, barred window, a few planks, a blanket and food pushed through a slot at the base of the door. The occasional sound of a flap being opened, a brief shaft of light. Being watched. Doing nothing.

And visits to the white room. Increasingly less often but always painful.

And now he was in the dark again. Where before he had seemed to himself dead and buried, now he was alone on an earth drained of life, the fading light just enough to see him home. He shivered as he sat on the bus; people avoided sitting near him.

Bearded, dirty, scruffy. Pedestrians moved away as they passed. Street lights heightened his drawn features. There was his car, slowly rusting, dirty, one tire flat. There was his front door. There should have been pleasure on his return. But to him they were now nothing.

He made his way to the first floor. Before he opened it, he knew that he was exhausted. His being was nothingness.

He slid to the ground, leaning against the door. He could not go in. Soon he fell asleep.

To be roughly woken by a kick. 'Get up,' said a voice. 'Get away, you don't belong here!'

When the figure had disappeared up the stairs, Mark lifted himself and put the key in the lock. As he pushed open the door, his hand came up to his eyes, brushing some straggling hair away, perhaps not wanting to see what lay before him: memories. And absence.

Absence. As he switched on a light he knew everything had gone.

No Alice, no human warmth, no love, no life.

Just the ransacked rooms, draws opened, books, clothing, anything, everything was lying everywhere. Ransacked.

And no Alice and so, no life.

But in the corner, on the wall a television screen. Mark stared at it, at the cheerful images of smiling people. He tried to turn it off but could only keep it silent. Throwing some clothes off his arm chair, he sat, resting is head on his hands, seeing nothing. The last words, blunt and impersonal, he heard from his captors, after he had asked after Alice, were: 'Oh, she's dead.'

Soon he was asleep.

*

Tuesday, 22nd December: *I am re-begot*
Of absence, darkness, death: things which are not.

Mark did not know what time it was when he opened his eyes. All was still, except for the ever-flickering screen. He stayed put for some time, not wanting, not able to move. At moments he stirred, but no more.

Suddenly, overriding the remote, a voice came from the screen: 'Today's lesson is that all who become lovers do so in the name of the greater good, in the name of everyone else, for we all belong to each other. From nothing will come nothing, *if* love is *selfish*! Love is for everyone! Happiness ever after.'

And so it went on for several minutes, emphases drummed through the airwaves.

But for Mark, where was love? Where was Alice? As she was dead, so was he. So was he? Whereas love had made him a quintessence from nothingness, now he was again all emptiness.

Somehow, he would raise himself, he would wash, even shave, go out to find something to eat, make a start at tidying, at living again. Somehow. Soon. Later.

He looked around him. Pictures, posters were hanging loosely, one or two even on the floor, Was that some damp spreading down from the ceiling? He noticed a crack in a window pane and curtains were hanging badly.

The books. The books which had helped make him, which had taught him that, when all is said and done, that it is choice, individual choice, that makes us human, makes us good and brings happiness. Books that had taught him that pleasure is good, too, but that happiness is better, that happiness has to be found in thoughtfulness and in selflessness and not in selfishness – these now lay scattered everywhere, some open, some torn and ripped, some even burnt. Happiness, he knew, could not be given by the State.

His eyes settled on one volume after another – and he could no longer believe.

An empty day, an empty life ahead of him. A few empty words came to him: 'And death hath no dominion.'

*

Wednesday, 23rd December: *I, by love's limbec, am the grave*
Of all that's nothing.

Dawn, and Mark was stirred by the sounds from the street below, car horns, engines, the occasional voices reaching up to him indistinguishable and mixing with the squawks of birds.

This was the chemistry of life now, the endless conquest of humans by other humans: slaughter and control. Secret policing has been enhanced by universal electronic surveillance. No move, no thought, no friendship was missed: all was recorded. Social credits awarded for good behaviour, jobs – and lives - lost otherwise.

And when one went to the woods or to a lake, together, to be as one, to be loved and loving, to make love because that is what you chose to do, you ended the day being tortured, separated, destroyed.

These thoughts. Mark had known them only too well. Now they were dead, however true.

It was the alchemy that had made Alice and him. It belonged only to them.

'Catch me!' she had called to him as she skittled into the wood nearby. Laughing she had run, only to hide behind the nearest tree.

And then, 'You *must* read this,' Mark had said of a poem or story or piece of philosophy he had found from previous times.

Or, 'Mm – this is de*lish*!' Alice savoured Mark's chocolate mousse. He knew she would want him to make love with her later. Soon.

And he would take her or she would take him. Ripping off clothes or not even bothering to. Arms, legs, hands, eyes: fierce and demanding. Or a slow, long love-making. They would lie together, and there would be nothing else, no other meaning to life or to love, but this, this moment.

And in their joy, the world would be washed away by tears as warm as the summer's sun.

In their chaos lay infinite simplicity.

And when it was over, when they had parted as all bodies must do, each felt that they were as one. Forever.

*

What is the meaning of 'meaning'?

Let us imagine that one is born without sensory faculties, no hearing sight, smell, taste or touch. Unlikely, but just imagine.

How would one learn what 'green' is or 'sweetness' or any of the myriad of words and terms we use to enhance our perception and understanding of the world and to communicate?

Let us now imagine that, by chance, hearing is restored. Someone is trying to teach one words.

‘That is a “tree”,’ she says.

“Tree”.

That is a sound made in the mouth. At this stage it can bear no objective reality: how could it be known to what it refers? It is not possible. The word – and *all* words – are merely sounds.

And we learn language as a matter of convenience and that without this convenience, then life has no meaning. And ‘meaning’ can have no meaning.

We are happy to go along with this as not to do so, well, that way madness lies.

Politicians, of course, want to control this ‘convenience’. To gather votes, to determine and control meaning as it so suits them, to control thoughts. Much of this is genuine and is the seat of conflict, of everyday politics, of advertising. . . .

But what happens when conflict is over?

All thought and argument and discussion is dialectical: I say something, you posit an opposing thought and, at best, we agree to differ or a resolution is arrived at.

Or not. The politician has won and determined that his thoughts and meaning are ‘correct’.

And so the authority of the state is the only provider of meaning – not that it means anything.

There is no choice in the matter, as Westerbrook and his kind will never stop reminding one.

*

Thursday, 24th December: *But I am by her death (which word wrongs her)*
Of the first nothing the elixir grown

Mark and Alice had had numerous friends, as all do. He had been a journalist, though all knew that they had to be careful. The days before the shooting of the agents in the café, four or five, Mark and Alice included, had taken themselves for a walk, beside a lake, along footpaths and over one or two hills, ending in a small village called Lowton. Where there was a small hotel and bar. And they started talking.

‘Praxis! Action for change, total change!’’

Leon had been the most vociferous of them. Others had tried to quieten him, but his angry enthusiasm had carried him away.

‘We must act, it is imperative! Create the world anew!’

And that was enough.

Nobody heard of him – or the others - again for a long time.

Westerbrook and his hands had them, in various ways.

And Mark woke again to his empty world.

Looking around him again, he took in the things lying around him. And there were books and clothes that he recognised of Alice’s, a dark red jumper, a pair of sandals, a necklace . . . .

But these meant nothing to him. Nor his phone nor his . . . .

He turned to the window.

The day lay ahead of him, as did all the days to come. He could sit here, he could go out, he could even breathe and sleep and die. There was nothing and nothing mattered.

Later, he did move. Almost as in a dream, he took himself out. A midwinter day left him shivering as he walked along the street, down to the river, which once before had been so calm and luminous. Where he and Alice had started.

It flowed grey and silently before him as he leant over the railing. 'Sweet Thames, run softly till I end my song.'

The words came to his mind. All it would take would be for him to lean forward over the railing.

He stood there for a long time. When before everything could be invested with love, with meaning, now nothing mattered.

Slowly, he walked home. Though he might have stopped anywhere.

*

Thursday, 25th December: *You lovers, for whose sake the lesser sun*
At this time to the Goat is run
To fetch new lust, and give it you,
Enjoy your summer all.

There was knock on the door.

Mark had woken late – standing now by the window, he did not know now what the time was. He turned. Could he be bothered?

He stood silhouetted in front of the grey daylight. There was a second knock, a little louder.

Shuffling his way across the room, Mark stopped, put his hand to the door. Not caring whether it was police or whoever, he opened the door. Mechanically.

'Hello, Mark. Good to see you back. We heard you moving around.'

It was his neighbour, Jim. But Jim, seeing Mark in his shabby state, found it difficult to look at him straight in the eye.

'My wife and I wondered if you would like to come to us for lunch today, with us and some of our family, my brother and his wife. The children will be there.'

Mark's response was silence.

'We'd love it if you could.'

It was hard. Not only had no kindness been shown him for many months, the only words he had heard had been orders snapped at him, questions forced upon him. He found himself resting an arm on the door post.

'Er. . . yes. I am sorry.' And where were *his* words now, words that were once *him*? 'Thank you. How kind.' He felt lump rise in his throat. 'What time?'

'1.00, OK?'

'Thank you.' His words were very faint, he realised, very weak. 'Thank you very much. How kind.'

As he closed the door behind once Jim had gone, Mark leant against the woodwork. Turned and looked again at the visible signs of his ransacked life.

When would it be summer again? He cared not.

In the time that followed, Mark sat, dozed; he walked through the apartment, picking up a book here, folding a piece of clothing there, then returning to his seat.

Hearing some sounds from next door, he raised himself. He did not choose to go; instead, mechanically he smoothed his hair, put on a clean shirt and a jumper . . . a jumper given to him once by Alice. He froze for a few moments and then made his way to the door.

On entering his neighbours' flat , the other adults looked at him, puzzled, askance, even worried. Jim greeted him.

'Hello!' he smiled welcoming, though Mark noticed that Delia, Jim's wife, well her smile was plainly a little forced. 'We're so glad your back. Have a glass. Have you seen Alice?'

Champagne. In a long glass. Where had Mark been just a few short, dark days before?

'Thank you.' His reply was barely audible.

'We know where you've been,' Jim continued. 'No matter. We are here for you.'

*

'Praxis.' A thought has no meaning without action. A revolutionary word, coined by Karl Marx to encourage action, intended for the overthrow of an unjust and cruel regime. Its implication is that since the regime won't allow for meaningful change, only violent action is possible.

It can also have milder connotations: support, sympathy and encouragement.

But when protesters take to the streets, sometimes not so peacefully, they are met with overwhelming armed force. We see this all over the world today.

Protective clothing, shields, batons, dogs, tasers: nothing is brutal enough to protect the regime.

Especially a regime everyone loves.

*

Christmas lunch – and a table full of plenty. Mark had forgotten what such colour was, vegetables, turkey, duck, all sorts of condiments and nibbles. Steaming gravy and a rich

Christmas pudding. But Mark could eat little of it, so unused to fine food as his stomach was. He smiled without looking, he passed over the dishes, muttered thanks, saw faces through the lighted candles, heard the children – three of them – laughing and joking, the adults watching, waiting and but not quite able to join in.

For Mark, this was as though in a film, a film without meaning, even though something in him recognised the kindness shown him.

'Now, Delia,' Jim said as the meal ended, plates had been removed, hats worn, crackers pulled and laughter at silly jokes and quiz questions had died down, 'now, presents!'

'Yay!' cried one of the boys.

'Quick,' enthused his brother.

And Jim's daughter, seven-year-old Lucy, as if prompted, withdrew into the room next door, a bedroom.

'She learnt this little game last year,' Delia explained. 'We are under strict instruction not to start till she has come back in.'

'Patience is a virtue,' Tone, Jim's brother, declared. 'Till Patience lost hers!' he sniggered.

They all found seats or places on the floor to sit. Jim dimmed the lights and the now dark room was filled only with light from the little tree in the corner.

And it was not long till Lucy returned. She had a circlet of Christmas tinsel on her head, her white dress was now garlanded with some holly and she held a candle in her hand. A beautiful, flickering candle.

Its light seemed to awaken the room with warmth, its rays and flickering marking out the features on the faces there.

'Delia,' Jim said, 'isn't she lovely, our Lucy.'

For a moment, it occurred to Mark that this little girl will have her spring. He saw her beyond now, well and happy. Though he was nothing - and the image passed at once.

Lucy went to the tree, picked up a present, read to whom it should go and took it to one of her cousins. Five more times she did this.

And then she brought one to Mark.

'Lux Eterna.' The two words floated silently into his mind.

He could no longer help himself. Tears burst forth. He cried. And he cried. And the others offered him comfort.

And then he smiled. And he knew he would have to act.

14

The Mau Mau: Recollections and Reflections on a most dark episode of Britain's Imperial Past

I am a child of empire – but I wonder if anyone even a generation younger than me can have any idea of what this means. I was born in September 1948, in a hospital in Nakuru, Kenya – a building, I understand, that later was to become the country residence of Jomo Kenyatta. My father was a farmer in the White Highlands, that central part of Kenya that has become synonymous with white expropriation of land for centuries the home of indigenous people, on a broad plateau called The Kinangop. I later went to an English prep school – such places were, at the time, referred to as 'cradles of empire', for its boys were one day to become the police and army officers, lawyers and administrators, the district commissioners and ultimately governors of the colonies of an empire that was the largest that History has ever known. And so, in a very meaningful sense, much of what I recount was done in my name.

All empires are created in death and destruction, though what they leave behind may be, paradoxically, admirable. It must be, surely, that our history, our histories must be understood for what they are and *not* for what we would like them to be. To be truthful – and we *must* be - the British Empire was founded on slavery and when this was ended, it prospered through colonialism which, to put it bluntly, is slavery with a few pennies thrown in.

This empire has long since died the death that all empires die, though perhaps even today we have not quite got over the influence that it bore on our national consciousness. I came to write this piece after hearing an item on the radio some years ago in which a then elderly man called Tim Symonds, who had been with the British Army fighting the Mau Mau, told how he had been with a unit that had attacked a gang in the Aberdare Forest. His face had been blackened for disguise, as was common. He recalled that as he was about to shoot, an African suddenly put up his hands, allowing himself to be arrested. When his name was asked for, he said 'Obama'[33].

---

[33] See this link: http://www.thisislondon.co.uk/standard/article-23620970-will-obama-forgive-britain-for-his-grandfathers-torture.do for an account of Obama's past Kenyan family.

Whether or not this was indeed the grandfather of the recent and first black President of the United States, my attention was drawn to the story, for my early life was closely determined by the Mau Mau – I can well remember being taken as a child on a family outing into the Aberdare Mountains, which rise to some 16,000 feet, for a picnic to see, perhaps, some elephants, and instead coming across four bodies hanging from a tall tree. We were quickly moved on. I came to understand much later in life that these had probably been killed by what was termed a Pseudogang, made up of settler farmers. Was my father one such? I will never know.

I was just four years old when this insurgency started, and though I never suffered from anything serious other than being threatened by a panga-wielding gardener, I had, I realised, very little knowledge of what it had been, other than a few family memories. I felt that I needed to read up on the subject. What I discovered has been both fascinating and deeply disturbing. What I am going to attempt to describe will not avoid even the most distressing aspects of what must be one of the darkest and most unpleasant episodes of British imperial rule.

I make no apologies for being, at least at the outset, somewhat personal. There is necessity. My father was a settler farmer. After going to school at Harrow, he went for a year to Cirencester to work on a farm, whence he took ship for South Africa, following his father, who had been attracted to South Africa to seek land under The Soldier Settler Scheme, 'for soldiers of the officer class'. Travelling through the Suez Canal and the Red Sea, my grandfather was persuaded, instead, to try his luck in Kenya. My father followed him, in 1930, just 20 years old. This he did, creating a farm out of untouched savannah, fighting in the Second World War, raising a family (in the process, losing a leg when his young bride was just four months pregnant with me), and finally selling up, some 35 years later, to move at last to South Africa.

Why Kenya – Kenya, with a long -e, till it becomes independent in 1963? Kenya was – is – beautiful – 'Officers and gentlemen to Kenya, other ranks to Rhodesia'.. It is a country created by Western Powers at the Congress of Berlin in 1884, during which, under the guidance of Bismarck, the Continent of Africa was divided up into the artificial countries that we have inherited today. There were rebellions against this in Kenya even before the end of the 19th Century. Britain and 'won' Kenya as it had now built the railway from Mombasa to Lake Victoria, to prevent Germany gaining control of the headwaters of the river Nile.

To a young man of his generation, as to those settlers who had come before him, stepping off the boat in Mombasa, the making his way up country to Nairobi and with no previous knowledge, it must have been a wonderful experience, commanding all his youthful ambition, sense of adventure and a rapidly awakening desire to make at least part of this apparently untended land into his own, his future, his life. Then he found himself the possessor of a spread of land of some four thousand acres on the North Kinangop, in the White Highlands. This was on a high plateau at about 8,000 feet above sea level. Tufted savannah grass, as high as one's waist and as sharp as a razor, covered the land as far as one could see. To the east, the Aberdare Mountains, behind which the Sun rose in splendour, and beyond which lies Mount Kenya, 'Keren-yagga' the 'Mountain of Mystery' of the Gikuyu and seat of their God, Ngei . Father's land slipped down over the Mau Escarpment into the

---

Great Rift Valley. Thirteen miles away lay our nearest town, Naivasha. On the left, is the extinct volcano of Longonot; to the right, Mount Susua, and in the middle, beyond, Lake Naivasha. Hippos wallowed in its shallows, whilst thousands and thousands of flamingos sucked up worms and marine creatures from its floor, accompanied by a million farting sounds. As one drove down the escarpment, one would see these pink, beautiful birds suddenly take to the air and, in great circles climb in their thousands higher and higher in the up-currents, become ever fainter in the blue African sky.

Soon, buildings appeared, sheds, barns and a homestead. Lines of trees were planted, fields laid out with what must have been miles and miles of fencing, ditching and tracks for the animals and machinery. Cattle, pigs, and sheep; wheat, barley, oats and pyrethrum (yes, pyrethrum, out of which DDT was produced, which killed all the birds, as Rachel Carson pointed out so clearly in 'Silent Spring', thereby bringing to an end an important source of income). Combine harvesters, tractors, electricity generators, the Jeep on which I learnt to drive, ponies for us children, hunters for the grown-ups; annual holidays at Malindi, seventy miles north of Mombasa, or safaris to Amboseli, or to Ngorongoro in the then Tanganyika. Fishing for blue marlin, seeking out lions at dawn or sunset or watching them hunt, then ourselves being chased by angry rhinos. Kilimanjaro slumbered, white topped in the hazy midday. Travelling for hundreds of miles along dusty, empty roads, except for surprise encounters with wild animals, gave rise to the expression, 'miles and miles of bloody Africa'. Never mind: after the First World War it was 'Officers and gentlemen. . . .'

This photograph, right, taken in a friend's light aircraft in about 1960, shows the family home, with its driveway, surrounding trees and the garden with its herbaceous border. Beyond this one can make out the vegetable garden, beyond which my father grew Lucerne for his cattle.

Kenya is a broad and varied country: tropical coastline, semi-desert interiors, proper desert in the Northern Province, where Somali *shifta* would come and raid their neighbours' cattle, great lakes and mountains, game reserves for safaris and for big-game hunting – we had a lion's pelt on our hallway floor. At night, the dogs barked in the great, blue silence, night birds called, in the distance the cows lowed, and overhead rumbled a BOAC Viscount as it made its way to London. My father made all this for himself and his family. I recall saying to myself one evening, safely ensconced in my Broadstairs prep school as I collected British and Empire stamps, that Kenya was to be our home for a thousand years – and where had I got *that* from? Was my father ever going to give this up? Was all his vigour and energy, indeed courage and perseverance, like that of 60,000 other white settlers, going to amount to nothing?

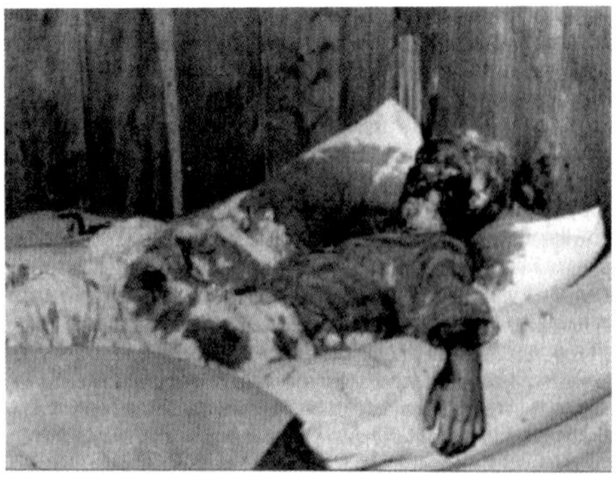

Postmortem photo of Michael Ruck after being hacked to death by Mau Mau insurg

Then, on the night of the 24th January, 1953, a little friend of mine, and his pregnant mother and his father, were murdered in their beds by a gang of insurgents. I can just remember Michael Ruck, a year or so older than myself, but one of my playmates. Whilst reading for this paper, I came across a picture of him, dead in his bed. His mother and father died with him. Their farm was but a few miles from ours, perhaps our nearest neighbours; perhaps we could have been the victims – it matters not.

This was not the first murderous attack on whites, but because of the death of the little boy, it is the one which gained world-wide attention and is the crucial moment in the development of the Mau Mau Emergency, of the insurgency or fight for liberation, call it what you will. It spread the first real panic and outrage amongst the settlers. My two siblings and I were sent immediately back to England, to be brought up more or less wholly thereafter by our grandparents, except for annual summer holidays. By the end of 1955, the insurgency had been defeated militarily; however, when we returned then, now my parents carried pistols and there was a detachment of the Black Watch camped on our farm. There was also, in a far corner, a 'protected' village, surrounded by barbed wire and watchtowers, for the black farm workers. The summer of 1962 was the last we spent in what was still the colony; a year later, Independence came and in 1964, my father sold up.

Why had my little friend died? To answer this, it is necessary to ask the question, what *was* Kenya.

It did not exist until the 1883-4 Congress of Berlin, at which the major European powers divided up Africa in order to control the spoils of the 'Scramble for Africa', which had exerted so much energy in the 19th Century. This resulted in the continent we know today, with its artificial countries created by the simple method of drawing straight lines back and forth across the map. Together with colonies in West Africa, Britain laid claim to, and got, a series of colonies from the Cape to Cairo. Indeed, I once met a wizened old settler called Captain Ewart Grogan who had walked that entire distance, never once leaving British territory. British East Africa, as it was then known, was constituted of Tanganyika (which was seeded to Britain after the First World War – Queen Victoria had once given her nephew Kilimanjaro as a birthday present), Uganda and Kenya.

Much of what follows is taken from Caroline Elkins' remarkable study of the Mau Mau Insurgency, *Imperial Reckoning* (2005). This was the first major study of the rising, a detailed work that relied on the testimony of many who had lived through this period. I draw heavily upon it. They were at the time elderly but their memories are detailed and extraordinary. Others have since contributed to our understanding. I also found Ngugi wa Thiongo's haunting novel *A Grain of Wheat* deeply moving as it gives substance to Elkins' work. Other works, including David Anderson's *Histories of the Hanged* which details all the black Kenyans imprisoned, tortured or executed (1090), give vivid accounts of the struggle. These are a very long way from Elspeth Huxley's *The Flame Trees of Thika*. It is also worth remembering that those who suffered at the hands of the British have long pursued for reparations in this country. Successive governments have successfully ignored this case, booting it into the long grass. Now virtually all the complainants must be dead.

In fact, according to Elkins, the British were at first most interested in Uganda, since they desperately wanted to control the headwaters of the River Nile. She suggests that the British were terrified that if the Germans got there first, they would shut off the flow, thereby starving Egypt of water. British forces would have to be withdrawn from Suez, leaving Britain's imperial 'Jewel in the Crown', India, indefensible[34]. Out of such stuff dreams are made on. The result, though, was the Uganda Railway, upon which Kenya, which finally became a colony on 1926, came to be built. Begun in 1896, it ran for 582 miles from Mombasa to Lake Victoria and beyond. Indentured Indian labour was brought in (the *wahindi* to the indigenous peoples). So dangerous and so epic an enterprise it was, that it became known as 'The Lunatic Railway'. Nairobi was at first merely a little staging post. As a boy,I once travelled on this railway, to the coast and to Malindi for our summer break; there was still a certain romance to it.

Because of its attractions, Kenya was, as I have indicated, for the rich and the upper-classes. The British, as they say, and perhaps the saying is as true today as then, go abroad to misbehave. Kenya rapidly became famous for its decadent life-style of drink, drugs, wife-swapping – the saying back in London was, 'Are you married, or do you come from Kenya?' The rich aristocrats and younger sons of aristocrats found the new colony an obvious attraction. But not everyone was part of the Happy Valley crowd or up to white mischief. For many farmers like my father, and for others like his siblings and many, many more, farming was hard work. Out of the virgin soil, as I have described, a living had to be made, and it was not really until the Second World War, when Britain was desperately in need of farm produce to feed itself, did farming lift off; thereafter it became very profitable. But it was hard, challenging and often lonely work. It was on its back that the Colony grew and prospered.

However, it was the indigenous people who suffered, and it is their story that must be told now. Kenya was made up, before the arrival of the white man in the late 19th Century, of numerous tribes and tribal groupings. There is a strong suggestion[35] that these groupings were largely exaggerated, if not created, by the new colonial administration in order to create some degree of order or, to put it more bluntly, to make easier the principle of divide and rule. The principal tribe in Kenya upon colonisation is, and remains, the Gikuyu. I use this spelling and pronunciation, as opposed to the Anglicised Kikuyu, in deference to Jomo Kenyatta, from whom much of what I am going to communicate about them comes. He became in due course the 'Father of the Nation', the 'Burning Spear' and its first post-independence President.

It is from his anthropological study of the Gikuyu, *Facing Mount Kenya* that much of my material comes. This work, published in 1938, when Kenyatta was a student at LSE, thus long before the Mau Mau Insurgency, gives the reader a very clear and detailed – and prescient - account of Gikuyu life, customs, habits, religion and social organisation until the era of colonisation. From then on, it tells a story of dispossession, betrayal, crude misunderstanding and prejudice, all descending into the brutality that was visited upon the Gikuyu by British Imperialism.

---

[34]. Elkins, p.2

[35]. Meredith, p.154-5

Before going any further, it is necessary to put the Gikuyu into their historical and geographical setting. They happened to be the tribe that was predominantly settled in what came to be termed the White Highlands, just, that is, where the most fertile lands lay – Kiambu, Thika, and Nairobi, though the Kinangop was Maasai hunting lands. There were of course numerous other tribes, but it was the Gikuyu who suffered most. Kenyatta's grandmother was a Maasai; neighbouring tribes such as the Wakamba, Embu and Meru also were involved, if only involuntarily. As I have indicated, one merely had to imagine a wheat field lying before you to realise it, so rich and productive was the soil. Coffee, tea, pyrethrum; sisal, carnations, and plentiful cattle, sheep and pigs thrived and flourished once established. No wonder the British simply stole this land from the indigenous peoples, for this is what it amounts to. This was justified on the grounds that the native was little more than a savage and needed to be taught appropriate ways of agriculture, parenthood, religion: empire always has its missionising justifications, and these should not be forgotten as this narrative infolds.

The question of land is central to the whole issue and, reading Kenyatta's work, one cannot come away without a profound impression of the deep significance it held in Gikuyu life, thinking and even religion. Without it, no man could consider himself an adult worthy of respect; no woman could feel herself part of her society, her family or clan without attachment to the land. Having read what I have about this subject, I can only conclude that the savages from the outset were not the indigenous peoples.

Gikuyu society was not hierarchical, in any sense that we might recognise that word. To be sure, it was patriarchal and patrilineal, with the greatest respect being paid to the elders of the tribe. But there was no centralised authority: there were no chiefs. This is a most important fact, and will be crucial in the development of the Colony's history up to and beyond independence, for the British wilfully or deliberately ignored this fact. This society of agriculturists was based upon the family unit, this unit being headed by a father, and being *identified* with a parcel of land that served to provide all their needs of clothing and food. There existed until the time of their removal from the land eight different degrees or types of ownership; these we need not go into here. Land was owned privately, and ownership derived ultimately from Mogai, the Lord of Nature. As the population expanded, so more land was taken in from the forests.

There is something beautifully Edenic in Kenyatta's account of this so perhaps we should not conceive of it all being as harmonious as he presents it. Nevertheless, the tradition of land ownership and its nature is so fundamentally different from British understanding that this led in part to the dismissive attitudes regarding Gikuyu society, with all its baleful consequences. Family being traditionally the all-important unit in the social structure, there developed a complex and careful system of relationship whereby clan or extended family, remained as a unit, and still tied to the same original land, however that might have been extended by purchase or by felling. Finally, in this brief and wholly simplified attempt to distinguish the nature of Gikuyu land tenure, it was intricately part and parcel of inheritance, marriage, payment and the system of seniority, as at all stages the rituals of such occasions were facilitated by the exchange of land and/or its produce. In other words, everything was done in respect of Mogai in all aspects of daily life; and, of course, by and large one's entire lifetime would have been spent in this one context.

What happened with the arrival of the Europeans, and the building of the railway? In short, the Gikuyu (as with other tribes) lost their land. Kenyatta gives an account of the early contact between them and the incomers, first traders and explorers, then railway workers and finally with those settling in the environs of the 'metal snake'[36]. Kenyatta's account is, of course, one sided, but it rings true since the Gikuyu did not bring upon themselves this change in their history and circumstances.

At first, he says, the Gikuyu, as was their custom, welcomed the newcomers with kindness and generosity, since they recognised them as being perhaps lonely, and certainly a long way from home. It did not take long for the strangers to recognise a good thing when they saw it. Soon tents became wooden huts, then these mutated into fortified buildings. Word had got back that this area of Kenya provided a valuable staging post on the route to Uganda and the interior. Kenyatta quotes one Lord Lugard: 'The object of a station is to form a centre for the purchase of food for caravans proceeding to Uganda,' for 'Kikuyu was reported a land where food was abundant and cheap.' So it began, and so it was why my father ended up there.[37]

Mt Kenya

However, indiscipline amongst the newcomers led to the theft of food, leading to reprisals from the Gikuyu, which in turn led to punishment from the Europeans, despite Lugard's making a kind of treaty with those he termed chiefs, one of whom was deported and died on his way to the coast. Outraged, the Gikuyu declined to trade any further, in the hope that the caravans would go away from their country. Some hope. Armed with 'magical sticks which spat fire' the incomers soon took over the Gikuyu lands with ease, the natives having nothing more threatening than spears and short swords, turned them into 'Crown Lands' in which the Gikuyu were to live as tenants of His Imperial British Majesty[38].In summing up this process of forced acquisition, Kenyatta writes with considerable anger: 'The Gikuyu lost most of their lands through magnanimity, for the Gikuyu country was never wholly conquered by force of arms, but the people were put under the ruthless domination of European imperialism through the insidious trickery of hypocritical treaties.' They were taught that 'might is right'[39]. In the end, the Gikuyu were restricted to the tribal reserves, whilst the British established themselves on territory extending along the line of the Great Rift Valley as far west to Kitale on the Ugandan border, north beyond Mt Kenya to Maralal, and south again to fifty or so miles south-east of Nairobi. The Mau Mau Uprising took place in and around Nairobi, in the White Highlands as far north-west to Nakuru, in the Aberdare Mountains and in the foothills of Mt Kenya.

However, it was not just land that was taken. Perhaps a less aggressive, greedy race would have recognised *something* of the pre-lapsarian nature of the existence of the indigenous people. The British, however, regarded the native Kenyans as being little more than primitive

---

36 . Kenyatta, p.21-2

37 . 'The Rise of Our East African Empire', by Lord Lugard. Quoted by Kenyatta, p.45

38 . From 'The Blue Book of Africa', no.18 (1893). Quoted by Kenyatta, p.47

39 . Kenyatta, p.194 etc

savages, in a state, at best, of ignorance and stupidity. This, as I have suggested, was far from the case. Kenyatta gives a very convincing and detailed account of all aspects of Gikuyu life, society, including marriage and sexual relations, and governance. It is very hard to believe that it would take, as the colonialists liked to claim, at least a generation for the African to even begin to come up to European standards and intelligence, if not a hundred years. In order to therefore 'civilise' the newly colonised, they set about destroying much of Gikuyu custom, habit and culture.

For example, Gikuyu governance, prior to colonisation was, as Kenyatta describes it[40], collectivist, lacking anything like the individualistic ethos of the European. In order that this way of doing things be maintained, authority was passed every thirty years or so from one generation to the next at what was termed an *itwika*. The first occasion this was to take place in the colonial times was in 1925-8. It would have involved a range of ceremonies and much singing and dancing. The Government, however, regarded this as 'seditious', and banned it. Thus, as Kenyatta puts it, 'the new generation had been denied the birthright of perpetuating national pride.' He becomes angry and bitter, pouring scorn on a British White Paper of 1923 which 'declared the mission of Great Britain' was 'to work continuously for the education and training of the African towards a higher intellectual, moral and economic level' than it was claimed existed when Britain 'assumed responsibility' for these people.

Instead, Kenyatta writes, as his people had been reduced to serfdom, so had his initiative in governance removed, his 'manhood killed'. Furthermore, since the lands were ancestral, and since they were always owned and cultivated with posterity in mind, this deracination takes on an even more destructive nature. 'The dead, the living and the unborn' were, to the Gikuyu part of an organic whole, through which 'custom, law and morality are maintained'[8]. It is not surprising that the *moral* nature of the people was undermined, and thereby contributed in no small way to the atrocities that the Mau Mau committed. Elkins concurs with this: 'Land and family entitled (the Gikuyu) to certain privileges' as 'without land, a man would remain socially a boy. A woman needed land to grow crops to nurture and sustain her family. . . . A Gikuyu could not be a Gikuyu without land'[41].

I will come back to this shortly, but it suffices to say here that the British replaced the collectivist rule of the various tribes with that one exercised through tribal chieftains, a concept that was very foreign to the Gikuyu. It was when one of these chiefs was assassinated on October 9th, 1952 that the Emergency was declared. Before that, however, the British had banned much of the Gikuyu way of life, as well as denying them the rights that the British, my father amongst them, had apparently fought a long and difficult war to preserve: freedom of speech, movement, association and so on. (Kenyatta reports that his own father even had his calabashes confiscated on the grounds that might have been part of some 'primitive' ritual). Indeed, I want to suggest in due course how the treatment of particularly the Gikuyu echoed the treatment of the Jews by the Nazis in many ways. There may not have been the gas chambers; there may well have been, though, a deliberate policy to exterminate them, or at least drastically reduce their population through starvation, illness and brutality. There were certainly concentration camps.

---

40 . Kenyatta, 213

41 . ibid

To begin with, the Gikuyu were forced into reserves, as increasing numbers of white immigrants took over their land. They were forced into a wage economy, something quite alien; they were taxed, and a tax was put upon their huts – and since many were not in employment, the tax could not be paid[42]. Furthermore, in a precursor to South Africa's hated Apartheid Pass Laws, all men leaving their reserves were obliged to carry a small tin container around their necks called a *kipande*. This held everything that would identify that man: name, tribal grouping, finger-prints, employment record and so on. This loathed item finally reduced the Gikuyu male to the status of animal: 'I was no longer a shepherd, but one of the flock, going to work on the white man's farm with my *mbugi*, or goat's bell, around my neck.'[43] Failure to have it would lead to serious punishment, a fine or imprisonment or both.

Detailed discussion of a whole range of further repressive measures, designed deliberately to inhibit black productivity in favour of white, is beyond the scope of this paper, suffice to say that they cumulatively acted to destroy and dispirit the local populace. One needs mentioning, however; I touched upon it above: the creation of chiefs. These men were co-opted, according to Elkins account, 'in order to enforce discipline and control over local populations'[44]. Loathed as they became, they were given great rewards, including large parcels of land, in order to keep them on side. As the Insurgency developed, the colonial authorities created two further groups who would act as their proxies and agents during it: the so-called 'Home Guard' and the 'loyalists', comprising those Africans who were coerced in one way or another into supporting the Government and its actions. The existence of these virtually assured that the Insurgency became a civil war between different Gikuyu groups. Only 32 white civilians, with about a further seventy military or police, were killed, whilst about 12,000 Mau Mau were killed in military operations. The number of civilian blacks killed ranges from the 'official' ten or eleven thousand to an unofficial 300,000.

Before I go into the response of the white government, both in Kenya and in London, the issue of coercion needs to be addressed. The absolute terror that an event like the death of my little friend created in the minds of the white settler community, especially those who lived in isolated farms, was manifest and obviously justifiable. There are also the on-going tropes of imperial rule: never trust a black man near your women, for fear of their rampant, uncontrolled sexual prowess, never trust the servants, all blacks are basically savages beneath a thin veneer of civilisation: these are all standard. There was one which, with some justification, filled people of *all* races with even great fear and disgust, and this was oath-taking.

The Mau Mau was distinct from other insurgencies in other parts of the Empire, in that it had a very basic, non-ideological basis: a powerful sense of grievance against the injustices I have described together with a powerful wish that the whites be driven form the ancestral lands, or be killed. It was as simple as this: there was no ideology behind it, certainly no communist or socialist thinking – or indeed, input from behind the Iron Curtain. Its intellectual leaders like Kenyatta were essentially conservative in outlook and idea (as he was later to prove only too conclusively); its military leadership, despite its adoption of British military ranks – Field-

---

42 . Elkins, p.14
43 . Elkins, p.16
44 . Elkins, p.18

Marshall Kimathi, General China – seem to me largely re-enacted the roles played in former times by tribal warriors.

It was the oath which bound the Mau Mau together. In its essence, it was atavistic, crude and repellent to Western minds – and, indeed to African minds, as it was meant to be. It came out of a dark part of Gikuyu culture; this needs to be outlined, and I want to argue that, given all that has been said above, its arrival was, in retrospect, only too predictable.

In *Facing Mount Kenya*, Kenyatta is merely describing the world into which he was born and in which he grew up. He knew it intimately, and although he writes with an academic's objectivity, one feels that it was a world that he loved; yet he is not uncritical of it. The penultimate chapter is entitled 'Magical Practices'. Most of it deals with beneficial practices; the last section, however, is concerned with 'Destructive Magic – Witchcraft. Orogi. Poison'. In essence, this section deals with methods of dealing with anyone who had cast evil spells. What is relevant here is as follows. The evil witch doctor, or group of them, known as an *arogi*, is able to spread real terror amongst the local people for their presumed powers. This was plainly then exploited by the Mau Mau in order to coerce and terrify their own people into supporting them. A gruesome poison – *orogi* – is mixed together in order for the evil to take place. Ingredients, as Kenyatta recounts, begin with ashes, poisonous herbs and roots. Animal parts are also added, especially the internal organs. However, also part of the mixture are human parts: 'the genital organs of both male and female, breasts, tongues, ears, hands and feet, blood, eyes, noses. These have been 'extracted from human bodies, the victims of the magician's work'[45].

These elements seem to coincide exactly with very disturbing and gruesome descriptions in Robert Ruark's 1962 novel, *Uhuru*. Whilst it is hard to exculpate Ruark from bias (he was a white American who cast himself in something of a Hemingway-mould, taking a powerful liking to Kenya, at least to *white* Kenya), I sense that his descriptions have veracity, though I cannot find any supporting evidence of human sacrifice. However, I must stress that Kenyatta's account is of the evil that this black magic amounts to, and the ways in which it was dealt with in tribal society. In no way does he approve or extol it[46].

The oathing ceremonies took place under a sacred Giant Fig-Tree. There seem to have been various degrees to it. At first, it was mild, even if dire in its consequences. It seems to have degenerated into something more and more ghastly as the Uprising went on, and as it faced its ultimate and predictable failure. In essence it meant: Are you with us? If not, you are against us, and we will deal with you. And if you fail to do as we demand in support of our cause and people, we will also deal with you – by death. Faced with this and with oppression from the whites, things could not have been easy for the Gikuyu people. If ordered to do so, an oath taker would have had kill a white farmer, his employer and his wife and children, as in the case I have already mentioned, for fear for being killed himself. It is reckoned[47] that 90% of the 1.5 million Gikuyu took the oath, for whatever reason, though we should bear in mind the powerful connection to land in Gikuyu mind.

Nevertheless, Oliver Lyttelton, the Colonial secretary during the first part of the Emergency, father of Humphrey and cousin & friend of my grandfather, wrote, 'The Mau Mau oath is the

---

[45]. Kenyatta, p.307
[46]. See Appendix B, for Ruark examples
[47]. Elkins, p.54

most bestial, filthy and nauseating incantation. . . . . I have never felt the forces of evil to be so near. . . . As I write memoranda or instruction. . . I would suddenly see a shadow fall across the page, the horned shadow of the devil himself.'[48]

As most unattractive as this might seem, this dark, atavistic ritual is, in my view, only the natural outcome of the deliberate subversion of a culture that had been up-rooted, turned inside out and its people reduced to serfdom, their pride and spirit broken. This type of thing seems typical: the destruction of ancient ethos and ways of life leaves little recourse but for its now deeply alienated people to retreat into actions and activities that would have been quite forbidden formerly, into the dark side of their tribal practices. After all, *these* were not banned, as being unknown. One thinks, for example, of the Taliban/Al Qaeda and suicide bombers. It is also the case that insurgents will turn upon anyone of their own people who they feel has betrayed them – recall the IRA, or the French on the collaborators after the end of the Second World War. From the Mau Mau point of view, it is perhaps the darkest part of their story – though not nearly as dark as what was to follow.

However, as is usual in cases such as these, the Insurgents are destined in the long run to win; the settlers and their local government, and the Government, first under Churchill, then Eden and Macmillan, were generally fighting a rear-guard battle. The settlers were desperate to keep things as they had been, the Governor, an aristocratic figure called Sir Evelyn Baring, a scion of the banking family, was forced to play them off against London. The British Government was well aware that the Empire was collapsing around them, and although it was willing to provide funds for the military operations and for the setting up and running of detention camps, it simply did not have the resources to do the job properly. It is interesting also, that virtually no outside countries came to the help of the Mau Mau, even though the Insurgency took place at the height of the Cold War.

In the first instance, the military battle was easily won by the British. The few guns, spears and occasional heavier weaponry were no match at all for the far superior fire power in the latter's hands. This is not to say that the fighting in the forests of The Aberdares was easy. The settlers established informal commando units – referred to as 'pseudogangs', such as I have alluded to in the anecdote about Obama *grandpere* above. These units were very ruthless and brutal, as the description from Ruark bears witness to[49]. But by the end of 1955, the war was effectively won. The Mau Mau military commanders, such as Dedan Kimathi, the most feared of all their commanders, were either arrested, dead or executed. Kenyatta himself, with five of his colleagues, had been arrested in November, 1952, and, after a show trial in which the sitting judge, imported from Britain at a cost of £20,000 (he later boasted that this was his price for the right verdict), and in which witnesses were also bribed (as they later admitted), was sentenced to seven years hard labour at a place called Lokitaung, a desolate outpost in the far northwest of the country and inaccessible to all but his guardians – and what a ghastly detail that must have proved. Kenyatta was 63 by this time and was expected to spend the rest of his life there. He died at the age of 88 after seventeen years as president. The uprising was easily defeated, but only militarily.

Why, then, the 10,000 or one hundred or three hundred thousand dead? Why the detention camps, the screening, the so-called Pipeline, why the uprooting of 40,000 Gikuyu and others

---

[48]. Quoted by Elkins, p.50

[49]. Also Appendix B

in April 1954 in Operation Anvil? Why the brutality, the torture, the mass executions, the 'villagisation' and the burning of huts and farm-land? And the Hola massacre, which brought it all to a pitiful end?

Lyttelton's attitude, as he sat in his London office, can be regarded as luridly self-indulgent. Perhaps, though, it was the attitude of the white settlers themselves displacing their guilt associated with the expropriation and general maltreatment - and the consequent fear of revenge - that lies behind what followed. The virulent, violent and hateful racism of the whites is quite astonishing, if Elkins is to be believed[50]. To the whites, the Mau Mau in particular, if not Africans in general, were 'vermin', 'animals' and 'barbarians' living in hovels seething with mud and animals.' Anthony Sampson, the journalist, reports hearing everywhere people asking, 'How many Kukes had to be gotten rid of, how many Kukes did you kill today.' 'The only good Kuke is a dead one.' I can go on, as Elkins does, at length. It makes for painful reading.

Even a more moderate settler, like Michael Blundell, the would-be Iain Smith of Kenya and lover of my aunt, called for 'drastic action' and a shoot-to-kill' policy. However, General Sir George Erskine, who took charge of military operations shortly after the start of the Emergency and who was grandfather of my first boy-hood passion, loathed with almost equal virulence the settlers: 'I hate the guts of them all. They are middle class sluts.'[51]

Perhaps behind it all was the fear a declining empire had of losing face. India had been the Empire's 'Jewel in the Crown', but no longer. Kenya became its replacement. Its administration and ruling elite had close ties to the ruling British Establishment, as I indicate. Ian MacLeod, the final Colonial Secretary in this shaming story, had a brother who was a Kenyan settler farmer. However, the more futile the struggle to maintain the status quote became, the more disgraceful the measures to try to do so.

The assassination of Chief Waruhiu on the 9th October, 1952 is in many senses the start of the Insurgency. He was the most hated of the Chiefs – he'd gone so far to have modelled himself on a particularly foppish type of upper middle class Englishman. The Emergency was put in place soon after, and there then started the process, as Elkins puts it, of 're-establishing colonial domination in Kenya' by 'creating one of the most restrictive police states in the history of the empire' and 'by deploying unspeakable terror and violence.'[52]

In the first place, there was mass deportation of those Gikuyu who had squatted on white farms – it had been the practice for blacks to live and work on unused 'white' land, often undercutting the owners' prices. Those repatriated were forced into transit camps, often for months – there was no space or place for them in the reserves – and this is a feature of much of what follows. Next followed a process termed 'screening'. This hated process apparently has no word in Kiswahili or Gikuyu. In essence, individuals were examined for supposed Mau Mau sympathies or allegiances, or to see whether the oath had been taken. There was much brutality involved, especially as the screening centres were mainly staffed by settlers or their acolytes, the so-called loyalists. Elkins quotes from two survivors of these camps she spoke to many years later whilst she was doing her research:

---

[50]. Elkins, p.49 etc

[51]. Elkins, p.50

[52]. Elkins, p.61

We would be asked whether we had taken the oath, and those who denied taking it were beaten badly until they were forced to confess. . . . many died from their beatings.

Another witness:

To be interrogated meant to be beaten. . . . You would be hit there, you would be beaten here [on the stomach, on the back] very hard. You would place your legs thus, and be hit on the ankle and the other. . . .

Elkins continues, her evidence garnered from scores whom she interviewed: 'Electric shock was also used, as well as cigarettes and fire. Bottles (often broken), gun barrels, knives, snakes, vermin and hot eggs were thrust up into men's rectums and women's vaginas. The screening teams often whipped, shot, burned and mutilated Mau Mau suspects.'

As seems to be so often the case, circumstances such as these allowed to rise to the forefront particularly savage and even psychopathic men, who led and even revelled in the torture. As their English names were not known, they were soon given nicknames by their victims; Kiboroboro, or the Killer, More More, the Whip, the One with the Crooked Nose. All these were white. There was a certain Dr Bunny, one of whose trademark techniques was to burn the skin off suspects' bodies, another to make them eat their own testicles. This man was, I recall, our family doctor. Given the attitudes outlined earlier, none of this is hardly surprising.

I make no apology for these horrifying details – there is much more in the same vein. One can only ask: who were the savages?

And the savagery was extensive, thorough and widespread, in the cities, towns and on the farms of the settlers. To be fair, the Mau Mau had themselves carried out two massacres, in March, 1953. The first was at Naivasha (our home town), when the police station was attacked. The second was at a place called Lari, outside Nairobi. Here was the homestead of the hated Chief Luka – who had been given vast land concessions. 97 residents were killed, young and old, male and female. The Government made this into a *cause celebre*. Vengeful reprisals accounted for more than four times that many. And in a small village near Fort Hall, government forces opened fire upon a large gathering at a peaceful meeting, listening to a young 'prophet' who was foretelling the end of British Rule. Nearly one hundred were murdered when police opened fire, their bodies afterwards dumped into a nearby shallow grave.[53]

Nevertheless, the Mau Mau, in these early days of the Insurgency attacked and indeed slaughtered in ways most cruel many of the chiefs, the loyalists and the members of the Home Guard. These, though, the Government continued to be handsomely rewarded for their support. But this was war, and terrible things happen in war. The British prided themselves on their 'civilisation', but as Elkins puts it, 'By relentlessly subjecting the minds and bodies of Mau Mau suspects to violence during screening, the British colonisers and their loyalist sympathisers were able to confirm in their own minds that the oath takers were subhuman and themselves paragons of civility.'[54]

---

[53]. These details can be found in Elkins, ch. 3. There is a very great deal more in the same vein.

[54]. Elkins, p.90

It is difficult in a short space to give a concise and accurate picture of the effects of British policy towards the Gikuyu in general and the Mau Mau in particular. (Other tribes were to be partially involved, though any trouble from them, like from the Maasai, was quickly and ruthlessly stamped upon). However, I will touch upon four central elements: detention and detention camps, rehabilitation and the Pipeline, villagisation, and the masking of the truth from the British public.

As far as the first is concerned, the crucial date is 24th April, 1954. On that day, General Erskine launched 'Operation Anvil'. Without warning, some 40,000 of Nairobi's black inhabitants were arrested. With what in hindsight has profound historical irony, this day became known as 'D-day'. District after district was sealed off, and the people taken into custody, with what was described as 'Gestapo-like' efficiency': 'Pack one bag, leave the rest of your belongings in your home. . . ,' blared the loudspeakers[55]. Some were lucky and were later released; most were not. A *gakunia*, a Gikuyu loyalist with a sack over his head to prevent recognition, had the power to send to detention anyone he felt like so doing with a quick a nod of his head. A screening centre, followed by a detention camp was the destiny of up to 70,000. Within a fortnight, Nairobi was 'cleansed' of all Gikuyu. And such it was: ethnic cleansing.

This presented the authorities with a serious problem: many had been rounded up beforehand and sent to the camps; these were now 'over-crowded and on the verge of ecological collapse.'[56] There were very many of these camps, of one type or another. When one takes into account the 'villages' created to 'protect' the Gikuyu left on farms and in the reserves, there were some 850 of them, of varying sizes. The largest of these was probably Manyani; there was a similar one at Mackinnon Road, both well away from the Gikuyu areas, on the road to Mombasa and the coast. There were about 20 other major ones, one of which was at Embakasi, now the site of Nairobi's international airport. Its runway was first laid by the prisoners. For the most hardened Mau Mau, there were two especially unpleasant camps. One was far away on Mageta Island on Lake Victoria, the other off-shore on Manda Island at Lamu, at the northern end of Kenya's coast-line. Prisoners here were kept in virtual isolation, with little hope of reprieve or escape, though there was an escape from the former. Men, women, boys and girls, often separated from parents, suffered terribly from malnutrition, cruelty, fear, loneliness and uncertainty - and the brutality.

The purpose of these camps was to weed out the die-hard 'terrorists', to force confessions and recantations of the Mau Mau oaths, and to generally terrorise the people. This was government policy. However, it left a serious problem: what to do with the thousands and thousands of Gikuyu in these camps. As indicated the hard-core were dealt with as above. The pressure on the reserves to sustain their populations was growing all the time; indeed it was exacerbated by the agricultural policies of the administration: land belonging to subsistence farmers, as it was seen, was regarded as being unproductive and useless. It was simply seized, and given to 'loyalists' and to the chiefs in ever larger portions. They did not know how to use this land. As prisoners were released, and returned to the reserves, it rapidly became apparent that there was nothing for them to go back to, so they migrated once again to Nairobi – thus indicating the utter pointlessness of Operation Anvil.

---

[55]. Elkins, p.121-3

[56]. Elkins, p.125

These camps were policed by white officers, with black guards or *askaris* doing much of the brutal spade work. But whites set the tone and the example. There was one, nick-named Kenda-Kenda or Nine-Nine[57]. He had 'a penchant for singling out the ninth in a line of detainees. . . . He would reach number nine, and whomever that person was, he would beat them mercilessly. He particularly liked stomping on people and there would be blood and brains splattered everywhere. . . . The unfortunate ninth man was sometimes rolled inside a coil of barbed wire by the *askaris* and Kenda-Kenda would start kicking him around, screaming at the man, calling him a "bloody Mau Mau".'[58]

I pick out just this one example; Elkins' central chapters are full of details and recollections such as this. They make, obviously, for painful and disturbing reading. These camps were dreadful places by any standards. It is interesting, though, to recall at this point that the British had infamously developed the idea of the concentration camp in the Boer War some fifty years before. These had been observed by a German officer called von Epp, who tried out the practice against the Namib and Herero peoples of what was then German Southwest Africa. He later advised Hitler on how to put in effect the Final Solution. As I commented above, Britain had just fought a war to put an end to this sort of thing.

However, there was an inherent contradiction in all of this. The so-called Pipeline was devised by an idealistic yet naïve Englishman called Thomas Askwith. A visiting Tory M.P. had urged upon the Governor the necessity for 'rehabilitation'. He had seen what was happening, and whilst generally supporting the Governor's and the military efforts, felt that things could not be left as they were. Urging upon Baring the need to 'win hearts and minds' in order to win the wider war, he pointed the way in which something could be done to redress the situation. Askwith, who was working with the Prisons Department, was charged with coming up with a plan. Indeed, he did come up with one, which went rather beyond anything the Governor was prepared to accept. Elkins comments that had it been put in place as intended, Askwith's name would have gone down as that of great social reformer.

However, as she puts it: 'The Pipeline was a microcosm where the contradictions and antagonisms between Kikuyu and European societies were brought to a boiling intensity and the world behind the barbed wire rendered utterly transparent, for the first time, the dark side of Britain's colonial project. The hypocrisies, the exploitations, the violence, and the suffering were all laid bare in the Pipeline. It was there that Britain finally revealed the true nature of its civilising mission.'

The idea behind the Pipeline was thus: the process of rehabilitation involved screening and then transfer from screening camp to detention camp, during which time an individual's affiliation to and attitude towards the Mau Mau would be determined. Prisoners were graded – back, grey and white – according to how hardened they were. The most hardened were sent, as mentioned, to distant detention centres and kept under very severe conditions. For the rest, a period of retraining, or indoctrination (including de-oathing ceremonies) and training in such areas as crafts, suitable (i.e. Western) agricultural techniques and so on would take place. Finally, the 'surrenders', as those who had recanted were called, were returned to their reservations, ideally to start a new life in the full realisation of the benefits of English culture now ingrained.

---

57 . Elkins, p.156

58 . Elkins, p.157

It will be no surprise to hear that it did not quite work out like this. As indicated, the process really involved nothing more than lengthy and multiple torture practices meted out in order to break the wills and minds of the detainees. Beatings, castrations, summary and often random execution – these seems to have been up to the inventiveness of the white guards and officers and their 'loyalist' assistants in devising ever more awful means of extraction confessions and recantations. Hard labour was also very much part of the process, like the building of the new airport for Nairobi. One former inmate recalled this at what became known as 'Satan's Paradise'[59]:

> *The askaris and the Wazungu (Europeans) did not need any good excuse in order to beat a Mau Mau to death. Some people used to go crazy during our porridge when they remembered they would go to the fields to do the back-breaking work. Some would go mad and pick up the toilet buckets and start splashing everybody while at the same time screaming. Some would place their hands on the ndaba (soil carriers on rails) so as to sever their limbs and escape from the work.*

On top of this were illnesses, brought on in very obvious ways: constant exposure to the weather, dreadful and limited food, and very poor hygiene. All this applied to both men's and women's camps. Starvation was an increasingly active weapon in the process of rehabilitation, it seems, and as I will outline below, outside the system. However, there is one aspect that needs touching on, and it is perhaps, in this section, the most disturbing. Rape, of one sort or another of forced penetrative sex of both male and female prisoners was widespread. Elkins offers an explanation of this[60]. It was bound up with the almost primordial white fear of the 'black man's purported sexuality'. This 'black peril' was, as she puts it 'certainly a threat to European male sexuality and, by extension, to Europe's ability to establish and maintain dominance over their African colonies.' This has about it the air of cod-psychology; nevertheless, such stereotyping would seem to be common-place in the literature and discourses about colonialism. Furthermore, since the process of colonial settlement in Kenya at least, as I suggested earlier, involved stripping the Gikuyu of their land, and therefore of their very manhood, and since the basis of the treatment of the detainees in the camps was to degrade and destroy them mentally, there would seem to be some coherence in this argument: to emasculate, de-nature, to dehumanise. But as I have mentioned before, the savagery came from one side only. If it is true – and I have only given you a glimpse of the horrors involved – then we are really at the nadir.

Though not yet. Chapter Eight of Elkins' work deals with what I consider the worst aspect of the whole matter: villagisation. I make no apologies in advance for some of the details I use to exemplify this. What did it involve? In the first place, it needs to be made clear that, prior to colonisation, and indeed today and throughout sub-Saharan Africa, the village, such as we know it, is not the basic unit of habitation. Gikuyu land-owning custom worked this: a few huts would contain the family and close relatives (like other African tribes, the Gikuyu were polygamous); there might be open space and hedged in sections, or *bomas* for the animals to be protected from predators. Finally, there would be the *shambas* or fields. Such an

---

59 . Elkins, p.188

60 . Elkins, p.208

arrangement would provide for the family, and there would be space between one settlement and another. Look at any photograph of rural Africa to see this.

In June, 1954, in other words just a few weeks after the fateful Operation Anvil was put in place, the government embarked upon its policy of 'villagisation', so that within the next eighteen months over a million Gikuyu were forcibly removed from their land and homes and put in camps surrounded by barbed wire, a ditch with spikes in, and looked over by watch-towers. Nobody was asked if they wanted this; it was to be for their good, however, to protect them from the Mau Mau. Indeed, the hapless Askwith, and one or two others, saw this as an ideal opportunity to further the rehabilitation process. To be fair to the British, the smallholders had offered a supply line to the fighters in the forests. The authorities wanted this cut off; they wanted a simple means of controlling every aspect of Gikuyu life outside the detention camps. It should also be born in mind that most of the people who found themselves in these new villages were the women, children and the old and sick.

Elkins description of the process of villagisation is graphic indeed: 'The sight and smell of the burning of wattle and roof thatching hung thickly over Kenya's Central Province throughout the second half of 1954.'[61] The forced removals in themselves appal: while British officers supervised, the Home Guards did the dirty work. Torching, beating and destruction were everywhere in those months. Confused and terrified Africans suddenly and without warning were evicted from their homes. Everything was lost: property, cooking utensils, clothing, farming implements, animals, and, worse of all, some were trapped in their huts and burned alive. What wasn't destroyed, was taken by the Home Guard for their own use. One elderly woman recalled for Elkins, many years later:

> *One only saved what one was wearing at the time! . . . During the move, I got separated from my children, and I could not trace them. They had been in front, leading our remaining cattle, but I failed to find them. During the whole night I could hear a lot of shooting and screaming. I cried the whole night, knowing that my children were gone.*[62]

And what were they moved to? Nothing, 'save a cordon of armed loyalists. . . . There was no shelter, food, water, sanitation facilities or medical supplies.'[63] In other words, the whole exercise was as a punishment of the whole Gikuyu community. It took months for the villagers themselves, with limited resources supplied by the government, to build their own camps. These consisted, as well as the things mentioned above, of small round huts in very cramped and close proximity to one another. In these up to ten families might be made to live, with communal cooking on inadequate stoves, with a bucket for a toilet. One recalled:

> *We were ordered to go into the forests to get logs and cut reeds, to construct more houses. Even me, with my two-day old baby, had to carry thatching reeds.*

Once the village was in place, it became nothing more than a prison, its inmates confined there at night and forced into hard labour during the day. This often consisted of the laying of terraces on the hillsides for rice to be cultivated – a crop quite foreign to Kenya. From morning to night, it appears that the Gikuyu – mainly women – were made to work as above,

---

[61]. Elkins, p.238
[62]. Elkins, p.240
[63]. Elkins, p.240

or doing pointless tasks, like digging trenches for no apparent reason. Slacking was instantly punished by a blow to the back or the head. 'Singing, talking, eating and drinking were all forbidden during forced labour.'[64] Deaths from exhaustion, brutality and hunger were frequent. Corpses would be thrown unceremoniously into the trenches.

I mentioned earlier that there may well have been a deliberate intention to kill as many Gikuyu as possible, though Elkins denies this. While there may not have been any articulated 'final solution', reading as one has done in the story of the Mau Mau leaves one with the definite impression that much that was done to them had this at least as an unspoken intention. Indeed, so much of the brutality seems spontaneous; it grew, feeding on the instinctual impulses of racism, then was repeated until it became habitual, the conSciences of the perpetrators dulled into silence by its frequency and its banality. Nevertheless, the brutal repression was encouraged and supervised by British officers and officials, settlers and police, even if much was carried out by their black underlings. These, as Elkins points out, did have choice, but they ran the risk of themselves being accused if they objected or disobeyed orders. Elkins quotes the Auschwitz survivor, Primo Levi, to answer the question of why it is that some can be made to act in ways that are inhuman to their own kind: "If one offers a position of privilege to a few individuals in a state of slavery exacting in exchange the betrayal of a natural solidarity with their comrades, some will accept."[65] This 'privilege' amounted to excessive freedom.

If a woman in one of the 'villages' was suspected of Mau Mau sympathies, she would be seized, thoroughly beaten and, then, taken to an *ndaki*, or underground holding cell. One such was filled with four feet of water and covered by a thick matting, making it dark. There might be a dozen or more other captives, struggling together for warmth and comfort, desperate to avoid snakes or vermin, presumably deliberately allowed to be there.

Once released the woman could expect further torture, such as the 'squeezing and mutilating women's breasts with pliers, pushing vermin or rifles into the vagina, forcing them to run around naked with buckets of excrement on their heads. Resistance could result in immediate execution.'

Rape was commonplace. All women lived in the villages in constant fear of sexual assault:

> *The white officers had no shame. They would rape women in full view of everyone. They would take whomever they wanted at one corner and do it just there*[66].

One poor woman records that one morning she went to work with her baby tied on her back. Focussed on her work for some time for fear of punishment, she was unaware that the baby had become silent. When she looked, it was dead.

Finally, the following passage sums it all up. One man, Simon Rutho, told Elkins this story. One of the few men left in his village, there was little he could do to help.

> *I remember in our village was a headman. . . from Kiamariga. He was a very cruel man. Whenever he desired a woman, he would take a beer bottle then*

---

[64] . Elkins, p.243

[65] . Elkins, p.185

[66] . Elkins, p.247

order an askari to hold one of the woman's legs, and another to hold the other, wide apart. Then he would insert a bottle into the woman's private parts and punch it up into the stomach. Many women died after being treated in this way. . . . Nobody cared about them. The village men would be told to go and bury them in the village when they died. . . . So many died. I remember a few years ago a farmer who was digging in his shamba exhumed a human skull into which a sweet potato had grown. The skull was taken to the local school, for the young children to see how it had been buried. The area around where the skull had been found had been the village graveyard, and if you tried digging there you would unearth skeletons of people who were buried at that time. Nobody cared about the village people[67].

Of course there was brutality by blacks on blacks, but it was with the deliberate acquiescence of the whites, in the way that Primo Levi's remark suggests. The terrible licence granted lead to horrors such as this, and to the haunting, almost unbearable poignancy of discovery in later years. And was the white fear of black sexual potency itself so terribly potent that it unleashed itself with such savagery?

*

By the end of 1955, the military battle was over. What was a rag-tag, poorly equipped, organised and led uprising of some 20,000 men and a few women armed with nothing more potent than rifles, often home-made, spears, *pangas* and *simis* or short swords, was no match at all for a force equipped with modern weaponry and fighter-bombers? Nevertheless, there was growing opposition in Britain against the treatment of the Gikuyu. A young Barbara Castle made her name as a parliamentarian to be feared by her persistent questions in the House of Commons; she also visited Kenya, earning the disgust of the settlers for her refusal to be hoodwinked. She earned the nickname of 'That Castellated Bitch', something I imagine her to have been quite proud of. She was helped by others such as the veteran Fenner Brockway. There was, too, some objection from Kenya residents, some black and Asian, and from some sectors of the white population, though many of them were in ignorance of what was being done in their name. Letters by the detainees were smuggled out of the camps, a few managing to get past the authorities; one or two even reached the Queen. Then there was Eileen Fletcher. She must have been a remarkable woman. She was a former rehabilitation officer, who had realised what it was really about. She was a Quaker, with impeccable credentials having been trained as a social worker, and had worked in Europe in the field after the War. Her articles, published in the Quaker periodical, *Peace News*. These had 'an electrifying effect'[68], and did indeed lead to improvements in conditions, especially for juveniles.

However, continued obfuscation, deceit, ignoring of requests for information and facts by both the colonial government under Baring, and by the new Colonial Secretary, Alan Lennox-Boyd, did much to keep the lid on things. The latter must have lied frequently to the House of Commons. Thus, although the Insurgency was largely defeated by Christmas 1955 (when we returned to a safer Kenya), the emergency was not lifted until 1960, following one

---

[67]. Elkins, p.245

[68]. Elkins, p.288

last outrage, the notorious Hola Massacre early in March, 1959. At first the Government tried to cover it up saying that the ten prisoners had died from drinking contaminated water; however, the truth about their violent deaths got out. This, following a showdown debate in the House of Commons on February 24th of that year in which an independent enquiry into the handling of the situation in the colony was voted down on party lines, made it obvious that the game could no longer be played.

In a further debate later that summer, about which Barbara Castle, who spoke for forty-five minutes, said that she was "trembling so much with anger that she could hardly get her words out,"[69], it was, perhaps surprisingly, Enoch Powell who called the Government's bluff, by demanding of the Colonial Secretary that he "ensure that the responsibility is recognised and carried where it belongs, and is seen to belong."

It was the beginning of the end. In fact, the British, in my judgement, had run out of will and interest. Macmillan's famous 'Winds of Change' speech in Capetown in 1959 had indicated not only this but a truth that had to be acknowledged: the days of the British Empire were numbered. All that remained was for negotiations with local leaders to arrange for independence. In Kenya, no leader would come forward: negotiations could not begin until Kenyatta was released. This was duly achieved in 1961; in 1963, Kenya became Kenya. There was an amnesty for all Mau Mau prisoners (though it was not unbanned till 2003). However, Britain got the independent country it wanted: a west-leaning, capitalist state under the conservative rule of an aging president, who had himself never been in favour of the Mau Mau. There never was an enquiry in to policies of the colonial government; no memorial was ever raised for the 100,000 or more victims of the repressions (half of whom were children), and even today, proceedings for compensation are winding their way at a snail's pace through the legal system. Kenya became the country it is today: over-populated, with vast differences in wealth, with corruption and cronyism at the heart all-pervasively of government because of the ways in which the British uprooted and destroyed a culture and a race, replacing it with one in its own image.

I end with Jomo Kenyatta's words, the concluding paragraph of *Facing Mount Kenya*:

> *If Africans were left in peace in their own lands, Europeans would have to offer them the benefits of white civilisation in real earnest before they could obtain the African labour which they want so much. They would have to offer Africans a way of life which was really superior to the one his fathers lived before him, and a share in the prosperity given them by their command of Science. They would have to let the African choose what parts of European culture could be beneficially transplanted, and how they could be adapted. He would probably not choose the gas bomb or the armed police force, but he might ask for some other things of which he does not get much today. As it is, by driving him off his ancestral lands, the Europeans have robbed him of the material foundations of his culture, and reduced him to a state of serfdom incompatible with human happiness. The African is conditioned, by the cultural and social institutions of centuries, to a freedom of which Europe has little conception, and it is not in his nature to accept serfdom forever. He realises that he must fight unceasingly for his own emancipation; for without this he is doomed to remain the prey of rival*

[69] . Elkins, p.351

imperialisms, which in every successive year will drive their fangs more deeply into his vitality and strength[70].

But this is not quite the end of the story; it really belongs to another old man. In 1980, some seventeen years after independence, and with Kenyatta now dead, I returned to the land of my birth, perhaps to recover some memories, perhaps for a little self-discovery. I went up one day to our former home and farm. The locality had been returned to a number of small holdings, as was the practice of the ages. However, our house, my first home, was now the property of a rich lady from Nairobi, one of the *wabenzi*, those wealthy Kenyans who drive Mercedes cars. I was shown around the house by an elderly man, the father of the owner; nothing much had been done to it over the years. Even some of the wall-paper was the same. 'Things were better,' he said, 'when you were here.' Why? Mama Ngina, Kenyatta's 'wife of his old age' and a terror throughout the country, had been ripping off the peasantry, for example by demanding they sell their limited produce to her or her agents. This old man took me to the courtyard at the rear of the house. There was a washing line strung across it; hanging there one item of clothing: a pair of boxer underpants. The design on it?

The Union Jack.

[70] Kenyatta, p.318

15

A Very English Garden

Germany should concentrate all of its strength on marking out a way of life for our people through the allocation of adequate *Lebensraum* for the next one hundred years. A. Hitler

There is the old photo, now copied and pasted into the laptop. It is of a house, apparently newly built. On the left hand corner of it stands a pram. It is in black and white and all the details are small and distant, probably taken by a Box Brownie of the period, immediately after the Second World War.

The baby in the pram is Little Christopher, as his parents come to call him. It is mid-afternoon, it seems. No one is in sight. It is very quiet and even today one can imagine the click of the shutter. A driveway, along which this photo is taken, reaches to the house. There is nearby a tall chimney, beneath which in years to come the geese will lay their eggs.

In the distance is seen a line of trees, probably, though one cannot tell for sure, of pines. Later there will be many, many more. Blue Gums, too. All in lines over the particular part of this plateau. In the distance is a line of hills, the Aberdare Mountains.

For this is Kenya, with a long 'e'. Here at eight thousand foot or more, is a farm, a settler's farm, the farm of Little Christopher's father and grandfather before him. The terrain is flat; this is a broad plateau, with an escarpment leading down into the Great Rift Valley. The little boy will, in time to come, marvel at the flight of thousands of flamingos as they rise in the air currents above the lake below.

This high plateau is extensive enough to allow for numerous farms; this one will, in its heyday, measure over 4000 acres. Though it doesn't look much now, in time it will prosper, and fencing will stretch for miles to contain large fields. Wheat. Barley, Oats. Cattle and sheep; a pigsty, too. And Pyrethrum, until Rachael Carson's 'Silent Spring' alerted the world to its dangers.

But this was not always the case. Before the boy's grandfather arrived, with more than 200,000 other British settlers before and after The Great War (the one to end all wars), the land had belonged to others. There were no fences or farm buildings or smart houses modelled on those of the English landed gentry or aristocracy. Instead of cows and sheep, there were antelopes and giraffes, even lions and rhinos. For centuries, the owners of the land – a term not to be confused with our meaning of it - had been the Maasai. Hunter-gatherers. No more.

The garden, the outlines of which can be seen in this photo, will be tended by a Maasai woman, Old Nalami. One day she will come to Julia, Christopher's mother, to say that she is being forced to leave the area by some Kikuyu men, who are not hunter-gatherers. They wanted the land - and in time they will take it. 'A man without land,' wrote Jomo Kenyatta, 'is not a man. A woman without land is not a woman.'

The driveway is in the shape of the letter D. Behind the camera, behind the photographer, it leads back to a gate and onto another straight drive, parallel with the house, one which leads from the main road, a few hundred yards away and to the farm itself, again some hundred yards or so away. The viewer now cannot see how the rest of the driveway passes the house and bends to the right to once again join the main drive. It provides the structure of what will be the garden.

This will surround the house on three sides; on the fourth behind the kitchen will be huts in which the household staff will live and keep white gowns, their sashes and fezzes. These three sides will be in turn subdivided: a rose garden, a wide area at the back looking towards the Mountains, over which the sun will rise. Two flower beds, twenty or so yards long, six feet wide, will point towards a gap in the pines, through which Sattima, the highest of these mountains fifteen miles away, can be seen. More flower beds face the north, with an herbaceous border running the entire length, behind which is a grassed walk. Halfway along, a gate leads to the kitchen garden – artichokes, potatoes, peas, carrots. Anything will grow and flourish in this soil. Beyond, Lucerne will be planted to feed the cattle.

Red hot pokers, a pepper tree, shrubs of many kinds; a pigeon house; agapanthus - a garden rich in variety and with extensive lawns. So very English. So Derbyshire.

There is also on the laptop a painting of the house as it was left in 1965. Rich in colour, careful in maintenance, comfortable and speaking of money well made.

*

April, four months in. Julia has become pregnant and is about to leave.

To leave what will become her garden, to leave her new home, to leave her five month old marriage. A year earlier she had met Jim. 'Love at first sight.' Perhaps. Mutual friends had brought them together after she had been sent to Kenya so that that she might get over her engagement to a naval officer. 'I have met Jim – and we are getting married!' she telegrammed home. 'Let's hope he's white!' retorted her father, a faithful servant of the Empire.

After a fashionable wedding in the cold December of 1947, she'd left for Africa. Where, one way or another, she will spend the next 45 years of her life. But now she wants to escape. Somewhere. Anywhere.

8000 feet up. 15 miles to the nearest town. Other than a growing farm yard, not another house in sight. No electricity; no running water. A telephone to connect with the world she knew before, yes but no friends to call, no party wall over which to chat with a neighbour. How would one not yet 22 feel?

Bored. Lonely. Not mature enough to look into herself to question the opportunistic streak in her that had brought her to this high plateau. In their courtship, Jim had, one evening, thrown his hat over the escarpment ; she caught it as it was returned by the up-drafting winds and was herself caught. Now, even the English garden is just a vague idea.

A 'boy' – for that is what the labourers whatever their ages on settler farms were called, their women were 'bibis',– was running to the door. His knock is, one has to say, frantic.

Vano, the 'houseboy' answers the knock. Julia, a magazine unread on her lap, does not move from the sofa just a few yards from the front door. As yet she had no grasp of Swahili, so the frantic message of the 'boy' concerned her not – till Vano, both urgent and self-deprecating, came quickly to tell her that there had been an accident. 'Bwana – the boss,' he said in broken English, 'has fallen off his tractor!'

'So? His fault, then. He can cope. Why bother me?' Julia's reply is silent.

'Memsahib, you must go to him,' were Vano's frightened words. 'Quickly. Njoroge tells he has lost his leg.'

Who's lost a leg? Njoroge? No, he is at the door. Jim? 'The Bwana?'

The thought is electric (even where there is no electricity). Julia, four months pregnant, rises quickly. She is needed.

'He is by his tractor, in the field beyond the new barn,' Vano informs her. This is difficult as his English is very poor. Away from the main road, to which Njoroge is now running.

Julia grabs her hat, puts on boots. Quickly she makes her way up the D-shaped driveway. 100 yards to the barn; turns to the left, into the field on the right.

Jim is lying there. On the newly ploughed earth, Julia sees blood, ever darker, mixing with the rich dark soil, in which anything will grow. His leg, his left leg, appears to be lying at a strange angle.

The tractor's engine is ticking over. Julia takes in the large iron spikes that have replaced the tires on the rear wheels. Orange, they are, for driving through the heavy soil. Jim's head rests against the plough.

Julia cannot take it all in. Jim stares at her, unblinking. 'Help,' he seems to be saying. But he doesn't really know what has happened. The tractor's engine ticks over. It is a hot day. One or two of the 'boys' stand watching, helpless. Only Njoroge had seen what had happened. Others are gathering.

Julia kneels down, utterly lost. What to do? What to say, except, feebly but frightened, 'What's the matter, Jim? What's the matter?' This time, almost shouting. Panicking.

'My leg,' he says. Just.

She looks down, to his right leg. But it is his left one that is at a strange angle.

'The wheel.' It is almost a whisper. 'I slipped.'

Julia looks at the wheel. Nothing wrong there. And then at the left leg. She tries to move it, rolling up the trouser-leg. She sees a great gash. The leg is apart, separated, splintered just below the knee.

But there seems to be some flesh still attached.

Julia is at loss. Little Christopher, as he will become, stirs in her womb. There is silence from the onlookers. After all, they only do what Bwana or Memsahib say. Julia does not know what to say. Or do. Jim is silent, his head leaning forward on his chest.

Njoroge is now at the main road. Main road? A dirt road leading across the plateau to the farms, to the hills in the distance. How much traffic on any day high up in the White Highlands? One, two cars? He does not know. The road is muddy, with puddles from recent heavy rain.

And then – and this is true – he hears the sound of an engine. A car approaches. He frantically waves it down. The driver, another white farmer – his first thought is that this is just another drunk Kuke (for that is what the Kikuyu were called).

But then, he does stop.

And Jim survives.

*

Julia stays – now she has something to do. Jim recovers his spirit. He is man of cheerful, positive outlook, his faced now rugged after nearly twenty years of African sun, wind and rain. And six years at war.

'Daddy-one-leg,' Little Christopher will call him, as will his little brother who soon arrives; and little sister, too. 'Daddy-two-legs', when he is wearing his prosthetic. Which thumps on the floor as Jim walks along. Nothing will ever stop him. Life is to be lived.

And Julia?

She stays. Pregnancies and births come and pass. Jim never complains. What would be the point? He recovers his spirit quickly after his stay in hospital, his life saved by one of his 'boys', a passing settler and an artery which was not cut.

She looks after Jim; she is no longer alone all day. Does she let on that she had been about to leave? She does not, though Jim notices a change in her. She smiles more tenderly. Bandages to change; soon, nappies as well.

Neighbours come around more often. Support. Comfort. She learns with Jim a new way of life. She also lays plans for the growth of her garden. As at her family home, back in The Mother Country, there are plenty of gardeners to help.

Life picks up – horses, polo, parties. Visits to Nairobi and to the coast for holidays, Jim learning to use crutches and his false leg. Little children come and play. Like Nicholas Betts.

Jim adds an upper storey to the house, two bedrooms and bathroom. One night, as Jim lies asleep beside her, Julia sees, or thinks she sees, a black arm come through the window.

*

One day in early 1953, a black tribal chief, who had adopted all the poses and dress of an English country squire, is murdered in his car. The Insurgency has begun, the rebellion against the taking of land and the impoverishment on the indigenous people.

When a country is invaded and occupied, its indigenous people will, in time arise, rebel, fight for their freedom. This is History – though it is odd that this has not happened in The Mother Country, after nearly a thousand years of Norman occupation.

Bloodshed. Oath taking at night, in the dark, under the tall tree. A dead goat, its entrails, eyes and testicles laid out in front of the oath-taker. Sexual stimulation, too. As reported in the English press, this is indeed savagery. 'You are with us. Or you are against us. Kill – or be killed, one way or another. What do you want? Who is this for? Attack the settlers and their families; attack those who do not support you. To fail us will bring terror and destruction to you and your family.'

mBatuni. The oath taken.

All his life, Christopher, no longer little, can just recall a little friend. Nicholas. How vague are our earliest memories – or do we just remember to remember them? That afternoon, Julia had taken him, his little brother and littler sister, just four months old, to see the Betts, only four miles away but some distance over very rough roads. And that morning, the 'houseboys' had played with little Nicholas, throwing him in the air, catching him with his cries of delight.

And when it was dark that night, as the panga came down on his head, Nicholas now screamed, just once. His blood staining his white sheets, his white skin. Chanting to Orogi, the spirit of these ancient people, the Betts' cook knows about chopping.

His father comes running. As he enters the room a second house boy, hiding in the dark, attacks him from behind. Death is instantaneous. In the next door room, in her bed, lies Nicholas' mother. Nicholas must just be having a bad dream. But that dream enters her room, carrying blood-stained pangas. It is too dark for her to see clearly. But the sudden pain tells her – and then it is over. Her pregnant stomach lies open as she breathes her last.

The story goes around the world, to everyone's horror.

The oath has been fulfilled.

*

It is not fulfilled often; perhaps only a dozen white civilians are so murdered and about one hundred British military killed. But the Mau Mau is no match for the might of the British Empire, even though it is now in the early stages of its decline. Dedan Kimathi, General China and their followers with home-made rifles and their pangas, hiding in the forests of the Aberdares or around Mount Kenya, their sacred mountain, Kerenyaga, are soon defeated. Some say that 300,000 Africans lost their lives in the insurgency, many killed indeed by the insurgents. But the British executed many thousands, tortured, imprisoned and put them to slave labour, for it can only be called so, in 'The Pipeline', a salutary lesson to them that rebellion was fruitless. It may have been 100,000. Or fewer: no one really knows.

The war was lost. Yet independence came soon after. And The Spear of the Nation, now President of Kenya, with a short 'e', in time will disown and discredit the Mau Mau.

*

But for Little Christopher, this was when he left home.

The shock and the horror and understanding were, of course, beyond him. He was years too young.

Three days later, a Land Rover with three officers arrived at the farm, telling of the terrible event.

Jim and Julia sit in silence, uncomprehending, terror slowly building. Just four miles away! Is it selfish for an early thought to have been, 'It could have been us'? The children are playing in the garden. Julia rushes to them, brings them in. A 'boy' is mowing the lawn.

Jim says to the officers, 'What happened? No don't tell me. Have they caught them? Are they hanging from trees even now?' These are garbled words, frantic. It could have been them. But it was little Nicholas and his father and his mother, now pregnant. Julia returns, falls into Jim's arms.

Christopher, many years later, can find the images on the internet.

'You will have to leave,' the officer in charge advises.

But they don't leave. The farm is work and home and livelihood and to leave, to leave the farm of Jim's creation? Wouldn't that be an admittance of defeat? And could they ever come back?

The White Highlands ('Happy Valley' is only a few miles away) are now filled with troops. Protection is, if not guaranteed, reassuring.

Little Christopher, his brother and baby sister, just a few months old, do leave. All he ever remembers is that he could not understand why the wings of the aeroplanes were touching. Or so it seemed to him. They left, for grandparents, boarding school and a life in The Mother Country.

*

Jim and Julia. Colonial settlers, they must have known, sooner or later, that that term will become redundant. Still, for the time being, life goes on. With no children to look after, the parties return, polo matches held and trips to The Mountains of the Moon in The Congo, to Amboseli and big game hunting - a lion's pelt will lie on the hall floor. The garden continues to grow, the farm to prosper. An aerial photo of the time will show many tall trees, lush lawns and flowered beds. Julia finds ways of being useful. She begins to cultivate and sell strawberries; one day Jim brings a lamb, abandoned by its mother, into the house. It thinks it is one of the dogs and rests on the sofa, to Jim's annoyance. It eats the strawberries, punnets and all. Ivan the Terrible.

After three years, it is now safe for the children to return – a detachment of The Black Watch is encamped on the farm. The children keep growing, to return to England, where they will finish their schooling.

In time, it is time for Jim to retire. The Kenya he knew has gone; his leg and hips cause him pain. He retires to South Africa, leaving, of course, Julia's garden behind. 'I will never be ruled by a black man,' he once declares to Christopher, now determinedly anti-Apartheid. And Jim dies just a year before Mandela comes to power.

And Julia? In time, she will return to The Mother Country, although no one now uses the term very much. Her children grow up, there are grand-children and even great-grandchildren and old age comes upon her.

Now, as her life closes down and she sleeps for most of the day, does she recall her garden, with its red hot pokers, rose-beds and agapanthuses, the pepper tree and the children clambering all over their father? Is her dream at last coming true?

Lebensraum

16

Big Brother

Consider the lilies of the field – they toil not, neither do they spin.
Matthew 6:28

Childhood days on a farm in Africa, Mark's earliest memories. Father had made it out of nothing, just scrubland, once the possession of wild animals – even at 8,000 feet – and ancient tribal hunter-gatherers. But these were gone. He and his elder brother, Jem, by the time that they could walk, had made it their own, had the run of the place. Echoes of its freedom, the silence, the winds and the mountains away to the north, The Valley to the south, remain long in their memories. Mark liked to follow Jem everywhere then.

A farm, with numerous buildings, tractors, a Caterpillar, cows milked each day. Long, hot days for most of the year. Mark will always love these memories. And the freedom to roam.

Except when it rained. 3 inches an hour. It could easily be measured. So it was, one July afternoon.

'Let's go out in the rain!' Big brother said. Marky – as he was then, at just 8 – was not too sure.

'It'll be OK, but don't be long,' Mother encouraged. She raised her voice to overcome to rain thundering on the corrugated-tin roof. One day, it will have solid, red tiles.

Jem said, 'We'll get a couple of sacks, turn them half inside-out and put them on our heads. Like the boys do. And the bibis.' He ran off to the garage, returning in a moment with two sacks, otherwise used for grain of one sort or another. Marky sat on the floor, playing with a toy.

'Come on, Marky,' Jem tried to be encouraging. 'One for you, one for me.'

The sacks came down almost to their ankles. They put boots on, too.

Outside, the rain was so heavy and falling so hard that the boys could not see very far. They walked up the driveway towards the farm buildings. Water was everywhere and the road surface was one continuous muddy puddle, deepening all the time and with large raindrops bouncing back up off the surface. Once or twice Marky slipped and nearly fell. The soaked sack now weighed him down. Jem was putting on a brave face. *He* would go on.

But Marky had turned back. Soon, Jem did, too.

In the garage, sodden sacks were left on the floor. Boots, too.

'Marky turned back!' Jem's scornful response was no doubt typical. He would lead the way. Always. Marky was then happy to learn from his elder and better. For the time being.

*

The driveway led up to the farm buildings, where it came to a T-junction. Just an earth surface, the diverging roads leading to fields and to the huts where the farm workers lived. In a compound, protected by barbed-wire.

A barn, where wheat was stored, or barley, oats. Inside was a dryer for pyrethrum. A pigsty and a shed for the tractors and combine harvester. Dusty, for so much of time, with evidence of wool from the shearing, chicken feathers and a Jeep, that Jem had taught himself to drive on.

'Internal combustion engine'. He'd heard the words at school, in a Science lesson. He understood them all right. After all, he was 10. He would show Mark, as he was called now. Even if he wasn't interested.

There was an old tractor by itself. Blue with large metal wheels, not tyres. Better for negotiating the mud. Some years back, Father had had a terrible accident on it. It was rarely used.

'Come on, Mark.' His younger brother, wanting to walk to the pigsty, stopped, turned back. What now?

'Come! I want to show you something.' Jem had climbed up onto the tractor, and was standing astride the seat. Mark looked up at him, past the tractor's wheel, saw bis brother's face, momentarily dazzled by a shaft of sunlight. Blue, blue sky and gently moving clouds. He wanted to get home for lunch.

'What are you doing? Why can't I go and look at the pigs? And I'm getting hungry.'

'You can, in just a mo. I want to show you something. It'll be good. I'm going to try to make this old tractor go.'

Mark shrugged, picked up a stick.

Jem had with him a box of matches. 'You never know when you might need them. It's what engines need. They need fire. It's called "internal combustion".'

Happy to be in charge, Jem had climbed up onto the driver's seat, then he leant over the steering wheel along the tank on top of the engine. There were three caps spaced along it. He took the first cap off. He lit a match. Dropped it into the tank. Nothing happened. Mark was getting uninterested.

Having put the cap back on, Jem edged along the tank. 'Watch!' he called.

Again, he took the next cap off. Dropped it in. Again, nothing, internal or otherwise.

Carefully, he put the cap back, edged to the third and last one. He had to reach just a little further, his nose not quite over the hole. Just enough to get the cap off. He lit the match.

'Here's the last one!' Mark looked up.

Whoosh! A flame leapt up out of the tank. Mark stopped switching at the grasses with the stick.

The flame had burst out of the tank. Mark saw it, looked away, looked back. Jem was lying along the tank now. Still. After a moment, he raised himself.

Mark saw that there was blackening on his brother's face. His eyebrows seem singed.

Internal combustion.

Mark ran off, homeward.

Jem got down of the tractor and, too, went back for lunch.

'What was that bang?' his Mother asked, looking her elder boy up and down. Was he hurt? He seemed OK, if a little, well, dusty. 'What on earth have you done to your eyebrows?'

Mark could not keep the story to himself. 'Jem always thinks he knows best!' he ended.

Father returned, too, for his lunch. He said nothing. But later he knew what had happened.

'So, my boy, you thought you knew how to make a tractor go. Well, this one won't ever go again. And you are so lucky you can still see me. And your Mother. And your Mark and your sister, Jill. Big brother. Huh!?'

*

It was a long, hot English summer that year. Perhaps it was the moment, Mark would recollect as the years went by, when it was that ideal time, that moment before childhood slips silently but inexorably away and bodily changes force new attitudes. It was, it seemed, an endless summer of croquet, ice-creams, of tents in the field – though Mark would *not* sleep in them. So Jem didn't either. There were cousins and a couple of girls from up the road. Parents were in Africa – there is always a little more license when Gran and Grandpa were in charge. And there was the air-rifle.

Mark was always following Jem - what to do, putting up tents, making a bonfire . . . And he would always remember the air-rifle. Jem had got the idea from somewhere. Perhaps even at that age, he wanted to go into the Army. Or the Police. He kept asking for one, till eventually grandparents acquiesced.

'Here you are, Jem, an early birthday present,' said Grandfather as he handed over the gun. 'We asked your Dad and Mum if this was OK. Take care, don't shoot anyone!'

Target practice in the wood, polishing and shining it, counting the pellets. It had a range of only 50 yards or so, but close up it could be dangerous. For Jem, it was as if he was in the Wild West, waiting for the Indians. Long, sunny days, though shortening through August. Mark went along with it all.

After lunch one afternoon, in their play-room. An air-rifle breaks in the middle, like a shot-gun, so a pellet can be inserted.

'Let's see what happens if I pull the trigger with the barrel open,' Jem said.

Mark looked up from *The Beano*. Jem broke the rifle, so that its barrel was at right-angle to the shoulder piece, the stock.

'Look what happens now!' Jem commanded. He pulled the trigger.

The barrel slammed shut.

Jem looked down.

'Aaah! I've cut my thumb off!'

In an instant, he was out of the door, clutching his hand. Mark followed as Jem ran, searching for a grandparent.

For the rest of their time in their grandparents' house, there would be drops of blood on the wooden staircase.

Jem had to stay in hospital. He had missed the start of the new school term. And his birthday. The wounded thumb turned sceptic.

*

Spring-time, on the edge of the New Forest, where the cousins lived. Bracken growing afresh, birds returning, the clocks having gone forward and the excitement for Jem of going to a new school in three days' time.

Mark did not want to play with Jem, not with his Chemistry set, not really with anything. He had learnt to shy away from any games, any experiments, with his elder brother. He did not know it at the time or, at least, he did not have the words to express it. Were they really brothers? Jem had been a prefect at school, though now he was moving on , but Mark resented being made to feel the lesser of the two, though, of course, this was a feeling hardly articulated.

Jem would never make it at Science, but on this occasion, he was keen on the set, given to him at Christmas. Chemicals and powders in tubes, a pipette, a small Bunsen burner. All carefully labelled. And a box of matches.

For some reason, the cousins had had their fireworks party a few days before and Jem had been allowed to take a spare rocket home. What would happen if he mixed some powders, added them to the firework. . . ?

It was nearly lunch time and Jem called Mark out onto the grassy patch by the bracken, where the cars were parked.

'Watch what happens when I set this rocket off!' He lay flat on the ground with the rocket, with added matter, just a few inches away from his nose. Mark, now feeling a mixture of irritation and worry and not just for his brother's sake, stood some feet away.

He blinked. A loud bang had filled his ears.

His brother lay on the ground. Afterwards, Mark said that Jem had been blown five feet in the air.

Maybe. But Jem's face was charred and blistered, his eyebrows all but gone. Even he felt a bit foolish, going indoors, trying to behave as if nothing had happened when he was asked what that noise had been. Mark hesitated not at all to tell the story. As he would in the future. Often.

But for now, Jem was furious. 'Why did you tell them?'

Mark just looked away. Perhaps a smile might have appeared as he recalled the sight.

'All I needed was a wash!'

Except that he had to be taken to see the doctor.

At his new school, he was at least an object of puzzlement. He resented this.

*

There was a family story told, too, that Mark heard from time to time. One day, as a toddler, Jem, not knowing any better, had found the car door open. Reaching up onto the passenger seat, he had found a packet – as the story was told in the family. Opening this, there appeared to him what looked like small sweets. He tried one, then another and more. Luckily (maybe) Mother had come to the car. Instantly, she realised what her little boy was doing. Smiling and eating. Eating the pills that had been bought that morning. Caponising pills for fattening up her geese, for neutering them. Seizing the packet in one hand and the boy in the other, she rushed in doors. Little Jem had to be taken to hospital, the nearest 70 miles away. And in the car, he turned bluer and bluer, with diarrhoea and vomiting.

He did not die. But from time to time, Mark would wonder.

*

And Mark knew that, from early on, they would lead different lives. They would meet, of course, perhaps even when Jem was in the Army, an officer in the forces of law and order. And when Mark, now radical, went underground.

17

Jane Austen on the Rise of Capitalism

A mark, a yen, a buck, or a pound
A buck or a pound
A buck or a pound
Is all that makes the world go around,
That clinking clanking sound
Can make the world go round
Kander and Ebb

Capitalism concentrates power in the hands of a minority capitalist class that exists through the exploitation of the majority working class and their labour; prioritizes profit over social good, natural resources and the environment; is an engine of inequality, corruption and economic instabilities; is anti-democratic.[71]

'Many historians now accept that out of the eighteenth-century transatlantic economy, based on sugar and slaves, evolved modern industrial capitalism, which during the early nineteenth century was based on textiles and cotton.'[72]

She was a genteel lady, younger daughter and seventh of eight children of a country parson, famous for writing stories about the narrow and class-determined existence that constrained her life. The only portrait of her by her elder sister shows a sharp faced and rather acerbic young woman. We would never have heard of her but for the novels for which she became so famous. Such seems to be the understanding of who Jane Austen was. It is almost wholly incomplete, for she must now be considered very much in relation to the above. She certainly needs to be.

She was indeed the child of a country vicar. She did have seven siblings and she did write these novels, and considerably more. However, despite everything above, she was worldly, well-educated and *very* well read; she loved to stay in London, especially with her banker and favourite brother, Henry, enjoying particularly the theatre (her family's amateur dramatics are well recorded). Born in 1775, she lived through a most turbulent time: 1776, the American War of Independence, 1789, the French Revolution, the Napoleonic Wars, in which her brothers participated, the great intellectual developments of her day – Davy, Galvani, Faraday, Franklin and above all the advance of Enlightenment thinking: these are all familiar to us. And in Britain, The Industrial Revolution was causing great social and economic changes. She was well aware of all these. And there was one issue above all which was central to the politics of the day: slavery.

[71] Wikipedia
[71]Sochan, George *Slavery and the Rise of Capitalism*

Mansfield Park is, perhaps to some, the least enjoyable of Janes Austen's novels. It is, however, her most ambitious, important and far-reaching novel. Some say that it is less engaging and amusing than other works because it is over-written, perhaps rather obsessionally so. However, as this essay hopes to show, it is her most important since it is a work that reflects the 'state of the nation' as its author saw it. This is not to say that it is overtly political – it is not, but that the time of its creation (1812-14) was a time of great events, revolution, war, scientific, economic and ideological and indeed, social mores and, although it will be perhaps another hundred years till sexual ones are challenged, this book is *also* Austen's most thorough examination of this last subject, since it is most intimately engaged with the personal status of it participants, giving the new found wealth from slavery the background to their lives. And although Austen enjoyed Gothic and Romantic literature, her own mode of writing always exhibits the rationalism of the Age of Enlightenment. Indeed, as this essay will try to show, Austen's greatness is because this novel alone establishes the place of 'the novel' as central to our culture. Through her pen, the novel becomes the key vehicle of social, economic and political criticism. Many authors have followed, but Austen made 'the novel' as we know it today.

All Austen's novels are about money, even her first whole novel, *Northanger Abbey*, given the mansion that General Tilney lives in. 'It is truth universally acknowledge that a man in possession of a good fortune. . . .' The famous opening words of *Pride and Prejudice* make it quite clear what Austen's intention is: money (and marriage). In *Emma*, money marries money. *Sense and Sensibility* is essentially a satire about money, who has it and who does not, whilst even her juvenilia, such as *Lady Susan*, show a prodigiously youthful and cynical awareness of the role of money in life; and *Sanditon*, her last unfinished noel is about capitalist development of a holiday resort. Even her most personal novel, *Persuasion*, has its hero, Captain Wentworth, return with money from fighting a sea battle against the French, the Battle of San Domingo in the West Indies (1806). Eight years prior to the novel's opening, Wentworth, was not allowed to marry Anne Elliott, as he had no money. After this battle, now enriched from the booty that Naval officers were entitled to, he is in a position to do so. This was a real battle at which, it appears, that the Austen sailor brothers had taken part. A year almost after Trafalgar, it saw the final demise of French naval power and allowed Britannia to rule the waves for the rest of the century. And at the end of the novel, Wentworth ensures that Mrs Smith can retain her income from the West Indies. This cannot mean that Austen approved of slavery. Far from it.

There are two principle themes in this work: 'new money' and a pilgrimage. As the novel concludes, the way of the world would seem to win out. After all, today we are all at the mercy of the corporate world. And it demands its price: happy, obedient buying.

This novel's principle character, Fanny Price, has often been seen as this work's most flawed aspect; indeed, she is often considered her least satisfying heroine. However, these two issues – wealth against the spiritual life - cannot be separated: Fanny Price is characterised as she is in order to reflect Austen's view of the world as she understood it by the time of this novel's creation.

Austen, of course, is admired for the minute dissection of the life as she knew it, its characters, families and the circumstances of the country gentry of her time and place. This work goes much further. Austen cannot be considered as being circumscribed by 'the small world as she knew it'. No one, educated or not, could have been unaware of the Napoleonic

Wars that raged through much of her adult life. Nor was she at all ignorant of the dreadful nature of the French Revolution: her cousin, Eliza, suffered the execution of her first husband, le Comte de Feuillide, in the Terror in 1794. They remained close, Eliza later marrying Jane's favourite brother, Henry, in 1797. Indeed, Austen's other brothers served in the Royal Navy throughout this time – some ships mentioned in *Mansfield Park* bear the same names as theirs. One became Admiral of the Fleet, the other a Rear-Admiral. Furthermore, Austen's letters abound with the life of her times: trips to London, to the theatre, to writers on many subjects, as well as the usual tittle-tattle and gossip of the life as it surrounded her (including mentions of ancestors of mine[73]).

What she *didn't* write about were experiences beyond her own or those of the people she might have known – famously, she never includes a scene in which only men participate. And though her novels are principally about the growth of their heroines from teenage youthfulness to married status, her moral view is much more complex. Perhaps Elizabeth Bennet is Austen's most loved character, for all her intelligence and flaws; the relationship between Elinor and Marianne in *Sense & Sensibility* often the most engaging, and it is Anne Elliot in *Persuasion* who is perhaps her most deeply felt heroine, languishing in spinsterhood till she is well beyond the contemporary age for marriage, until Captain Wentworth comes back into her life. Her loneliness and patience are deeply moving.

That is, until we consider Fanny Price. While it cannot be said that Anne Elliot's state mirrors Austen's, as the latter had eschewed a marriage offer, determined to remain single and to be able to write as she wished. Had she become Mrs Harris Bigg Wither[74] she would probably never have become what she did, despite the offer of a very comfortable existence. Her children were to be found life in her imagination[75]. It is Fanny, however, who, it is said, more closely reflects her creator, for Jane was never in love with her suitor. This, though, is not the complete picture.

Many, as mentioned, have found the characterisation of Fanny at best inadequate. For example, "Nobody, I believe, has ever found it possible to like the heroine of *Mansfield Park*," declared the great critic and Austen aficionado Lionel Trilling. Marilyn Butler thought that "Fanny is a failure is widely agreed". Others have been fiercer. Kingsley Amis called Fanny "a monster of complacency and pride concealed under a cloak of cringing self-abasement".

None of this is so. Though in the initial stages of the novel, Fanny is quiet, subdued and subjected, she grows in stature as she matures, Trilling is right up to a point, though he plainly fails to notice the distinct and purposeful development of her character by Austen. The intent of this essay is to suggest, indeed, that, far from being 'a failure', Fanny can only leave the reader with a profound impression that she, Fanny, has been made to progress from girlhood to womanhood intact in more senses than one *and* as one who is both vital and wise.

---

[73] My several times great-aunt amongst them; her father was the Rev John Benn, vicar of Faringdon, about 2 miles south of Chawton, Hampshire, from 1797-1857. He has come down to us as 'The Hunting Vicar'. Austen and her mother read *Pride and Prejudice* to Miss Benn on its first being published, 'By A Lady'.

[74] December, 1802; Jane was approaching 27, Anne Elliot's age in *Persuasion*.

[75] There were one or two other affairs, in particular with one Blackall; he apparently died. Interestingly, long ago a Lesbian friend once told me that Austen thought and wrote just like her.

As for Kingsley Amis' view, well, he appears to be ready only to approve of women who were quickly beddable.

To be fair, it is not easy to see where Fanny derives her moral principles. Her father is irresponsible and dissolute, her mother not strong enough to avoid being overwhelmed by parenthood and by circumstances. Her one aunt, Lady Bertram, is indolent, lazy and vacuous; the other, Mrs Norris, is an energetic and intensely selfish bully. And at the start of the novel, when Fanny is but 10 years old, when she goes to Mansfield rescued from the chaos that is her Portsmouth home, she is, indeed, timid and sickly, though why this should be a surprise is itself surprising. Whilst Lady Bertram insists that she is respected and cared for in her new home, Fanny is not to forget that she is only the poor cousin, secondary to the other children. Under these circumstances, it is not surprising that Fanny in the early chapters is so shadowy and quiet, disregarded by her new family in its entirety, except by Edmund. Her new home is utterly different from anything else that she had experienced, reflecting, from her own point of view, place, peace and order, if only to be found in the isolation of her own attic room.

But perhaps it doesn't matter where Fanny's moral understanding or nature come from, except to say it comes from Austen herself. It beggars belief to think that her heroine, embodying the work's moral and indeed religious meanings, should be regarded without great care. It seems that Austen puts her heroine through a series of trials which reflect very definite challenges, deriving from the Christian tradition and into which Austen was born – her father and two of her bothers were Anglican pastors. This is not to say that these trials are identifiably Biblical, except to say that they are there. Austen was, though, a great admirer of Bunyan's *The Pilgrim's Progress* and Fanny is Austen's pilgrim.

The first trial, of course, is Fanny's initial removal from Portsmouth. This is the overarching challenge of the work, with the heroine coming out happy and married. The second is the amateur dramatics, the staging of the play *Lovers Vows*. The final one is the series of attacks she undergoes subsequent to Henry Crawford's proposal to her, from Crawford, then from his sister, Mary, then from Sir Thomas and finally, and most painfully, from Edmund. I think that the first of these can be identified as the distinction between the steep and narrow path to redemption and salvation, with, perhaps Fanny's sojourn back in Portsmouth reflecting Bunyan's *The Pilgrim's Progress*, in particular the Slough of Despond[76]. Indeed, she is sent back by Sir Thomas so that she might perceive the error of her ways in not accepting Crawford. Whilst she is there, assailed again by this young man and by the atmosphere of her parental home with its noise, disorder and discomforts, the place virtually overwhelms Fanny, old neuroses threatening their return. It is certainly the case that Austen puts her heroine through the mill. Repeatedly.

The second challenge deals with the ways in which people play roles in life as well in dramatics and deception is its main thrust. With Sir Thomas absent still in Antigua, the younger generation have free rein. It is not necessary here to go into this in detail, save to say that it provides the spur, through its exploration of sexual attraction and deception, for Maria's and Crawford's later elopement; nor is it necessary to follow the arguments put forward to encourage Fanny to accept Henry, except to say that they go to the heart of the

[76] Very shortly before her end, Austen was asked if she wanted anything, she replied, quoting Bunyan: 'Nothing but death'.

meaning of the work, that is the contrast between the Christian values – spiritual and moral - that Fanny (and ostensibly Edmund) embody, and worldliness, for want of a better term.

Austen famously wrote in a letter of the time that this novel is about 'ordination'. There has been much coverage of this matter. However, it cannot just be about Edmund's progress to taking up Holy Orders. As should be obvious, the issue is not just the clerical life but its contrast with the world as it is represented by both the Crawfords and the Bertram family, and even by Edmund as he falls for the charms of Mary. It is central to all the arguments put against Fanny in the second half of the book. In short, Austen makes it absolutely clear that Fanny will marry *only* for love, and so Fanny is made to stand alone against the world, as Austen depicts it here. Thomas Hardy quotes the young German poet, Novalis, in characterising the differences between Henchard and Farfrae in *The Mayor of Casterbridge*: 'Character is Fate[77].' Austen would have readily agreed.

We are familiar enough with the limited life of the country squirearchy and minor nobility known well to the author in her lifetime and social orbit. But what else was taking place? Obviously the French Revolution had left its scars even on Austen's family as mentioned above; it had also left the British establishment terrified. The government at the time put in place strict rules of censorship and meeting. The Napoleonic Wars, though never described by Austen, were well known to her, again as mentioned. It was a time of considerable trepidation and fear. 'Bony' remained a means of terrifying little children into good behaviour for the rest of the century.

But it was also a time of great change and development, in the Sciences as well as in politics and economics. It is fair to say that Mercantilism with its aggressive insistence on ruthless acquisition of wealth and its nationalist imperatives was giving way to the *laissez-faire* economics, which laid down the foundations of modern economics, enshrining as it did much more dynamic and individual processes and which suited Britain's imperial ambitions much better[78]. Austen's younger brother was, for a time, a successful banker. But there is one further matter which has a much closer bearing on the book's meaning.

The Bertrams, as it has been observed, are what we might now call *nouveau riche*. Rushworth represents old wealth, his rundown estate ready for improvements such as Humphrey Repton might have made and which Henry Crawford is only too willing to give voice to, regarding his own boastful expertise. Though Austen does not explain how, except in contrast to the wealth of Rushworth and that it is of benefit for Maria to marry into 'old wealth'[79], it is clearly meant that the Bertram wealth has come from slavery. In 1804, the Act of Union between The United Kingdom and Ireland (the Anglo-Irish Ascendancy) came into force, bringing, as it did, a hundred or so new MPs to Westminster, and it was with their backing that Parliament saw the abolition of the Slave Trade in 1807[80], just a few years before the composition of this novel. It is no wonder that Sir Thomas is so disagreeable in the early chapters of the book, before he goes to his estate in Antigua.

---

[77] Hardy quoted from *Novalis* which was the pseudonym of Georg Philipp Friedrich Freiherr von Hardenberg (2 May 1772 – 25 March 1801), a poet, author, mystic, and philosopher of Early German Romanticism.

[78] See William Dalrymple's *The Anarchy* about the East India Company.

[79] It is perhaps permissible to see in Austen's rejection of marriage to Harris Bigg Wither the threat of boredom that Maria, on being married to Rushworth, appears to have motivated her at the end of the novel in elopement.

[80] March 27th, 1807. The Whig government of Grenville fell two days later.

This is not the place to go into slavery, though it is at the core of this work. It is whilst Sir Thomas (and his elder son, Tom) are away in the West Indies that the dramatics take place, epitomising as they do, unbridled flirtatious licence. On his return, not only does he put a stop to them, but something else happens: Fanny is now 18 and her resolute dislike of the activity has made life extremely difficult for her, though Sir Thomas comes to respect her all the more for it. It is essential to note that she is now a young woman, a sexual being ready for marriage, in terms of contemporary custom; we read of Edmund plainly telling her so. Though Austen never puts it like this, she makes it quite clear that this is the case.

Firstly, Fanny has a completely changed relationship with her uncle. He now likes her and they have lively conversations about Antigua. But there is more. Fanny's room, in the east wing of the mansion has no heating; Sir Thomas orders a fire to be put in place and laid for her. On the one hand this is a considerate act; on the other it is purposefully symbolic, suggesting as it does the actual nature of Sir Thomas' attraction for his niece, albeit unacknowledged.

This is harmless enough, however real. But there is a crucial moment in the book, perhaps the most crucial of all. Chapter 21 begins with a conversation between Edmund and Fanny. This begins with discussion about the Grant's and about Sir Thomas' return having restored things as they were before his departure. Edmund then gives the reader and Fanny a very clear idea of the changes that have taken place in her: 'Your uncle thinks you are very pretty. . . your uncle never did admire you till now. . . . Your complexion is so improved – and your figure. . . . . You must try not to mind growing up into a pretty woman.'

It is clear from this that what has been said above is most germane. But now occurs the most important moment in the work. Edmund comments about how much his father seems to enjoy talking to Fanny, and implying a criticism that she does not talk to him enough. She mentions that she asked him last night about the slave trade. All she gets in response is: '– but there was such a dead silence!' . . . and her 'cousins were sitting by without speaking a word.'[81]

Sit Thomas had been delighted to talk about Antigua, but *not* about the slave trade; it appears the others were embarrassed, too. Why the silence?

As Austen implies, the wealth of the Bertram family is dependent on slavery. As much as the Napoleonic Wars were a central matter of the day, so was slavery. In 1788, the Anti-Slavery Committee had been established; there were boycotts of sugar taking place up and down the country. And as has just been mentioned the trade in slaves had been recently abolished, though not slavery itself. Sir Thomas' silence on the matter suggests at the very least his angry resentment at its abolition. Slaves died often more quickly from the appalling condition of their lives than they could be replaced by new ones from Africa, no pleasing circumstance for a slave owner before and even more so now. But is there a deeper feeling of moral confusion, and one unrecognised?

That slavery was and remains a monumental evil is an idea common with us today; the idea was growing so in Austen's time. She had, indeed, read Thomas Clarkson, he who travelled a reported 35,000 miles, mostly at night, around the country agitating for reform and abolition. Austen notes in passing in a letter of 24th January, 1811, that she had 'loved' Clarkson. It is Clarkson and *not* Wilberforce who should be regarded as the real hero of the abolition

[81] Page 213, Penguin edition

movement. It is known that Nelson was very much against the abolition of the trade, as he felt that it would advantage France (it would not have done after 1805), as Britannia ruled the waves for the rest of the century.). He did not live long enough, of course, to fight this battle in The House of Lords.

However, there is another reason for his antipathy: having spent a considerable time in the West Indies, Nelson had become very friendly with slave owners, as indeed had many of his officers and men. Plainly he had turned a blind eye to its horrors, just like Sir Thomas, whether he approved of it or not. It is not known what the two sailor brothers of Austen thought of slavery. They had served in the Indies, were known to Nelson and knew him. Nevertheless, this moral vacuum at the heart of the nation is well reflected in *Mansfield Park*. Abolition would have meant serious damage to Britain's imperial ambitions, in terms of trade and power and of personal wealth. The earlier loss of the American colonies would have been a stark reminder of this. It is worth recording, though, that in the ensuing decades, the Royal Navy did much to curtail the trade in slaves.

This is thus the crucial moment in *Mansfield Park* and perhaps one of the most significant moments in all the literature of this genre.

At this point, I make a digression. I offer no apologies for the rather personal nature of what I say. In about 1875, my great-great-grandfather, who had become very rich in Manchester, moved his home to the Derbyshire countryside, where he built a mansion with at least 24 bedrooms, It had extensive garden and its estate still contains various tenanted farms. He was said to the 'the richest non-aristocrat in England.' How had this come about? Directly or indirectly through slavery. The family, originally small landowning framers, leased out land upon which the slums of the workers in the cotton mills would live. The Manchester Ship Canal ran through some of this land; the family also made very fortuitous marriages.

But my point is this: I have lived a comfortable middle-class life. I suspect, too, that anyone who considers themselves white, middle-class, Anglo-Saxon or whatever will have benefitted even today from slavery and its subsequent and concomitant successor, colonisation.

It is not till the very end of the book that Sir Thomas undergoes a considerable degree of self-questioning, following the elopement of his two daughters, as does Edmund. The latter finally comes to realise the mistaken affection he had for Mary for what it is: a result of seduction. Bertram realises that he has never paid proper attention to the up-bringing of his daughters, he has not taught them values that would seem to be very close to Austen's own: those Augustan values of modesty, self-restraint, balance and objectivity, or more properly, the Christian values into which she was born.

Austen's work makes abundantly clear the basis of this prosperity. And so she explores the worldliness that is being born as she writes.

It has been said by more than one commentator that Fanny Price and Mary Crawford represent two sides of Austen's character. Certainly, Austen's surviving letters reveal a most complex character. These are fully of vitality, right up to the approach of her death. They are amusing, enjoying endless social comment or tittle-tattle, references to a huge range of literary and contemporary events and people. They are witty and acerbic, even at times revealing not very pleasing attitudes. In short, they are most worldly. Mary Crawford could well have written these.

Fanny could never have done so, for reasons suggested above. It seems that one must never forget Austen's up-bringing, especially its grounding in the Protestant faith. Though she never bangs on about it, it is always there. Thus, it is Fanny's destiny to marry into the Cloth and become a parson's wife.

But what exactly is it that finally brings about the end of the relationship between the Crawfords and the Bertrams? It is embodied in what Edmund tells Fanny about his final meeting with Mary. What appals him is her, Mary's, insistence that Maria's and Henry's elopement (disastrous though it proves) is not its absolute wrongness but that it is 'folly', folly that their reputations will be ruined. Its moral and spiritual wrongness, however, is most emphatically to be understood in terms of 'ordination': Edmund has by now taken up Holy Orders, and has been most hurt by his sisters' actions. For marriage to be so treated as something that can be easily disposed of goes right against the sacramental place of marriage – and indeed, sexual relations – in the Christian faith, as then understood and practised. Pre-marital as much as extra-marital sex are, thus, profoundly wrong, as they cannot be understood as part of God's purposes[82]. This must be all part and parcel of the concept of Original Sin. In not understanding this, Mary reveals her shallow, worldly and opportunistic mind. Her last 'saucy, playful smile' with which she tries to invite Edmund back into her company as he finally takes his leave of her, is the most appropriate gesture that Austen gives her.

It is mentioned above that Mary's attempt to win Edmund is a seduction. It begins perhaps on the occasion of the outing to the estate of Rushworth at Sotherton, continues through the dramatics and nearly results in her victory prior to the disgrace at the end of the novel. Edmund so nearly falls for it, despite Mary's rejection of the priesthood largely, as she sees it, as being uninteresting, even unworldly, being her hidden meaning.

This is as much a seduction as Henry's attempt to woo Fanny. Indeed, when he tells his sister that he intends to make Fanny fall in love with him, this is surely meant to mean 'seduce her.' It becomes the central issue of the second half of the book and is as much at the heart of the work as is slavery. Why is it, then, that he runs of with Maria? This is all very much at one with their flirtation at Mansfield and their loose natures and follows most naturally. Austen is known for her disapproval of those who spend their time going rather purposelessly from place to place. Although Henry has his estate at Everingham, he is rarely there. His lustful desire for Fanny (for it is only this) takes him back to Mansfield and even to Portsmouth. The Crawford's continual restlessness is symbolic of their moral looseness, and this includes especially sexual looseness. It cannot be believed that he can ever love Fanny. Austen suggests that he might do so, though leaving it up to the reader to read between the lines: his sexual frustration from failure with Fanny can only result in finding release with another woman. In rejecting him so forcefully, in rejecting the offer of an easy comfortable life as mistress of Everingham, Fanny's refusal reflects, amongst other things, Austen's own refusal of the offer of marriage to Harris Bigg Wither and a comfortable life at his country estate at Manydown. Henry's securing promotion for Fanny's naval brother is not done out of good will for William, but to make Fanny feel grateful to him. She does not fall for this, though. So much does Henry deploy, the more Fanny rejects, though this is not to say that this is easy.

---

[82] Well, as far as the male is concerned. Orgasm, it is suggested, is, in the state of marriage, to touch the Divine. For women, this was regarded as hysteria, irony of ironies, the word deriving from the Ancient Greek for womb. Implements could be bought to prevent women from this horror.

Austen reminds us that the straight and narrow path is *never* easy. And as Maria should so willingly accept Henry's advances, her final destination at the novel's end only serves to punish her not for her behaviour, but for her shallow and selfish own regard, bored as she is with Rushworth and no doubt, greatly regretting her marriage to him rather than to Crawford, though she was in competition for his attention at the time of the dramatics with her sister, Julia. And Sir Thomas bitterly regrets his part in this, his failure to bring up his daughters correctly.

And so it is that Austen has laid the ground-work for the novel in the 19th Century and beyond, as it serves as a critique of establishment ideas and practices by, for example, Mrs Gaskell, George Eliot, Dickens and Robert Tressell's *Ragged Trousered Philanthropists* and so many authors beyond.

The work effectively ends with Mary's last, 'saucy smile'. Thereafter, Austen finishes off things pretty promptly. The affair between Henry and Maria ends after only two months, with its suggestion of violence. Her destiny is to spend the future punished, with the dreadful Mrs Norris, well away from Mansfield, while Henry will no doubt carry on in his own, spoilt way. Mary will float around the world with her half-sister, Mrs Grant, since the latter's husband has died following three 'institutional dinners', thus allowing Fanny & Edmund to move into the parsonage at Mansfield, once the latter has recovered from his affliction and seen the error of his ways. Julia and John Yates settle down, more or less, and Fanny's sister, Susan, more robust, perhaps, than her elder, moves into the big house to take Fanny's place, one day maybe to marry the reformed Tom Bertram.

And does not Austen's masterpiece signal the great divide between the spiritual and the material, between a settled, ages-old way of life, now increasingly defunct and challenged in numerous ways as The Age of Enlightenment progressed in the burgeoning Capitalist way, in which its purpose is to allow those who have it to make money out of money. And as the spiritual life of the Nation has declined in the two hundred years since Austen's – and Darwin's time, does not this novel illustrate Spencer's most famous response to *On the Origins of Species*, ' the survival of the fittest'?

Who knows? Austen has been criticised for fluffing her endings. But Austen is ever the ironist. If she doesn't allow her hero and heroine a final kiss (unlike in the excellent BBC version of *Persuasion*), it is not just because she doesn't want to offend decorum. 'I have told my story, she might say, 'the people and events are fictions, aren't they, even if the themes and ideas are real. Take them or leave them as you wish.' But in contrasting the spiritual life with the worldly, are not both fictional? In dashing off her ending, does not Austen provide the reader with an uncomfortable question: what is real and what is fictional? Yet her overall meaning *is* clear.

And I wonder what Austen would have made of a young man kicking a football around a football pitch, for a million Pounds a week?

Capitalism: Capitalising on capital.

And responsibility?

18

Empty

Alice sat on the edge of her bed. Her hands under her.

It was a single bed. The room was painted white and there were old blue curtains on the solitary window. She never closed the curtains at night. Now all she could see from this room on the fourth, or the fifth, floor was a grey day with the town spreading into the far distance on this grey, cloudy morning.

The sheets were dishevelled. She could never, these days, be bothered to make her bed. A pair of fraying slippers was nearby and all Alice was dressed in was an old T-shirt and nickers. She sat on her hands. It was like this every morning – every day and every night. A pair of jeans and a jumper, a coat for cold days, a bite to eat before work.

She knew it would never leave her. That cold hand. And those hours in the torture room. And what had happened there.

'Time to get going, Alice!' The chirpy voice was happy and oh so pleasant. Donna, who always wanted you to know that you were never alone, that there was always someone there to help and who knew your every move and thought.

Alice sat still, head down, her thoughts apparently far away. Not that she had any thoughts these days. After all, why should she have, when the State provided everything, work, food, home, entertainment, sex parties?

She could think no more. She and Mark – what remained of him – and her – had lain on the Cathedral steps for hours. In time relatives came for the dead. Alice had been wakened by a constant weeping and crying. Then operatives had picked her up and bundled her into a van, having ripped her hand from Mark's.

These were the memories that persisted through the weeks and months since. Home: grey, lonely and empty.

She got up, walked slowly to the window. Paused. Lent into the corner and slid slowly to the ground, her head coming to rest against the wall, her legs folding.

All she could think of was that day, when she and Mark had made love by the lake. When she and Mark had been tortured. When that man had forced himself into her.

'Come on now, Alice.' After a while, Donna's voice was perhaps a little more commanding now, a patient mother, perhaps, trying to get her child ready for school. 'A bite to eat will do you good.'

Alice knew too much to be taken in. She knew what would happen, too. Raising herself, she picked up a towel, wiping her face as she went to the living space – a small kitchen in the corner, a chair, a table, a sofa in front of a screen.

Some bread and a glass of milk, thin and beginning to be sour.

'Come along, now,' Donna encouraged. 'You've to be at work in 20 minutes. The hallway and stairs need a thorough going over. Everyone here will be so grateful.'

It was not as if Alice minded all this. Perhaps she was beyond caring. Donna had not been the only one to attend to her, to encourage. But Alice could sleep, sit for hours in silence, elbows on knees, chin resting on her hands. No thought, just memories passing through her mind, uninvited but ever-present. Memories.

And however bright it was outside her, inside it was not even dark. Just a void.

*

Ian McEwan's latest work, *People Like Us*, tells the story of the relationship between its central protagonist and an android that he buys to satisfy his every need. It is a brief addendum that he concludes with, called *Dussel*. . . In this he advances the idea that robots or androids will become so like humans, in behaviour, feel and nature that it will be impossible to tell the difference. In fact, it will become, McEwan suggests, very impolite to ask someone sitting next to you at dinner if he or she is 'real' or not.

Perhaps, though, McEwan misses the point.

It is not that robots will become human, but that humans will become robots.

In a sense, it may be that humans have *always*, in some sense, been robots. They have done whatever their leaders have asked or programmed them to do – toil in fields or factories, bred to ensure replacement workers, to be willing to be marshalled into regiments and platoons to be massacred and slaughtered 'for King and Country' – all to the profit of those who control their lives, their world, the monarchs and their priests. And in their millions, billions, humans have acquiesced in this.

But this was ever in the time before robots.

Homo Deus, Yuval Noah Harari's famous 'Brief History of Tomorrow', is a witty title. It was Hegel who propounded the notion that 'God is Man'; it was Marx who reversed this: 'Man is God'. Mankind, for Marx, must rise up and remove, in bloody revolution if necessary, the shackles that have ever bound him.

Harari's title is ironic. Although he is happy to advance the idea that humanity is successfully overcoming war, poverty and pestilence, his work is a dire warning of the threat of what he calls Big Data, the Internet of Everything. An Internet that embodies all knowledge *including* all knowledge of the thoughts, feelings and activities of every human, and in so doing, controls those aspects that are essential to life and to being human.

Man will *not* be God, though humans might well be told they are. The gods will be, Harari contends, those very, very few people who will come to control the internet.

He does not say when this will happen. But it is happening now.

When once humans were conditioned to toil and to suffer - the Human Condition – now they will only have to consume and have pleasures. So long as they do not attempt to change anything. Is it not the case that the ruling classes – aristocracies and monarchies, international capitalists, whoever – learnt one lesson from the French and Russian Revolutions: do not let the people starve? If they do, they surely will rise up.

And if nothing can be changed? Humans will be robots.

*

It was not long after they had met that Mark and Alice, not long after they had been out together a couple of times – to the cinema to see cheerful films of happy citizens, even to the 'parties' organised by the state in former churches. It was what everyone did, especially the young.

They were sitting on a terrace. For once the day was cheerful, even spring-like. The river below flowed silently and softly. It was their days off work – or 'pleasure' as all were expected to call it. There was a pause in their chat. Alice and he were relaxed, looking at each, at the water, at the people in little boats below them. But there were no fish jumping.

'I think we can make each other happy,' Mark suddenly said, gently but looking at Alice with delight in his eyes. She took his hand for a moment.

Alice stood up, drawing Mark with her. She stepped towards the railings above the river, still holding Mark's hand. She paused and with her free hand gently brushed her dark, red-brown hair back.

They stood looking at each other. She put her hand on his shoulder looking up into his eyes.

'Yes,' she said, almost silently. And she put her lips to his. It was their first kiss, their first full kiss.

It was her choice.

As it had been his.

It did not matter that there were one or two others on the terrace that midday. But this was to be something more. Mark led Alice to some steps that took them to a pathway along the river. After walking a little way, they came to a secluded spot. Here, they fell into each other's arms.

As their mutual, newly discovered love filled them, so did the trust that it would always be like this for the rest of their lives.

But there were electronic devices recording their every move and sound.

19

Dreamland

All happy families are alike; each unhappy family
is unhappy in its own way.

Leo Tolstoy

"It will be Spag Bol tonight," Mark said to himself. "Or something."

He had been in the kitchen now for an hour or so, reading the paper. As ever, full of bad, worrying or disturbing news. His team had just been demoted from the Premiership, too. But at least he was alone. The family – now out at work or at school – knew only too well when he was in a bad mood. But to him, the kitchen was *his* room. His wife, Alice, was only too happy with this.

It was a large room, with just one window, looking out over the lane that lead up through the old village, with its ramshackle and varied buildings and down which huge tractors and other farm equipment would rumble and roar. In front was the sink and work surfaces. Cupboards, once fine but now a little tired looking, went from the left and then along the wall away from the window, a couple of dressers, a table and another cupboard was by the door, whilst a second door led through to a little sitting room and then the garden. There was a sofa in the far corner, blue and covered in cushions, perhaps his favourite place in the house to sit. A large table filled the centre of the room, the centre of family life. Six wheelback chairs.

All this – and the rest of those – had once been his all alone. But then, rather late in life, he had married. He was happy, now. But he lived as much in his own mind as he had lived before.

And now there were children – the 16-year-old twins, Jamie and Sally, and little Annie, now nearing 11.

Does a family have a recipe? Is life like a recipe? Ingredients, time, cost, effort, oh, and hope. And love.

But Spag Bol was easy enough, if that is what it was to be, and there was a Tiramisu he'd prepared yesterday. They liked that.

But did he ever have a recipe for marriage, for love? Did it all, well, just, happen? Eyes open or eyes closed?

But he liked the room, his home all a bit higgledy-piggledy, for to him it looked lived in. But only up to a point, even though Alice had a touch the of OCDCs about her. Lived in, warm, homely, unfussy. How could it be otherwise, with teenage children?

Fresh vegetables on the sideboard, wine on the rack. Pictures on the wall – an old print of the 'Fighting Temeraire' from his schooldays – and plenty, one way or another for the eye to take in: prints of pigs, sheep and cows.

Mark had finished lunch – cold meat sandwich and an orange – an hour or two ago; he had been reading 'Ordinary People' and was now into his second, or third, bottle of pale ale. He let his mind wander.

*

He'd travelled, read many a book, played Bridge, considered himself left of centre politically, been an estate agent, a time he recalled as a 25-year-chore. And as it is, his body, like some casserole dish, had mixed these elements with those that he had inherited, had mixed them, braised them, to produce a dish, well, self-satisfied some might have called him, but he was largely at peace with himself and the world.

Then he had met Alice. That special something added? A secret ingredient?

Where does one meet the one whom you will marry? On a train, in the pub? To tell, the truth, he found it hard to recall; she had just been around, he had just been around and gradually they had drawn closer. What had done this? Reading, yes, cards, no. Travel, perhaps to Weston-Super-Mare but no further. Just liking each other's company? Cooking? Yes. They had even been on courses. She was much more capable than him but, somehow, they were more and more together until she moved in, unmarried (still) – and then the children appeared. Alice returned to work; Mark continued to develop his cookery. Up to a point.

*

His lunch of a sandwich and beer, followed by an apple, had been enough. Now he was feeling just a little dozy.

Comforting himself on the sofa, kitchen life came alive in his mind. It wasn't as though he was a great cook, but he enjoyed giving the family a good meal.

And all those family meals, seeing the children growing up, sometimes argumentative, much of the time competitive, with each other, with their parents. Fish dishes were Sal's preference – fish pie especially, with cheese on top, cheese which Jamie would push to the side. The creamy sauce, the varied fishes, prawns a few capers and mashed potatoes. Jamie was all for chicken whilst Annie, well she would eat anything that wasn't too spicy.

Mark lay there, he could smell those dishes, mixing with talk and chatter, school stories and his wife's willingness to be pleased. Tomato in Bolognaise sauce, rich gravies (he could never produce the same one twice) and puddings he'd made long ago suddenly made their presence felt.

And in the casserole that was his mind, these will all come together. Coq au vin, pork in cider sauce, bacon and eggs for breakfast. He himself loved profiteroles – and fruit salad, especially with bananas and plenty of syrup, with a dash of Cointreau, to tell the truth. And his 'signature dish': chocolate mousse.

Children's parties, and then dinner parties for friends. If these ended before midnight, he felt he had failed!

And so he was drifting slowly, pleasantly, through middle age. And what did all these ingredients add up to?

*

The door opened noisily, and he woke from his reverie. Annie was back from school, dumping her bad on the floor by the door, and removing her trainers.

"Hi, Dad," she said as she cuddled up against him. "Did I wake you?"

"Oh no, I was just thinking of what to do for dinner."

"Oh yeah, you was snoring! Snoring loudly!" She held him tight.

"Well, does a good snore make for a great supper?"

"Of course!" she exclaimed. "What are we having?" She felt she was not really getting a straight answer from her father.

"Mmm. . . ."

"Liar! You were just dreaming. And snoring. Loudly!"

"OK, you win. What would you like? Spag Bol? With your favourite ingredient, sundried tomato paste?"

"Yeah, lovely. But we had it only a day or two ago."

He remembered now. "Fish pie?"

"Yay!" She gave him a big kiss on his cheek.

"Have you any homework to do? Well, sit at the table, get it out, get it done and when you have finished, you can help me."

"Pudding?" she asked.

"Tiramisu."

"OK."

"And we will make a fruit salad, too."

She sat herself at the table, put her headphones on and was lost to the world writing a short story and listening to music she loved. She moved gently in time to it. Then it was time for Maths. Multiply and divide!

*

Coq au Vin, it turned out to be. Chicken breasts, thighs and bacon, perhaps some slices of chorizo, mushrooms, peppers, onions, sliced carrots. And Garlic, lots of it. Salt and pepper, *and* pepper corns. Not forgetting a few raisins. Peas. And a dark, wine sauce, some mustard perhaps. A little 'cheat's gravy' for thickening, essential. Potatoes, peeled, cut up and put on to boil, and red cabbage. Dark arts, reflected in the wording on his apron: 'Dark Knight of the Kitchen!', a Christmas present a year or two ago.

Cutting, shaping. As gentle as he could: Mark had always been a great believer in light hands. Don't rush, savour the ingredients even as they are taken from the fridge. He loved those Dutch 16th Century still-lives of fruits and vegetables, chicken or swan or rabbit ready for preparation, all fresh and colourful. Then the faces of the 16th Century Arcimboldo, with faces designed out of all sorts of vegetables and fruits. He'd shown these to Annie, who had loved them. And he was doing this for his little girl.

She was just beginning to grow out of childhood. He recalled her and a friend once at the beach. They had dressed themselves in hats and dark-glasses and in their bikinis they had called out, "We're Beach Babes!" as they ran laughing to the sea. It was always her enthusiasm that held him.

*

Annie banged her books shut. "Finished," she said. "Easy, peasy!"

"Come here and help me, then, to make the fruit salad. There's the knife. Peel and slice those three bananas – a couple of millimetres each slice. I have made a syrup, very sweet and a little gooey."

"Yum!" She was leaning against the of the kitchen-top, just tall enough to watch her father. She took hold of the bananas and the red fruits, strawberries, raspberries, bilberries. Leslie opened tins of lychees, pineapple segments, oranges. She prepared them with loving focus, whilst Leslie started prepping the main course. "What are you making? Fish pie?"

"Wait and see."

She gave her father a doubtful look. Fish? Or something else?

He did not quite know how this was going to turn out. Chicken thighs and breasts, cubed. "OK, what next?" he thought. He opened the fridge.

"Hi, everybody!" Sally burst in, dumping her things on top of her little sister's. So absorbed were her father and sister that it took them a moment to react. 16 years old, as with her brother, young and living fully for now, but reaching out beyond, she knew not where, to the life that beckons her.

"Sally!" Her father came to her and gave her a kiss. "Had a good day? Where's your bro?"

"Yeah, great. Jamie's got Football practice." As Mark recalled. "And I've made a new friend. This is Domino."

Mark and Jenny suddenly realised another at the door. He was embarrassed, not the least because this was not his name. But the ensuing silence let the other two notice this lad – a year or two older than Sally? – shy, but striking, with a grand halo of black hair, Afro, slim and dark-skinned. Annie was almost in love on the instant.

"Domino," said Mark, "very good to meet you. Come in, come in, make yourself at home."

"Can he stay for dinner? *Please*!"

Mark waved his hand, "Of course, take a seat. You can help me chop the food – here, a couple of onions – know what to do?"

Silently, Domino sat, took the knife, the onions and uncertainly got to work.

"Dad!!" Sally exclaimed. "He has *not* come here to cook supper."

"Well, then, *you* can do the tomatoes."

She took the tomatoes, the knife, sat next to Domino, got to work. He looked coyly at her, struggling with the onions. Gently, she showed him how.

Mark continued to look into the fridge. Peppers, sauces, garlic, mushrooms – all would go into the pot. And something a little spicy.

Chat, giggles, oohs and ahs. Sally kept her new friend busy, Mark collected the onions, put them on to fry gently, then, in due course added the other ingredients. Annie put some music on – Alicia Keys, was it? – and Sally shrugged, giving Domino a look that said, "It's only Annie."

"Have you voted today – remember you're 16 and you allowed to?" Mark asked.

"Of course! Sally replied. "And I'm not telling you who for!"

The room was warming up, the windows steaming.

"We're going to do our homework, Dad," Sally declared. She wished she and Domino had just quietly walked out.

"Great," Mark said. "But go to the sitting-room with Domino and not upstairs, won't you, please?"

Sally sighed.

"Why's he called 'Domino'?" Annie called as Sally was following her boy out of the room.

Sally turned and gave them a mischievous look. "Because he's my dominant male!"

Physics, Maths and Chemistry: how she loved these!

*

Jamie burst in, breathless. Dumped his kit and bags on Annie's. His football kit was climbing out of the top, but his knees and hands and face all showed signs of footballing battles.

"Hi, Jamie. Had a good time?"

"Yeah, s'okay."

"No! Don't sit – not till you have had a shower!"

Jamie gave a short scowl.

"Then you can do your homework with your sister. She's in the siting-room with a new 'friend', Domino."

" 'Domino'! Hah, he's Seamus."

"Homework?"

"Right."

"Then I'll need you here."

Nothing new in this for Jamie, but he didn't mind all the family pulling together. Anyway, there were lovely smells filling the kitchen. He knew what was coming.

As he was going out, his mother entered. She kissed his cheek, made the usual comments, checked that she now had no mud on her and gave him a hug.

And Alice's mother, Angela, was with her. Suddenly, to Leslie, the room seemed somewhat smaller.

"Hi, Gran," Jamie said, going out.

"Grannie!" Annie exclaimed, running to her.

"Hello," Mark said, giving her a kiss on the cheek.

"I'd love a cuppa," declared Angela.

"Angela's staying for supper," Alice said. "Her cooker's not working."

"So she said," thought Mark. "Yes, do. That's great. Tea coming up. One for you, my love?"

Of course, he loved Angela, everyone did: a force of life she was. All bling, carefully brushed and bushed hairstyle, energies and a great way with people for she had a great heart and was so generous. Many of these traits Alice had, too, especially a love of jewellery. But whereas her mother was grand, she was petite.

Soon, they were all sitting at the table, drinking tea, chatting, enjoying the warmth of the house on this autumn evening, not long after the clocks had gone back. Sally and Domino were back and a cleaned-up, Jamie, too.

And Angela was listening, drawing them all out of themselves. "Why are you 'Seamus', Domino?"

The lad looked at Angela, to him a very old lady. He spoke softly, "My Mum's Irish, my Dad Nigerian."

"How interesting – we lived in Nigeria, once upon a time. . . ."

*

Darkness had fallen and the kitchen blinds were down. 7.00 and supper was ready. Annie had finished the fruit salad, the bananas and the syrup she had made just to her taste, Alice had done the red cabbage, with lardons added, whilst Mark's casserole was gently simmering away, sending its aromas around the room.

Everyone had a bit to do, not just the cooking: laying the table ("How many curses, Dad?" Dad scowled. "Sorry, just a joke. Two? Just two?" Jamie, the wannabe chef, had asked, hoping for more.) Angela was trying to get conversation out of Domino, but even she found this hard work. Sally had fed the dog and now was, well, texting.

"I didn't ask," Mark said to his beloved partner. " Have you had a good day?"

"I wondered if you would ask – thought you never would." Then she drew close to him, as he was opening what will prove to be the first of at least a few bottles of wine. "Yes," she said. "Very good." She put her arm in his and gave him a squeeze.

Mark and she were quite tactile, even after so many years together. But this *was* a little unusual. He turned and looked at her. In her gentle smile he sensed she was really wanting to tell him something.

"And?"

"Guess."

"You got the sack?"

"Stupid. V cold!"

"Well?"

"I had a great surprise today."

"OK, what's so hot?"

"Hot money!"

"Oh, tell me!"

"Promotion!" she whispered.

Leslie looked at her, smiled; she nodded with proud smile. He took hold of her, hugged her off her feet and kissed her so very warmly.

"What to?"

"Director." For a moment, it seemed even the casserole stopped simmering away.

All conversation stopped. This was not usual behaviour. Dad hugging Mum in front of all. Domino looked down.

Soon the champagne was out, pink and very bubbly. Fizzy pop. Pop!

Even Domino managed then a smile.

*

Soon they were seated for the meal. The overhead lights were off, two candles lit on the table and four lights placed around the room. The vegetables were on the table, and Jamie was lifting the casserole of the stove.

"Ladies and Gentlemen!" he declared as he put in from to his father. "Dinner is served. First course – Roast Leg of Insurance Salesman! From our *in*famous chef."

"Yummm. . ." went Sally.

"Yummy," crowed Annie. "My favourite."

"Lush, lush, lush," purred Angela.

"Ya-Humm. . ." murmured Alice, as she leant forward, anticipating.

"Mmm," Domino offered.

And Mark?

Silence.

Then, quietly, but getting louder, Mark started to sing:

"Eating humans is wrong! I don't eat humans. I WON'T eat humans! Eating humans is wrong!"

"Why not – they're good for you – they're delicious – they like to be eaten – there are too many of them and they come cheap!" Such cries raced around the table.

Half an hour later, after seconds had been served and approving sounds had been uttered, all that was left on the plates were bones and bits of skin.

One or two with some well-cooked bird feathers still in place.

Of course, everyone loved Annie's fruit salad. And the Tiramisu.

*

Much later, when the house was dark, when Angela and Domino had left and, when was still and quiet, Mark and Alice sat close together on the blue sofa.

Tired and relaxed, they listened to some gentle music, piano pieces by Chopin.

One standard lamp provided the only light.

"What a day!" Alice said softly. "What a lovely dinner. Annie's fruit salad was the best bit of all."

"Not the casseroled insurance sales. . . ."

"Pah! Not a patch. Might have been better if it had been a bank manager. You got all the ingredients right, in those around the table *and* in the dishes. And as for the other pudding – what was it? Oh, yes. A Tiramisu. What's that mean, tell me again?"

He told her. And so they held each other.

20

The Beatitudes

Blessed are the pure in heart

The Bible

When the last speck of dust had been swept away, when the last window-pane was spotlessly clean, Alice's supervisor told her that she could go.

Putting on her coat, she could sense his eyes looking at her, askance if not directly. The hallway was empty of people; a bench ran along one wall and there was a screen showing happy people frolicking around a swimming pool. Everything else looked, to Alice, a little shoddy. Not that she cared. It was all the same to her. Sitting for a moment on the bench, she wanted nothing but rest and a moment's solitude. She sensed the man moving towards her.

Immediately, she stood up, looked around her and, without giving him any sign, briskly took herself out through the swing doors.

Outside, it was darkening, grey, cold. Street lights, sparsely placed, threw shadows on the street and sides of buildings. Shop windows, doorways, rubbish bins: all were sentinels. Her footsteps were watched, her breath was her only guide. Ought she return to her flat? Not whilst he was in the hall. An uneven pavement, cars sluggishly passing, other humans avoiding: she did not notice.

Around the first corner, high on a wall opposite, was a big screen, lighting the way with laughter, splashes, trays of drinks.

'Blessed are those who are hungry and thirsty,' a chorus appeared to be singing from somewhere. 'For you will have plenty!'

The green of the palm trees, bright sunshine, the blue of the sea and water: Alice glanced up but saw nothing.

Though a memory did rush through her, a memory of just such a day with Mark, a day of laughter, sunshine, swimming and cocktails. With Mark.

She almost asked herself, 'Who was he?'

She made her way to a river, but it was now dark and so were its waters. A little light flickered on the surface, wavelets splashed gently against a stone wall. Dead leaves covered the ground as Alice leant against an upright. She knew she could easily slide down, sit on the decay and never get up again.

Soon the chill of the evening got to her and, almost unwillingly, she turned and made her way back to the block of rotting flats that was now her home.

*

Alice was alone; she had been told this on her release, that she had some work to do, that the people would be grateful for this and that she would have somewhere to live. But that was all. Now, she knew not where she lived, nor cared.

Days would come and go for her – at times she felt she would rather have been in prison still. She was indifferent to her routine, as she knew that there was nothing else for her. Mark was gone, she knew not where, her past was gone, her future she cared not for and her present, well, every day was her now and the same.

Slowly she made her way home. The message was clear, as the screen in the hallway told her: 'Blessed are those who humble themselves, for then the people will give them everything.' The supervisor was gone and she made her way to her small flat.

The screen in the corner; Donna sitting so patiently on the corner table. Alice took a little food out of the fridge and a glass of water, sat on the edge of the sofa and waited – for what? For tiredness to take her over? For sleep to let her forget? The screen would not let her sleep nor forget. Almost with reluctance, she peeled the skin off a banana. And there was a knock on the door.

She did not move. Again the knock, this time much more aggressive. Perhaps police were about to break it down.

The she heard a woman's voice.

Slowly, she got up and went the few paces to the door. And opened it.

For a moment, she froze before throwing her arms around the woman before her. It was her mother.

Whom she had not seen or heard of for all these months.

At first, her hold was fierce, tight, then she felt a weakness coming through her and her mother had to hold her up.

With a certain brusqueness, she guided her daughter back into the room and closed the door. 'Alice. Alice! Alice – my darling.'

Alice quivered, gave a little cry. And the tears began. Great, ghastly cries even wails, from Alice. From her mother, gentle tears. Gentle pats on the back.

Alice found herself being led to the sofa, being seated and hugged. Her strength had almost dissipated. But soon her mother's warmth and soothing voice calmed her.

'Blessed are the poor in spirit, for the people will love them.'

Alice moved back and, wiping the tears from her cheeks and eyes, looked at her mother. And then held her again, tight around the neck.

Soon, her mother said, 'Now, now. All will be well. The people will love you. You have learnt so much.'

For some time, Alice remained silent, except for the occasional sniff.

'Why have you come? Why has it taken you so long?'

‘ “Why have I come?” Why do you ask, my love? To see you, to be with you. I am your mother. I am here to show I care, to show I love you.’

Alice was silent. For some time. She rested her head on her mother’s shoulder. Silence filled the room. And then her tears and ever more of them.

Only the flickering screen seemed to offer any life with its images of lovely, happy people, advertisements for all being well with the world.

In time, Alice, almost in a whisper, asked her mother this. ‘Where have you been all these months and weeks?’

Her mother remained silent.

‘Do you know? Did you not miss me? Did you not wonder?’

For a moment, her mother bowed her head before looking at Alice in the eye. She smiled. ‘They told me. You have been in prison.’

‘When did they tell you?’

Her mother shrugged her shoulders. ‘A few days ago, or so. I don’t remember.’

‘Oh, Mother. Mother!’

She paused. The asked, ‘Have you come to take me home? Can I come back with you?’

‘I – don’t know. I’m not sure. . . .’

The day had descended into darkness, only the neon strip providing light, but no colour or warmth, into the apartment.

Alice stood. ‘Did they tell you to come here?’ She walked to the window. ‘Did they allow it? I don’t even know where I am – how did you know?’ She was by the window, looking out down at the darkening street below. Street lights. Shop windows. And a black car.

‘Do you know where Mark is?’ She saw her mother pause, looking vacant. Her voice rose. ‘Do you know what they did to me? What they did to me?’

‘Who is this “they”?’

‘Mark’s dead! You know that don’t you? Don’t you?’

Her mother shook her head. ‘You were arrested when the officers were shot in the bar. That’s all I know.’

‘ “They” – oh, I think you know who they are. *They* arrested us, *they* took us in, threw us in cells, took us into their torture room. TORTURED us, raped me, yes *raped* me and killed Mark in front of me. Is that all you know? Couldn’t you guess?’

Her mother stood and came over to her and stroked her daughter’s cheek tenderly. ‘Blessed are those who are persecuted for righteousness sake – for you will soon be in the kingdom of the people.’ She smiled gently.

Alice sprang away. ‘You’re one of them! Aren’t you? Aren’t you?!’

*

It is perhaps unnecessary for the ordinary person to understand in any detail the nature of The Theory of Relativity or of Quantum Physics. Certainly, this writer does not and cannot – nor does anyone know how to relate them.

However, there are implications that should be available to all. In the first place, to grasp that time cannot exist without space and that space cannot exist without time, for Einstein's theory stressing how they must interact and that the one can affect the other, implies that time may have no beginning and no end and so that the vastness of the universe – incomprehensibly vast – is in itself, a paradox. Put another way, the enormity of the universe is mirrored only by the infinitesimal smallness of the parts that make up the atom, String Theory, in particular.

Einstein famously distrusted Quantum Theory. 'God,' he declared, 'does not play jokes.' Not that he believed in God. On the other hand, Quantum Theory, dealing as it does with the infinitesimally small – the elements inside the atom (which itself has largely had only theoretical existence until recently photographed) – being its subject matter. In particular, one is familiar with Schrodinger's Cat, which is both dead and alive. In this famous metaphor, Schrodinger captured the essential paradox of the photon: it is both a particle and a wave. Here, the answer does not matter, except in so far as there is one conclusion that follows: it is a matter of chance. Therefore, the arrangement of all matter at the subatomic level is a matter of chance. Fortunately, Quantum Physics, though dealing as it does with the random arrangement of sub-atomic particles, postulates that although we can wake up in the morning reassured that one's nose has not turned green, since this current arrangement of matter is extremely predictable, our nose or our galaxy or our universe, though a matter of chance, is reassuringly likely to remain the same, in so far as we are alive.

But are we alive? Is it this terrible uncertainty which, amongst other things, allows us to turn to tyranny for our comfort and safety, to make us believe that life has a purpose?

*

'One of them? Who? What do you mean, my darling?'

'I – we – were tortured! Don't you understand? And after all these months, you appear out of the blue!'

'I came because I love you. I do!'

Alice moved away as her mother tried to embrace her.

They stood, looking at each other.

Alice spoke first, almost in a whisper. 'Tell me the truth. Tell me why you have come – and why do you ignore what has happened to me?'

She drew the ragged curtain.

'I wanted to see you. We have despaired for all these months, your father and me. Our lives – well, our lives have been, well, different. Our jobs, you know. . . .'

‘And that black car in the street, there. It’s for you, isn’t it?’

‘I have come, yes, to bring you back to us, to our lives in this country where we have so much – plenty of food, entertainment, the lovely sex parties –.’

Alice looked baffled. Pained and baffled.

‘And I have come to help you see that you, who are so pure in heart, will be blessed by the people. You will find happiness in all that is provided for us.’

Alice sat. Never had she felt so alone. Resting her head on the arm of the chair, she let out a loud, angry, moan.

‘Six months!’ She shivered. That lovely day, that terrible day, those terrible months. And now her mother. Was she helping her? Had she betrayed her? And did she know the difference? ‘What’s happened to Mark?’

‘Mark?’

‘Yes, Mark! My Mark. I love him so much.’

‘Oh Mark, your Mark. The police told me he was dead.’

Alice looked at her mother as she tried to take in these words. Were they as dead to her as all else had become?

Her mother, in her comfortable jersey and sensible shoes, came to her, put her hand on her daughter’s shoulder. Alice jolted away.

Her mother pulled up a tattered kitchen chair. Gently she said, ‘Blessed you will be if you mourn, for you will be comforted. The State gives us everything. Be happy, my love, be cheerful. Come back home with me.’

Alice looked up, first at her mother’s smile, then around the flat. She recalled the apartment she had shared with Mark, the home that she had been brought up in with all its comforts and plenty. The munificent State.

‘Do I have a choice?’ she asked, almost only to herself.

And she knew the answer.

*

It may well be that we are not products of a beneficial life or even of god and kind creator. As yet, no one has been able to unify the two great theories of the nature of matter. This maybe because Evolution has given the capacity to determine the nature of things only in so far as this enables us to pass on our genes.

Darwin, in his Theory of Evolution, made it clear that, on the biological level, all creatures that have life are the result of chance mutations. In time, he came to regret the term he had used in the subtitle to *On The Origins of Species*: Natural Selection. This, he recognised, gave the impression that there was a driving force behind selection, that is a determining nature. Organisms, little and large, appear as mutations, live, pass on their genes, and survive as long as stronger forms of life do not destroy them. For this reason, all existence is only temporary (even if it has been around for 500 million years or so): extinction is the inevitable outcome. This applies to mankind as much as it the smallest virus.

How then, should we perceive life, as we go from moment to moment, from day to day? When all is purposeless.

Isn't the answer straightforward?

21

'Nature, red in tooth and claw'

A Meditation on Freedom

The egg lies, perhaps, on a bed of fresh straw; there may be four or five others. It may be warm in the barn, it may be colder in the shed out in the field. The hen is pecking away at grains left by the farmer, but never far from her brood. The straw is dry, or it is soiled, but there is an accompanying silence which strangely reassures as one pauses to see if all is fine. There is mud on the boots, but there is, perhaps, an unacknowledged sense of pleasure as life is felt making its progress. You pause and listen – something has attracted the attention. It has been heard many times before in locations everywhere – a tiny scratching is coming from inside the egg. It has been three weeks in gestation.

You bend down to hear more clearly; then there is a slight cracking – and a crack appears on the surface of the egg. And, as the crack gets a little bigger, the beak of the infantile bird pokes through. It is moved a little from side to side, trying to make the hole wider. Then, you see it thrust forward, outward, the whole beak, the eyes and then the head, with the shell breaking off in little pieces. There is a push, and then another as the body of the chick breaks out of what has been its home. It is out. It shivers, staggers, its wings flap for the very first time. The little creature, infinitely delicate and vulnerable has broken into the world, into the life that has been beckoning it, that will nurture it or destroy it. Its mother gently brings it under her wing.

There is a photograph, of a Crocodile, one of Nature's most fearful creatures. It is lying, with its mouth slightly open, open sufficiently to allow one to see the teeth, the ferocious teeth that can snap a man's leg in two, and with its cold, watching eye. Maybe it is looking at the camera, unblinking. The viewer sees the impassive eye, takes in the rough, ridged scales, and sees the teeth. Fear is instinctual, even though the viewer is safe in his sitting-room. But there, at the tip of the jaw, which is open a couple of inches, sits, on its mother's lip, a tiny infant. No more than two or three inches long. The mother could, of course, snap its jaws and the infant would be no more. But she does not. It is reported that, amongst other characteristics, the female Crocodile is one of Nature's tenderest mothers. It has, after all, no predators – except man.

But the Dik-dik, the smallest of Africa's antelopes, standing at no more than about 15 inches high, is not so free. It ranges across the bushveldt of southern and eastern Africa. You will see these, perhaps, on the plains of Amboseli, in the flat interior of the Ngorongoro Crater or in the Kruger Park. Being so small, they are also so vulnerable. So, driving on safari one day in one of these nature parks, you see a Dik-dik being born. The mother is standing as she gives birth and as her off-spring comes out into the world, you will see something astonishing: it is standing and able to walk almost immediately. Evolution has given this creature this striking ability – in order to give perhaps only a fractional advantage over its predators. It is also capable of running at 25 miles per hour. Its existence is widespread over these lands.

There is, too, the Spatulate Hummingbird. You will find this only in one place on this planet, but it epitomises all the beauty of evolution, of biological life. It is found in a very small part of a forested and mountainous district of Peru. It is tiny, just fifteen centimetres long, including a normal tail but much of this length is taken up by two long tail feathers, at the end of each is a dark blue feather, shaped a little like the Ace of Spades. This little creature has a turquoise gorget, a white body, blue crown and dark green body. When courting, it flies vigorously around its environment, but can only keep this up for a short while, not more than fifteen minutes. Its fragile existence is under threat from human predation, including logging.

In the rondavel of a hotel on the shores of Lake Naivasha in Kenya, a Paradise Flycatcher was found resting on the lamp-shade. This is, again, a tiny, beautiful bird. Orange in colour it usually is and small enough to fit in the hand, except for a long tail that at least doubles its length.

Meanwhile, outside on the lawns of the hotel, wildebeest and waterbuck rest on the grass; on occasion, nature's most dangerous creation, a Hippopotamus, or 'horse of water', might wander around.

*

The infant becomes the chicken, the antelope, piglet, the calf, the kitten or the child. He or she will totter, and walk and run, ever farther from the parents. The chick will have no choices, the crocodile will not need choice as she can have whatever is needed and the dik-dik's only choice will be dictated by its ability to evade its predator by running into a thicket – it has been conditioned so to do. He will be ordinary. Like most of us humans. Meanwhile, for all its preternatural beauty, however much this Hummingbird will display its charms to its much more dowdy potential mate, she might well decide that he is not beautiful enough, whilst the Flycatcher must hope for the best. And the Hippo – Evolution has turned him into the most violent of animals as he has to contest with other males of his own size and strength in order to mate. This is *the* ultimate alpha male.

In his working life, a former teacher guided, or helped to guide, his charges to whatever lay in store for them beyond his classroom. He always admired they ways in which they lived life for now, yet reached out to the life that beckoned them. Their abilities and talent being fostered, they could make choices, choices that, one way or another would define their futures. Such freedom of choice, if that is really what it is, plays little part in the lives of those creatures above, or in any creatures. But freedom and choice are inextricably linked.

Freedom to, freedom from? And how much do we, *can* we actually choose? In most cases, the child will, in time, flee the nest, he or she must kill its parents, metaphorically speaking, to be free.

We strut and display like the best of them, we can compete for partners and mates, for territory and place. And power. And in writing this, its author is free to make choices all the time, in every word and sentence, in topic, theme and structure. But can these questions be answered with clarity? Can this one?

And we struggle against those politicians who would rule us, those who control the media, the judiciary and government and the language of politics. We have to watch so carefully that this is not happening at any time.

George Orwell, in *1984* depicted a world, a people, under the thumb and control of a brutal yet anonymous state – anonymous in the sense that only Big Brother – the ultimate alpha male, unnamed, secret and ruthless, but universal - was in charge. Winston Smith and his lover, Julia, attempt to defy the regime, with dire consequences. Orwell has them escape the city, with its grim and endless controls, into the woods and fields beyond. There they make love. It is a return to nature, an attempt to give rebirth to Adam and Eve, perhaps, or at least to regain their natural and instinctual selves, selves who are both biological and conscious. It is, as Orwell puts it, 'a political act'. The choice they make is disastrous, for Smith will betray this love.

A terrible choice is forced upon him. Freedom is denied him, either way. Betray Julia – or protect himself?

Smith surrenders to necessity. Is not all freedom, all choice, curtailed by necessity?

It has often been said that there is no creature more cruel, more bloodthirsty than the human creature, particularly the male of the species. This does not need illustration. Yet what is it that make us so violent when there is so much to find in life so much that is beautiful? Why does Smith have this choice thrust upon him?

Our generation, now in perhaps in the last phases of life, has inherited the terrible consequences of war, but we have, by and large and luckily, never been involved in such, though we see it all around the world. What produces the warmonger, the tyrant, the torturer? And *why* do so many follow such? Why do we torture, execute?

> First they came for the socialists, and I did not speak out—
> Because I was not a socialist.
> Then they came for the trade unionists, and I did not speak out—
> Because I was not a trade unionist.
> Then they came for the Jews, and I did not speak out—
> Because I was not a Jew.
> Then they came for me—and there was no one left to speak for me.

These famous words from Pastor Niemoller (1892-1984), giving voice to his own shame at not speaking out against the rise of the Nazi Party in pre-war Germany, have echoed down the years. They were echoed by Hannah Arendt (1905-75), famous for her comment following the 1961 trial of Adolf Eichmann about the 'banality of evil' as it reflected on the former Nazi's woeful lack of moral imagination in being the agent who managed the transportation of millions of Jews to the gas-chambers. Arendt explained further: 'The sad truth is that most evil is done by people who never make up their minds to be good or evil.'

Arendt came under some criticism for her famous statement, as it might have suggested that there was an excuse for the terrible deeds of Eichmann, indeed for the Nazis in general and for all totalitarian actions. However, it is the second statement that makes it more interesting. We are reminded that Eichmann and his ilk were – and are – humans. In other words, the torturer will torture at the behest of his superiors because he is unthinking. Perhaps this applies to us all in our minor ways from day to day as we are confronted with those very elements which makes us most human: choice and necessity. The refusal of choice is so much easier. But are we ever free to refuse choice? And if we accept the rule of the totalitarian, the tyrant, explicitly or implicitly supporting him (ever 'her'?), do we deny our own humanity?

There is an image that refuses to fade. In the fading months of his Presidency of the USA, the Horror then occupying The White House claimed that he had Covid; after three days in hospital (superior being that he is), he had recovered and returned. He stands on the balcony of the famous building, shrouded in a golden light and, as ever, framed by Stars and Stripes. He salutes – whom? The people of America? Himself?

A few weeks later, 70 million of his fellow Americans voted for him. Thankfully, it was not enough, but he won't admit it. How could he, when his pose would have delighted Mussolini and all the other tyrants, little and large, that have strutted upon the stage in our times, before and no doubt after?

But why do we allow such?

*

In the rondavel of a hotel on the shores of Lake Naivasha in Kenya, a Paradise Flycatcher was found resting on the lamp-shade. This is, again, a tiny, beautiful bird. Orange in colour it usually is and small enough to fit in the hand, except for a long tail that at least trebles its length. Wanting the little creature to be free, the occupier opened the windows and door as the bird flew around desperate to get out. It came to rest again on the ceiling lamp. In order to take it to the window, he put his hand gently towards it, slowly. Gently. In an instance, the bird had flown and was gone through a window, finding its freedom in its natural element. The man was left holding the feathers of the tail.

Evolution had given this creature the means of escape. It took its freedom in an instant.

Spatulate Hummingbird

22

***The Fall** – A Parable*

And therefore never send to know for whom
the bell tolls; it tolls for thee.
John Donne

Westerbrook strode towards the door with his usual purposefulness. Tall and upright and, as ever, neatly, precisely dressed, he made no effort to be, as it were, in charge. Indeed, those around him, both below in the pecking order and above, felt that they knew where they stood with him and that they were, as one might say, grateful for this. Such respect was never to be articulated. It just existed. He felt comfortable in the dark corridors of The Castle; he enjoyed the polished touch of the old wooden staircase.

He knocked, entered without waiting. The Secretary was at his desk, the large window behind almost making a silhouette out of him. He beckoned to Westerbrook to be seated. The walls of the office were panelled, a radiator on the left. Landscapes from a different century decorated them.

'Good evening,' Westerbrook said as he leant against the radiator, folded his arms and inhaled from his cigarette.

The Secretary could be seen clearly. Westerbrook observed, as he often did, the lines on the man's forehead. Inwardly, he chuckled. The meeting would not last long: both wanted to get home.

'How has it been today?' The Secretary had no need to ask this as all was followed on screen and recorded. But it was just a formality. He liked to think that he was putting his junior colleague at ease. He need not have bothered. 'That young couple . . .'

'Yes,' Westerbrook interjected. 'We dealt with these. They won't ever be any trouble. Nor will their friends. To think that even if they go out into the hills that they will be free to say and think without our knowing!'

'Yes, yes.' The Secretary did not need to be told what he already knew, though he knew that Westerbrook needed to be reminded of *his* place. 'Well done. I am sure it gave you all a lot of pleasure.'

This sort of conversation had been taking place for so long that each could recite it, just the names being different. The usual small talk followed. One or two vaguely bawdy jokes, best wishes to the family. . . .

'Right,' said Westerbrook, putting out the cigarette in The Secretary's ash-tray. 'I'll be of, then.' He raised his right hand, giving the open-palmed salute that was *de rigueur*. 'All is in control.' He left the room.

The Secretary was glad that he was not sitting opposite Westerbrook, for he disliked his torturer's eyes. One was green, the other blue. He picked up his phone.

*

All and sundry manifestations of police tyranny and autocratic outrage, in addition to the evils connected with the economic struggle, are equally "widely applicable" as a means of "drawing in" the masses.
Vladimir Lenin, Essential Works: *What Is To Be Done and Other Writings.*

*

Westerbrook made his way downstairs. As he was crossing the road to his waiting car, something jarred in his mind. He put the thought to one side.

'Home, please, Jankowski.' The driver nodded and he drove off.

Watching the passing scenery, Westerbrook reflected on his day. He was pleased. Though he knew, like everyone else, he was being watched all the time by micro-cameras, he felt he could relax. After all, who was going to come for him? All the same, he was not without ambition. Not at all. He did not want to remain a torturer for ever. Rather, he would supervise the torturers – and who knew better how to do it than himself? And if The Secretary, or anyone else, was going to stand in his way, well, he Colonel Westerbrook will have something to say. General he will be – and thereafter?

He was disturbed in this revery by the sight of an advert having fallen partially from its position. And what was it that had made him feel uncomfortable. Indeed, not 'what' but 'why' had he felt that momentary, unfamiliar intrusion into his mind?

Electronics are better at reading the mind than the possessor of that mind.

*

Privacy advocates are concerned about the threat to privacy represented by increasing storage and integration of personally identifiable information; expert panels have released various policy recommendations to conform practice to expectations of privacy. The misuse of big data in several cases by media, companies, and even the government has allowed for abolition of trust in almost every fundamental institution holding up society.

It is argued that a new kind of social contract will be needed to protect individual liberties in the context of big data and giant corporations that own vast amounts of information, and that the use of big data should be monitored and better regulated at the national and international levels.
Wikipedia: *Big Data.*

*

Peter and Tom were waiting downstairs this evening, though they were not playing with each other. Tom was reading a war-story in his comic, whilst his elder brother was reading with his mother, sitting on her lap. An ordinary, domestic scene, though these day's Mary's features were increasingly drawn. That afternoon she had confided in a friend that it had been a long time since she had laughed. Westerbrook had learned of this almost soon after.

The driver had dropped him off at his front door. 'Same time, tomorrow morning, as usual, please.'

He breathed in deeply as he entered. All was just as he liked it, as he liked it after a day's work. The cellar, the 'White Room' as it was called, could often leave him feeling somewhat tense.

'Right, what do we have here?' he said, examining Tom's comic. 'This looks good. Glad to see you are reading about tough and brave men.' Mary gently put Peter's book down on the floor, beside her.

'Ha! Why are you hiding something? Give it here, Mary. Now!' Mary did as she was told. 'What's this? A cookery book! A *cookery* book? "Twenty Recipes For Beginners". Well and good! Be a cook, then, if that's all you want, young man. You can cook supper for me this evening. No, Mary, you will not help him! It had better be good.'

Peter looked at his Father, then at his Mother. Still and chilling water filled the space between them.

It wasn't good. An omelette, of sorts. Peas, chips from the supermarket. Ice cream.

'Tom, you will understand, won't you? Why am I so tough on you? Because I want you to be strong, I want you to understand how we work and live these days so when you come to be grown up, you will be ready, ready for service, duty and for living for The Party.'

'What's Democracy, Dad?' Peter asked. 'Teacher told us this morning.'

'Did he now?' Westerbrook will remember this. 'What did he say?'

'She, Dad. She said that, once before, everyone could vote for the government they wanted. What 'before'?'

'Well, we don't have that now! There's no need. Everything is as it should be. Everyone has all they need and The Party helps everyone.' The teacher, Westerbrook told himself, should not have been talking about this.

Mary remained silent throughout all this. Even when she and her husband were alone later, she could only pretend to agree with her husband.

'So, you haven't laughed for ages? As you said this afternoon? Don't you realise The Internet catches everything – *everything*! Lucky you, being married to me. You could have been arrested, as your friend has been. A foolish conversation indeed.'

Mary's thoughts were kept very silent.

Later, in bed, as the light was turned out and after Westerbrook had exercised his right, he realised, as he turned over, what had so vaguely troubled him after his meeting with The Secretary. The Secretary had not asked him to sit in the usual chair.

For the first time for a very long time, Westerbrook found it difficult to get to sleep.

*

But a democracy is bound in the end to be obscene, for it is composed of myriad disunited fragments, each fragment assuming to itself a false wholeness, a false individuality. Modern democracy is made up of millions of frictional parts all asserting their own wholeness.

Democracy and equality try to deny the mystic recognition of difference and innate priority, the joy of obedience and the sacred responsibility of authority.
D. H. Lawrence

*

Then it was a flashing light that woke Westerbrook. But before he could raise his head, there was a loud crash from downstairs, the rushing of numerous booted feet, monosyllabic commands – and the door to his bedroom burst open.

Mary sat, pulling the sheets around her as the heavily protected police – as she thought them – with their helmets, body-padding, truncheons, tasers, radios – and guns pointing at her, at her husband. Cameras on helmets.

Terror filled her as Westerbrook was roughly pulled from his bed – naked, as so he always slept.

'Dress! Quick!' came a command, as rough hands threw him towards some clothes on a chair.

Westerbrook straightened himself. Refusing to dress. Naked, he bellowed, 'What are you? Do you know who I am? Do you know what's going to happen to you?'

But he would not have been able to identify one of these 'officers' of the State, of his state of *his* Party.

He was instantly slapped around the face. Still, Westerbrook was defiant.

He saw the face of little Tom at the door.

'Well, if you don't want to dress, we'll take you as you are.' Tom was bundled out of the way as his father was pulled, driven, even hurtled out of the room. Naked.

Tom ran to his Mother. Peter joined them. Terrified.

Another officer, again, fully militarised, these agents, so familiar in countries around the World. 'Get dressed. One bag only!' The rough tone did little to explain – or rather it did much. ' You will be moving out, going elsewhere. Oh, boys, you won't be seeing your Father for a long, long time. If ever.'

Suddenly, Westerbrook was back in the room. Still tall and defiant, momentarily he had broken free, and rushed back to get some clothing. A shirt, trousers, slippers. Not a glance did he give his cowering family. Guards dragged him away, his clothes only half on. Sirens blared away, into the distance.

Mary sat on her bed, facing the empty room, empty of her husband, empty of reason, empty of her life. Her boys had sought comfort, one on either side of her. She held them close, very close. A Pietà.

She, though, felt, if incoherently, something. Something liberating?

The three sat together, on the bed. Silent. Peter buried his head in his Mother's arm; Tom sat looking at the door. The room was still dark, but dawn was slowly rising.

Mary, her arms around her boys, held them tight to her. Stillness, everywhere. Silence. She opened her eyes from time to time. All was still. Some clothes, usually so immaculate, lay on the bed, on the floor. The door was ajar. At one moment she thought she could hear her husband coming upstairs. The walls, usually so white, the house, usually so tidy, now silent, empty.

The violence of the scene – the figures dressed in protective clothing, the guns, the helmets, radios and tasers – was replayed in her mind. Again and again. At least the boys were safe.

She knew – as her husband would often warn her – that her world had utterly, completely changed.

She had been told to pack. Just one bag. Between them? Each? Even this she could not answer. Nor, certainly, where would she be in an hour or two?

*

'Jesus died to save all? No, no, no! Jesus died to save himself. Just as now one must die to save others, to save the State. One man's death can *never* diminish me. One man's death elevates me. And everyone.
'So – *Death to Traitors!'*
Ramon Rodrigues *The New Jerusalem.*

*

Westerbrook knew what was coming. After all, he had been one of its main practitioners. Practitioners of one of the State's 'purification' processes. He knew that everyone had every reason to be happy. Anything else had to be dealt with. After all, did not The Party provide all, even the most basic pleasures? Sex parties?

Nevertheless, he would do his best to shake free of his captors. And seek redress.

The door of the van opened – he knew exactly where he was, his second home, no, his main home. He stared defiantly at the officer, Taser pointing at him. He refused to move. The Taser fired, just once. Westerbrook fell.

He did not know how long he had been unconscious, but when he woke, he was in a cell, just four feet by five, with just enough height to enable sitting. He felt a chill. He was naked. He knew the meaning of it all, of what was to come next.

It was the white room, with its chair, bolted to the ground in the middle, fierce spotlights on it. But, then, he had helped design this space. There were stains on the floor.

Now his arms were bolted to the arms of the chair, cold metal when he first was seated so very roughly. His ankles were also tied tight to the bottom of the legs, keeping his knees apart. A cloth had been tied around his head and between his teeth, his mouth forced open to prevent speaking.

He knew what this was for, too.

Around the room, on tables, on shelves were instruments, tools of the trade. There were no windows.

After some time, Westerbrook saw a chair being put in place a few feet before him. And then, someone sat on it. Comfortably, smoking a long, thin cigar. The Secretary.

He did not speak for some time. He was enjoying the moment.

He was dressed comfortably, in a three-piece suit. Legs crossed. 'Attendants' waiting in the shadows.

'So.' He smiled. 'We meet again.' He did not add, 'For the last time.'

He saw Westerbrook struggle against his bindings.

'How does it feel to be in here again? And naked?' He knew there could be no answer.

'You're an ambitious man, aren't you?' Suddenly, The Secretary's voice had hardened.

'Naked! Did you really think that nakedness was a physical thing only? You like strip-shows? Oh yes, we've told your wife this. You know everyone is followed. Everything – *everything* –

is on the Internet. Even the slightest thought. And the Party knows how to govern. We control the judges and all the media – it's obvious, isn't? But you know this. And we know how to control how people vote, too. It's the end of History, isn't it?'

Westerbrook knew that there was nothing to do, nothing to say. Nothing was coming. Very soon.

'A man must die, for the good of everyone. So *you* have practised for so long. Pleasure and then happiness! Huh! You have thought yourself above all this.'

He paused, for some time. The Secretary was enjoying this.

'So long.'

He nodded at one of the men.

The last Westerbrook heard was the sound of a switch.

Click.

First his legs. Then, so quickly, his hands, his head. The pain, excruciating, filled his body, a wave, and another and another, each more painful. A very bright light. Brighter than anything. All in a very few moments.

Then nothing.

'Deal with him in the usual way,' commanded the Secretary. He drew on his cigar and left the room. *He* had done his duty.

Later that morning, the guards took Westerbrook's burnt body to the crematorium, the same crematorium to which Waterbrook had sent so many.

In the afternoon, a bag of ashes, of human waste, was casually shaken out into the nearby river.

*

And Mary? And Peter and Tom? Westerbrook's boys were taken away and given to the State's adoption service. They were never to see their parents again – or each other. Mary never smiled again.

She was placed in a small apartment in a distant town. She was given, too, a job as a school cleaner. And there was a young woman neighbour, who cleaned the stairs and hallway and who also cleaned in the local supermarket. And never smiled.

The State looks after everyone.

23

To Have – or Not to Have. . . .

God save our. . . .

On 29th April, 2011, a young woman stood for a moment at the top of the steps leading to the entrance to Westminster Abbey. She is as beautiful as one could imagine for such an event and in her hands she holds a lovely bouquet flowers that epitomise all the beauty and glory of majesty. She pauses, looking up at the ancient carvings, members and figures that make up the ornamentation of the ancient doorway. She lowers the flowers, walks over to a young soldier on guard duty and hands them to him, smiling. She turns, walks back down to the car that had brought her to this moment, opens the door. After a moment, it drives off. She is never seen again.

Inside the Abbey, the great and the good, headed by the Monarch and her family, sit waiting for the moment when she will be escorted down the aisle by her father to be handed to the young Prince, waiting by the altar steps. As is common, these Royal events are timed and organised to perfection, to the minute. And, so, when the young woman does not appear as rehearsed only the day before, gradually a shuffling begins to be heard, faces turning down the aisle.

Soon, a young man, an officer in splendid Guards unform, comes quickly down the aisle. No, he is not going to marry the Prince. He is not quite sure who to tell what happened. He has never had to do anything like this and never will do such again.

In desperation, he tells the groom's father. *He* tells his mother; she gathers herself together and, with as much of the dignity as she is accustomed to showing, she leads the family, all in some confusion, down the aisle and out.

Meanwhile, television cameras have beamed the scene across the world to billions watching.

*

'Good for her!' said Andy in the pub that evening. 'I saw it all. End of the Monarchy, I say!'

'Good riddance!' Freddy replied, bringing the first pints. 'Plainly, she did not understand what was going on. Chickened out, I say. She could never have been our Queen. The Monarchy will survive without her. She was just a commoner.'

'Hm! Is that what you want, then?'

'Of course.'

Andy had known his friend for years and though he had respected his views, they were often very different from his.

'You know how I feel – Monarchy is good for us, it helps us, it makes us feel who and what we are. British!' Freddy tried his beer.

'Hold on,' Andy interspersed, taking a first sip. 'Why should I look to someone else to tell me who I am? I am me. I eat, I play football, I have my work and family. That's me! Just like you.'

'Of course. Just like me – we play in the same team, after all. But how do you feel when we won the World Cup back in '66? I know we were neither alive, but we are forever being reminded of it. Bobby Moore and Geoff Hurst's hat-trick and all that.'

'And why have we never won anything else since? Anyway, are you saying we won the Cup *because* we are a Monarchy? Was Phil the Greek part of the team? Oh no, he would have been playing for Greece!'

'Now you're joking. No argument there. Except that at the time it made us all feel good.'

'Really? Because we are a monarchy? Where there any Scots playing. Or Welsh. Or Irish? Our Monarch always likes to remind us that together we are 'Great' Britain. Tell that to the Scots or Welsh or Irish! Besides,' Andy went on, 'I'm part Welsh.'

'OK, but Monarchy is much more than sport! You know that. It's our *history*, it's the past running through today and into the future. Think of Victoria, think of Queen Elizabeth – the First – the ways in which Monarchy held together the Empire.'

'Hmm! You touch on a lot of topics here, *big* topics. Empire! Don't get me started on *that*. Let me ask you,' said Andy slowly and looking at his pal sharply, 'were any of these monarchs ever elected? Did we ever *vote* for a King or Queen? No, of course not. Shouldn't we vote before the next Monarch is crowned? Monarchy is based on conquest.'

'No! That would make him – or her – a president. Why should we ever do that. It's quite foreign to our natures. Anyway who would you have as president? Tony Blair?'

'Maybe, but that's so simplistic. Look around the World. As I understand it, only 7 percent of all countries in the world have monarchs, the rest presidents, of one sort or another. Of course there are good presidents and corrupt, cruel ones, but most of those monarchies are not just figureheads, but themselves tyrants. There are plenty of wonderful people in the country who have achieved so much and who might be willing to represent us as Head of State for, say a fixed term of four years. *If* we need one at all.'

'But how could we ever agree on who would be Head of State? Appointed? Elected? Who by?'

'Quite! By something called the electorate.''

'It's so much better,' continued Freddy, warming to his theme, 'to have a natural process of becoming king or queen. As I said, this makes us feel all part of a one big family, breaking down those differences between, say, a Yorkshire family and one from Cornwall, between rich and poor. And just look at the younger generation, even in the papers today, a smiling, happy, ordinary family. Just as we are or as we *can* be.'

'Oh,' Andy answered defensively, 'I have no objections to the Royal Family as they are, despite one or two oddballs. They are decent enough people. But why should someone, a little child, be born to such privilege, to such untouchable comfort, ease and vast wealth, none of which they have made for themselves? Does *that* make them ordinary? I think not. And their lives are shrouded in security, isolation. . . . My round,' Andy continued, getting up. 'This is getting interesting. You Monarchist, you! Same again, Old British Windsor Ale?'

Andy made his way through a growing crowd to the bar, whilst Freddy sat twiddling his beer-mat. He knew Andy certainly had been a republican, ever since the death of one of the family, more than twenty years ago. All that excessive out-pouring of grief, those acres of flowers, the funeral beamed across the world. Of course, it had been a terrible loss to her family, but to the rest of us? We had all shared in it. Freddy felt more adamant.

Andy, meanwhile, was reflecting on just the same topic. He remembered that day so well, as he presumed, Freddy will have done, for very different reasons. A brilliant sunny day, millions in the streets and around the world, the family walking in solemn procession behind the cortege, the service. The country had stopped, united for the moment in grief. That was true. But hadn't it been all *so* over the top?

'Here you are, mate,' Andy said.

'Come on now,' Freddy said, raising his glass. 'You must admit that all those ceremonies, weddings, funerals, coronations, are wonderful. If only because they entertain us. Though, of course, they do much more than that.'

Andy looked at Freddy. 'Yeah, well, if that's what you pay your licence fee for, that's your choice. But it is *more* than entertainment. It's also propaganda, it's all about creating a myth, a myth of, how do they put it, 'national identity'. Look, I think that monarchy goes back to the oldest times, when tribes and clans needed, for evolutionary necessity, to have a strong leader, an alpha male – or female. Occasionally. Yes, to give coherence, connection, protection. But *now*? Well, we must grow out of that. We are democratic and monarchies and their religions and dynasties have lead only to endless wars.'

'And that's just why we must continue with monarchy, for we always need meaning, connection and assurance. Aren't you proud of being British? Isn't that what you and I are?' Freddy shuffled, pulling his jacket tighter around him. 'Have we, our nation, not achieved so much, aren't we, as they say, exceptional?'

Andy was a little taken aback by burst of emotion. 'Hold on! That's just it, the myth. Of course we've achieved a lot, but what modern country has not? And let me add that most of what we achieved has been achieved through slavery, imperialism and later colonialism. I was reading only the other day that if you are white and middle-class in this country, you will have benefitted, one way or another, from slavery. Funded by imperial gain. Queen Victoria? Pah! Empress of India? Did any Indians vote for her? Or not – our antecedents, all good working-class people, were made to toil in mills and mines and factories all to live in poverty. Come on, you know this. And what did any monarch do to respond to this? Nothing. Ever!'

'Oh come on now. Our Monarchy is renowned around the world. This *is* the case. Don't you know it? You ought to. And if our kings and queens were so bad, so. . . casual, would this be the case? As I said, Monarchy binds us together, rich and poor. . . '

'And keeps the difference between rich and poor all the time.' Andy was getting angry at his friend's, his old friend's ignorance. 'But let's start again, he continued. 'What is the opposite of Monarchy? Democracy, yes? Of course. The people have struggled for centuries to achieve democracy, but this has so often just been handed down to us, making us grateful. Pah! And do you know what 'sovereignty' means?'

'Yeah, it means we are free to do as we like as a nation. No one can boss us around – tell us how to play football!'

'Bollocks! We don't need anyone to do that, do we? The first part of the word comes originally from the Latin, "super" meaning 'above" us. So we live *under* the king or queen, under their *supreme* authority. Meaning we are under the monarchy, we are 'subject' to it. Were the monarchs ever elected? No! I say I am a citizen – and a democrat.'

'Oh. Come on. Democracy needs Monarchy and Monarchy needs Democracy. Each protects the people from overbearing government. We've agreed on that long ago. What about Magna Carta, eh? And the Commonwealth in the 17th Century – The Glorious Revolution of 1689. The Great Reform Act. None of these could have happened without a monarch, for the monarchs at the time had to go along with it – or look what happened to Charles I. Cromwell's rule ended and we had to get our monarchy back.'

'Really?? Never! Democracy begins from the ground up, NOT from on high down to the lives of ordinary people. The people, in that way, are their own monarchs. They MUST be. And if that makes life a little anarchic, then great! Democracy must never mean 'handed down to us'. And remember, a monarch reigns over us, does not rule us.'

'Bloody hell!' Freddy was too flustered to think straight. 'You are on your high horse now. If you don't like Monarchy, what would you like to replace it?'

'We mentioned this before, don't you recall. To tell the truth, perhaps no one. Why do we need a 'Head of State'? To meet people at airports? To enjoy extravagant banquets? Is that what you'd like?'

Freddy took a swig and looked at Andy with a glint of triumph in his eye.

'No! No! Royalty should engage us, embody our past, enrich the present and help forge the future. They can't enforce, no, but they can lead. They can forge public opinion. . . .'

'Blimey, you're getting poetic in your old age! Enslave us, mythologise the past, steal the present and. . . well, forget about the future. What's left?'

'Monarchy! "God save our gr . . . ." Freddy gulped the last of his beer. Perhaps he was growing aware that their altercation was attracting attention.

*

Of course, she didn't do that.

24

***The Seasons** – A Parable*

2021

Saturday, 21st March – The Spring Equinox
Monday 21st June – Midsummer Solstice
Wednesday, 22nd September - Autumn Equinox
Tuesday, 21st December – Winter Solstice

No one of course, can remember those first moments, moments when, after perhaps some hours of painful contractions and after months of proud pregnancy, the birth happens. First, it was her head, with, indeed, some black hair all wet, untidy and straggling over the crown. Then a face, not, one might think, happy after those months of warmth and containment, and so ready to wail, then her shoulders, and so much more easily, the rest of her body. There is still the umbilical attached, but that goes very quickly as she is held in the nurse's hands. From foetus to infant has taken just a few minutes. Dorothy.

Mother lies back, still with her legs apart and knees up as she is cleaned. And though she is exhausted, her new-born is put into her hands, into her arms, as tears of delight run down her cheeks. Never again will she be so close to her child; never again will her little girl mean so much as in that moment. And father, he sits next to her. Silent. Proud and never again will he share quite such happiness.

It is December 21st. Darkness has fallen and Christmas is just four days away. And by two minutes every day, the days will get longer.

It is many decades later. As she lies dying, memories of the life she has led take over. Dorothy does not recall this scene, of course, as no one will, but she sees those little pink wellies with a frog on front as she stumbles through a muddy lane, just four years old. Dolls and teddy bears and all the toys of childhood – and the squabbles with her little brother. But then she feels the warmth of her father's clothes as he picks her up after a stumble when trying to kick a football.

A kite floats through her mind, and then, on a day, a small plane. It is a warm, early spring day. Dorothy moves slightly on her bed – her hand is gently held. Was it at that moment in childhood that she knew that she would be, when grown up, a pilot? "What do you want to be when you are older?" A voice she no longer recognises, and the old question's answer evinces a chuckle.

What was it? Flight, soaring flight? Exploring, seeing the world? Being a bird?

And as she grows, the days become longer. The grey of mornings, the dampness, the snows and the frost – skating on local lakes, even some skiing holidays – snowdrops and daffodils competing for space, green shoots promising colour and new life and on the hedges little buds and new leaf begin their reach for the sun, as hellebores and camelia fade after their winter flowering.

Schoolgirl. 11 years old. New tights to go with her uniform. A moment's anxiety, a moment's pride, passes through the old mind. Then, as so much in life, competition and laughter. Laughter at each other's jokes (so soon to become childish), laughter at teacher's peccadilloes, at parents' obvious limitations. Competition for attention, for doing better at Physics, for parents' encouragement.

For boys. When was it that nature took its inevitable, but no less surprising turn? The days become longer, as do her days at school – games and plays, music lessons and extra time thinking about, learning about aeroplanes. There are boys seeking her attention. Rob, with his skate-board; Tom, who told her about Jimi Hendrix. Barry from Australia – such promise. She happily goes out with these and the others – she has no shortage, and she laughs with her friends about the boys and yet, and yet, which would 'pop her cherry'? Giggles and apprehension. As A Level approaches, Dorothy senses, as her mind fights against the closing down, she is the sole girl taking the subjects best suited to her ambition. Her Form Mistress replies, 'Oh, you mean an Air Hostess?'

The day is darkening, although it is early afternoon. She stirs a little. 'Mother.' Her son, Freddie is holding her hand. But there is no Alice there.

Caribbean waters, blue and warm flow beneath her as she pilots the Cessna. She ferries the rich and famous, with money to spend and time on their hands, to private islands. Even occasional royalty. She is comfortable on her deathbed, the warmth of those days filling her now. And as in a dream, she is now flying a Boeing over the Himalayas. Proudly craggy and snow-covered and safely well below.

A thin smile on her lips when once there has been much laughter.

March. The time when the clocks go forward into Spring, when day is as long as night and when all around is new in colour and form. She sees the buds have been waiting for some time, of course, but as winter fades, it was then that she knows, knows beyond any doubt – and in a very few moments, that the young man who has just entered the room is to be the father of her children. Tom. Dorothy and Tom, Tom and Doro, Tom and Dotty. Her bedroom – her death room - now fills with the light of love.

And so it was to be. Freddie, and then Alice, summer babies each one. One of each made each happy. They had travelled, Tom and Dorothy, the World, an airline pilot married to an accountant. Mount Cook and Table Mountain, the skyscrapers of New York and Chicago, the lakes of Central Africa, Arctic wastes and the greatest of cities, London, Paris, Rome. St Petersburg. Floating through her slowing mind, she is happy.

The raspberries, the strawberries, Oil Seed Rape yellowing the countryside, wheat and barley throughout the warm days of summer. But Dorothy had not always been so lucky – she feels a mood change within.

Some farmers burn the stubble, others quickly plough the fields and it only takes six weeks from initial diagnosis to Tom's parting. Other faces, other women come before Dorothy now, but she knows Tom has never been unfaithful. But then he leaves her. For ever. There are the usual processes of dying, of funeral, of love and support and these soon fade and she is alone. Bereft and trying to start again. How quickly does that summer fade into to autumn?

Dead leaves on the pavement in the park. Golden, but turning. Freddie senses his Mother move just a little more.

And then the winds and rains of autumn, the autumn woods in their brilliant afternoon sun, so temporary. Alice. She opens her eyes for a moment. There is no Alice. That grey, grey day in the black car when the authorities allow her one visit to her daughter. Alice who has lost her, who has lost her Mark, who had lost everything. She knew not where.

Dorothy hears her now, on that grey day in her sparse and lonely apartment. 'They tortured me! They raped me.' Does Dorothy now blame herself for the support she gave to The Party?

Her losses. Now she opens her eyes one more time. A little. Outside it is cold, inside she feels no warmth but maybe a sinking feeling; Freddie feels the cold in her hand. Once more she sees her son. It is darkening, it is all darkening into the longest night.

25

From First to Last: Recipes for Life

Chewing the food of sweet and bitter fancy

Shakespeare

Leche de origen temprano, con amore

The little infant, not minutes old and now wrapped in a towel, lies in its mother's arms. Its face, wrinkled as in old age, its eyes shut. She, exhausted from her labour, raises her right hand, opens the gown and her breast appears. The baby's lips open and without any encouragement or effort, they fix on the nipple.

A surge of love filled the mother; the father, sitting now on the bed's edge, smiles as he has never smiled before. He weeps. The baby cries its first cry. Dribbles.

Baby food. Splash into the pot, milky porridge, sweet apricot – splashed around its mouth. Her spoon is banged on her little high table. Dad feeds her gently, smiling.

Soon, she will unwrap her own sweeties, eating enough, leaving some. Wanting more!

*

Chorizo and charred spring onion rigatoni

The Full English. He had given up living on Mother's milk – that's for little brother. Now he was with Dad. Be like Dad.

Dad is spooning breakfast into his mouth. Two fried eggs on crispy fried bread. The yellow of the yolk, the lad observes, spreads over the plate. Two rashers of bacon, well cooked, crispy. Baked beans, tomatoes. Mushrooms, of course. With Black Pudding, at least one big slice.

Slowly, Dad devours the lot. Not exactly savouring, for this is for every day. Certainly relishing.

Toast and marmalade to follow. A cuppa, though now a little cold.

Then, hey! It's off to work, off to school.

All prepared by Mother.

*

Pollo alla Generosi Domenica non economica

Sunday lunch. En famille. 'Yay!' as the granddaughter says. Sunday roast.

Beef this week, or is it chicken? Pork sometimes. Cauliflower cheese, steaming in the dish. Carrots, warm, orange and waiting.

Who's pouring the wine? Two bottles of Merlot (perhaps). A beer or two, pre-prandial.

Cabbage, but lightly cooked. Roast potatoes. Crisp on the outside, golden brown with some darkening. Gently hot. And gravy. Clear, shiny , not too thick, not too thin!

Dad carves (of course); all help themselves.

Key Lime Pie. Ice cream – well, OK Aldi's best in a tub. Perhaps, if lucky, a little dessert wine.

A globe of Brandy, half full.

Let's go for a walk. No, no. Snooze time.

*

Matambre arrollado

Fatten up the World! The Juiciest Hamburger ever! And it's lunch again. My favourite, too.

Ground beef, eggs and bread-crumbs. Milk and cheese (plenty of it!) Garlic, and the buns, thick, soft and crisp on the outside.

But make it all double layered. The cheese nice and sticky, too. I dig my teeth in, hold this delicacy firmly in my podgy fingers. Dig in, bite, chew, buttocks slipping around the stool. Meaty, tomatoey, lettuce summery green. Yum!!!

I'll go out and shoot a pig, good sturdy fence between it and me. It has a few bushes to hide behind. Least I know where my meat comes from.

Fattened up for the kill. Capitalism kills, OK?

*

Glace de la Maison, chocolat et gingembre moulu

But today it's Chocolate mousse. One's 'signature dish'. Four eggs, separated, whites and yolks. Whisk the whites, add sugar, whisk on till firm, little peaks. Melt dark chocolate, mixing to ensure thorough smoothness. Add the yolks, feed the whipped whites into the mixture. Slowly. Not feed, fold! The whites darken, slowly, streaky at first. The spoon turns it over. Slowly, you enjoy the change. Ever darker, till it is all consistent. You dip your finger in. Yes! Needs a dash of Cointreau, though. In it goes.

You pour it into your smart bowl, cut glass preferably. You level it, turning the bowl, shaking it, gently. You cover it, put in the fridge for some hours.

Later you will maybe add cream, then some strawberries. Or indeed, a raspberry jus. Even better.

Chocolate to delight your guests (if you have not kept it all for yourself). Rich. Smooth. Deep.

Unctuous.

*

Garlic kangaroo with guasacaca sauce

The young man sits, opposite a young woman. It is, perhaps, a summer evening in an old tavern. They only met a few hours ago. Each has a full tumbler before them. They chat. They flirt. Lips part, eyelids flutter. Life is good. Where are you going? Oh you live here, what do you do? – Dishes are placed before each. A whole roast chicken, that's all. Eyes meet and, not for the first time, there are smiles. Seductive, happy ones.

At first, knives and forks are used. The tasty meat is made to linger for a few moments, then into the mouth. Savoured. Then again. More quickly. Fingers tear the flesh off the bone.

Impatience gets the better of the two. She, temptingly, pulls off a leg; then he does. Then a wing. Each pulls at the carcass.

And, no doubt, beer, plenty of it, helps.

And that night, they pull at each other's flesh.

It is only later that Tom Jones, for that is the young man's name, learns that he had slept with his mother.

*

One-pan pierogies with Brussels sprouts and kimchi

The Souls. Well, that's what they called themselves. In the hedonistic days before the First World War, led by the example of their King, these aristocrats liked to gather to discuss, to mark their upper-class superiority by talking – about philosophy or art or music or the Empire. Or of their 'conquests' along Oxford Street.

They would also eat. And not just banquets fit for those who were born to banquet, but menus that were made up of some hundred courses. Some hundred.

Meanwhile, 8-year-old children were working down the mines, like their fathers and grandfathers, six days a week, 12 hours or so, too.

Such privilege.

*

Nona's torta di pollo melassa nero

Tonight it's curry – curried chicken, like Mother used to make it. Turmeric. Chilli. Cardamom. And Black Treacle.

To the side: tomatoes chopped small, sliced bananas, coconut ground small, onions in a light dressing, oil & vinegar. Maybe cucumber.

Rice, of course, sprinkled with some chopped raisins. Sometimes, saffron.

Curry: to make one sweat, to purge the body of impurities.

For a treat, Father allows the elder ones a glass of Lager each. Orange juice for the youngest.

And to follow: Ice-cream. Home-made, too.

So, nowadays curries are never so hot or tasty. Perhaps nothing is. Well, who has impurities?

*

Pulled jackfruit tacos with chipotle, charred corn and coleslaw

Elizabeth David (1913-1992). She who rescued us from grey cabbage, tough lamb, dull suet puddings and all the rest of the dreary food of our childhoods? Don't you recall the like?

Eggs that were tinned apricots fried in bacon fat. Stewed crow.

Mediterranean Food. Then *Italian Food* - and last and first, *French Provincial Cooking.*

Suddenly, by the mid-Sixties, whole new worlds were being opened up. Generations of master chefs, gastronomes and home cooks have benefitted directly or indirectly from her work.

In the last of these books, the recipes are there. But no quantities.

That's how to learn!

*

Bang bang partridge salad with crispy noodles

What would one cook for, say, The Queen, for the dinner of your life that you will never cook again?

Anyone of these dishes mentioned here? Doubt it. Let's stick with good old English – now that we are free of the European yolk!

Nibbles, first. Quails eggs, Mayonnaise and celery salt? Then for the Starter: Asparagus rolled in smoked Salmon (*not* Scottish, of course). Followed by one's famous Coq au Vin – sorry! Partridge in Red Wine, with bacon, chorizo (oh, OK, just one little indulgence), onions and assorted vegetables, as available; sweet potatoes, red cabbage. Or maybe Coronation Chicken?

Finish with the Chocolate Mousse. Of course: 'Off with his head!' if t's not there. Fruit salad with Kiwi Fruit (well, they are our kith and kin, aren't they?).

Just some ideas, but what could be better?

Just remembered, the wines. Well, there are now up to 4000 vineyards in the UK. Lots to choose from! No need to drink Italian. Or French.

*

Mushroom and black rice chachouka cakes

Afternoon tea. After the Tennis on a summer afternoon. Five or six of us, more or less appropriately dressed for sport and tea and self-satisfaction.

Here it is: sandwiches – salmon (smoked), raspberry and/or cucumber. And the scones, home-made, with rich double cream and strawberry jam.

Ginger biscuits. Chocolate cake and Jaffa cakes (only because the eldest loves them).

Hats off now, for they have moved into the shadow of the great Oak tree. One or two hats are fanning warmed cheeks. Or batting the flies away.

That night, Daphne and young Lionel might well make it together. Game, set and match! Future assured: the Great Oak will long outlive them.

*

Aparachi trota con patate dolci vivanco

Cocktail time! Autumn is setting in, so let's make the most of a sunny evening. Down to The Golden Swan, seats on the bank as the waters silently glide by.

For Jilly, a Cosmopolitan – vodka, Cointreau and lime, in a cocktail glass. So elegant. For Gerald, the masculine one: Bloody Mary, vodka again, tomato juice and, essentially, Worcester sauce. Down – almost – in one.

For others, Mojito, a Sidecar and a Singapore Sling. All well iced (does the barman mix more ice than necessary and less alcohol??), and nibbles to go with.

And for Old Man, well, just a pint of their best bitter. To begin with.

*

Mchwa, tambi za kupanda-miti

The last supper. Flutes of Champagne, Bollinger (2008, of course) with oysters and a turnip (from Belarus) and asparagus canape. The fizz flows, tongues loosen.

Caviar, Sevruga, as much as you want. Then Smoked Salmon, freshly imported that day from Alaska. It takes time, but what is time during the last supper?

It melts in the mouth, the fillet steak. Nothing more to be said really. Just add sweet potato, your greens and an unctuous but not too strong a gravy.

Chateau Petrus (2015). At least: £4,000 a bottle. Plenty of it.

Cheese course, before the dessert, a la Francaise.

Dessert: the finest chocolate mousse (again) and the real speciality: Ginger ice-cream made especially for today.

And Château d'Yquem - the world's greatest, most expensive sweet wine, enjoyed so much by Hannibal Lecter.

*

Posho Africana Chwala

Many, many years later – or before, who knows? - a priest, a nurse, a son or daughter, holds a glass. In it is water, fresh water. The rim of the glass is put to the old man's – old woman's – lip. In the darkened room the old features, known and loved for so long – or hated – have collapsed. One last drink, one last sip, a tiny drop – but it is not taken in. Tired, old eyes, eyes that have seen so much, taken in so much beauty and horror, open a little, just a little. Not that they see anything.

'Let it be death, then.'

In a moment, behind the eyes is the void, void even void of the awareness of void, a void beyond the deepest of sleep.

The nurse, the son stay still for minutes. Silence in the darkening room. Two fingers place a parting kiss, bowed heads in sorrow and sadness.

The doctor raises the sheet, draws it over the face. To mask the hungry grimace of death.

Such recipes. Such creativity!

26

Infinity Rooms

Cleanse the doors of perception
And see Being for the Infinity that it is.
Blake

I reach out to you, Yayoi Kasuma, from across the continents, across the oceans and through time.

You reach to me, unknowing but knowing all, across the oceans and all the lands between us.

As you have reached out to all the World.

From your youngest age to your old age, from deep inside you to the widest vision of all life.

From darkness and illness to light and joy. Your world is and is not our world. Your world is and is not.

Yours is a life of endless struggle – and triumphant success.

Paradox is everything, though your art is you as you are your art. Which created which? Who created whom?

And now in your tenth decade, you create more and more, even though you have created so much more since your youngest days, when all you could do was to draw and to paint. "If it were not for art, I would have killed myself a long time ago."

You broke away from the traditional *nohinga* art of the Japan of your youth, though it all goes deeper than this. Picasso, Renoir, Manet – so many from our side of the Universe have done such, rejected the old, the conventional - to find and to be themselves.

You drew into yourself, into the hallucinations and to the troubles of your childhood – a father who was unfaithful, a mother who sent you to spy on him and would even beat you and who did her best to stop you as an artist from a very young age. War-torn Japan saw you fixing parachutes from the age of 12. Happiness was not your inheritance.

And then came your darkest period: 'Atomic Bomb' (1954). Your country trying to come to terms with what had happened. Your image is of darkness, of violent reds; yellows and reds fly across the image. A monster, indeed.

Once , you wrote this:

'One day I was looking at the red flower patterns of the tablecloth on a table, and when I looked up I saw the same pattern covering the ceiling, the windows, and the walls, and finally all over the room, my body and the universe. I felt as if I had begun to self-obliterate, to revolve in the infinity of endless time and the absoluteness of space, and be reduced to nothingness. As I realised it was actually happening and not just in my imagination, I was frightened. I knew I had to run away lest I should be deprived of my life by the spell of the red flowers. I ran desperately up the stairs. The steps below me began to fall apart and I fell down the stairs spraining my ankle.'

Millions of others, carrying with them torments and uncertainties of their childhood, react and fall into the arms of demagogues and tyrants. Your struggle has been to confront yours through your art – and you have committed yourself not just to painting, but to literature, fashion. Your 'self-obliteration' is ironic. It is still Yayoi Kusama who paints and writes, even at 92. Endlessly trying to liberate – self-obliterate – yourself from these hauntings and dreads. And in becoming your art and your art becoming you, you have triumphed.

Darkness, anarchy in your New York days (oh, the Happenings. Heady days!), your dread of sex, your obsession with the phallus. Yet, your anger at the Male, for it is the male – me and all that half of humanity – that has brought so much war, so much sorrow and destruction, over so many centuries

Dots and nets. (Whole streets and buildings are now bedecked with them: A polka-dot has the form of the sun, which is a symbol of the energy of the whole world and our living life, and also the form of the moon, which is calm. Round, soft, colourful, senseless and unknowing. Polka-dots become movement. . . . Polka dots are a way to infinity. Such have they been defined and determined.) Pumpkins and your wonderful Five Tulips. Endless works you produce, day in day out even now in your studio near to the mental hospital you checked yourself into on your return from America in 1973.

And now: Infinity. It seems that you have long reached out for infinity. Or it has reached out for you. But here's the paradox: an image of infinity, as above and below and so very many others, top is defined. Here it is framed on the page. Or it might be on a wall, in a gallery or on a page in an art book. Infinity cannot be so defined, for this is the contradiction: it limits it.

And yet, the infinity is in your mind. And you invite me in. *Us* in.

I float. There is no limit and gravity has no pull. I see others – but no, it is me again as I was or as I will be.

But no, again, it is just my arm floating in the dark, in between the spectral light. And then a leg.

Or is it my brain, synapse flickering shining, flickering on and off, here and in the far distance?

Now or yesterday. Then. Whenever. Forever.

A strange entanglement of electrons seeking one for the other, or photons on and off. . . .

And in the infinity is a Cosmos, indefinable, a Multiverse, without beginning, without end –

A beauty beyond beauty.

All about your love: ‘Art has taught me about the fantastic world, home to life, death and the human race which has endured for hundreds of millions of light years, personal peace and love, the mystique of the cosmos, and many other things.’

And you look out at us in your pumpkin dress and red, red coiffure, with your dark, dark eyes that draw one into your world, your cosmos.

But I must return to the here and now.

27

***The End** - A Parable*

Is it like this
In death's other kingdom
Waking alone
At the hour when we are
Trembling with tenderness
Lips that would kiss
Form prayers to broken stone.
T.S. Eliot

He looked at the broken window. Cobweb in a corner above. Old grey walls, a door not closed properly. Clothes dotted around. Stale smell of food. He had done no washing up. Distant sounds he did not recognise - only his breathing. It was like this each evening, once he had returned from work. Slumped in his chair, his hands sore, his arms aching from chopping, digging, sweeping. Soon the screen will come alive, with its endless propaganda interspersing hearty but empty programmes - bread and circuses. Then maybe he would be hungry enough to eat something. Maybe not. In time, sleep would come, where he now sat?

It had been like this now for weeks, for months – Mark could not tell. The pains from his torture had gone, but scars still remained. It was not the physical evidence, though, that now bore down on him so heavily. The neighbours had been kind, but he kept away, for they were watched – and watching. Where was Alice? Why did he feel no longing for her? Drugged, had he been, drugged to remove memories? He did not know where he was. One morning, he had woken up in his new living quarters. That day, officials had come to tell him how he was to live, to work, to sleep. To be. The State, The Party. All will be well, and all is well. . . .

Every day.

Alice's hair, fallen over her eye. Gently, he removed it. Kissed her.

He knew that every day, every move and thought – these are being and will be recorded. In time, he has been told, he could gain 'social credits'. *If* he earns them. But how could he not do so? Something had gone from him. The capacity for joy, for love. Almost, for behaviour. Almost.

A table and chair. On the table a few sheets of paper, a pen, taken carefully from work. He had, at times, been writing. A few hundred words, often rambling, even incoherent, disorganised. But each with pain. Doodles in the margins, scrawls. But still, these were what remained of him.

Young, they were. Young. In the corner, in the room, sat a girl. Hair over one eye.

Then one day, she was naked. Both were.

He arouses himself, goes to the desk. Picks up the paper. It – crumpled now, full of scrawls – is enough to kill him.

Democracy. That's the only true starting point. It belongs to all.

A slice of bread, jam, left over from the morning. He eats. The last.

Democracy. Cannot be controlled!

Standing, for some time, he looks at the paper. At what has been written. Was it by him?

No one is 'subject'. All are citizens. That first word is disgusting.

Outside it is grey, though late summer. He looks out at the fading day.

How can one live without love? Or without self-restraint?

Soon, he will go out.

But now, he lowers his head, puts a knuckle on the top of the table, rests himself.

No human should ever be tortured. No human should ever be a torturer.

For a time. He will need to go out.

No human should ever be watched. Damn the sensors, the endless cameras, the microphones hidden away!

Soon.

Their car. The afternoon by the lake. What were those times, time that keep rising in his mind? Impinging, without feeling. Why? Why?

Why should the State know everything about one? Anything??

Slowly, he turns. Makes for the door. He doesn't yet know it, but he will never come back here. To this room, this grey room of no meaning.

He cares not to not lock the door as he goes out. Laughter from next door. Down the stairs, a banister loose somewhere. Linoleum tatty, loose.

Outside, it is still warm. Pedestrians ignore him. So? Two men are chatting, eyeing women, perhaps.

Mark turns, walks down the street, past dull shops, posters and adverts for coming 'parties', 'festivals', celebrations of the merger of The State, The Party. Potholes. A broken window, signposts graffitied. Mark does not notice these, head lowered as he slowly walks. Along the street, down. Down to the river. The bridge. He could recall being there, long, long ago.

Alice putting her arms around his neck.

'Shove over!' The man forces Mark off the pavement.

His lips on hers; hers on his. Gently to begin with. The river, the bridge above. Cameras, sensors hidden.

This time, Mark stays above. Brunel's' arch offers no protection now.

Half way across. He leans over the balustrade, its columns, stained, roughened, holds a collapsing parapet.

I want to dance to the tune of the infinite, the dance that is all being, is me - but not mine.

The water flows, silently, softly. Lights glisten, ephemeral on the surface. Is it a face he sees there?

He leans. Waits. For the end of time?

Making love is this dance!

The paper is in his pocket. Soon, in his hand.

Opens it, reads what he can, folds it.

Damn The State! Damn The Party!!!

He waits. He cannot move at all. Silence, despite the noises around. Silence inside speaks louder.

Then he tears it, first once.

Then twice, then as many times as he can before it is too small to tear.

The shreds fall through his fingers, floating gently, elegantly to the river below. Some caught in a gentle breeze. The waters carry them slowly away, some fragments caught in the weeds, some on the stone work.

Time will tell all truth.

Marks watches, vacant. Tired.

He turns, lean against the balustrade. Looks to walk back. Turns his head. Two men, he sees. They watch him. Not minding if now he sees them.

Mark leans back, looks the other way.

Two more men. Coming now towards him. Just yards away. One smiles. 'We have you, now,' the smile seems to say.

Mark leans back. It is not a decision. As the four get nearer – within touching, grabbing distance – he tilts back, raises himself. Leans back over the balustrade, into the space between the bridge and the water, between life and death.

Gently, he tilts, passes the balance point. Drops.

Into the river below.

Just another bit of paper.

The men shrug. 'C'est la vie!' says one.

They do not even bother to look down to the body. Smashed on the stone work. Blood merging with the murky waters of the darkening evening. Slowly flowing away.

28

Sweet Thames, Run Softly

A story in three times – or none

It is gloomy, that space beneath the National Theatre and the art galleries nearby by. Dank. After several decades, when once this area would have been fashionable and architecturally novel, it is now tired and uninviting; parts are enjoyed by kids on their skateboards and rollers. The concrete is old and dark in feel. A few yards away, the waters of the River, as they have done for centuries, glide silently eastwards, quiet and still, and the far hum of city life seems to enhance the silence. This southern embankment, as it has done since Shakespeare's time, has housed theatres, taverns and brothels – in his time one and the same thing. Cars, neon lights and office buildings now crowd the spaces, where before The Rose, The Bear Garden and The Globe once offered entertainment for London's citizens. Indeed, there is still a Globe Theatre there today.

The playwright sits there of an afternoon. Across the water he can see the City of London, with its twenty-five or so church towers and spires, all dominated by St Paul's Cathedral, though this is not the one Charles will see when he comes from Bromley to London, seeking out pigeon breeders. Going from the one bank to the other is the old London Bridge, grand with its houses on top. To the east is The Tower, place of many an execution; in the distance are windmills on the hillside that is Hampstead Heath, deep in the countryside. And to the west are small fields with a few cows and sheep and vegetable gardens. Westminster is far to the west, out of the picture. At the southern end is the gateway to the city; here one can see on poles, atop the castellated gatehouse, the heads of the executed, to remind visitors and residents to be careful with what they say and do. If south of the river is a place of life and license, then north of it is puritanical, at least. On this day, as he passes, Charles counts eighteen heads.

Will is tiring. 'He who tires of London, tires of Life.' Not, for once , his words, but it is how he feels. All the World has passed through his head. He sits on a log, or is it a bench? Before him, wherries and other small boats carry passengers and bales of straw, an animal or two, upriver. Busy it looks, though on the far side of The Bridge, he has noticed, more and more often, many large ships, traders waiting for the wind and the tide to take them to The Indies, West and East, or to the ports of Europe. Only a few years before, The East India Company has been given its Royal Charter. The seeds are being sown. Will feels not the confidence that this sight instils in so many. A gentle breeze freshens him, but only in so far as it alleviates the stench of the city, for all around him is poverty. London. He has determined to be back in his beloved Stratford, but he still has one or two plays to see the light of day. 'The Tempest'. This, he hopes, will be his last word, then to retire in meritocratic quiet. For a year or two.

But now he is not alone. An elderly man is making his way towards him. They have met here before, at this time, about three in the afternoon, but who can tell if the clocks are true? They have come to know each other, not well though. They are now more than just passing acquaintances, meeting here on the South Bank from time to time to share ideas. Now there is a new bench, for the tangled slum of houses and brothels, of waterlogged ditches, abandoned clothes – and bodies – has been cleared away. Just a few years before, the new Embankment, here on the south as well as on the north of the River, has left all clean and tidy. The mudlarks have gone. There are benches, too, for pedestrians and where once there were pleasure houses there are now The Cremorne and Vauxhall Gardens, by day places for family outings but after nightfall, other sorts of delights are available. On this afternoon early in November, the crest as it were between autumn and winter, it is not warm. Charles sits.

He is, like the other, tired. Perhaps he has been tired for many years. No one asked him to do as he has done, no one asked him to become famous, yet, despite endless illness – nausea, eczema, weakness, digestive problems, all sometimes lasting for months - he has kept working. He has learnt the term for this: 'workaholic'. Today, his eyes are hollow and shaded, his beard straggling and thinning, thereby not hiding the scars on his cheeks as he once intended it. He wears a cloak over his shoulders, and a hat, with its rim upturned. His stride, once the stride of a young man who had circumnavigated the World, now remains strong, but it is not quick. He stands a moment or two before Will as a lad on a board races noisily by, two girls giggling nearby. Old men.

" 'Behold the swelling scene'," Charles nods as he recognises Will. " 'Earth has nothing more fair to show.' " A grey day and its autumn chill make the eyes of each water a little. "Just think," the old man continues, "the smell, the dirty waters – do you know that until very recently the River was declared dead? *Nothing* could live in it. Even when I was young in the early part of the century, the streets were full of horse-muck, even the best ones. Now, of course, it is fumes and engine noise." He sits. He likes his new friend but will be at his brother's before the afternoon is over.

" 'That time of year'," the other replies, " 'thou mayest in me behold when yellow leaves or few or none, ...' " One or two streetlights flicker into life on the north bank.

"You know, something," Charles continues, ignoring Will's gentle tease, "I have read all your works, that is, Emma and I and our children. We loved doing this. You showed us – everybody – life in all its great variety and muddle. The World. No television then, no Netflix. They gave much pleasure, then the children grew up. A welcome break from the barnacles, though."

"Barnacles? What are they?"

"I don't suppose you get them in Stratford, too far from the sea. Little molluscs - sorry, creatures in tiny shells that cling to rocks and the bottom of boats – I had to do it." Charles pauses as Will turns to look at him. "But please, don't ask why. Eight years and four books." Charles raises his stick in welcome to a wherry that has just drawn up in front of them. A vital memory lies in the pause.

"I won't."

Charles is struck by how similar Will looks to the memorial in Stratford-upon-Avon church. Bald, plump somewhat, hair now greying around the ears, holding a quill in his right hand. But Will does ask**.** "Something to do with what you called 'Evolution', last time we met, I should imagine."

"Hmm. I don't talk about it much, though I had worked out the matter some years before, after I had returned. But we do love your plays."

"Thank you. *The Origin of Species*. I have read it now. Thank you. Did I understand it? Not much, even though you claimed to have written it for the average reader, not just for a - what was the word? - a scientist."

Three children are throwing breadcrumbs for some birds which peck away.

Children. Charles sees his young Annie walking with him, around the Sand Walk at Down, dancing, watching, observing with the eager engagement of childhood all that her father noted and said. Her joyous nature never dies in him. He could never bear to take himself back to Malvern, where she died and lies buried. Just 10 years old. Nearly twenty years ago.

Will sees his young Hamnet, dead at the age of 11. 'In sad cypress let me be laid.'

Neither yet knows of the other's loss – or losses.

"Yes, I had to prove that I was a scientist, if only to myself. Do you know why you wrote? What was it – just to make a living?"

Will pauses, fidgets a little, looks at Charles, looks away as a pleasure boat steams its way towards Chelsea. "It is a tale told by an idiot, signifying nothing." He'd *like* to say this but, well, but he cannot. "I loved reading, I read everything as a boy. Thought I could do better. I became everything and nothing for the more I acted, the more I wrote, the less I was within, as that Argentinian put it. What did he write? That I 'started out assuming that everyone was just like him; the puzzlement of a friend to whom he had confided a little of his emptiness revealed his error and left him with the lasting impression that the individual should not diverge from the species.' I can't put it better."

"Ha!" Charles's surprise surprised Will. " 'Species'. Well, well. That's what I have spent my life thinking about. He was wrong. Individuals *do* diverge from the species. They have done for millions of years."

"Millions! Didn't life begin 6,400 years ago as that Bishop claimed? Put here by God? I know – I read you book. But *why*?"

Charles looks puzzled, unsure as which question Will is asking. He'd rather talk about himself, if he has to. "Maybe – maybe because there was an emptiness in me too. I lost my mother when I was eight. I would roam around the countryside, collecting stones and other objects. Trying perhaps to fill the hole. It was the same when I went around the World in that little ship."

"Named after a dog?"

"Yes, *The Beagle*. I was very young. I was full of energy then, oh, yes. Forever walking away from that boat, to be on dry land. Collecting all the time, sending much home. Shooting, too. But where were you in your early days? No one seems to know."

"At war. Somewhere over the water. Religious wars, wars of independence. I don't like to remember."

"And your plays are full of wars and battles and dynasties but little about religion. Are you Catholic or Protestant?"

"God is dead."

"Ah, yes indeed. Indeed." Charles pauses as a skateboard clatters noisily against a nearby pillar. "I think I was losing faith after I returned. Then our little Annie died - ."

"You, too? We have more in common than you might imagine. I lost my son. My Hamnet. Bubonic Plague. It was terrible."

Charles looks at Will; he seems momentarily far away. What a terrible death. "Nobody knew the cause then. Now, we think Tuberculosis."

Overhead a passenger plane heads for the airport to the west, unsighted in the cloud.

They sit. The silent River sings a wordless, soundless song that filled the space between them.

"Do you have other children?"

"Yes, two daughters. Married. But I don't see them much now."

"Seven, Emma and I."

"Seven?"

"And two others died. One child at birth and our little Charles at three, from a fever."

"I am so sorry."

Bells from Southwark Cathedral ring out. Will and Charles sit still. Greying skies, some litter scurries in the wind from them.

Then, Charles: "How can there be a God? Why should there be a God who kills little children? 'Suffer not the little children to come unto me. . . .' Pah!"

The two elderly men sit still. Passers-by pay them little attention, thinking that the one in doublet and hose must be an actor from the nearby Globe. The two girls are moving on, the screens of their mobiles their only focus of attention.

"But it was more than that," Will, after a time, offers, "wasn't it? 'After you returned', you said just now. Reading about how 'the fittest races survive through natural selection' told me something, something perhaps I know but could not put words to."

"And you *the* master of words! How we loved your language, your poetry and the characters you brought to life through them. In war, in love, in the struggle to survive. I am a scientist – or so I like to think – you are a poet and playwright. So full of life and death, your plays. And poetry."

"Thank you. Such kind words." Will holds his attention on the old buildings opposite that seem to be tumbling into the waters. "But in the end, what is there? Just greying skies and London smog."

" 'O, for a muse of fire that would ascend the brightest heaven of invention'! But, Will, what does it all lead to? 'Monarchs to behold the swelling scene. . . .' 'Swelling'! Blood and bloated bodies, dead and dying, left lying in agony on sodden battlefields whilst scavengers looted their bodies, arrogant monarchs and dim-witted soldiers, Bardolph and Pistol and *all* the rest, in their thousands, their millions – 50,000 killed in one day in 1815, as you will recall. God is dead. Indeed he is!"

"Mmm." A few years back, Will might well have been burnt at the stake had *he* uttered such words. A painful death, but perhaps now it's death he would welcome. And so might Charles. "Was that what I was trying for? When you read my plays, even my poetry, did you think I was seeking a moral, a reason for hope that good would triumph over evil? All those churches on the other side, the cathedral just a few yards away on our right. Look at St Paul's."

"I know, monuments to hope. At least beyond this world. And yours is not the St Paul's that today is virtually hidden by tall buildings and drowned in the noise of traffic. There was a plague, yes, Bubonic, then a great fire. A great cathedral burnt to the ground. Mysterious ways." But curiously, Charles still has some love for the city.

Then it was endless waste, human and animal; now, it is litter, noise, pollution. Carbon. Methane.

"What was it you said to me last time?" Will continues. "Something about looking into the dark night of the soul. I thought about that. Well, I know – Lear goes mad, lovers fighting in the forest, Romans plotting each other's death, infidelities, of course, greed and ambition. And the Prince of Denmark. If ever I failed it was with this one. He goes off to Norway, has his two friends killed, returns to Denmark uttering a few platitudes and then, as my audiences like so much, there is the usual bloodbath to end with. All too easy. Yes, you're right. So many die. And if you are honest, I don't think I see hope any more. Lear's redemption wishful thinking and Prospero will fall to his brother, sooner or later."

" 'Slings and arrows of outrageous fortune.' An endless struggle between meaning and meaningless. Is that it? Shall we get a drink in the café, just behind us? I'll pay." Charles is feeling the damp of the season. He knows the struggle only too well.

As they enter, there is a hush as all goes mute, if only for a moment. People look up, pause, think, seeming to recognise. It's only a couple of actors. Will asks for a beer: it's all he knows. Charles takes tea, some biscuits.

They sit, Charles stirs his sugar in. Solid flesh melted into a lukewarm dew. He is reminded of a joke – was it a 'joke'? – his father, Robert, once told him. A woman accosts him in a meeting, a party, challenging him as to his faith, or lack of it. "Doctor, I know that sugar is sweet in my mouth," she said, " and I know that my Redeemer liveth." Did she not know how we came by sugar? Slavery. Such ignorance!

"Do you recall the full title of my book?" Will drinks, shrugs. "*On the Origin of Species by Means of Natural Selection, or the Preservation of Favoured Races in the Struggle for Life.* It *is* a struggle, isn't it? This *is* what you wrote about. All your life. All the time. Even in your comedies. Actually, I came to regret the term."

"Struggle for life?"

"No. 'Natural Selection'. The latter, yes, because Nature does *not* select. But the first word suggests something driving it. There is nothing driving it. Except accident, chance. All is blind, all life is happenstance. You and me, too."

"But isn't history behind it all? Isn't the Queen a reminder of the idea that in time, all will right itself?"

"Which Queen?"

"Our Queen."

"Just another human. History seems to determine that humans are better off with a monarch than otherwise. Anyway, 'History' is just an old-fashioned word for 'Selection'. Selection by chance. Or 'Evolution', if you prefer."

"And love. I wrote about love, didn't I? I loved writing about it. *Much Ado*. My sonnets."

"Much ado about nothing. And your sonnets, aren't they about failed loved? Of course, there's love. We breed. Love is part of religion. I take my family to the church door every Sunday, but I won't go in. How can I, when there is no God?"

"Can I get you another drink? I need another."

"No thank you, Falstaff."

A young man passes. He notices the dark, hollow eyes of the old man. As Will returns, the man thinks, "Weird. Well, you can wear what you like these days."

Will sits. He looks at his friend. How tired he appears. The eyes sunk, the skin so poor and everything about him so gentle. So gentle. 'Beautifully benignant, benignly simple.' He tries to recall who said these words about Charles. Wasn't it a young American writer?

Charles smiles at his friend. "I wonder if he plays Backgammon?" he thinks. Better than this conversation.

"But," says Will, "if there is no god, can there be *any* meaning? I loved finding meaning, all the time. Language is my life. OK, I have wife and daughters. Have I ever loved them more than I loved words?"

" 'The barge she sat in burned upon the water.' Yes, that's a wonderful speech, beautiful. Beautiful. But it wasn't yours. You took it all, word for word, from Petrarch."

"Well, yes so I did. But I ended it my way. 'The holy priests praise her when she is riggish'. No, I didn't make it up, but I did enjoy it, the word. A good old farmer's word. The word, I mean. And, all right, it!"

"Well, I know you started young, with a woman rather older than you. But that's life. We breed. All organisms breed. And there is only one purpose to this – to pass on that which makes us a human or a bee or anything biological. 'Riggish'! What a word."

"And that is all? Can't we hope, can't we love? Don't we have children to hope, to love? That their lives might be better?"

"Even if we send them off to war?" Charles pauses; it is some time before he starts again. Will knows not to hurry him. "You love to have numerous bodies lying about the stage at the end of a play. *Hamlet*, as you mention. Morality! Of course, we must, *must* try to be moral. But beyond our near ones, it is very difficult. That other phrase – 'The survival of the fittest'. No, I didn't make that up. It was Herbert Spencer, the economist. And scallywag. You've seen all those ships on the river at the far side of the Bridge, going to far-off lands to demonstrate who is the fittest? I have been proved right about History, sorry, Natural Selection. The *only* thing that remains to us is responsibility. " Coming from one so apparently frail, Charles' passion shook Will.

"But all my life," Will tries to avoid a sense of desperation, "I have been filled with a sense of life, of its endless variety. Oh, I know you are going to quote William Blake – 'Life is made for joy and woe. . . .' – and I have always been compelled to face this. It's all summed up in here." He taps his forehead.

"Actually," Charles breaks in, "I was going to say, "Cleanse the doors of perception and see Being for the infinity. .' "

". . that it is.' But *is* it? I'm going home. Soon."

Charles looks into his teacup, which is almost drained of tea. Will downs the last of his beer. People stand and leave, others take their places. He feels Charles' gentle eyes looking hard at him.

"You do know now, don't you, that all you ever wrote echoes everything that I have written?"

"And vice versa!"

"Henry V invades France conquers and mates with the daughter of the conquered king. Benedick and Beatrice show sexual display before accepting each other – and all those lovers in *Love's Labour's Lost*! Henry VII overcomes Richard III, the fitter has survived, if only because the latter's horse has galloped off – only to face endless struggle till he dies, too. Don't you see, Will, all is paradox. Lovers end up tragic, happy endings are only thc poet's choice and life and death go on. And there is the only end of life, for the individual and for the species. Extinction."

"But humans go on, we develop, don't we? We learn!"

"Of course. But why is it that some win and some lose? Because, by chance, one has an advantage – better weapons, better diets, better swimmers – you name it. At this time, one side has sufficient and powerful enough weapons to completely destroy an enemy. That enemy has such, too. What happens when that balance is upset?"

"So, at Agincourt Henry V was better equipped than Charles VI of France?"

"Of course. Longbows. And Charles was mad. It's not just weapons. Humans can spend so much money developing vehicles to take them everywhere in the world. Vast cost, vast waste. Yet a bug can grow, hop into bodies, fly around the world for free. . . ! It doesn't intend this, it just happens. By chance it finds a suitable environment."

"It could infect all?"

"Indeed. I am reminded now of the cuckoo that ejects its foster-brothers, of ants that make other ants their slaves, of the Ichneumonidae that invades the bodies of live caterpillars to lay its eggs. Such pain. Endless, voracious destruction. As my friend on the Isle of Wight put it, 'Nature red in tooth and claw.' Alfred Tennyson. Heard of him?"

"So that's what I was writing about?"

"Yes. But it isn't all, you know."

"I think that all I ever said was what kept on filling me. Such abundance! Was that life? With a big L – Life."

"Yes! I recall that time we stopped off the coast of South America and I went into the jungle. Such growth from the smallest insect – and beings too small to see – to the tallest of all those giant trees! And the *noise*! It seemed to me as if this was the great song of life itself. Everything in vital fruition, struggling in vast quantities to survive and then, endless decay, rot into death. And now? It's all over, bar the last act. I think I know what you will say. Something about 'cloud-capped towers and gorgeous temples'. Yes? 'The great globe itself' – what will you say?" Charles waves his arm, gestures in the emptying café, with the daylight fading beyond. "All 'shall dissolve . . . and leave not a rack behind'."

"So, you have been cheating!" Will responds. "Well, let *me* say how you will end your great book, summing up the struggle for life, the war of nature, famine and death, its very last sentence. 'There is grandeur in this view of life. . . and while this planet has gone on cycling according to the fixed laws of gravity, from so simple a beginning endless forms most beautiful and most wonderful have been, and are being, evolved'."

"Touché! 'And our little lives are rounded with a sleep'."

Could anything so beautiful have ever been written?

"I must go now. I am expected."

"Oh, we are always expected. Everywhere."

And so they part. They will never meet again. Will returns to Stratford, Charles to Westminster Abbey, where others wait. Imagination has given to airy nothingness a local habitation

Signifying

29

Walking In The Hills (2)

I wandered lonely as a. . . .
Wordsworth

It is about 5.0 pm of an August afternoon. There is plenty of sunlight, but given clouds and the mountains surrounding the lake, it is darker than it might otherwise have been. I had taken myself off the beaten path that would later take me to the top of Helvellyn. The first ascent from Glenridding is steep, but after a while the climb is less strenuous. Below the path is a tarn about the size of a football pitch, ahead the way to Striding Edge and the top of the mountain. To my right, off the beaten track, was a level area of ground. I decided to explore.

The walking was of no difficulty, short, tussocky grass stretched away all around. I was not at all sure where I was heading, but after a short time, I was well rewarded.

Immediately before me, the ground fell away. I stopped. It was a moment or two before I could take in the wonder that lay before me. Some way below, to my right, I could see the roofs of Glenridding. And, then, to the north and east, stretching for twenty or more miles, lay Ullswater. In this light, the waters of this most beautiful of lakes was a dark blue, almost tinged with purple, in fact, The mountains, hills and valleys opposite, were covered in bracken, grasses and willow herb, blue and mauve, whilst to my left, covering the road to Pooley Bridge, narrow and twisty, was shrouded in woodland. Small boats dotted the lake.

The only sound, the gentle rustle of a fresh breeze, served even more to highlight the beauty of the early evening.

I seated myself on rock, staying there for many minutes, fearing that any move I might make would disturb it all.

It was the Romantics who taught us to see in Nature more than just the picturesque. Nature for them is essentially elevating and spiritual. There is a painting – I forget who by – that epitomises this. A small group is making its way through a barren, rocky and dangerous mountainside to its summit, beyond which can be see a brilliant light, the light of achievement, of liberation, even of unification with the divine. The symbolism is obvious.

I am not sure how many of us understand or respond like this, but Sheffield Crag has long remained in my memory.

*

It is many years ago since I used to holiday in the Lake District. Since 2001, when I bought my house in the Limousin, France, I have rarely been back – there was one occasion, though, which I will describe later. But for all the years that I remained in teaching and then, since retirement, I have spent the school holidays and the summer months pleasing my Francophile self. But those summers spent in rented cottages, as the 20th Century drew to a close, have long lasted in my memory. Many people have the idea that the Lakes are forever covered in cloud and soaked with rain. In the summer at least, this is far from the case, as the evening I mention above bears witness.

Of course, many thousands, indeed millions go to the Lakes each year, but I learnt how to avoid the crowds. Essentially, this meant keeping well away from Ambleside and Windermere, though I have visited Beatrice Potter's old home. On occasion, I rented houses on the east side of the M6 motorway, under the lea of Crossfell, the highest point in the Pennines. Another occasion, I recall, renting a very small cottage on the south side of the lake, not far from the famous Sharrow Bay Hotel. One afternoon, I was reading *Scoop*, laughing out loud to myself, when a small group of late teenaged girls, on their Duke of Edinburgh's Award expedition, must have heard the racket I was making. Their knock quickly quietened me – and I was soon to learn that one had been stung by a bee. Perhaps with some disappointment, I directed them to the nearby campsite, where I presumed someone would be able to help.

Otherwise, my orbit took me from Helvellyn, as mentioned, to Great Gable to Scafell Pike to Coniston – these and many more were my destinations, Keswick, Penrith, Derwent Water, Hawes Water and Buttermere, too, as well as Ullswater. But there are two or three walks which I recall here. Of course, many greater walkers than me have done much more and written so much – Alfred Wainright of old, or the remarkable Robert MacFarlane more recently, have shown the way, though I am happier to sleep in a bed than in a bivouac in a dip in the land of a winter's night, as the latter recounts.

*

I suppose it must be thirty years or so ago that I walked the length of Ullswater – more than twenty miles, I measured it. I had rented a cottage near Penrith, going for a walk every other day. This one was to be the last of that holiday. I parked the car at Pooley Bridge – the same bridge that was to be washed away in floods some years later – and set off, leaving the tourists and the shops and cafes behind. I had planned the walk from there to Howtown, half way down the south side of this great lake, where there is a pub, for lunch; from there, I would make my way to Glenridding, to catch the ferry back to the car. I doubt very much I could do anything like it these days.

At first, the route took me through fields and farmland, caravan and camping sites, with the waters nearby. Slowly, the incline steepened and I was through to Barton Heath. Wanting to break away from all that was civilised, I left the footpath and made my way across grass slopes that headed higher and higher. On the right was a wooded section, not unnatural plantation, but a wild wood. On my left, was a steep cliff, not high though.

I am not one for planning a route in detail, preferring a modicum of adventure and, anyway, Ordnance Survey maps are so good that one can hardly get into trouble. So, after a short while I came to another footpath, this time more formal and well used. In fact, it is an old Roman road, which runs, like so many others, along the tops of the hills so that the Roman legions could avoid ambush in the wooded valleys below. I took this and was soon walking along a crest. To the south and west, I could see, miles away, Haweswater, whilst Ullswater was far below; Watermillock was nestled in its valley opposite, whilst farmland stretched far north into the distance; a little yacht basin, which I will come to know later on, lay there too. I had made good progress.

I think I prefer to be a solitary walker, though what follows might seem to give the lie to this. Many years later, I will take this route again, and a very different experience it will prove.

Soon this old roadway divided, but I kept along the ridge in order to maintain height and the views – there was still some way to go before I could get a drink. It was easy walking, with heathers and grasses brushing my legs. Much of the surface was peaty, meaning frequent steps up and over little mounds. It was not long before I realised that there was a modicum of danger before me, for the land in front was dropping quite rapidly away. I scampered down easily enough towards the lake, taking another pathway, less obvious this time, and it was not long before I was in Howtown. Halfway.

Howtown is not much of a town, more of a village. In past times, it must have been very isolated and lonely, but with today's tourism it is, at least in summer, a most welcome place, with its pub, and it is here that the little passenger ferry stops as it makes its way up and down the lake.

Lunch with a pint or two was most refreshing and I was ready for the more exacting part of the walk.

There are varied ways one can get to Glenridding from this point. One can keep to the lakeside and make one's way around a small hill to Sandwick; or one can go inland, again around this hill, rejoining the path and following it first to Patterdale then on. However, I took the longer, more difficult way: from Howtown, I walked along a lane up the valley, southwards from the lake. This lasted a mile or two. Through Martindale, I headed towards Sandwick, but instead soon turned left, once again away from the lake along Nettleslack Valley.

Easy going so far, but I soon realised that the hillside to my right, which I had intended to go up was becoming more and more of a cliff. I had to go up and across this to make my way to Patterdale or walk all the way to the end of the valley. I made the latter choice.

At the head of the valley, I made my way carefully up a steep incline. It was well worth it. For the view, all 360 degrees of it, was breathtaking. To the northeast, all the way down the valley to Martindale, thence on up the lake until its end at Pooley Bridge. I turned and looking almost due south, were the hills and mountains of this northern part of the Lakes. And there, below me, nestled amongst trees and hills, lay Glenridding. Helvellyn towered above.

What is it that so elevates the viewer when he is isolated far above the life that is normal? Is it the silence, silence marked only by the wind and the flight of the bird, of the skylark so far above that it can only be heard and not seen? Perhaps it is this, too: home is the familiar, the place of our being, of everything that is, at least for as long as we can make it so, ours. But there is perhaps a contrary impulse, one that has been with us for millennia: the need to explore, to find new homes or to subject our very being to new definitions. Is this what the Romantics were suggesting?

Maybe. I made my way carefully down the steep slope, almost stumbling over small boulders and broken decaying logs. Here and there, wool fluttered in the wind left behind by forgotten sheep and even occasionally, lay the bleached skull of a long dead ewe. Soon I came across a path that took me to Glenridding, though first I had to find a way through a barbed-wire fence.

I suppose that everyone must feel a great sense of joy at achievement and of great pleasure at those aspects of Nature that one has experienced on the way. Perhaps this *is* just what Coleridge and Wordsworth meant. But one is also, well, knackered.

I had made my way to the ferry. This *faux* paddle steamer takes it passengers by diesel engine up and down the lake. It was now about 5.00 pm on this lovely summer's day. On the benches and seats of the boat were many of what was then to me the 'older generation' – a pensioners' outing from Bury, perhaps.

I sat down on what must have been one of the last seats available and within minutes, I was asleep. For but a few moments.

I had broken wind. Very loudly.

*

Many years before, well, decades, as a schoolboy in the CCF, I and some of my peers had been sent on an 'Arduous Training Course', for a week in the Lake District. Perhaps it was then that the seed was sown that would bring me back here later in life. That week, in 1966, was, as I have often thought, one of the best in my life.

Arduous it was meant to be, arduous it was. But I thrived. We camped out all week, in every conceivable weather, wind, rain, snow and sunshine, cooking our meals in bonfires made of sodden wood. One day took us to Helvellyn, not from Glenridding, but from the west, from the northern end of nearby Thirlmere. As the weather worsened, I was greatly pleased for the rubberised cape that was part of our uniform. How useful it must have been in past wars. But we never made it to the summit – the fog became thicker and thicker and, between us schoolboys, we reckoned it wiser to descend again to our rendezvous. A pity, in a way.

Many years later, I finally returned to Helvellyn with my friend, John. This time we made it. We ascended from Glenridding and finding ourselves near the top, we faced two last obstacles. The first was Striding Edge. This is a narrow strip lasting about three hundred yards, rocky and dangerous, for on either side, the cliffs fall away almost vertically for, what 500, 600 feet. I was, er, sensible, and took a path just below the ridge, whilst John was braver, taking the narrow path along the very top. We made it all right, but then in front of us was a slope of scree, a couple of hundred feet or so. We battled our way up this. And then we were there. Some years later, we tried this again.

As we reached the foot of Striding Edge, the morning drizzle had turned first to sleet and then to snow. Gradually the path had become covered so that it was difficult to know where to put one's feet. There was, then, a small group of other adventurers, students, probably. Plainly, they were deciding whether to go on or not. We stopped and gave the matter brief thought – and turned back down. What those others did, we will never know. If sensible, they might have taken our unspoken advice.

On another occasion, we and another friend, Stephen, were tackling Scafell. No real problem, except that the latter was a PE teacher and he was, well, the typical mountain goat. At one point he indicated that we should follow him, up a long and very steep gulley. He darted ahead, I followed behind with John after me.

Across the gulley, about halfway up I came across a large boulder. No problem: a pause for breath, and steadying myself, I took a leap, grabbing a tussock to pull myself over and onto the top of this rock.

John was soon behind me. He didn't pause, steady himself. He made a jump at it, faltered, stopped and looked with panic in his face, straight at me. Over his shoulder I see way down almost vertically beneath, some hundreds of feet, a stream.

For a brief moment, I paused, then grabbed him to pull him up and over. He is not and never has been a heavy man.

Unfortunately, the summit of Scafell was shrouded in mist that day.

*

It is to Barton Heath that I must return, for one final memory.

I had rented for three or four nights one of the Helvellyn Cottages, up the valley from the village. John had joined me. He wanted a break, as it had been a very emotional time for him and his family, great sadness and joy mixed as one.

Our first walk had been from Howtown to Glenridding in a day that had poured with rain; the following one was our failed walk to the top. John then had to return home early next morning and, as I had time on my hands, I thought I would return to the Heath to do at least a part of my marathon of years before.

This was the middle of November, that time when autumn is passing into winter. Nothing could have epitomised this so well as that morning.

The rains that had flooded the valley and halted our walk up Helvellyn had passed through so that now there was not a cloud in the sky. A strong, bright blue it was, with the rays of sun in the east filling the valley below and colouring the hills all around.

As I walked up to the top of the Heath, I was unaware that I had dropped my jumper. I did not care, for Nature had provided one of the most wonderful sights.

Set against the blue of the sky, all the mountains had been capped in fresh, white snow. From Crossfell in the Pennines to the east, to Blencathra in the north and Helvellyn, to Coniston and Great Gable and to Scafell, this wonderful land was surmounted by a most glorious crown.

As with Sheffield Crag, this, too, has never left my mind.

And I found my jumper as I made my way back to Pooley Bridge.

30

Mobster Quadrille : Four Fugues

And we should call every truth false which was not accompanied by at least one laugh.

Nietzsche

'Halle - .' whispered Glu'Free.

'-loo -,' went JayEss.

'-yaH!!' burst Wammy.

'SHHHH!' BB went, his voice authoritarian. 'Sh!'

'But that's -,'

'-quite a place!'

'The jewel in the crown!' declared JayEss. 'Magnificat!'

'Shut up, all of you!' commanded BB. 'Do you want us to be found out?'

It was not yet fully dark on this warm summer's evening. The four men, hidden in the bushes on a rise a little above the large mansion they were observing, were silent now.

BB was their leader, tall, gentle of manner, if not ruthless in action, smartly combed greying hair and a penchant, it was said in careful whispers, for teenage boys. Yes, in his time he had read his books. Karl Marx, too, class conflict, exploitation and all that. Much had, though, fallen on deaf ears when he tried to talk to his gang about it. He had known them for many a year. Did he like them? Not really but they had become used to doing his beckoning and they had a, shall we say, certain notoriety. Together, they weren't to be messed with, the Four Fugues. But *no one* knew their real names.

Glu'Free and JayEss were, to BB, his two heavies. The latter, indeed, as he had sired so many children, twenty it was said. His 'drive' had driven one poor wife to her early grave. Once tousled haired but now balding and fond of schoolboy expressions, he needed to be managed with a firm hand. Plump and a lover of good food, JayEss was very much the jack in the pack.

Glu'Free – no sticky fingers for him! – was almost exactly the same age. No wife, no children. People wondered about him. Like his boss, he was gentle in manner, but quick indeed with the knife when required. Some said that he was foreign; certainly, he had something of an accent, from somewhere not London. A key member of the party.

And Wammy the Lad? Well, he was the trickster, the likely lad, the chirpy, skinny one who could scale up drainpipes as well has he could women. Married he was, and constant though his wife was, she had long learnt to put up with his infidelities. His playing of the hornpipe was famous in all the pubs east of Charing Cross.

And what on earth had BB brought them to? An establishment. *The* Establishment? And it *was* large, a beautiful mansion pale yellow in colour. Below them they could see a tall, porticoed entrance from a terrace to the mansion, with rooms and three stories stretching on either side and above. And below the terrace, a large swimming pool, darkening blue now in the fading light. As they watched, two lights came on. A middle-aged man sat on a long-lounger while a young, dark-haired girl in a gown walked to the water's edge. She didn't sit down but, as the man indicated, she disrobed. The gown fell to her feet. She was naked.

'Yah!' Wammy's excitement had to be restrained, BB's hand grasping his shoulder.

'Wakey! Wakey!' whispered JayEss.

'Mmm!' purred Glu'Free. 'Oh, a dear, a female dear!'

'Sh!' commanded BB once again.

Then two more girls appeared, very young. They sat close to the man.

'Cor! Lucky bloke!' muttered Wammy. 'A Hareem - high jinks!'

'Bit old, n'est-pas?' Glu'Free was watching carefully.

'I know 'im!' JayEss declared.

'So do I,' BB smugly responded. 'It's why I brought you here. Cabinet Minister, he is. Called Mr Perfumo. He spreads it around a bit, and he owns a large company selling . . . perfumes!'

'Mega rich?'

'House full of. . . .'

'Gold!'

'Silver!'

'Birds!!'

BB quietened them down. There was a gentle splash as the girl slid into the pool, the other two drinking with Mr Perfumo. Keeping him company.

'Now's the time,' BB said. 'Baklava's on, gloves on.'

Dressed in black, the four men were now indistinguishable, except each wore a different coloured badge on the shoulder. And white surgical gloves - catching the light, dancing in the light as the excitement and nerves built up.

'No talking, no coughing, no noise. We walk round the edge of the house. There's a door at the side, and in we go. Bring your sacks! Got your keys, Glu'Free?'

On went the headgear, on went the gloves. Out came four figures, of varying sizes, all dark except for eight white hands that caught whatever light remained.

Down they went to the edge of the garden, in through a gate and then tiptoeing behind a tall hedge. Half-way along was a gap. As each of the gang went by, they glanced through to see the scene by the pool. Had Mr Perfumo not been so focussed on the curves of the girls as they moved in front of him, he might have seen these eight hands dancing by. BB, however, hastened them on.

They made their way to the gravel driveway, to the side entrance of the mansion, but walking so carefully on the grass verge. BB had warned them of this – he had 'cased the joint' last week, posing as a delivery man.

Glu'Free, safe-breaker house-breaker extraordinaire, fiddled with his 'toys'. The others froze, but in a minute of two, there was a quiet click and the door was pushed open.

Inside was a passageway. The passageway gave onto a kitchen. Gumboots, coats, even a shotgun?

'Cor blimey!' Wammy could not believe in what he saw. Modern, all shiny, spacious - money well earned, well spent. Lots of it.

Glu'Free dipped his finger into a bowl filled with, to him, black fish-eggs. 'Mmm!' he went. As ever.

'Some great grub here!' went JayEss, helping himself to some smoked salmon.

'Salmon or no salmon,' BB whispered, 'we've got a job to do. Wammy, through there, into the dining-room and sitting-room. Glu'Free, to the right to see what you can find there. JayEss, with me along the corridor. And, for God's sake, put your masks on properly! And full bags, please.'

And each went his way, picking up this or that, shoving, moving, bustling even. Silver spoons, an old clock, a box of cigars, coloured handkerchiefs, ladies' scarves, stockings and shoes. Even a box of condoms. 'Might come in useful,' Wammy thought. 'JayEss won't have no need of these. Nor the other two.'

And in the dining-room, Wammy found two bottles, one of Chateau Lafitte '64, the other something called Hirondelle. Not that he would have known the diff, once in his bag. But there on a chair was a large gold bangle, jewel-encrusted. 'Wow!' he said. 'This could get me anything! Better *not* tell the wife.' He tucked it up beneath his jumper. This was for him. He made his way back to the kitchen, keeping quiet being increasingly difficult.

JayEss was now in the library. Not that he knew much about books, though he *did* know that a second-hand book *could* get in a bob or two from the right fence. But his first look fell on one or two dodgy looking journals. Hidden under 'Country Life' were two Playboy magazines. Into his bag. 'Teach my eldest boy the facts of life,' he thought. And there, on the arm of a sofa: a plump, old, leather-bound book. Beautiful condition. He thumbed through it. Musical scores – he knew that much. Pieces called 'cantatas', whatever they were. To JayEss, it looked too good to be true. Up inside his jumper it went. He made his way back to the kitchen, doing his best to keep quiet.

But Glu'Free knew a Picasso when he saw one, not the least when it was signed. There it was, on the wall in the middle, just behind the D of the snooker table. It was a portrait. Was it of Shakespeare? Glu'Free did have *some* cultural or intellectual pretensions. His sticky fingers were not going to touch it, were they? His bag was already too full. Off the wall, into his jumper it went, quick as ever. It almost slipped out as he was returning – so quietly - to the kitchen.

And the ever-suave BB knew a good thing when he saw it. Now in the study, with its papers, books and comfy chairs, desk and family photos, his eyes fell immediately on a couple of handsome, well-cut tumblers. An ice-box – and a tantalus. With three beautifully cut decanters. Unlocked it was. He sniffs at one: a very good quality whiskey; at a second: a fine brandy. And the third? A rich, deeply coloured – what? Port? He doesn't bother to try it. On go the stoppers, down goes the lid. He locks it, into his pocket goes the key. And the tantalus – too big for the jumper. Into his sack, it went. He won't tell the others. He tiptoes back to the kitchen. For once he smiles. Silently.

And as Wammy entered the kitchen, so did one from the garden. It was the girl who had been swimming naked, now drying her hair. Her gown was on, wet hair swept back.

He saw the beautiful young girl; she saw a curious figure, carrying a sack, wearing a balaclava and fancy white rubber gloves, with something up his jumper.

He dropped his bag; she tightened the gown around her, holding it tight up to her throat.

He said, 'Hello. You look nice.'

She said, 'Hello. I can't tell if you look nice.'

He takes off the hood. She saw a mischievous looking face and tousled dark hair. She recognised his accent. 'What are you doing? Where are you from?'

'Stratford East,' he said.

'So am I,' she said.

Somewhat opportunistically, he said, 'Can I give you a lift home? What are *you* doing here?'

She sat astride a chair. 'I just want to go home.'

'Quick, then. What about the other two girls?'

'Oh, they'll be OK?'

' Let's go, then. We, er, I have a car. What's your name?'

'Tina. I need my clothes.'

Wammy picked up his bag, took her hand, saying there was no need for them. He lead her out into the driveway, the way they had come in before, as quiet as mice. He was risking nothing.

And there leaning up against the wall, smoking, was one of the other girls, the blonde one. She was smoking, something Wammy knows well, something smelling sweet and a little sickly. She smiles happily.

'Hello,' she purrs, giggling. 'Have a puff. Tina? Where are you off to? Somewhere in the bushes?'

'No, Wendy. No! He's taking me home. Want to come?'

'Mmm. He looks dishy.' Have a puff.' She giggled again. 'But don't Bogart that joint!' she crooned softly.

Wammy has a puff – then worried about the sounds being made. 'Let's go! Quick!'

As they walk back the way that Wammy and his friends had come, they pass the gap in the hedge. Mr Perfume might just have noticed something – white gloves, a lighted joint, a blonde girl - had he not been looking very hard at a mole the third girl had on her neck, just beneath and to the right of her chin.

When they reached the 4x4, Wammy put the girls in the back. Wendy is giggling. 'I love a pink car.'

'Even when it's red?'

'Well,' Wendy tickled Wammy under his chin, 'you would say that, wouldn't you?'

Wammy thought to himself, 'A lump of gold and two luscious birds! Not bad for a night's work.'

Meanwhile, the others, gathered briefly in the kitchen, could no longer wait for Wammy. Too bad if he got caught. But, as they reached the car, there he was, sitting on the ground, smoking the last of the joint, and singing, 'People get up to all sorts of things', a favourite from home. 'Yay!' he exclaimed on seeing the others. Jumping up and dancing a little jig, he showed the two in the back of the car to his mates.

'Grimes!' said BB, 'What have you got here?'

'Jesus!' exclaimed JayEss. 'What a joy for a man's arousing.'

'Leave off! They're *my* friends,' Wammy sang between puffs.

Tina was sitting nervously in the rear compartment. Wendy had now fallen asleep, curled up against her, dreaming, no doubt, of yellow baboons dancing in strawberry fields.

'Joy to the World!' Glu'Free muttered. 'What would Judas Mac make of this?'

But BB was having none of it. 'Into the car – quick!!'

And they bundled in, sacks full of loot, and personal property hidden in jumpers.

As the vehicle had been parked carefully, facing down a steep slope, there was no need yet to turn on the engine. And whilst it rolled slowly but ever faster downhill, so Mr Perfumo was happy with the new love of his life, Lila. She was happy, too. Wasn't she?

She would be paid now for all three. So she imagined. Anyway, she would have to be gone early in the morning, before Mrs Perfumo arrived. But perhaps not, there might be 'friends'.

BB, Glu'Free, JayEss and Wammy – well they slid happily back into the big city. In time, perhaps, a signed Picasso portrait of the Bard would turn up in some auction house in Singapore or Beijing, whilst an 18th Century volume of cantatas and fugues would sell for a very pretty price. A beautiful ancient Egyptian bracelet would find its way back onto the market, to be bought by the latest lover of one Tatiana, the third – or fourth? – Mrs Perfumo. And as for the contents of the tantalus – well, they would remain for one man only.

Anyway, they would all do well enough out the contents of the sacks. So they imagined, passing through Parliament Square on their way home. Class conflict in action and wealth redistributed. Life was good!

But it is possible, perhaps, that, as they slid down that hill, they did not notice an elderly man walking his elderly dog back up the hill, back to the mansion. It is possible that this was old Mr Perfumo, the first Mr P, founder of the now global business.

And he still had all his marbles. He could easily remember the number plate of the passing 4x4.

The Players –

Georg Friedrich Handel, Wolfgang Amadeus Mozart, Johan Sebastian Bach & Benjamin Britten.
A former Secretary of State for War. Christine Keeler and Mandy Rice-Davies. Lila: the one who got away.
And with apologies to Lewis Carroll.

Well, 'to those that have shall be given; to those that have not, even such as they have will be taken away.'

31

The Steps - Postscript

. . . . It means there is nothing beyond life; but it does mean that there is life, in all its wonder and tragedy. In my life, I have tried to pass on the keys to those that have sat before me. I cannot go with them. You will pass them onto your children, in one way or another, and every step will be an ending and a beginning.

And our story might end in your lives, or in your children's lives or their children's, when the Icecap melts and methane will fill the world. Or when intercontinental missiles are sent from one side of our planet to another. But then, maybe the human story will last another six billion years, when our Sun, running out of hydrogen and time, will expand and inflate itself like a greedy emperor, gobbling up the planets nearest it, including our Earth. It will then collapse in upon itself, finally to be quite extinguished, leaving not a rack behind but a darkness and eternal silence in our little, unimportant corner of the universe that will last for all eternity.

Select Bibliography

Darwin's Journey

Aydon C *Charles Darwin – His Life and Times*. London, 2002.
Boulter M *Darwin's Garden – Down House and The Origin of the Species*. London, 2008.
Bowlby J *Charles Darwin – A New Life*. New York & London, 1990.
Darwin C *Beagle Diary*. London 1839.
Journal of Researches in to the Geology and Natural History of the various countries visited by H.M.S. Beagle. London 1845.
On The Origin of Species by Means of Natural Selection, or The Preservation of Favoured Races in the Struggle for Life. London, 1859.
The Descent of Man, and Selection in Relation to Sex. London 1871.
Autobiographies. London, 1986.
Evolution: Selected Letters of Charles Darwin, vol. 1, 1822-59, vol. 2, 1860-1870. Cambridge 2008.
Desmond A & Moore J. *Darwin's Sacred Cause – Race Slavery and the Quest for Human Origins*. London, 2009.
Gribbin J & White M *Darwin – A Life in Science*. London 2009.
Healey E *Emma Darwin – The Inspirational Wife of a Genius*. London, 2001.
Keynes, R *Creation – The True Story of Charles Darwin*. London 2001.
Stott, R *Darwin and the Barnacle*. London, 2003.

Damn You, Johnson

Geoghegan P *Democracy For Sale*. London 2020

On Atheism

Aquinas T *Quinquae Via*, or *Five Ways: In Summa Theologica*. c.1274.
Dawkins R *The God Delusion*. London 2006.
Hitchens C *God Is Not Great*. London 2007.
Figes O *The Whisperers*. London 2007.
Frayn M *Copenhagen*. London 1998.
Milton J *Paradise Lost*. Book 1. London 1667.
Rovelli C *Helgoland*. London 2021.
Sophocles *Oedipus Rex*. Athens c.429 BC.
Stoppard T *Arcadia*. London 1993.

Frankenstein's Heirs

Aeschylus *Prometheus Bound and Other Plays*, ed. Vellacott, P. London 1961.
Borges J *Labyrinths*. London, 1964.
Chatwin B *Utz*. London, 1988.
Clarke A C *2001: A Space Odyssey*. London, 1968. First published as *The Sentinel*. London, 1951.

Graves, R The Greek Myths. London, 1955.
Larkin P *The Whitsun Weddings*. London. 1964.
Shakespeare *The Complete Works*. ed Wells & Taylor. Oxford, 1986.
Shelley M *Frankenstein or the Modern Prometheus*. London, 1818.

Films:

Metropolis, directed, Fritz Lang. Berlin, 1926.
The Terminator, directed by James Cameron. 1984.
Terminator Two: Judgement Day, directed by James Cameron. 1991.
Terminator Three: The Rise of the Machines, directed by Jonathan Mostow. 2004.
Alien, directed by Ridley Scott. 1979.
Aliens, directed by James Cameron. 1986.
Alien 3, directed by David Fincher. 1992.
Alien Resurrection, directed by Jean-Pierre Jeunet. 1997. All 20th Century Fox.
Mary Shelley's Frankenstein, directed by Kenneth Branagh. Columbia Tristar, 2004.
The Matrix, 1999.
Matrix Reloaded 2003 &
Matrix Revolution 2004, all three directed by the Wachowski Brothers. Warner Bros Films.
2001: A Space Odyssey, directed by Stanley Kubrick. MGM, 1968.

Nocturnal upon St Lucy's Day

Donne, John *Nocturnal upon St Lucy's Day.*

The Mau Mau

Anderson D *Histories of the Hanged.*
Elkins C *Imperial Reckoning – The Untold Story of Britain's Gulag in Kenya*. New York, 2005. This Pulitzer Prize winning work seems to be the only major study of the Mau Mau Insurgency. It is a major work and impresses by its extensive detail and thoroughness of research. This Harvard historian spent many months living amongst the Gikuyu people, interviewing hundreds of survivors of the period.
Kenyatta J *Facing Mount Kenya*. London, 1938. As a young man, Kenyatta studied under one of the founders of modern Anthropology, Bronislaw Malinowski. Those such as he and Margaret Mead studied tribal society not in relation to civilised societies, but in evolutionary terms. These societies had existed so long because they had adapted to the environments in which they had settled. Food being abundant and predators easily dealt with, further adaptation along evolutionary lines was never necessary. Until the arrival of colonists.
Ngugi wa Thiong'o, *A Grain of Wheat*. London, 1976. This work by the foremost Kenyan novelist of the day, tells of these events very hauntingly from an entirely different perspective. He himself was imprisoned for a year without trial by Daniel arap Moi, Kenyatta's successor as President.
Ruark, R *Uhuru*. London, 1962. This, as with others of his novels, sees Africa as very much a place for which the white man, having tamed it through courage and energy and

enterprise, had a moral right to ownership. There are no 'good blacks' unless they are in some role of subservience.

Others have written creatively of the period, including Elspeth Huxley and Adam Faulds, a finalist in a recent Booker Prize competition. His *Broken Word* is an account of the Mau Mau in verse.

YouTube also has plenty of interesting material, including film clips from the period. One shows – in grainy black and white – whites going out hunting, somewhere in the White Highlands, but as if they were with The Quorn. I remember it well.

There have been various cinema accounts of the Uprising, including the suggestion that James Cameron's *Avatar* owes its inspiration in part to these events.

Jane Austen and the Rise of Capitalism

Austen J *Mansfield Park.* London, 1816. All other of Austen's work are implied in this essay.
Bunyan C *The Pilgrim's Progress*. London 1678.
Chapman R *Jane Austen's Letters*, OUP, 1952.
Dalrymple W *The Anarchy.* London 2021.
Halperin J *The Life of Jane Austen.* Harvester Press, 1984.
Honan P *Jane Austen: Her Life.* London, 1987.
Tomalin, C *Jane Austen A Life*. London 1997.

Empty

Harari Y N *Homo Deus*. London 2015. (Referred to on various occasions in this book.)
McEwan I *People Like Us*. London 2020.

Infinity Rooms

Kusama Y *All About My Love.* London 2019.

As ever, in these days, Wikipedia has proved invaluable, at least in so far as it allows one to appear learned.

Numerous other work have been mentioned in passing.

There are various illustrations used in this work. Some are by the author. The copyright to the others is not always known. Please address yourself to the author for any queries in this regard.

Printed in Great Britain
by Amazon

72489125R00150